I0645571

BLUE I.C.E.

BY

SAIF A. RIZVI, M.D.

In no fix'd place the happy souls reside. In groves we live, and lie on mossy beds, By crystal streams, that murmur thro' the meads: But pass yon easy hill, and thence descend; The path conducts you to your journey's end." This said, he led them up the mountain's brow, And shews them all the shining fields below. They wind the hill, and thro' the blissful meadows go.
— Virgil, *Aeneid* (6.641)

A

PZYKLON

Black Sun Production

PRODUCT

My Father always told me to dream first, but then sometimes we don't wake up from that dream.

The Grand Plan.

1

FIRE

Delta Force Operator Tor Krush awoke sweating in the cold Louisiana morning, and he checked the time —— 5.28 AM — read the neon green numbers on the digital black clock on his bedside counter that so adorned millions of American bedrooms all across the USA. He was having trouble sleeping since his tours in Iraq, but today he was happy to have woken up early. It was November 8th, 2016 — a historic day dawning on the USA. It was Election Day and he pushed his own troubles aside with money and his separated wife, not to mention thoughts of suicide that he'd been having lately. But today was one of those days that you were kinda glad to be alive. He turned on the radio channel —— *96 Rock* —— playing *Metallica's Unforgiven*, while he replayed Ronald Trump's words in his mind that had stuck.

"I don't care if you're dying. I don't care. Die after you vote for me!"

Those were strong words, but Tor was in a dark place already and he had only smiled when he'd heard Ronald. That guy knew who he was talking to. *The trash of America.* The Americans who lived a life of misery, so much so that it was a good day when you didn't feel like dying. Pain lived inside of him and he looked for a bottle under his bed. There. The reassuring touch of a still-not-so-empty Jim Beam. Good old Jimmie, he smiled, as he hauled it up to unscrew the cap off gingerly, and he wasn't done till he'd drained a quarter neat. The alcohol seared his insides, but it made him feel alive. Still Tor Krush, French company, Delta Force, but suddenly images of gunships replayed desperate night missions in the desert, while taking out hooked nosed *Hajïs* by the dozens. The Arabs didn't mind dying and they died in the thousands. For Allah. But then came the question. *What was he there for? Government orders? The American Dream?* Rage filled him —— at his wasted ten years in Iraq and he smashed the bottle from across the bed and watched the alcohol drip from the wall as shards of glass stuck to the paper-thin cardboard that was supposed to be a fucking *wall.* He let out a desperate sob, but then he needed to be there for Ronald today. No one cared about him, but his V.A benefits were the only thing keeping him alive and Ronald was the only guy who seemed to care about them. So many of his buddies had committed suicide in the last year alone. He was one of the few survivors of his French Company. One guy had blown his head off in front of his wife just last Saturday at fucking *Arby's*, but Tor had been too drunk to even make it to his funeral. Shit, he'd known that guy, Sinker. Had been his best man, but now he just didn't care. Sinker's wife had called and sobbed on the phone after that, but he didn't have any emotions left. He didn't know what to say to her before he'd hung up on her. The boys of French Company knew they were all dead men. They had seen too much to live.

He somehow got into a pair of jeans that hung loosely on him as he gazed at himself in the mirror and at his hollowed-out stomach, but the stringy muscles still packed a mean wallop. Just then his phone buzzed. His sister inviting him to her *Instagram* account filled with pictures of her newly born baby in Los Angeles. He thumbed unemotionally through her pictures, filled with her attractive friends, but somehow managed to smile as he saw his happy sister with her husband and their new baby. They lived in another part of America that was alien to him. He couldn't imagine getting a job and working in a big city, wearing a suit like a pompous cunt. Tor's family had come from a long line of Alligator hunters, and they had made their living for over a hundred years through selling 'gator meat —— with the swamp only a stone's throw away, while alligators roamed his property freely and one of the reasons that they could never keep dogs. 'Gators loved dogs and some of the caymans moved so fast that escape could be hairy. But they never bothered Tor's family as Tor picked up a Sig Sauer .45 caliber pistol from the bedside and made sure that the clip was full. It was Election Day and there was talk about stealing the election. Well, not in *Baton Rouge*. Not today, when he was headed there with his I.D and gun permit in his wallet, as he got into his super-charged red Dodge Ram 1500. No state trooper or highway patrol was going to stop him today with that Supercharger that he'd paid partly out of Tracy's alimony. She was only going to blow it on drugs and the 7,000 dollars looked mighty fine under his hood. He thought about his past where his elite Special Forces unit called *French Company* had been permanently retired by the Pentagon. There had been talk of war crimes and the press had tried to throw it up in the air. A massacre in an Arab village, with 40 villagers executed in cold blood, and then their village burned to the ground. Not now, Tor told himself as his mind threatened to go back to that repressed memory of what had happened. You can think about it after the fucking vote, he told himself staring at the empty highway ahead. He was legally drunk and behind the wheel, so he kept well under the speed limit even though the highway was eerily empty. Wasn't everyone going to vote today? Or did he have the wrong day here. He swore to himself. His phone rang. It was his ex, Tracy, well still his wife legally.

"Yeah?" he asked her gruffly.

"How are you feeling?" she asked. She was calling about the fucking check that he'd already spent.

"Cut the crap. You know I don't have the money," he snarled at Tracy.

"Tor, you need to get a job," she said sadly. She had married a young man, but now a bitter man who hated the world was on the other end of the phone line. After his dishonorable discharge from Iraq, she had felt that she was with a stranger. A stranger who had brought back demons from Iraq, but the worst part was that he didn't want to talk about it. Even with the doctors. And now she needed money now to support her fentanyl habit that she'd picked up just trying to deal with Tor, and Tracy's descent into hell had been quick.

"And you need to quit on the heroin!" he shouted now into the phone. "You're the addict here and not me!"

"You're the one who's gonna die first, Tor!" Tracy screamed as she disconnected the phone line.

"Fuck!" hollered Tor into the phone. He took his eyes off the road as the phone slipped onto the passenger's side floor mat. Suddenly, he looked up to see a car just in-front of him and he swerved violently to avoid it, but it wasn't any ordinary cruiser, as suddenly the wail of a siren started up behind him. Cops. Fuck. He screeched his Ram to a halt in the service lane as a cop car pulled up behind him. Tor was in a violent mood now and for a minute his hand went to his Sig .45. He could just blow the cop away. *Then what?*

"Come out slowly from the car and put your hands on the hood!" screeched the megaphone mounted on the Louisiana patrol cruiser's roof. He emerged to rest his hands on the truck, as the sunlight glinted off the cop's silver shades, and who quickly patted him down and took his Sig.

"You got a permit, boy?" grinned the cop.

"Yeah, it's in my wallet," snarled Tor. "Look Gary, it's fucking Election Day." He knew Gary Portman alright. He'd been in high school with him.

"I can smell your breath already, Tor," grinned Gary some more. "Right from over here."

"Well go to hell," snarled Tor.

"Poor life choices lead to all these kinds of problems," clucked Gary shaking his head. "You know you were the best athlete in school and look what the glory boys at *Delta Force* did to you."

"Yeah, like you care," replied Tor. More bullshit. Even from the fucking cop.

"Who're you voting for, Tor?" asked Gary enjoying this immensely. While Tor had gotten all the girls in school, Gary had been the weirdo. Well now the shoe was on the other foot, as Gary adjusted his hat in the bright sun and took off his sunglasses to polish them with his tie. He was a regulations cop. Yes sir. Doing his duty for the good old USA.

"Hillary!" snarled Tor. Gary burst out laughing, trying to picture Tor holding one of those blue posters saying *I'm with Her.* He had to hold his sides now as he shook with laughter. *Today was going to be just great.*

"Well you do know that your high-school sweetheart *wife* of your's is in worse shape than even you are," said Gary now playing with handcuffs that he held up playfully in his hands. Now Tor turned around.

"I know you wanted Tracy, but she married me," said Tor.

Gary winced. The rejection. He couldn't believe it after all these years —— the pain was still there. *Fucking high school.* That's why he'd become a cop, while Tor had become the celebrated military hero of the town. *A Medal of Honor hero.*

"Yeah, look what you made her into," said Gary and now all the mirth had gone out of his eyes as he suddenly swung a meaty fist into Tor's stomach, who saw it a mile away, but decided to take it as he bent over. "That's for Tracy."

With that Gary began to walk back to his cruiser.

"Aren't you going to arrest me, officer?" asked Tor bitterly. The last thing that he wanted was pity from this loser cop.

"Fuck you, Tor!" swore Gary now, his face red in the bright sun. Fucking hicks, he swore to himself. "I still care about Tracy and I check up on her now and then, something that you don't even do. She's gonna die pretty soon, and y'know that."

 Tor shrugged.

"She's got a new habit ——— the *Red Devil*," said Gary, as he climbed back into his car and revved the engine viciously to drive away kicking up asphalt into the air.

The *Red*, thought Tor, and a slow shiver coursed through his spine. Once you were on the Red, the *Devil* was riding your back. A new import from Mexico, *crystal Meth*, but ten times dirtier. The Mexicans didn't know how to make drugs ——— they only knew how to kill you.

Cheaply.

The Voting booth

10.00 AM

"Can I see some ID?" asked Linda, running the voting booth at the *Baton Rouge High School* ———Tor's high school teacher back in the day. Tor grinned at her, and she grinned back, while leaning over to hug him. But Linda was troubled to note Tor's pale and ashen face with bloodshot eyes.

"What's wrong, honey?" she asked.

Tor just hugged her tighter. His parents had died in a car crash at an early age, and the small Mississippi town community just outside *Baton Rouge* had taken care of Tor, and Elizabeth, his younger sister. Linda knew everything about him, and she had been a frequent visitor to his Uncle's house, who had now moved away to Florida with his wife.

"Ah, nothing seems to make sense anymore," finally admitted Tor. She nodded understandingly.

"Look, the country is in deep trouble. The USA is not what it used to be when I was your age," Linda said.

Tor nodded and turned to all the Trump supporters wearing red MAGA hats everywhere.

"He's really the only hope we have," said Linda.

"Yeah, I'm also hoping that the Pentagon is able to sort out French Company soon enough before we all die out," said Tor quietly. Everyone in town knew the trouble French Company was in. They were all from the *Greater Baton Rouge* area and it was just terrible for the folk to see their sons dying as if they were infected by some deadly mysterious virus. Like something from the swamp was coming to get them, but only this time it was from a land far away.

Tor went to the voting booth, where lay the electronic machines and without hesitation picked his candidate, though he wasn't religious, but he actually said a prayer, some sort of gibberish that he cobbled up together for Ronald Trump.

15 days later

The Pentagon, Virginia

Tor is seated with seven of the remaining soldiers of French Company at a military tribunal convened for an investigation into possible war crimes.

"The evidence against you and your company is damming, gentlemen," said General Hammersmith, lead Prosecutor, leafing through the files full of grisly photos of executed and burnt Arab bodies. "I have no doubt that French Company is guilty, and they should be punished severely."

French Company sat unemotionally through the proceedings.

Then the tribunal head, General Marcus also from Louisiana, a tall and lean man of 70 years, and in an impeccable Pentagon uniform shook his head at all the evidence presented in front of him.

"This all looks very bad," he said, aghast that the men would do something like this while wearing American uniforms. The men from French Company didn't say anything but looked at the polished floor.

Their defense lawyer hadn't even shown up, such were the odds lined up against them.

"Would any of you like to say something in your defense?" he thundered.

None of the men said anything.

"Then I have no option, but to confirm your dishonorable discharge and fifteen years of hard labor in jail," he announced, and shut the file with vehemence. In all his years of dealing with American War Crimes tribunals, he had never seen a massacre this large.

"You are all a disgrace to the American uniform and I have no sympathy for any of you!" he thundered angrily. "Military police will take all of you into custody immediately."

The men still didn't say anything as they were led away.

January 1st, 2023

"Prisoner Tor!" announced an officer of the 42nd Military Police Brigade, as a groggy Tor woke up to greet the New Year. For him it had been just another day in prison, no celebrations here at the Northwestern Joint Regional Correction Facility at *Fort Lewis* deep in Washington State. "You have a phone call."

"My lucky day," said Tor, and wondered who it could be, and with a wiry grin he got up from his bunk, while his stomach hurt from the crunches that he'd been doing at the prison gym. He grinned at the stiff guard, fucking MPs.

"Happy New Year to you too!" Tor said as he exited and waited for the guard to put on the mandatory handcuffs.

"No, something's happened," said the guard with a nervous look in his eye now.

"Well, nothing happens in my world except for bad things," grinned Tor, as he stretched out and yawned, his heavy biceps were eighteen and a half inches now. Prison had actually saved him from certain suicide. He had needed the discipline that they had here and more importantly, he had family with French Company here, all of them working out together everyday. Shit, they were all in top shape. *All they needed was another war.*

"Fall behind me, soldier," ordered the MP, and led the way as he unlocked a host of iron gates to a control room, where a phone handle lay innocuously on the table. Tor at that moment couldn't have imagined how his life would change as he picked up that cream-colored receiver.

"Hello," he said winking at the female guard sitting at the control desk.

"Oh Tor!" cried a familiar voice and he immediately recognized Linda.

"Hey," he said. She sounded like she'd been crying, and he tried to think what might've happened, as his body stiffened into a combat stance.

"Tor, they killed Lizzie," she said, and Tor's jaw hardened into a knot. A round ball that formed at the angle of his jaw which most of his friends knew was trouble and a dangerous glint in his eye that the control room female guard noted worriedly. She already knew though what had happened, and she quietly radioed for back up, scared now to be alone with him in the room without any shackles —— a clear violation of military prison protocol.

"They killed Lizzie and her baby," wailed Linda becoming incoherent. Suddenly the line went dead. Tor wondered at that point what to do. His last blood connection to this world had been cut, not that he'd cared or ever had wanted to see his niece, but something moved inside him. A deep wound was opening, and it would form slowly, but there would be blood. Of that Tor was sure. He was suddenly back in Iraq on a cold night.

THWACK! THWACK!

Gunships with mini guns blazing orange tracers into the surrounding mountain village. Dead Islamic fighters lay everywhere on their night vision, when they had landed in the hot LZ. Bullets whizzing by!

"Incoming!" shouted Sinker, as hot lead threaded the air like angry hornets.

"Return fire!" ordered Tor, as the company was surrounded suddenly from all sides by the enemy. Sunni fighters in the craggy Anbar mountains were a vicious lot and American soldiers were dropping left and right as the chopper was hit by an RPG and it crashed and burned into the valley down below.

"It's a trap!" yelled Sinker in panic. Panic. Major panic.

"Sir!" shouted a pair of MPs' grabbing his shoulder causing Tor to snap out of it and he crashed back to reality. He was back in *Fort Lewis,* as he blinked under the fluorescent light at the men, who were armed with taser guns just in case.

"I'm ok," he said shrugging, and relaxed his shoulders. "She voted for Hillary anyways."

He was trying to tell himself that it didn't matter trying to fight the rising panic in his system. The panic attack wasn't going away, and his heart rate revved up a notch and dizziness grabbed him by the throat. Something like being thrown off a plane without a parachute.

"Sir, you need some fresh air," urged a black MP with a baton in his hand and Tor wondered if he should *neutralize* this threat. The muscles in his back bunched together and he was stiffer than an ironing board.

The female guard came into the picture.

"Breathe, sir. Breathe. You're having a panic attack and let's get you outside," she said, breaking protocol again to take his hand and somehow Tor Krush followed her lead with the human touch comforting him greatly.

The Oval Office at the White House,
Washington D.C.
2 A.M

President Ronald Trump is sitting in the Oval Office, while wondering where to fit a large gilded frame containing an oil painting of President Andrew Jackson, and just when he'd found a spot on the wall, there was a knock on the door.

"Come in," he said standing up. It was the retired five-star General Felix Schwartzkopf, who had become his Chief of Staff.

"Just the man that I wanted to see," Trump exclaimed. "Come and help me find a spot in the room."

Schwartzkopf seemed to be upset, but he smiled anyways and got on the job. Ten minutes later, Trump and Schwartzkopf had found a place on the wall just behind Trump's table to the right.

"You've got it," Trump said holding a silver hammer. "Absolutely awesome spot."

"Yes sir," said Schwartzkopf, while removing the drill from the power socket, and both men had rolled sleeves.

"You think it's straight?" asked Ronald Trump, after both men had heaved the large painting onto the wall. Then he went across to the other end of the room. Schwartzkopf joins him and nods.

"Well, it ain't crooked," he says, and both men burst out laughing. Trump slaps him hard on the back, but Schwartzkopf doesn't even notice.

"Sir, there's been another murder," he says, suddenly turning to the matter at hand.

"And?" asks Trump turning to him, while narrowing his eyes.

"It was an illegal, and the murder victims include a newborn child," said Schwartzkopf, pulling out glossy photos from the LAPD. "It happened on New Year's Eve. Apparently rape and murder, and the perp is still on the run, but we have him on video surveillance and have positively identified him as an El Salvadoran national, Hernandez Rodriguez. But the reason that the DoD is interested is for something else."

Trump rocks on his heels becoming very quiet, while nodding to himself, as he holds up a photo with a blonde's slashed neck along with pictures of her dead baby inside their car, and then glances at a photo of her husband slumped over the steering wheel.

"Apparently, the couple gave the illegal a lift," said Schwartzkopf. "Final details are still being gathered, but we have a confirmed rape along with the perp's DNA."

"You know, I want to call a press conference on this and highlight this case at a national level," says Trump calculating the press reaction and how this could be played out with the Democrats. "Who is the next of kin?"

"Sir, Elizabeth Krush was born in Louisiana with only one living next of kin, her brother. A war hero apparently, and who is currently in military prison," said Schwartzkopf with a gleam in his eye.

"What?" Trump glances sharply at Schwartzkopf.

"Yes sir, that's why the DoD is interested in this case. He's a courtmartialed Medal of Honor recipient, *Delta Force,* and sentenced to 15 years in jail for war crimes."

"Unbelievable," says Trump. "What is this country coming to, General?"

Schwartzkopf also shakes his head.

"I've run a background check on the soldier and the case is really murky with the CIA giving evidence against his entire Company."

"You mean Barrack Ovadia's CIA?" smirks Trump. "Something stinks."

General Schwartzkopf nods as he looks at his boss, Ronald Trump, who is now fixing his hair in the mirror.

"You know, like my hair, I don't like things out of place," said Trump.

Schwartzkopf nods again.

"We're going to get to the bottom of this, General. Oh, and we're going to have fun fixing this."

Ronald takes out a banned CFC containing hairspray and liberally sprays his blonde hair back in place.

Three days later at Fort Lewis

Tor is working out at the gym with his buddy, Flipper —— 250-pound bench presses —— when an MP stares at Tor from above.

"Help me up, Flipper," wheezes Tor, as they pull the 250-pound weight off his chest and the barbell clangs heavily on the metal stand as Tor springs up pouring sweat.

"Sir, you have a visitor," said the MP.

"Who?" asks Tor, while the men from French Company gather around.

"I'm not at liberty to say," says the MP stiffly.

"Ok, let's go," says Tor, while grabbing his protein shake. His heart thuds harder at what might this visit bring. The MP leads him past the control room and out into Fort Lewis, where much to Tor's surprise they board a jeep and drive over to the Commanding Officer's HQ.

"What the hell?" questions Tor, still slurping whey protein from his shaker, as he gets off the jeep and is saluted by guards. Adjacently, there are black suited men in dark shades, along with five important looking *Escalades* parked with blackened windows flashing blue lights silently. Looked like the Feds were here or something, thought Tor, as he entered the building's conference room where men in Army uniforms saluted him all the way. What the hell was going on? Since when did these guys salute a jailbird?

"They salute you, son, because we're going to clear this mess up," said a voice from behind him. The MP stiffens and salutes smartly again. Tor recognizes him from TV.

"Vice President Mike Rense!" exclaims Tor also stiffening and saluting.

"At ease, gentlemen," says Rense, and then leads him into a room where General Schwartzkopf is seated with the tribunal head, General Thomas Marcus, the one who had sentenced them three years ago.

"Sit down," nodded General Schwartzkopf, and Tor was awed to see so many smiles directed at him, but most of all he trusted General Schwartzkopf, who was an army legend.

"Delta Operator Tor, first of all we wish to extend our heartfelt condolences to what happened to your sister in L.A, and this is one of the reasons that we are here today, but also at the miscarriage of justice that is suspected in French Company's court-martial.

"Permission to speak," interrupted General Thomas Marcus of the 75th Army Ranger Squadron, who had turned red as a beetroot.

"Save it," cut in Schwartzkopf brusquely. "We don't have time for this, but it has been learned that the previous administration had ordered the CIA to eliminate French Company from the Anbar province!" Schwartzkopf dropped the bombshell, while pulling out a heavy file which he tossed on the table.

It was stamped with TOP SECRET all over and General Marcus quickly grabbed it to leaf through it to examine the evidence, where he read all the damming evidence of a *frame up*.

"Yes, it appears that the CIA didn't want Delta Force to wipe out their precious Sunni fighters that they were nurturing as a future ISIS army, but French Company was showing no signs of letting up against them."

General Marcus now has sweat on his brow and takes a sip of water.

"If all this is true then why didn't you speak up, Operator Tor?" he asks bitterly.

Tor stares stoically back at him and shrugged, *"We were up against the CIA."*

"Sad business, Operator Tor, but we have a full pardon for you," said Mike Rense pulling out an envelope from his suit's breast pocket and slid it over to Tor. The camp commander made a note of it and was already signing the release form for Operator Tor.

"Sir, with all due respect, I can't do that," said Tor.

"Why not?" asked a surprised Rense.

"Not without the entire French Company," he said staring straight ahead. "My men come first, and then me."

Tor slid the pardon back to Rense.

"Yes, of course," said Schwartzkopf, nodding at Colonel Davis, the camp commander, who hastily rewrote the order for the release of the entire French Company. Rense, meanwhile, made a few adjustments to the written letter as he scratched out Tor Krush's name and replaced it with French Company.

"There!" he exclaimed. "Justice has been served."

General Marcus was meanwhile writing out an order countermanding the court-martial.

"Thank you, sir," said Tor expressionlessly. The outside world had nothing for him, especially since the death of his sister.

"Now Tor," said Mike Rense looking straight into his eyes. "How would you like to work for the government and get some payback?"

"Sir, I don't know," replied Tor.

"What we have in mind is I.C.E, or the Immigration and Customs Enforcement," said Schwartzkopf, and Tor looked bewildered. He was looking to go back to war as a Delta Operator.

"Permission to speak freely," said Tor.

"Granted."

"I want to go back to Iraq and finish off ISIS," he said.

"Tor, we're asking you to go after your sister's killer, and a whole host of other bad guys operating right here at home. Try it out for a month, and if you don't like it, then we'll transfer you back to your Special Ops Command," promised Rense, and now he had Tor's undivided attention. "ISIS has already been dealt within the years that you were in jail."

"This country is full of illegal Mexican and Central American violent criminals who are bringing death and drugs to this country," said Schwartzkopf gazing at Tor squarely in the eye.

"Tor, I also want to tell you that President Trump has his eye on you too, and he is the one who organized your pardon," added Rense.

Tor nodded.

"If the President wants it, then I'm at his command," said Tor solidly.

"Thank you, Tor, we're going to need patriots like you to take back our country," said Rense getting up.

Tor shook hands with him.

"Sir, I take it that French Company is also going to join ICE?" asked Tor, as Rense and Schwartzkopf got ready to leave.

"Whatever you want, sport, you're going to be an ICE operator with an independent command, and with your own discretionary powers," said Rense winking at him as he left.

President Trump at the Funeral

Hundreds of mourners had gathered in L.A at the Westwood Village Memorial Park cemetery, when President Trump's motorcade entered from the Wilshire Boulevard entrance, though the Secret Service was already there positioned all around the cemetery. Tor was there too, with his French Company in full Ranger military uniform, while scanning the crowds to see Lizzie's friends and stood near the casket with his sister looking pretty and almost alive, a testament to the mortician's abilities to present the dead well. Tor looked at his sister, and he hadn't seen her for the last five years —— serving in Iraq and then time in Fort Lewis. She had also intensely disliked his wife Tracy and they had gradually drifted apart, with Tor being Republican and Lizzie turning into a social justice warrior.

The crowd was surprised to see President Trump coming in for Lizzie's funeral ——— mostly young women and some of them were sobbing.

"Lizzie was the nicest person ever," announced one blonde in a black miniskirt, and a lot of them were wearing veils. "But she wouldn't like it if President Trump came here and gave a speech against everything that she stood for."

Tor stared at her, while standing next to her and said nothing, but his muscles bunched on his jaw. Hard Republican. She hastily left as someone else came to pay their respects.

A priest waited and then Flipper, another French Company Operator, beckoned to Tor, as they saw Trump entering with a posse of reporters and Secret Service. Tor spoke into his com.

"High value VIP is here," he said alerting French Company, as Ronald Trump waved to Tor who saluted stiffly.

"At ease, Tor," said Ronald Trump pulling up to Tor and clasped his hand. "I've heard a lot about you."

"Sir, it's great to finally meet you."

"Yes, I'm so sorry for your loss."

Tor nodded gravely while holding Trump's hand.

"Is the priest about to begin the service?" asked Ronald Trump as the casket was lowered, and French Company, who were no strangers to burying people, joined in to carefully lower it into the freshly dug earth that Tor alone had dug as a way of his own penance. He would miss his sister, and even though he had told no one of his sorrow, a piece of his soul had died with her. Meanwhile, few of the mourners were inclined to meet with Trump, while the priest had begun his service and concluded quickly with *ashes to ashes, and dust to dust."*

Tor threw some earth on the casket and took one final look at his sister. He looked up to see Ronald Trump staring at him and he nodded as the ceremony quickly terminated. Trump then came over and asked to meet with the gathered *French Company.*

"Yes sir, this is Flipper, Kim, Drew, Xander, Ron, Chico, and lastly Dee. All that's left of us."

"You men have been through a lot," said Trump oblivious to the dirty looks that a lot of the *Leftie* crowd gave him. Most Californians couldn't believe that Ronald Trump was here in the first place, and it had been a secret and unannounced visit. Some of Lizzie's friends tried to say goodbye and give their contact details to Tor, but the Secret Service didn't allow them —— instead collected their visiting cards and pieces of hastily scribbled notes with promises that it would reach Tor shortly.

"Sir, we did what we could for America," said Kim, a stocky martial arts expert from Baton Rouge and a survivor of countless battles in the Middle East, most of them highly classified.

"And now America asks you to clean up her streets right here at home," said Trump, as the sky suddenly turned grey and a light drizzle started. The Secret Service immediately had Trump under a large black umbrella.

"Yes sir, with Lizzie's death we've realized that a far greater enemy lurks at home," said Ron, a tall man with the build of a wrestler, but he was known to move at lightning fast speeds and was the fastest shooter in the Louisiana based *French Company.*

"Here is a letter for you," said Ronald Trump. "It contains an Executive Order of mine allowing you unlimited authority as ICE deputies on loan from Special OP's Command, but you answer only to me directly. I want you to kick some serious ass out there with no one to stop you. And I know you're the right crowd for the job. Whatever you want, choppers, guns, money, all of them are available to you with my Executive Order."

"Sir, we are more than anxious to begin *Operation Dark Sorrow,"* said Tor, the ranking officer-specialist in French company now. "For my sister."

"And we're going to save a lot of innocent American lives from those illegals," said Trump shaking hands with the team one last time.

It had begun to pour now, but none of the boys moved as they saluted Ronald Trump and stood at attention till his motorcade left.

Delta ICE

"Flipper, what d'ya think?" asked Tor settling down on his dead sister's expensive couch, and French Company had billeted themselves into her house causing it to resemble a military barracks now instead of her usual tastefully decorated bourgeois house. There were racks of AR-15's placed in the corners of the living room —— while her beloved potted plants had been unceremoniously deposited in the garden. Expensive paintings had been replaced by maps of downtown L.A which plastered her walls now, while everyone wore army fatigues with low-slung Sig Sauers on their gun-belts. This fashionable West Hollywood house was going to be French Company's new operating HQ. The house was in Lizzie's name and since there was no will, it had passed to Tor as next of kin, and by L.A's property value, the house was valued at three million dollars, but then Tor was a Louisiana boy and he missed the swamp and 'gators there.

"Well, the checklist is almost complete," grinned Flipper. Dee, a rugged man with a blonde beard and a military style baseball cap came in holding more supplies. New MacBook Pros, and iPhones for everyone with California state government issued phone numbers.

"What about cars?" asked Kim, the squat bodybuilder.

Chico smiled, holding a beer can, while flicking through the Samsung 4K OLED TV's cable channels.

"They should be here today," said Chico. "I placed an order for three bullet proof Escalades and a couple of Dodge Demons."

"Fuckin' *white trash*," chuckled Xander, tattooed and heavily muscled also from Louisiana, and also the tallest in French Company, while Chico, the shortest as the only Hispanic in the group from Costa Rica, threw a pillow at Xander. Ron came back with a six-pack of Heineken beer from the kitchen, which was now stuffed with beer crates. He passed out the beer, while Drew pointed impatiently at a map of downtown Los Angeles. Both Ron and Drew were from *New Orleans.*

"Ladies, look sharp, we need to comb L.A since there are over 250 neighborhoods here," said Drew, who had hacked into the ICE database. "We are getting a live feed of ICE data as they see it."

Everyone looked impressed, while no one had thought of making contact with ICE itself, as they saw multiple illegals moving around. Apparently, a lot of them were wearing tracking ankle bracelets.

"Which neighborhood is Hernandez in?" asked Tor, narrowing his eyes hungrily.

"That's the thing," sighed Drew, as he clicked on the guy's file in the ICE database.

ACCESS DENIED

"We need to get ICE to open up to us," said Flipper, Tor's deputy.

"How?" asked Xander pulling up his laptop and powered the Mac and logged in.

"Wait, did we just hack into ICE?" asked Chico.

Suddenly, a wail of sirens.

"Jesus Christ, Drew!"

The sirens grew louder and filled the neighborhood.

Tor groaned. This was not how he'd imagined the operation.

A megaphone opened up outside.

"This is the police."

A hard knock on the door and Tor saw heavily armed ICE operatives when he opened the door, whose eyes widened when they saw the racks of AR-15's and the tough men lounging around in there.

"What the fuck?" demanded one of the ICE operatives —— a woman. The other one was looking carefully at the men.

"Are you guys some kind of a White militia?" asked the freaked out Hispanic girl as she radioed for back up.

"We wouldn't have Chico with us, would we then?" retorted Xander as everyone burst out laughing, and the bald Chico, a Vin-Diesel look alike glared at Xander.

"We're on *Special Assignment* to help ICE find an illegal murderer," said Tor pulling out his military ID, as did the others. A beefy ICE officer went around to collect their ID's.

"What the fuck have you guys been smoking?" demanded the girl with a touch of a Spanish accent in her voice. Xander's lip curled into a sneer as she continued. "And where the hell are all your accents from?"

"The girl's questions are legit," said Dee laughing, while she glared at him. Kim sat quietly wondering how to explain this mess.

"Um. We're on a mission from President Ronald Trump and we're all from Louisiana, ma'am," replied Flipper innocently, and pulled out the envelope from the President and was about to give it to her, when Tor gripped his hand.

"Our mission is classified," snarled Tor, taking the envelope away. "On a need to know basis only. Call your chief, 'cause they should be expecting us by now."

More sirens in the distance.

"Well ok, hot shots," said the girl. "We're out of here, since LAPD is here, and you'll have to explain your weapons to them. You guys appear to be U.S citizens so that's the end of the line for us."

Just then two detectives from the LAPD walked in holding French Company's military ID's.

"Ok, you guys are in the clear," said one of the detectives, flashing his LAPD badge which Tor examined closely. Full situational awareness. "My name is detective Terry Farmer."

"Hey man, fuck this shit. Let's find our guy, blow him away and get out of this town," said Xander suddenly exasperated with all this pussyfooting, and everyone nodded.

"Well, what you country hicks don't realize is that we have procedure over here in the big cities, and not like a war zone where you just pull the trigger," said the girl, amazed that they had turned out to be legit.

"Ok, why don't we all sit down and have an inter-departmental conference right now," suggested Terry Farmer. "I am covering your sister's homicide by the way." Terry had now turned to Tor.

Everyone was electrified in the room now and the girl looked really embarrassed now.

"Ronald Trump has really ordered a Special Ops hit on the illegals of South LA?" she asked finally.

"Yes, everyone should just sit down," said Kim.

"I'm getting my boss on the phone right now," said the girl as she punched in a number on her cell phone.

"See, this sure as hell beats looking up ICE HQ, and instead, they just come straight to us," remarked Chico happily.

"Ron, get some more chairs from the dining room," said Tor.

"On it," said Ron, as Chico and Kim accompanied him.

Soon the four ICE and LAPD agents were sitting with French Company with their bosses on a conference call.

"What?" snorted the ICE chief Brandon Lashbrook. "Does the president think that we're not going to do our job?"

"No sir, we're just here to help," said Tor, trying to smoothen the ruffled territorial feathers here.

"Your ID's check out on the LAPD side as ICE contractors," said LAPD chief Remmy Colt, "but we will need you guys to carry your ICE ID's with you at all times, especially when you're going in heavy."

Tor looked at the girl who nodded and posed a question to her chief.

"So how do we coordinate with these guys operationally?" she asked glancing at Kim. A quiet squat man with a long beard. A killer with a Yogi's calm.

The ICE chief was meanwhile speaking to DC on the other line.

"I just spoke with Vice President Mike Rense and promised him that these guys will be getting their ICE badges and uniforms," said Lashbrook with new respect in his voice.

"Just who the hell are you guys?" demanded the girl again shaking her head. She had never dreamed of meeting these types of shadowy men here in LA.

"We're military. Delta Force," leered Xander, flexing a heavily tattooed bicep that read "Kill 'em ALL". "Can't you tell?"

The LAPD detectives grinned at them appreciatively, while the girl's mouth had turned into a big O.

"Yeah, the guys you see in the movies. That's us," said Xander enjoying the moment even more, as Tor frowned at disclosing their identity, though this wasn't a covert OP.

"Ronald Trump doesn't kid around, does he?" whistled the LAPD officer.

"Yes sir, and our operation *Dark Sorrow* is a go," said Tor, while glancing out of the window and at the gorgeous fiery sunset of L.A.

Oh, they knew how to bring a piece of hell here alright.

2

Dark Sorrow

Chesterfield, South LA.
Last known whereabouts of Hernandez

"So, this guy *Hernie* was just a homeless bum?" demanded Xander, wearing his new night-vision goggles, while the men stuffed themselves into the two brand new Escalades, now bristling with guns. Then they took off at top speed to ignore quite a few traffic lights with their blue police sirens screaming in the late L.A. evening.

"Where the hell did you get those goggles from?" demanded Tor, driving expertly as if he was back in *Fallujah*. A few cop cars got excited, but their flashing black unmarked Escalades convinced them that this was a government OPs alright.

"Army surplus store," replied Xander with a grin. Behind him were Chico and Dee in full combat gear, while following them was the other Escalade driven by Flipper, containing the rest of French Company.

"Well Hernie is here with his long time, but also illegal girlfriend," said Tor, as Xander accessed the ICE file on Juanita Ramirez, working in L.A as a nanny. "That's her address in Chesterfield. So, what are we supposed to do? Just go in and blow him away?"

"Oh, yeah. This guy is never going to see a courtroom in his life," swore Tor grimly. He would enjoy killing him and do what he was trained to do. To kill. No arrests tonight. No witnesses.

"Well, we can't talk about it then. Not now, not ever," said Dee tersely.

The two Escalades pulled up on 2100 East Florence Avenue, where rows of high-rises greeted them.

"Fucking projects," snarled Flipper, as he exited his Escalade, while pulling out a police battering ram.

"Ok guys, on me," said Tor, as everyone checked their gear one last time and stormed through the entrance of the building, which had no doorman or elevator. A strolling couple, holding hands, saw tremendous movement as eight burly and metal-clinking men rushed by. A man, smoking in the distance in the cool night, dropped his cigarette when he saw ICE written on the men's backs. He immediately called his cousins to let them know the US Government was in the building.

Meanwhile, the men clambered upstairs determinedly with Tor leading the pack, while holding his HK-416 fitted with a silencer and an extended magazine.

"Ok, we're here on the 4th floor. Room 416," radioed Flipper.

"Copy that, Red Leader."

"Get the battering ram ready."

"Copy that."

"Thermal imaging reveals two bodies in the room," said Xander, while unlocking his weapon.

"GO!" Flipper smashed open the wooden door, while the team thundered in, with Dee on the stairs, and Drew covered the back alley outside.

The men storm into the small apartment to find a couple in bed, clearly terrified and who raise their hands slowly into the air.

"Please don't shoot!" shouts the woman, as the men surround Hernandez, a swarthy bearded character wearing a host of gold chains and rings, while his right arm is covered with gang tattoos.

"Ok start talking. Names!" shouts Tor and pulls off the covers to reveal two naked people, but no weapons.

"My name is Hernandez Marcos," says the pleading man.

"Check his ID," says Tor viciously butting his head with his rifle's stock.

A sickening thud as the man recovers shaking his bleeding head while the female trembles even more.

Xander dives into the Hispanic's Levi's that lie on a rocking chair and fishes out a wallet.

"Nothing," says Xander. "Fucking Illegal!"

"Talk motherfucker!" screams Tor. "Did you murder my sister on New Year's Eve?"

The man's jaw drops open and he babbles a stream of Spanish.

Just then wailing sirens.

"Red Leader, we have LAPD here," crackles in Drew's voice.

"What the fuck?" shouts Tor.

"Shoot him now!" Xander has his gun ready now. The woman is screaming shrilly. Tor doesn't like the situation.

"This smells like a setup," says Tor.

"Yup," chimes in Drew on the com.

The sound of thudding police pounding up the stairs.

"LAPD!"

Uniformed SWAT bursts into the room holding Ron and he enters as a human shield.

"Hey, this is an ICE OP!" protests Xander, and lowers his gun as do the rest of them.

In walks Mariela with an ICE team.

"Let us do our job and we don't need you glory boys killing people on our beat," she says, as Hernandez and the woman gratefully get dressed and are handcuffed.

"What the hell is this?" demands Tor ripping off his night vision googles.

"Look, I had no choice, but the Mayor got wind of your presence and she's very nervous. Do you know the heat that you would bring if you'd shot him?"

"Well, he had it coming," argued Tor, pissed to have been cheated out of his quarry.

"This is not Iraq," she says turning to Hernandez who appears bewildered, while his girlfriend is paralyzed with shock. Tor turns to punch Hernandez real hard in the face. A broken nose which spurts blood all over the room.

"Oh, you're a dead man alright, motherfucker," snarls Tor, while Xander kicks him hard in the gut. He's wearing combat boots with carbon metal plated tips. The crunch of a rib breaking.

"Stop it!" shouts a furious Mariela pushing Xander aside.

"I don't know who the fuck you think you are, you *fucking 'spic!'* shouts Xander, as an ICE officer comes in between Xander and Hernandez, and then leads

Hernandez away coughing and wiping blood. The girlfriend is screaming as she's lead away too.

"What did you call me, White boy?" demands Mariela, and she tries to slap him, but Xander sees it from a mile away and has her on the floor before she even knows it, along-with a heavy knee on her back. One push and he can break her spine.

"Stand down, *Delta Operator!*" orders Tor, knowing that Xander was as dangerous as a rattler in these situations. *He'd killed for far less in Iraq.*

"She started it," protests Xander, as he gets off her in one fluid motion. Mariela is breathing hard with rage now, but too furious to speak as she glares at the grinning Xander.

"You're all assholes!" she screams, and storms out of the apartment, with ICE and LAPD SWAT evacuating the building quickly after her.

Xander now punches a hole in the paper-thin wall, literally, and the men stare in fascination at the torn lilac paper in the hole, as Kim and Ron leave the apartment. Flipper radioes Tor to rendezvous back at the West Hollywood safe house.

"Fuck man!" swears Xander examining his leather gloves. "I thought we were fucking untouchables here in LA. Man, we've even got Trump's letter."

"Well, I guess not," says Tor now with a thoughtful expression on his face. "The Californians don't give a rats ass about his *Executive Order.*

"That fucking Latino!" exhales Xander.

"Come on, let's get the fuck out of here."

"If she screws with me again, I'm gonna break her neck," swears Xander.

"She's a sexy Latina," grins Tor. Xander calms down a bit realizing Tor's logic. "But I ain't having kids with a *spic,* "says Xander, but realizing that she wouldn't be a half-bad shag.

They descend the stairs leisurely, while a host of angry eyes watch them —— however, a door opens ominously accompanied by fierce whispers of arguing hotheads in Spanish.

"You just get yourself a nice swamp girl from Louisiana," continues Tor meanwhile, when suddenly there is movement on top of the staircase behind them. A masked man with a gun. Xander has already fired his assault rifle, while Tor is turning.

RAT-A-TAT!

The masked man falls forward filled with 5.46 mm high velocity bullets, while there are shouts and screams coming from the wooden floors above. Rapid

Cholo Spanish followed by multiple clicking of magazines locking into automatics.

Xander and Tor have a split second to look at each other before there is a metallic *clink* and a grenade thuds downstairs to make its way agonizingly slowly towards them.

"Jump!" screams Tor, but Xander is already in headlong flight downstairs before Tor, while the grenade explodes in slow motion. More clinking of steel pins and hot fiery balls of fire roll over their heads as the men stay down on the landing of the staircase. Then the thud of more rapid footsteps.

"Arriba! Arriba!" scream guttural voices.

"Hostiles!" screams Tor into his earpiece, while getting up and is relieved to see Xander do the same. They had just escaped multiple grenade explosions and charred wood on all sides greet them from the cheap project's walls, which are also on fire now and wisps of smoke quickly fill the air. There is a piece of wood sticking into Xander's Kevlar jacket, which he is oblivious to, but then on his night-vision he observes two silhouettes with guns up above. He leaps forward to fire a long automatic burst into the staircase above. Two bodies roll down as Xander nips back expertly accompanied by intense return automatic fire.

BLAM! BLAM! BLAM!

"They have illegal automatics too," grins Tor, as he sneaks forward to retrieve a grenade pinned on one of the dead bodies, and in one motion pulls the ring and tosses it up while bullets whip all around him. Xander has no choice but to cover Tor's retreat and unleashes a firestorm of accurate fire with his night vision and more bodies tumble down the stairs.

"Fire in the hole!" shouts Tor to remind Xander to take cover, and at the last minute Xander pulls back as tongues of wicked fire followed by an explosion rock the building. By now, flames are chewing through the creaking wooden staircase. The smoke quickly becomes overpowering, while more automatic gunfire rakes their former positions.

"Jesus, this whole building is filled with *bandits!*" shouts Tor, ripping off his night vision goggles, as the inferno is making it impossible to see. Thick black smoke clogs their lungs as the fire begins to leap forward cutting off their exit.

"*Evac now!*" screams Xander into his earpiece, as he hears voices and thudding of footsteps making their way up from down below. They were trapped in between the fire and the *Cholos*. "Clear the building!"

Tor coughs as he hastily descends the stairs with his rifle's mag-light piercing through the smoke, while Xander is covering their retreat down. No panic. Measured steps, steady heart rates. No sweat. All systems go. Xander's mind sees the flames and he fights to keep images of burning villages in Iraq out. Civilians screaming with babies crying, along with bleating goats. *Yep, Arabs and their fucking goats.*

"Delta OP!" yells Tor, as he grips Xander's shoulder and yanks him into the thick cloud of smoke. The building was on fire from the ground up. Women and children are crying now still trapped in the project, and the Delta Operators realize that they're dealing with a very ruthless enemy, ready to burn civilians along with them. A grenade explodes frightfully near them, and they feel the blast cut into their Kevlar boots. Too close for comfort.

"Window!" points Tor. It's still the second floor though, but without thinking the men charge towards the window, while firing their rifles to blow the glass away, and Tor leaps out headfirst with his elbow protecting his eyes along with Xander who does the same. They have measured the distance and like expert divers' somersault onto the grass below to break their falls with extreme precision. They're now in the front lawn of the building, but behind them gunfire follows as bullets THWACK all around them into the weed covered grass. Just then their two black Escalades pull up in front of them —— doors open with Kim kneeling, and Dee resting his assault rifle on Kim's shoulder, while giving covering fire.

RAT-A-TAT-TAT!

"Get in!" yells Flipper firing his assault rifle from the other Escalade, as Xander and Tor squeeze in.

"Shit!" wheezes Xander as the cars screech to take off into the night, while bullets thud into their trucks from all sides, but the bulletproof exteriors hold.

"What the fuck just happened back there?" shouted Flipper.

"We should go back and finish the bastards," argued Xander in full combat mode. In the distance, the Fire Department was charging towards the scene along with scores of LAPD police cruisers.

"Or maybe not!" grins Xander. He puts up his hand to high-five Tor. "That was a good fight!"

"Yeah, that felt good," said Tor, and that familiar adrenaline thrill was like heroin coursing through his body like a relaxing drug. All the boys in French Company lived for that high. *To kill or be killed.*

The U.S 75th Ranger motto was, *Rangers lead the way!*

Breaking News on CNN

"Tonight, a fire broke out and details are emerging about a murderous standoff between renegade ICE officers and unarmed immigrants in this *Sanctuary City* of Los Angeles," announced a breathless blonde in front of a burning building. "This is one of the poorest neighborhoods in South L.A," blared another woman for the BBC also with a picture of the blaze, which was still not under control. "The death toll threatens to be one of the highest in Ronald Trump's second term America, where instead of giving succor, innocent immigrants are pursued with bullets and the strong arm of the law."

"Just who were these renegade ICE officers?" demanded an African American woman for NBC. "We'll tell you as soon as we come back from this break."

"Jesus Christ!" mumbled Drew as he watched the news in Tor's inherited house in West Hollywood.

Everyone else was quiet, while nursing their Heineken beers, but Xander had a look of disgust, and Chico finally switched off the OLED screen with a remote.

"Fuck this shit!" he said as everyone turned to look at him. "They're gonna hang us high and leave us to dry."

"He's right," said Kim. "Maybe we should leave the state or something."

Just then there were sirens outside.

"Too late," said Ron, squeezing his empty beer can and tossing it expertly into the now overflowing trash can.

"Any news trucks?" asked Tor.

An angry knock on the door. Flipper opens the door wearily, and in storms that woman, Mariela, but behind her are two men in suits.

"Jesus Christ, not you again," says Xander with disgust.

No one says anything, as the men stand there, not with hostile eyes, but with a look of deference.

"Who the fuck are you?" demands Chico rudely now, while flexing his biceps in his sleeveless military vest.

"Oh, we're so sorry," said the older white-haired man. "I'm the LAPD police chief, Remmy Colt, whom you spoke on the phone with earlier."

"And I'm the ICE chief, Brandon Lashbrook, also on that conference call," said the other man while remaining standing. Mariela is also unusually quiet with a curious look in her eyes.

"Yeah, your fucking lovely *immigrants* were armed to the teeth in that building," sneered Xander looking at Mariela.

"Does he always have such a big mouth?" asked Mariela, and now everyone burst out laughing while Xander turned red at this insult. It kind of broke the ice and now everyone sat down on whatever they could find.

"Yeah, I mean despite what the press says, I think that you guys are lucky to be alive," marveled Remmy, the police chief. "Don't get me wrong, I'm all for Trump's immigration policies, but this Democrat Mayor is breathing down my neck."

"Same here," agreed Brandon, the ICE chief.

"But 35 people died," said Mariela. "And we also found a lot of guns, and partially destroyed drugs. A lot of fentanyl. Like more than a ton, and apparently that house was one of the main storage depots of MS-13."

Tor whistled.

"Comparable to Afghanistan," says Kim, who had served there and knew Heroin well.

"Well we don't know what to do with you, give you guys medals or put you in jail," said the LAPD chief shaking his head wistfully.

"Yeah, we live in a twisted reality where we can't really go after the bad guys, as long as the mayor remains this *Gonzalez* woman, an Ovadia administration holdout."

"Maybe she just needs a good banging," said Xander, looking sharply at Mariela, who turns her nose in the air and decides to ignore the pointed remark.

"Ha ha, I wish it was that easy. City hall is full of bleeding liberals," said Remmy now quite bitterly. "We know it better than you, and we have stopped policing most areas of South LA, while the press ignores these so-called *minority* crimes as much as they can."

"So, Ronald Trump was right," said Chico causing everyone to nod, but the Californians do so warily, like a guilty pleasure that no one wants to 'fess up to. The men of French Company who are used to a more direct line of action and plan are disgusted by this hypocrisy.

"But we have a plan," counters the chief now, and French Company respond to it warily.

"Yes, since Ronald Trump is backing you all the way, we can give you a free hand for about two weeks," says ICE chief, Lashbrook, who is tired of rounding up criminals, only to have them released later by the county jails. He is also tired of not being able to enforce the law and the American constitution, and so he wants to seize this opportunity. Even Mariela cracks a smile.

"What about Intel?" asks Tor. "And what about Hernandez?"

At this everyone becomes very uncomfortable.

"Hernandez is being processed by the law and unfortunately we can't do anything except prosecute him to the fullest extent of the law, though he'll probably be deported back to his country before that," explains Lashbrook. Tor digests the information, while the rest of French Company grin evilly as macabre plans form in their minds. The ICE chief smiles knowingly at them.

"Of course, you will have complete access to our database, and I am even assigning Mariela to your team to further coordinate your activities..."

There is pandemonium, while Xander has already leapt to his feet in protest. Tor smiles as he realizes the game.

"A fucking embed!" screams Xander at Mariela.

"A spy!" cries Dee.

"Gentlemen, I trust you will treat the only female on your team with respect," says the ICE chief.

Kim is shaking his head, while Chico is smiling.

"What I mean is that she will be coordinating and supplying you with Intel, 24 hours a day. You guys will really need her."

"You don't know who we are!" roars Tor, as visions of hell at Fort Benning — —— what they called training —— torture that very few soldiers had experienced.

"I don't intend to join Delta Force, but only to direct your power more efficiently," she says earnestly trying to bury the hatchet and sticks a hand out. Xander's eyes almost pop out. Xander retreats like a caged animal, but then lowers his eyes and takes her hand, and then glares at French Company for loving his discomfort.

"We're all law enforcement here and on the same side."

"The great Xander shakes the hand of a girl," giggles Chico, while Mariela smiles, as Xander holds it for a few seconds too long and then retreats to the sofa to sulk.

"So, then it's settled," says Lashbrook with a sigh of relief, but the LAPD chief, Remmy still wears the look of a condemned man.

"Now I have to explain the climbing body-count to the Mayor," he says mournfully, and no one envies his job as he gets up wearily looking awkward in his baggy suit and exits into the night.

Life in LA

A beautiful girl in yoga pants was jogging past her old friend's house in West Hollywood, when she saw an odd sign outside the house.

"Private Property. Trespassers will be prosecuted."

She went up and rang the bell. There was no answer, so she tried to peer through the curtains, but which were pulled tightly together. Then she tried going around through the back, where she found lots of wooden crates with strange military markings. Very odd. Her friend had been murdered but she hadn't been in the United States at the time of the funeral, so she wondered who was living in this house now. She tried to peer into the crates —— where the smell of cordite greeted her, but being naturally curious, she lifted a crate to examine it.

"Looking for something?" asked a man in an underwear while holding something behind his back. She was startled but recovered her composure quickly.

"Oh, I'm so sorry, I didn't know if anyone was living here," she said eyeing the six-foot-two inches and well-built blonde.

The man turned his head questioningly.

"Well, Lizzie was a good friend of mine," she managed.

"Oh, I'm her brother, Tor," he said putting his hand out which she took awkwardly. He wondered what to do as she didn't budge while holding his hand. "Well any friend of Lizzie's is a friend of mine. Come on in."

"Oh, I don't mean to intrude," she protested, but the man was gone, and she hesitated momentarily to follow him inside the house that Lizzie had built up so lovingly, but now it had taken on a whole new character. The kitchen had stacks of beer cases, with piles of empty pizza boxes, not to mention Chinese takeaways, along with sacks of empty and crushed beer cans.

"Oh, sorry about the mess," said Tor and waved to her to come through into the living room, where she saw neat racks of assault rifles and ICE Kevlar vests hanging in the wardrobe racks. There were enough boots to kit out a school along with maps plastered all across the walls of Southern L.A.

"Oh my god," was all that she could manage.

"They're not all mine," said Tor enjoying her reaction, as he slid into Lizzie's husband's dressing gown. "The guys have gone grocery shopping."

"So, you're ICE?" she asked.

"Yeah, and you know why," said Tor grimly.

At this, the woman lowered her eyes and sorrow flooded through her. She wanted to talk, and maybe it was a good thing that the guys weren't here.

"It's just not fair what happened to her," she said, and Tor nodded grimly.

"Yeah, nobody deserved what happened to her," said Tor.

"It's funny, but she talked so much about you," she said looking into Tor's eyes. Tor felt embarrassed, but he hadn't had the fondest of feelings for left-wing Lizzie and her political activism for Hillary had cut her off from him. But he wasn't going to admit that to this woman. Not yet.

"She was so proud of you, Special Forces and the Medal of Honor," she said, and Tor realized that she was something of a close confidant.

"Why weren't you at the funeral?" he asked her.

"I was in Paris closing a corporate merger deal that couldn't wait," she said while lowering her eyes. "I know, I feel shit about it."

Then she burst into a sob. "But I don't think that I could've made it for her funeral anyways."

She was crying now, and Tor wondered what to do. He was never any good comforting women anyways, and he thought of his estranged wife, Tracy. A heroin addict. Jesus Christ.

"But Tor, she wanted you to know that she loved you even though you guys were politically against each other," she said opening her wide blue eyes.

Tor saw a very healthy woman with toned muscles, and he compared her body to Tracy's wasted heroin ravaged body back in Louisiana, though Tracy used to be a real looker back in high school.

"Please don't hate her for her political beliefs," said this woman.

Tor didn't even know her name, and he was suddenly having flashbacks of Iraq with crying Iraqi women, with death in their dark kohl laden eyes. Panic and pleading and it was there in this woman. He got up to sit next to her and hugged her instinctively causing her to melt into his arms. A weird feeling after three years in military prison to now cradling this beautiful woman.

"Lizzie was so afraid that you would commit suicide," she said causing Tor to let go of her in a hurry. "Yeah, we saw the military suicides in the news everyday."

"You know too much about me," was all that Tor could muster embarrassedly. He felt like such a gimp for ever contemplating suicide.

"Yeah, well we were close, and her baby daughter was like my own," she said.

"Wait, what's your name?" asked Tor.

"Claire," she said.

"Where do you live?" he asked her hastily trying to get out of this emotional minefield.

"I'm the big red house from across the street," she said, also relieved to change the subject. Feelings were never easy.

"And what do you do?" he asked her.

"I work for *California Asset Acquisitions* as an executive," she said. "Though I work from home."

Now she had a bright smile on her face, and all was good again. Tor hesitated.

"I used to be against all the ICE roundups, but now I'm not so sure," she said. Tor breathed a sigh of relief.

She smiled. "I know you're a terrible Trump supporter and Lizzie hated you for that, but you were always her brother."

She was needling him. Tor smiled too.

"Well, that's why I'm here," he said grimly.

"I can't believe it," she said getting up, while Tor admired her toned thighs in black spandex and her pink sports bra with a healthy swell to it. *"Tor Krush from Louisiana here in L.A."*

"Well Claire, I hope to see more of you," he said also getting up. Just then he heard the roar of the Escalades outside. Then loud men slamming SUV doors. Tor was petrified while Claire cocked her head.

 The door was roughly thrown open and in trooped French Company.

"Well, I'll be!" roared Xander holding more pizza boxes, with Chico almost dropping the cheesy dips. Claire gawked at the tattoo laden muscular arm of Xander's.

"Come on in, guys," smiled Tor. "She won't bite."

Tor was sure though that Xander would manage to be his usual asshole self again. He was great as a combat buddy but shit as a wingman.

"Claire was just leaving, but let me introduce her to you," said Tor artfully and Claire nodded. "Claire, this is French Company."
She shook hands with all them men who stood rooted to the spot as Tor then artfully nudged her out into the sunny front lawn.
"Hey Tor!" yelled Xander from inside, and with a grin threw a cellphone which Tor caught, as Claire grinned from cheek to cheek.
"Your boys are real smooth," she said, as Tor stared at the radioactive phone in his hand. "Well yeah, please take my number before I leave you to your *French Company,* even though they don't look very French to me."
Tor squints in the sunshine to cover his embarrassment as she takes the phone from him to enter her digits, while the men hoot from behind.
"Oh, someone just got lucky!" yells Drew.
"I love you too," howls Xander, as Claire decides to hug Tor and then kisses him languidly on the cheeks under the hot sun.
There is dead silence now.
"See you later, boys," she says waving to the boys and smartly breaks into a jog while putting her earbuds back in.

Stake out

A large house in a Hispanic neighborhood of South LA, suspected to be a MS-13 cartel's safe house, and to where ICE had tracked some recent mules from the border. That information had been the relayed to French Company. It had been a weeks-long sting operation and Mariela had a grim expression on her face sitting in the Escalade, as she counted down the seconds for the operation. Drew sat shotgun with a laptop monitoring surveillance cameras covering different parts of the building, while Pantera's *"Cowboys From Hell"* played on the radio in the background, though Mariela hated this white boy music. Latin rock was where she drew the line when it came to the guitar as she turned off the radio.
"Ok, we have two guards sitting and smoking in the front driveway," whispered Drew into his mini-earpiece com. *"And then two bad hombres out at the back stacking a black minivan with contraband."*
"Any other guards?" asked Kim itching to storm the building sitting in the other Escalade. He was dressed in full body armor and a Kevlar helmet.

"Wait, let me fly the drone towards a window," said Drew, taking the risk of being spotted, as a small micro-drone flew below the roof of the two-story house and peered through the windows serially, while Drew took photos. It was a tiny drone copter no bigger than a coffee mug but filled with powerful microwave transmitters. The guards below smoked and didn't notice the little drone as even their wide brimmed sombreros blocked out most of the sun.

"Four men inside and four outside," whispered Drew.

"Ok, let's go," ordered Tor, and suddenly the men jumped out of their Escalades with big ICE letters emblazoned all over their uniforms and stormed the front door of the house led by Kim, Ron, and Dee, while Flipper led Xander and Chico towards the back from across the street.

The two guys sitting up front were startled to see blue helmeted men charging towards them with guns.

"ICE!" yelled Tor. "Drop your weapons!"

He sprinted towards the men, who remained paralyzed on their chairs as Tor reached them, while Kim and the rest continued to charge into the building. Surprise was key. Tor, meanwhile, patted down the guys and Mariela came running to cuff them and take them into the Escalade.

"Ok, I'm going in," said Tor then and sprinted in as the sound of gunfire filled the neighborhood, while pit bulls barked ferociously knowing that their masters were in trouble.

"Hostiles down," announced Xander's grim voice, while Mariela rolled her eyes. These guys still thought they were in Iraq. Tor continued to sprint towards the front of the house, where he saw Kim bash the front door in with a battering ram.

Gunshots.

"Incoming!" shouted Tor, his HK 417 rapidly emptying a clip while charging into the house. A body hit the wooden stairs with a loud thump, but another volley of gunshots as the men followed Tor in. Kim saw a grenade roll up to his feet and he could even hear the fuse burning inside, but Tor's gloved hand has scooped it up to quickly send it flying back upstairs. A huge explosion rocks the house. Meanwhile, Xander has entered from the rear and reaches the staircase at about the same time as Tor. FLIR nightvision switched on.

"One bogey?" whispers Xander as his sharp ears hear some faint sounds above.

"Possibly two," replies Tor approaching the top of the stairs, bathed in bright green on his scope, since the perps have cut the lights. He steps over a body.

 BLAM! BLAM! BLAM!
The shots are wild, but Tor fires off a shot automatically. A body crumples, long curly hair flying — a woman, meanwhile, Xander has gone forward with his gun glued to his eye to enter a bedroom. Excruciating silence ensues, as Tor moves into another bedroom. In the green, he identifies the bathroom, and the shower curtain moves, while a drop of sweat enters his eye causing him to blink momentarily. In that moment, he feels a hot metal slug thud into his chest, and as he falls, his gun goes off to plug the guy behind the curtain. A body crumples past the curtain and onto the wet bathroom floor.
"Shit, man down!" announces Xander loudly into the com, and Tor glares at him while viciously pulling a .45 caliber slug out of his Kevlar vest.
"Shut the fuck up," he growls weakly, but Xander grins and heads out as Tor shakes his head. He was getting old. He'd never taken a bullet in Iraq, sure a few close calls, but he'd dodged ISIS mortars and missiles. *Now he'd just taken a slug from a Mexican in a toilet.* He gets up to his feet and he can hear Xander on the com.
"Clear the area, LAPD says they're on the way," announces Xander exiting the house quickly with Tor shuffling in slowly behind him. Lucky it hadn't been a hollow point. Those things went through Kevlar like butter. He staggered into their Escalade as it roared off into the street with barking dogs and neighbors all watching the lightning fast daylight raid.
"Did you take care of the minivan?" asks Tor.
"We blew out the tires and then the guards," grinned Flipper. "That's what happens when you fall in love."
 A round of laughter from the boys as Tor turns red in the face. The Escalades with their blue flashing lights clear the Southern L.A Chesterfield neighborhood fast and heading towards West Hollywood.

Newsflash

"Another day of infamy!" blares a CNN reporter. *'More undocumented civilians gunned down by Trump's goons."*

"One of the biggest hauls of fentanyl in modern day history today suspected to belong to the ruthless MS-13 cartel," announced a tall and broad-shouldered BBC reporter.

"Our Sanctuary cities are not safe with Trump's death squads on the loose and he will face intense heat from California Senator, Chuck Zucker, who has promised a Congressional inquiry into this mayhem," vowed a reporter from the L.A Times.

"We cannot evade due process of law and must let these presumed innocent Mexican citizens have their day in a court of law," fumed another reporter. "These poor undocumented Mexicans are often exploited people who need sympathy and rehabilitation and not an ICE bullet."

 Xander roars with laughter at this description.

"Those bastards were rocking grenades in combat boots," said Chico, shaking his head at the idiocy of the mainstream media, while Kim stared impassively at the TV in the living room, almost like he's meditating. He is itching to work out, and that's his best way to relieve stress, when a cellphone rings. Drew stares at the screen.

"A Miss Claire," he whoops, and tosses the phone over to Tor, who groans as he catches it, and then quickly heads to the basement gym, where he takes the call.

"Hi," says a female voice.

"Hey," says Tor.

"I just saw the news," she said.

"Yeah."

"They're calling you guys all sorts of ugly names."

"The fucking press," Tor shakes his head. Goddam civilians.

"Hey, do you want to get a beer?" she asks, and Tor is surprised at the thought of hanging out with her. He hasn't done that in a long time.

"Yeah sure," he said. Never turn a good beer down was a tried and tested maxim.

"I'll pick you up in five minutes, soldier," she said.

Meanwhile, the doorbell rings as Tor runs up to change. Drew already has the house wired with cameras from every angle and Mariela is seen from multiple angles on the front porch. The men are now whistling for another reason. More beer cans come out, but Drew has been a survivor from countless Army Ranger operations for over a decade and he knows that the enemy can strike anytime which causes him to abstain tonight.

Mariela enters to high-five everyone and is apparently getting accepted by French Company.

"Where's Tor?" she asks, and Tor winces as he slips into his jeans and notes his rock-hard abs in the mirror. A round of laughter and he can hear her voice too, when to his horror he hears the doorbell ring again and he's getting his boots on, when he hears more whistles.

"Lover boy is putting on his make up," said Xander in a falsetto voice. Tor's fingers slip while tying his shoelaces. He curses and thunders downstairs, only to be greeted by a festive sight of everyone holding beers with Claire in a short black dress and high heels. Mariela is not too impressed by the Californian blonde, whom she regards as a classic bimbo, but then if Tor likes her then that was his choice. She turns her nose, only to see Xander grin evilly at her. She turns red and heads over to the serious Drew who is programming a satellite flyby every 15 minutes giving him neighborhood status updates, while his algorithm was looking for any unusual activity around their house.

"So, you feel safe now?" she asked grinning.

"That's the way I was trained," he replied tersely taking a sip from his black coffee. She turns to see Xander leer at her again, while Tor is captivated by Claire. She sees sparks and feels jealous. She's had a few broken relationships with some police types, and she wants to avoid those kinds of burned out men now. But then there is that six-foot-two hunk of a military asshole, Xander. He's hard to avoid as he slides over to her.

"So, you impressed?" he asked her.

"Well you managed to kill everybody again today," she said, and Xander takes it as a compliment.

"That's what I'm trained to do," he says shrugging his shoulders. "Hold my beer and watch this."

He turns to Claire as Mariela holds his almost empty beer can. "Hey Claire, Tor took a bullet today."

Claire now has a horrified expression on her face, while Tor shoots him a venomous look. Xander cackles along with the rest of the crew.

"You know that's not funny," scowls Mariela with her eyes flashing. "Asshole!"

She storms away to get another drink as Xander rolls his eyes.

Tor hastily departs with Claire, but the boys know he's been set up real good as the door closes. Nothing like telling a woman a bullet story —— a guaranteed to-get-laid story.

Plumas National Park

"Do you know how much we lost over there?" screamed a Chinese in a suit at a Mexican while waving a gun at him. The Mexican seemed to be fearless, this was his turf, but the Chinese were the new people with the fentanyl money. The Chinese Triad was visiting the Kali Cartel's HQ in California.

"We lost a lot too," protested the Mexican. "We lost six of our best men."

"I don't care!" screamed the Chinese, Hong, whose pedigree dated back to the Ming dynasty, and he belonged to the original ancient Triad. He grabbed Ramirez by the lapels, as the Mexican pit bulls were held back by their handlers. Hong then released Ramirez to suddenly pull out a gun and shoot one of the dogs.

BLAM!

The rest of the dogs were snarling with rage now and in the pandemonium their Mexican handlers let them loose —— the dogs charged towards Hong to avenge their dead comrade. Hong, without losing a beat, began to shoot them one by one, straight in the head, and four dogs lay dead by his feet.

"Don't worry, we're Chinese and we will still eat these dogs," he said grinning happily. Ramirez was a Californian drug lord and had at least 50 murders to his name, with death warrants in Mexico, El Salvador, and was also on the FBI's most wanted list for at least 35 dead Americans. But the Mexicans were losing out to the Chinese mass-producing factories of Fentanyl and its derivatives causing billions to pour into Chinese pockets, while allowing them to become a force to reckon with.

"Those were our best dogs!" screamed Ramirez with his hand on the trigger of his Kalashnikov, and he wondered if he should shoot these Chinese bastards, but then the truce with the triads would be broken.

"What are you going to do?" leered Hong. "Shoot me?"

At that the Chinese men all began to laugh, and it was a cruel laugh, but somehow the bloodthirsty killer Ramirez stayed quiet and swallowed his pride. One day, he would boil all of them alive in oil and then feed them to his dogs.

Then he looked at his dead dogs, his notorious pit bulls that had mangled so many, now lay dead.

"So, what do we do about this new vigilante ICE group?" demanded Hong getting back to the main issue at hand. "We lost a lot of money today."

"I've told the Mayor and she says that she's doing her best to call off these American dogs," said Ramiro.

"That Mayor bitch doesn't know what she's talking about," sneered Hong. "I spoke to Senator Zucker and he told me that it's a bunch of racists."

"White Supremacists?" demanded Ramiro. "White boys?"

"Trump has declared an unofficial war against us," said Hong thoughtfully.

"Believe me, we'll find out where they live and burn them in their sleep."

"It's not going to be so easy," replied Hong.

"I will get the best killers from Mexico, you know the ones that beheaded and burned 200 people in Acapulco in one night," gloated Ramiro.

"Yes, you better, or we will have to step into this game," said Hong looking disdainfully at the Mexicans. "From what I've heard, they're Special Forces or something..."

"If they're human, then they will all die. Their wives, their families, whoever they have loved in the past, we will kill them all."

Hong nodded and the Chinese men in suits and dark glasses all quietly disappeared into the bright California National Park. There were rumors of brown bears roaming the park causing the men to gaze warily into the undergrowth as they left the Mexican enclosure that the Cartel had carved out for itself inside the national park.

Tor goes for Sushi

"Yeah, I wanted to bring you out of your comfort zone," Claire said, and Tor didn't really care as he entered a fancy restaurant with blue lights —— appropriately called *Blue Fin*. Tor felt out of place as he entered the plush restaurant.

"Ah..." protested Tor, but Claire was testing him —— to see if he could fit into L.A society. Fancy people with money and Tor had always sneered at these. city folks.

"It's my treat," said Claire, as they were ushered to their table laden with fancy silverware. People were using small silver spoons to scoop out caviar from champagne glasses. Tor, who usually dined on swamp 'gators back home had no problem with seafood though, much to Claire's relief.

"I thought we were getting a beer," he said, as the Japanese waiter smartly pushed a mostly wine menu but just as quickly flipped to its tiny beer section. Tor chose a Hefeweizen blonde on tap.

"Tor, what happened today?" she asked with a sudden serious note in her voice. Tor raised his eyebrows questioningly.

"The bullet, goddammit!" she swore loudly, and suddenly there was pin-drop silence in the restaurant, while Tor wore a sheepish smile, but Claire was not smiling. "I just lost your sister, and I don't want to lose you now."

She laid her hand on his and Tor wondered about his wife, Tracy, probably high on Fentanyl, or whatever she could lay her hands on. *A voice told him to relax.*

"It's real nice of you Claire to care, but I had my Kevlar on me," he shrugged, and everyone resumed eating in the restaurant. Her grip on his hand tightened.

"Lizzie would want you to live. Please take care of yourself," she said with emotion in her eyes, as his phone buzzed and a text message flashed, *"Did you get laid yet?"*

Tor could imagine the guys chortling back home.

"Yeah, I know," said Tor rubbing his chest gingerly and Claire's eyes widened as she imagined him taking a bullet and horror filled her thoughts.

"Anyways, come on Claire, let's enjoy ourselves," he said, when suddenly the TV flashed *"President Trump orders air strikes on North Korea!"*

Tor was stunned. Another war.

"I think that we just invaded North Korea," she said looking up excitedly and she wondered what Tor would say. He shook his head wearily.

"You know North Korea means big trouble," he said. Claire shook her head too.

"I don't know what's wrong or right anymore in this world," she said as everyone in the restaurant was now pointing to the TV and had stopped eating.

"All I know is that the drugs are pouring into the USA and Trump is trying to stop it," said Tor. Claire looked at him and thought of her co-workers in her finance building. Mostly nerds and execs, all ruthlessly focused on getting ahead in life.

"I'm so proud of your service to our country, Tor," said Claire, and Tor looked up at her.

"I thought you would be like my sister, anti-Trump and all that," he said looking closely into her eyes to see if she was faking it.

"Well, I've been in and out of politics, but with China's trade war, I think that we need to take some sensible border precautions," she said.

"Your accent is slightly off," he said.

Claire started to laugh loudly.

"Oh my god, have you heard yours?"

"Well it's a Louisiana drawl," he replied grinning. Oh, no wonder everyone was looking at him all weird in L.A whenever he spoke.

"Well, I'm from England originally," she said.

"Oh, well I'd have never guessed," he said. "What's it like over there?"

"Oh, you've never been?" she asked, and it always surprised her when she met Americans who had never traveled anywhere else.

"Yeah, only to war zones," he replied bitterly.

"Americans are such a suppressed people, and that's what I feel after having lived here in L.A."

"Yeah, how come you moved here?"

"I was married once and I moved here in my twenties for love," she said. He nodded as she gazed at his wedding band. Shit, he still had it on.

"Yeah, but Lizzie told me that you guys had split up."

Tor was relieved.

"And that's why I asked you out," she said coyly. His phone buzzed again. *"Are you in her panties yet?" Xander texted.*

"Can I sit next to you?" asked Tor in a strangled voice.

"Sure, as long as you switch off your phone," she grinned, and Tor stabbed the power button ferociously to slide over next to Claire's crossed thighs and with her dress riding high, but just then the waiter brought his beer and Claire's expensive wine.

The Cartel's vengeance

"Arriba, Arriba," whispered Mexican ex-paramilitary Colonel Osvaldo Montoya, as they approached the West Hollywood house in darkness. Two squads of ex-Guatemalan Special Forces, the Kaibils, emerged from SUVs a block away under the cover of midnight, and stealthily approached the marked house.

Meanwhile, the party was in full swing with Xander on his tenth beer, when Drew was alerted by his algorithm and he quickly put his Red Bull down to see his infra-red drone transmitting bone-chilling images of crouching men approaching the house from the backyard.

"Incoming!" Drew screamed over the music and Xander hastily snapped out of an embrace with Mariela who looked up dazedly. "We've got hostiles!"

Kim was already cradling his Heckler and Koch and heading up to the roof. Just then gunfire erupted!

RAT-A-TAT! RATATATAT!

The first floor was raked with bullets as windowpanes shattered and Kalashnikov slugs slammed into the woodwork, but Kim was already on the roof with his FLIR optics and he had begun to fire, single action, like a sniper.

CRACK! CRACK! Two men crumbled, but the other men were firing from the tree line through the backyard, but they still hadn't spotted Kim on the roof. A man came running forward in the dark night with a flaming bottle, but Kim shot him down as the bottle exploded in his hand burning his already dead body. Kim smiled through his thick beard and could feel the old adrenaline picking up, but someone threw a long arcing bottle that landed by the backdoor where it burst. Shit, they didn't have much time as French Company opened dense fire into the tree line, but no more men appeared. Xander and Chico were up there calling the police and Drew had already dialed 9-1-1, but their phones were being jammed. Big trouble.

"Shit, I think we're on our own here," whispered Drew to Xander who nodded. They were in trouble. Flipper descended with a fire extinguisher and there was pandemonium in the house, while Ron covered him as they made their way through the thick smoke. Another burning bottle smashed into the back door. And then a metallic clink, followed by others. But even more ominously, the grenades kept rolling. *The back door was open.* Suddenly, a speeding 18-wheeler white truck with headlights appeared from the front and broke through the front garden's fence to horrifically smash into the house.

The whole house erupted into a giant fireball. Kim opened his eyes wide as a howling inferno hurtled up coming for him and he gazed at it calmly. He had often wondered how death would come and here it was, in the fucking streets of L.A where he'd least expected it. The red explosion melted Chico in front of his eyes before he too was swallowed up.

The explosion was so big that neighboring houses caught fire too, as people came running out accompanied by blaring fire-truck sirens in the background now.

The Dinner

"Do you want to get out of here?" Claire asked eventually, as they broke off a long kiss after three beers and a bottle of wine. Tor was glad that his phone was switched off as she paid the bill and they headed to the car. They got in where Tor went in again to kiss her and tried to push his hand under her dress.

"Not here," she protested, staring at grinning passersby's through the windscreen and pushed his hand away. "Your place or mine?"

"I love that question," said Tor hoarsely. She put the car into drive to slowly drive home.

"Well I think that my house will definitely be better," she said. "Those friends of yours are something else."

He nodded and wasn't really thinking right now.

"I hope those cops don't stop us," she said, noting flashing police cars up ahead worriedly as they entered West Hollywood only to have a policeman stop her car.

"Oh shit," she groaned, as Tor tried to focus his eyes hazily on the situation.

"Ma'am, do you live here?" he asked her leaning into her car through the window.

"Yes," she said trying to keep her mouth closed and not let the alcohol float over to the cop.

"Can I see some ID?" Claire's heart was in her shoes now and her heart thumped worriedly. A fucking DUI was the thing that she needed as she handed him her driver's license, which the cop examined seriously.

"We have bad news for you," he said. Now Tor snapped awake, when he heard that tone.

"There's been an explosion on your street, and it's been sealed off as we investigate," he said. Tor was instantly awake, and he reached for his phone. It was off. Shit. He turned it on. 15 missed calls. *Motherfucker.*

"Can we go to the house?" he asked as he dialed his voicemail. No messages.

"I'm ICE," said Tor pulling out his ID, and the officer's eyes widened.
"Yes, go right ahead," he said, though he was sure that both of them were drunk, but then seeing the ICE ID, he let it slide.
Claire put her foot down on the pedal to screech into the night, while Tor now had a sick feeling in his heart. A gut instinct told him that something was wrong. Very wrong.

3

Payback

Cedar Sinai Medical Center,
Beverly Blvd.

"Sir, the patient will see you now," said the nurse and Tor got to his feet, with Claire sleeping on a patient bench in the waiting room. 9 A.M in the morning. He headed into the hospital room to enter the SICU.

"Hey Tor," grinned Xander. Tor stared at him, barely recognizable through his bandaged head while lying in bed. Tor rushed over to hug his friend.

"Tor, any news about the others?" asked Xander, with his brow darkening now.

"Flipper, Ron, and Chico didn't make it," replied Tor with a forlorn expression on his face. "Drew is ok along with Mariela. Drew said that you guys ducked into the basement while Kim and Chico took the roof."

"Kim?"

"They found the tough son of a bitch in the neighbor's swimming pool. He must've flown quite a distance, but luckily the pool wasn't empty."

"Shit, we let our guard down," cursed Xander.

"It was a fucking setup," snarled Tor angrily.

"It really looks like that," said Xander. "We got cocky."

"It's not our fault. We were in our home country and as law enforcement," said Tor shaking his head.

"This country is not really ours anymore," growled Xander, as a Hispanic nurse came in with a Chinese doctor. Tor also stared at the new reality.

"Mr Alexander, you have recovered very rapidly, and your labs and vitals are fine so we can discharge you today in the evening," said the young Chinese doctor smiling at him, and Tor felt bad for the kid. The doctor was just doing his job and he smiled back at him, even though Xander stared hostilely at him. The nurse was already un-bandaging his scalp and face, though 15 stitches remained on his scalp for deeper lacerations.

"Ok, thanks a lot, and what about Kim?" Tor asked.

"Follow me," said the doctor, while Xander jumped off the bed, but no one argued with him, while the nurse hastily took out his I.V lines and bandaged his bleeding needle sites. The doctor then led them to the medical ICU where they entered to see Kim on the respirator, while Drew was already working on the computer. He stood up relieved to see Tor.

"Jesus Christ, I'm so sorry that I wasn't there," said Tor feeling bad that he hadn't been there in the battle.

"Dude are you crazy?" said Xander. "That was a car bomb and not even the best soldiers could've escaped that."

Drew nodded and gave Tor a big hug.

"You would've been an unnecessary casualty, besides we needed someone to avenge us."

Tor nodded grimly. There was going to be hell to pay for whoever did this.

"Those guys were experts. No ordinary attack," claimed Drew.

"You're right about that!" boomed a voice from behind them. It was the LAPD chief Remmy Colt.

Tor turned a dark shade of red and Xander swore under his breath. The police chief put up his hands in the air disarmingly.

"Look guys, I'm just as shocked as you are," Remmy said, and tried to shake hands with the men but no one took his hand.

"Why are you here?" demanded Xander hostilely.

"Look I have something to tell you," said the police chief and he leaned closer. "There was a leak, but at the highest level."

Tor nodded.

"It was that mayor, wasn't it?" demanded Xander, and the chief's eyes jerked in surprise.

"We had our own hunch," said Tor, and even Kim stirred now on the respirator. His eyes flew open and the men went to him.

"You're going to be fine, Kim," said Tor holding his hand.

"At least you have your beard, look at my hair," Xander pointed to his scalp's shaved areas filled with stitches and Kim gave a thumbs up.

Next there was another knock on the door, and it was the ICE chief, Brandon Lashbrook accompanied by Mariela who had her left arm in a cast, while appearing very shaken and frightened. She saw Tor and hugged him.

"I'm glad you're safe, guys," she said gripping Tor's hand and clasped it to her breast. Claire at that moment appeared with everyone gathered.

"Is everything ok, Tor?" she asked noting Tor's hand resting comfortably on Mariela's bosom.

"Give us a minute," said Xander. Claire realized that they were all police here and feeling self-conscious, hastily left.

 Everyone dropped to whispers now.

"It was that bitch, Gonzalez," hissed the ICE chief. "I have wiretapped evidence." He pulled out a thumb drive and slipped it into Drew's hand.

Tor and the LAPD stared at Brandon who was pissed.

"The heat that's coming down in the face of this attack," he said. "Not to mention the casualties French Company took." Brandon looked forlornly at his feet.

"They were family," said Tor, with reality slowly permeating through. Life was so unpredictable, but as soldiers on active duty, they were prepared for seeing their friends die. Numbed inside by the long list of deaths of comrades.

"We're going to organize the funerals. Where would you like to send the bodies?" asked the ICE chief.

"To *Baton Rouge*," said Tor. "But Ron was an orphan, so I think that we will take care of his private burial arrangements."

"Sure thing," said the ICE chief.

"Yeah, ship 'em over to *Baton Rouge*," said Xander. "We'll be there on the next plane."

"I think that Kim will be ok in a day or two, so we'll fly with him," said Tor. "The bodies are already on ice."

"Meanwhile, we have some unfinished business with the Mayor," said Xander. The ICE chief and the LAPD chief nodded grimly, while Kim put up another thumb, and Tor looked at Xander intently.

"The Getty house is just around the corner on Windsor Square.

The Mayor's house

Two police cars stood outside Mayor Elena Gonzalez's Residence when suddenly the lights went out. The policemen outside realized that something was wrong and thought about getting out of their cars, as they chewed slowly on their creamy *Dunkin' Donuts,* but then the lights came back, while the evening sky was filled with thunder and lightning.

"Nah, some kind of a power surge," said one of the cops, and the men shook their heads at the shabby power lines of Central L.A. The infrastructure was crumbling here, and it was poetic that the Mayor's lights had gone out. Maybe she would do something about it rather than just making sure that LA stayed as a *Sanctuary City.* The cops were disgusted by it.

Meanwhile, Drew, Xander, and Tor had bypassed the security system to enter the house, while Drew made a beeline for the basement where the electrical system was installed, and got to work interrupting the video live feed with a fake loop, as Xander and Tor made their way through the house. It was 10 PM and the mayor was an early sleeper according to intel, when they saw the light on in the study —— where a thick female sat visible through a crack in the door.

"Is that the *'spic?'* demanded Xander pulling out a Bowie knife. She was on the phone and clearly agitated, while Drew was tapping into her conversation with an ultra-powerful mic amplifier that could pick up even a sneeze in the neighboring house. She was speaking in Spanish very rapidly and Drew grimaced wincing as he tried to keep up with the Mexican dialect, but he was also recording it for later.

"Anybody else here?" asked Xander, and Tor nodded, pointing upstairs.

"Kids."

"Ok, let's make it quick," said Xander pulling on a balaclava mask and so did Tor, and they burst into the room with Sigs pointed to her head. Mayor Gonzalez dropped her cell phone and was about to scream, when Tor clamped her mouth in an instant, while resting a Special Forces Ka-Bar knife under her chin.

"Do exactly as we say and you might live," he whispered ominously into her ear and she trembled. Mounds of fat on her neck —— probably two inches, and it disgusted Tor to even hold her.

"You're a cartel rat!" swore Xander. "We know you betrayed those ICE agents."

The Mayor experienced visions of terror and began to sob.

"Please don't, I have children," she gasped, and Xander laughed ominously to come closer to her with a 10-inch Bowie hunting knife, while Tor pushed his knife deeper now into her considerable Adam's apple from behind. Any other person would've been decapitated with this amount of knife movement, but Tor was slow and deliberate with his pressure and depth.

"Please, I don't know anything," she gasped through Tor's fingers covering her mouth, while the knife choked her windpipe.

"Gut her like a pig," swore Tor, and now Xander came up with the knife and pretended to sink it into her stomach with a mighty heave. She tried to scream but Tor pushed her forward and she fell, though Tor grabbed her at the very end. Now she was beyond terror when Xander grabbed her curly hair.

"Ok niggah, we gonna cut you up real good now," he grinned in his best Louisiana drawl.

"Please, the cartel will kill me and my family," she whispered now looking up beseechingly. Both Tor and Xander laughed with even Drew on the com line sniggering too. She saw no mercy in their eyes. "MS13 gangs just distribute the drugs but you don't know the parent Kali cartel," she said shaking. "You have no idea who you are asking about. They have supernatural voodoo powers." Tor and Xander sniggered some more. She continued.

"I have family in Mexico City, and I had no choice but to share all the details on those ICE agents," she said.

"Who is your contact?" demanded Xander now slapping her hard across the face. *"Fucking voodoo nigger."*

Tor was still playing her mouth like a mouth organ and making sure that she couldn't scream but only whisper.

"Oh, call me what you like but you have not seen hell as I have in Mexico. You think you have seen evil, white boy. You have seen nothing!" she whispered hoarsely while pointing to her cell phone on the ground. Xander picked it up and she unlocked her iPhone with her contorted facial features, and Xander made her turn off the password and facial recognition software.

"The contact's name is Samuel Fuego and the passcode is 76123," she said, though now smiling in a nasty and unhealthy way. Like she had nothing to live for. Tor might have felt bad for her, but she had the blood of Ron, Chico, and Flipper on her and there was no forgiveness here. She continued.

"Fuego means fire," she said, "and he will burn you White Devils from the inside out."

Xander slapped her now with his backhand that sent her eyeballs spinning as Tor didn't let her head budge, while her lips and nose began to bleed.

"Where we come from, we feed your kind to the swamp as 'gator feed. So, you best never get involved with ICE after this."

She viciously spat out a gob of blood and mucus, but Xander was miles away from her and quickly laid a punch into her fat gut. Her eyes glazed and she couldn't breathe for a few seconds after that, while Tor then let her fall heavily to the ground.

"Don't forget her iPhone," reminded Drew, as the men then slipped out of the house like they'd never been there. Meanwhile, the cops were now on their fourth round of donuts —— their windows rolled up tight —— as fat drops of rain began to pelt their police cruisers, when there was a mighty crack of thunder that caused the cops to let go of their donuts in a hurry. It sounded like a bomb had gone off in the Mayor's house and they dashed out to investigate.

After the Funeral

"What do we have?" asked Xander at an ICE safe house in Oakland, California, freshly back from the funeral in *Baton Rouge*, Louisiana two weeks ago. Someone there had hinted that the DEA was going to get in touch with them to pass more Intel over to them about the Kali cartel.

"Nothing new," said Drew. "All the numbers on the Mayor's phone are in Mexico City, while there is one number here registered to the Golden Dragon restaurant and the funny thing is that the call was placed at 6 A.M.

"You mean we might have some Chinese mafia involved here too?" asked Mariela who was nursing Xander's scalp back to health, and they somehow made a nice couple against all odds. But her local Hispanic intel made her indispensable for them to carry out their operation.

"You want another one?" she asked reading a text message from her phone. Something in her tone caught the men's attention and she looked uneasily at them.

"You know your Hernandez guy?" she said displaying the text message to them. "He just got deported to Mexico last week by an LA immigration judge."
 The men looked grimly at the phone.

"So, when do we leave for Mexico?" grinned Drew looking at Tor.

The Mexican Border

Two Escalades followed by two Dodge Demons stopped at the border crossing with Mexico where Tor flashed an ICE badge on the San Antonio, Texan side and then proceeded to clear the Mexican border to pass through followed by Xander in the next Escalade, who leered at the suspicious Mexican immigration agent.

"We're going to give those illegal bastards hell that your country is full of," grinned Xander, as the Mexican immigration official took his time with Xander's ICE pass.

"It says here you're from Louisiana," he said staring at Xander, and then at Mariela who flashed her ICE badge and spoke rapidly to him in Spanish and explained to him that they were in hot pursuit of some criminals. The official knew they were trouble and he glared at the White boy who seemed to be too cocky for his own good. *Xander was not finished.*

"We're going to finish that Wall real soon, so we don't have to be chasing after your illegals anymore," gloated Xander, and then drove away on the dust laden highway.

"Bastards!" muttered the Mexican official after the Escalade.

"We're in Mexico!" Xander said turning to Mariela, who looked worried mostly at Xander's racist mouth. He was trouble alright. They had been driving for two days now with a lot of pit stops in California, while also a good way to cool off and mourn the deaths of their comrades.

Kim and Drew were in the Dodge Demons behind and also quickly roared into Mexico without any trouble, but they knew how to keep their mouths shut, a very important attribute in Ranger school. Their cars were armed to the gills with weapons, including C-4 explosives, while Kim packed a .50 caliber in his car along with a host of small arms. Drew, meanwhile, had four Mac Pro towers with him, souped up to super-computing levels that could crack any government website, along with DARPA's latest miniaturized weaponized drones. All of French Company wore carbon-plated body armor. It was to be a dirty but fast operation.

"Head straight to Mexico City," said Tor, switching on navigation and was relieved to see Mexico City light up. "It says ETA in six hours and the highway looks good."

"I read you, Gold Leader, but I think our squaw wants to hit the toilet before that," grinned Xander, as Mariela's dark eyes flashed with embarrassment. It wasn't her fault that she had a small UTI infection, something to do with Xander giving her a rough time in bed.

"If you hadn't been so brutal with me," she protested as memories of making passionate love filtered through.

"So, happy to be in your home country now?" Xander grinned, as she aimed a punch at him.

"I told you before, I'm of Spanish origin," she said. Xander snorted, as she shook her head in disgust and she had to have her head examined for shacking up with this guy. He wasn't even her type.

"Hope you're not pregnant, darling," he added, and her mouth dropped open just when she thought that he couldn't shock her anymore.

"Why, you piece of white trash from Louisiana!" she cried, and Xander had her on *"broadcast"* on the com.

 Kim was heard chuckling.

"Is he giving you a hard time?" asked Tor cutting into the conversation.

"Cuff him," said Drew.

Mariela flushed red as the men broke into laughter finding all this very funny. *"White trash,"* pronounced Tor.

"That's us, buddy," said Kim.

"That's why we all voted Trump," chimed in Xander, and now Mariela realized that they were trolling her with Trump now.

"Look guys, we still have some heavy driving ahead of us," reminded Tor, and he was right. "We don't even know where *Hernie* really is. So, we're going to search Mexico City, and then proceed to Acapulco. Hopefully, that Mayor bitch is scared enough not to be passing anymore fresh intel.

"We should've finished her," said Xander remorsefully, sending chills down Mariela's spine, even though she knew that's what the LAPD and the ICE chief had been expecting, but somehow French Company had let her live.

"Don't say that over the radio," she said, and Xander gave her a hard stare.

"Then that contact of hers, that Samuel Fuego guy of the Kali cartel," said Drew.

"Yeah, they're in a part of the Yucatán peninsula where even the military doesn't go," remarked the quiet Kim, and everyone hastily consulted their navigation maps to see how much driving lay ahead.

"Jesus Christ, it's like three days away," said Xander, as Mariela pinched in and out of Google maps on the Escalade's navigation system.

"Well, we've got a lot of errands on the way," said Tor.

"Jesus Christ, Tor, are we supposed to take on the entire Kali cartel all by ourselves?" demanded Mariela worriedly. "How do we even find them?"

"We have cell numbers from the Mayor's phone, and I've compiled a DEA file on most of these guys here," said the efficient Drew.

"Anyways, you don't find the Kali cartel, they usually find you," said Mariela who was long experienced with the ruthlessness of the cartel. But *French Company* didn't care, and after surviving that truck bomb, something had changed inside them. Running riot in Mexico was not her cup of tea, but Xander's animal magnetism had been irresistible causing her to volunteer for this mission.

But it was going to be her last assignment.

"We need food," said Xander, as he saw something come up on his GPS. *A diner.* He turned his more than 90 miles an hour speeding Escalade onto the dirt road that spat up small pebbles from under his steel reinforced tires to screech to halt besides the red and blue garishly painted, but empty diner. Xander's Escalade was followed by Kim's and Drew's Dodge Demons —— souped up to 1000 horsepower. They weren't gonna go down for a lack of a good getaway car. *No sir, no red-blooded American would ever settle when it came to cars.*

As the cars rolled up, the diner's owner gazed worriedly at them through the large windows and fished out his cell phone to bark rapidly in Cholo Spanish, while stroking his forehead worriedly. He scowled as the *Gringos* entered. The tiny cigarette that he was smoking fell from his lips, when Xander towered over the small Mexican at six feet and three inches of pure muscle and bone.

"Hola Señor," quivered the owner now, while looking beseechingly at Mariela for help over the filthy and greasy counter.

"Señor, can we sit down?" she asked apologetically in Spanish realizing the effect that the Americans, even though they were in casual clothes, were having on the five-foot two-inch Pedro.

"Sure," he said, and looked relieved that they weren't here for him, but just in case he had already informed the Kali cartel contact that some DEA looking fellows had pulled up. Now it was their call as the camera zoomed into the guests and focused on them. Pedro looked up at the camera and smiled, while sweating profusely. Mariela snuck up on him and startled him.

"I need to pee," she said. He looked relieved and thumbed her towards the back, and she took off in a hurry. Then his phone buzzed with a *"Whatsapp"* message. He scrolled through his Huawei phone with his fat and greasy fingers and saw the message. *"Delay them for as long as you can."*

Pedro cursed at the men wearing casual long jackets and jeans. God only knew what they were packing under them. Usually DEA agents just took choppers and went for the big guys. Why were these guys driving? Very unusual.

"Señor, what can I get you," he tried to ask cheerfully. "Some fried pollo?"

Xander and Tor stared at him with their frozen blue eyes, while Kim regarded him impassively, but Drew was already hacking into Pedro's Wi-Fi network.

"Your WI-Fi password, please," asked Drew, and Tor tried hard not to chuckle at the ludicrous request, as Drew was already in the man's WhatsApp account and was scanning his recent messages with an auto-translator. Now Pedro grew very relaxed as he rattled out a Spanish name and a simple password.

"We'll all have the *Pescado*," announced Mariela returning and trying to end this standoff. Pedro looked miffed, as he had about ten pounds of fried chicken ready to be served, but the frozen fish was going to take time to cook. Dam! He cursed the gringos under his breath, while moving his fat waist to yell at his wife inside, watching a soap opera, to go cook the fish. She grunted, engrossed in the middle of a heavy sex scene, and got off the bed to peer at the customers, and also cursed them under her breath. *Gringos.* Her niece, who was such a beauty, had just been deported back to Guadalcanal, and there was a race traitor among them, a curly dark-haired pretty woman of obvious Hispanic origin. Oh, she seemed to be in love with one of the gringos. Her husband approached her nervously.

"They're police," he whispered, and his wife, Noel now stared at them with more apprehension. "And the Kali cartel is interested in them."

She was alarmed now and remembered how they had recently killed her cousin for stealing drugs from them. He had been beheaded along with four other teens, and it hadn't even made it to the local news, forget about American T.V as her husband sent out another WhatsApp text. Then maybe these Gringos were here to free the Mexicans from this accursed drug cartel, but then she didn't really pin her hopes high. Their karma in this life was to suffer and she went back to watching another swarthy Mexican make out with a plastic over-made up peroxide-blonde doll, while her mind tried to make a tough decision between the unopened two-liter Pepsi bottle over a pound of deep fried chicken that bathed the room with the heavy aroma of grease.

"So, they're not really making us Pescado," smiled Drew, and displayed a WhatApp message from Pedro saying. "They are waiting for their never-to-be-cooked fish." It ended with a smiley, but Drew was already tracing the number to the owner and hacking into his life.

"It looks like a Chinese Triad member from his Facebook profile linked to this number," noted Drew, and Tor was impressed. Concrete evidence linking the Triad.

"Shit, but our priority is to snuff out Hernie first for what he did to Tor's sis," said Kim sagely, and everyone turned to him as he rarely spoke, and they nodded at him. Just then two Dodge vans pulled up and out popped four Mexicans and two Chinese, who made no bones about hiding their Kalashnikovs.

"Let me handle this," said Tor, and Xander nodded. Both of them were wearing tan colored long leather jackets with *Sigs* stuck in their holsters under them, while Kim's overcoat packed a HK MP-7 submachine gun. The men stayed seated, as the Mexicans rudely entered, while breaking the bell that sat atop of the entrance door. The Chinese stopped at a distance from them.

"Hey, you!" shouted a Chinaman with his finger on his Kalashnikov's trigger. Pedro and his fat wife watched from behind the corner wondering what would happen, while hoping that the Chinese would pay for the damages at the very least.

"Yes, can we help you?" asked Tor looking up into a Mexican's Kalashnikov, but the men still remained seated.

"Get up or die," said the Chinaman menacingly, and he pointed to the Mexican who laid a hand on Kim's shoulder. At that moment, French Company sprang to action, while time slowed down. Tor had his Sig .45 out, while Xander had already fired the first bullet which plugged nicely into the Chinese man's forehead, dead center, and Xander smiled for a fraction of a second, and then turned to the other Chinaman. But he was disappointed to see that Kim had already sprayed the area with deadly MP-7 high velocity bullets. All the men fell to the floor before Mariela had even pulled out her gun. Suddenly, the time came back.

 BLAM BLAM BLAM BLAM!

"What the hell!" she screamed uncomprehendingly through the deafening roar as all around her bodies crumpled to the floor. But by this time, Tor was already on top of one of the wounded Chinese who was still alive.

"Talk motherfucker," he growled. "Who sent you?"

"Come on," said Drew irritably, as he pulled out his Sig and sent a bullet smashing through the wounded man's head. "I've got their phones."

Tor jerked back in surprise as the .45 bullet tore off half the Chinaman's small head.

"Smart ass!" shouted Tor wiping blood and brains off his face.

"Times have changed, boy," said Drew now strolling into Pedro's Kitchen and in a few minutes returned with three kilos of pure Fentanyl. "Street value of a million dollars."

"Please, they will kill us," pleaded Pedro from the back, as Kim viewed him with narrowed eyes.

"Well, you're lucky that we don't kill you," said Kim, as his terrified wife hastily pulled Pedro back into the kitchen.

"Hasta la Viejo!" shouted Xander cheerfully as they exited, though the door chime was broken. *Much like Pedro and his wife.* Xander got Mariela, still in shock from the encounter, back into the car, while Kim thought about his .50 caliber and imagined different scenarios where he could've used it mounted on top of his Dodge Demon. Tor tore away onto the road rapidly accelerating to 80 miles an hour in a few seconds, with the rest of French Company hot on his heels. *Next stop Mexico City.*

Mexico City

French Company came to a screeching halt outside a *Best Western Hotel,* and Xander was aching for a shower. They had driven non-stop for 20 hours at breakneck speeds at 120 mph and were now dead tired, having decided not to stop anymore along the way. The highway seemed to be a drug conduit more than anything else in Mexico. Now they parked and shooed away the valets, since they had too much ordinance in there for these fools to see.

Xander trooped into his room along with Mariela, while the boys winked at her as she went in with him, still excited about spending the night with this animal again —— as passionate memories stirred in her. But to her disappointment, he dropped into bed only to pass out. She was wide awake like a cat and not at all sleepy and took out her cellphone to make a few phone calls while making sure that Xander was really asleep.

Meanwhile, Drew released a small security drone to hover over the hotel. He went through a Chinese suspect, Chino Lee's Facebook —— live-streaming a brand-new Lamborghini right here in Mexico City. Drew geotagged the post and tomorrow they would pay this guy a visit, as he slowly got into bed and restful sleep overtook him. If they eliminated him, the Chinese supply line would be interrupted. At least for the time being.

Tor was sleeping when a sudden nightmare overtook him and he was back in Fallujah, with small arms fire following him as he ran through the deserted streets, and he ducked behind a pillar in 120 degrees temperature. Sweltering heat and he saw a dead marine on the street lying face-down among the strewn rocks and mud and shook his head. Not a good day to die on, with sweat running down him, and he checked his SAW magazine. Meanwhile, the whoosh of an RPG! Fuck! His pillar was hit, and it crumbled into dust and flames, while Tor rolled away in the nick of time, but the searing heat of the blast burned though his body as ISIS bullets followed him relentlessly.

"Die motherfucker, die!" screamed the bullets, but he gritted his teeth and pulled his body behind another wall miraculously unscathed. No filthy third-worlder was going to kill a Delta Force OP in open combat. Just then, as he rested his body weight on the wall, the thunk of a mortar, and there was no outrunning this one as a big red explosion covered him with the collapsing yellow mud wall.

"Fuck!" roared Tor as he got up sweating and screaming in bed, his body in full combat mode, when he suddenly saw his wife, Tracy, now staring sadly at him, as she plunged the needle of pure Fentanyl into her veins one last time.

"Goodbye Tor," she said and disappeared into the inky darkness of the hotel room, and somewhere a police siren sounded mixed with some Mexican reggae-tone music. His own PTSD had been too much for the fragile Tracy and she had taken to drugs for psychic relief, as Tor woke up every single night dying on a different battlefield, dreaming and sweating.

Just then the phone rang. Tor snatched up his cell phone.

"Hello!"

"Tor, it's Linda."

"Jesus, don't tell me it's Tracy?" Tor pleaded. He would drop this mission right now and go back to sweet Tracy and make everything right. Just this one last time, God. He prayed as Linda paused.

"Tor, she died of an overdose a few hours ago," said Linda in a tired voice. "I was with her in the hospital for the last three hours in Baton Rouge."

Tor let out a sob. His beautiful Tracy, that high school cheerleader who had loved him since he was 16, when he'd been a football star, and the first thing that they did out of High School was to get married, before Tor was selected by the elite Army Rangers.

"Tor, come home," said Linda. "We're going to have the funeral soon."

"I don't think I can make it, Linda," sobbed Tor. His door was suddenly yanked open and there was Xander, who usually slept with one ear open. The lights came on and Xander immediately sized up the situation. Between Delta comrades, they always knew the score, and it was a fatality. *A close one.*

Xander messaged Drew and Kim on their phones and they were there soon to find Tor on the floor holding his head. Mariela tried to knock on the door but realized that she wasn't wanted.

"If only I had one more chance," he sobbed into the phone. Linda was still there.

"Tor, there's nothing we can do about it, but the fentanyl was from Mexico according to the police, and way too clean," said Linda, while everyone could hear Linda's clear Baton Rouge tinged Louisiana drawl. All of them winced. Tor now struck his forehead in despair with the palm of his hand. Xander took charge now and took the phone from Tor's trembling hand.

"It's ok, Linda," he said in a firm voice. "We'll get him through this."

"Tor, she left you a long time ago," said Kim now cradling Tor's head on the floor with his big bushy beard on his face.

"I drove her away!" screamed Tor seeing her lovely face and then her wasted body. The drugs, and a vicious anger coursed through him.

"Put me on speaker-phone," said Linda to Xander.

"Listen to me, Tor, you're in a position to help other Americans. Tracy isn't and won't be the only one. Thousands of red-blooded Americans are dying everyday in the USA. You need to do something about it."

The fierceness in the voice of gentle Linda startled even Tor out of his misery. Linda continued.

"Yes Tor, we are counting on you to wipe these drug-lords out."

Right now, for the surviving members of French Company, who had all gone to school together, had been taught by Linda since grade school, her words were more powerful than even Ronald Trump's could ever be.

"Do you hear me?" she demanded. "Search and destroy, soldiers!"

"Yes ma'am!" roared the soldiers of French Company now all grown up, while grade-school memories of them playing Cowboys and Indians filtered through with a youthful Miss Linda watching over them affectionately in *Baton Rouge.*

The Raid

"Suspect is in sight," announced Xander, lurking besides a garish painting in Carlos Habib's vast *Modern Art Museum.*

"Pretend at least that you're interested in the art," whispered Mariela by his arm, while playing the romantic couple enjoying a day at the museum, and no one gave the gringo Xander another look, but the gringo was trailing a Chinaman —— with his new Chinese girlfriend, who had just arrived from Beijing, while showing her just how successful he had become off the fentanyl trade.

"Suspect is headed to the toilets," said Tor watching the hacked videos from the Museum's security feed that Drew had tapped into. "Hit him there."

"On it," said Xander, as he followed the Chinaman into the toilet and found it empty —— probably in the cubicle, and ferociously kicked the door open to find the Chinese guy wiping his ass, only to slam his head onto the side-wall and then he took him by the neck and quickly broke it. The man would have no chance to survive this mortal wound. Within a minute, he would be dead. Xander hurried out of the museum where Mariela was waiting, when there was a shrill scream inside the museum —— apparently the murder had been discovered. Xander got into the Escalade with Mariela and screeched into traffic, while Drew erased the video of Xander ever having been there in the museum from his hotel room in the Best Western Hotel, before getting up to hastily pack. Their job here was done in Mexico City. Now began the part where they would get *Hernie,* and that would be some solace for Tor, who was still recovering from Tracy's death.

The men quickly hit the highway to close in on Xander's GPS location.

"Did you kill him?" demanded Mariela, now frightened by this extra-judicial killing. She wasn't very comfortable knowing that her mission was quickly turning into a blood bath.

"Look, he was a key part of the fentanyl invasion of the USA and probably his fentanyl that killed Tracy."

"Yeah, but we should've kept him alive for questioning," she argued.

"We know all their secrets," said Xander, and there was no arguing with him.

"Focus on the next task, the Yucatán Peninsula, the home of the Kali Cartel," he said, causing a chill to go down her spine, and not in her wildest dreams had she imagined that as an ICE agent she would go there.

Xander picked up speed along with Tor leading the charge at a brisk 120 mph, way above the legal limit, but then there were no cops here to stop them.

"I've never gone so fast in my life," whispered Mariela, as the Escalade powered through the well-maintained highway.

"You haven't seen Tor drive then," replied Xander, while remembering Mosul in Iraq, where Tor had driven a HUMVEE through a minefield of IEDs, and into a hornet's nest of heavy ISIS machine gun fire. Tor had been a legend in Iraq, but now he was chasing Narcos straight into their home base.

"Hey, guys something is going on in the United States!" yelled Drew grimly.

"What?"

"Looks like North Korea launched a nuclear missile at South Korea," said Drew, and everyone had their cellphones streaming CNN's breaking news coverage. Trump had declared war on North Korea a month ago, but no one expected anyone to actually launch missiles, and even the United States had been in deep negotiations trying to end the *"official state of war"*.

"Jesus Christ!" swore Tor pulling to a sudden halt followed by the rest of French Company on this empty stretch of road in the Yucatán.

Xander stood now on the road along with Mariela while pointing in the distance. *A giant mushroom cloud was visible on the horizon and rapidly gaining on them.* Tor put his hand on Xander's shoulder hurriedly.

"French Company, move out!" Tor shouted. "Possible WMD situation!"

Everyone snapped out of this unbelievable situation and headed back into their cars.

"Fuck, fuck, fuck!" shouted Kim as he thought of his loved ones at home. He was divorced, but he had kids whom he hadn't seen in five years ever since his wife had slapped a restraining order on him. Fuck that bitch, thought Kim, as he got into the *Demon* and gunned the engine to roar out to a 135 miles an hour speed effortlessly, followed by Drew who for the first time was now emotional and shaking his head terribly, while Tor had the radio on.

"Emergency Broadcast!" blared the radio, while Tor fiddled with his cell phone which had gone silent. No signal. Darkness was falling, a shadow over the desolate Yucatán Peninsula where the meteorite had landed killing the dinosaurs. An utter wasteland here. Fitting for the nuclear mushroom cloud that chased them.

"THIS IS THE PRESIDENT OF THE UNITED STATES," blared the emergency broadcast on their police radio accompanied by a lot of static.

"We are now in a Nuclear War with the Republic of North Korea. At 1700 hours, North Korea destroyed the city of Seoul, South Korea," said the gravelly and hoarse voice which the men recognized as Ronald Trump's instantly. *"The cities of Washington D.C, New York, Los Angeles, and Miami have been hit with nuclear warheads from North Korean or possible Russian submarines. We have launched over 75 thermo-nuclear ICBMs at important North Korean sites. We have totally destroyed Pyongyang. That city no longer exists. Meanwhile, I have declared Martial Law in the United States and I have suspended the US Constitution. The United States National Guard and the US Army have been deployed across the United States. Local militias have also been deputized to maintain law and order. All matters are now to be settled by the militias or the Army and they will be the judge, jury, and if need be, executioners of all looters and criminals."*

Ronald Trump paused as the *Star-Spangled Banner* played in the background. He seemed to be in shock too, when suddenly the transmission was cut off.

By now, the men had put some distance between the mushroom cloud and themselves, but they had been trained for Nuclear War, and they knew that they needed to get to a forest, where they would be safer from radiation than in the current open landscape. Their GPS systems had all gone blank and there was only radio silence from every single local station.

"Fuck, I wouldn't even mind that *reggaeton* shit right now," whispered Xander, while Mariela had tears in her eyes. Her family, including her mother and father, had all been in Los Angeles, and the news that it had been hit with a nuclear blast was unbelievable.

"You guys are Delta Force," she turned tearfully to Xander in the car. "Do you think that we will make it out alive?"

Xander grimaced. He was in shock too, and even though they had trained for this day, they had no equipment for it. He looked at his cell phone again, dead, as even Mariela furiously restarted her phone itching to dial Los Angeles one last time. She let out a sob, but Xander now switched on his xenon high beams and accelerated to more than 150 miles an hour catching up with Tor and pulled up besides him. The highway was still eerily empty.

"Hey Tor," he said and pointed to his dashboard. "I'm running low on gas."

 A road sign with Texaco written on it up ahead, and they roared into the rural gas station which had seen better days, as the sign flapped in the late evening. The lights were on as the men hastily exited their cars to yank open the gas station's glass door only to find it eerily empty inside. There was no air conditioning in the musty small station with narrow lanes of dented canned food lining it's aisles. The cashier was also missing.

"Hola!" Mariela tried to call out to the store clerk, while the men got busy stuffing cheap, canned sardines and mackerel into their bags. Xander was meanwhile pumping gas into their fuel tanks.

"Fill these Jerry cans here too," said Tor, emerging with loads of canned food and tortillas. God only knew when their next meal would be. Xander gathered a few empty Jerry cans strewn about near the toilet.

"Start packing, honey," shouted Drew, as he piled in heaps of cheap batteries and Mexican cigarettes into his car.

"Aren't we stealing?" Mariela asked.

"There's a nuclear war going on out there!" protested Drew, while staggering through the small doorway to his Mustang, where he threw the supplies into the trunk. He stood for a moment in the hot night and tried to absorb the magnitude of the event, when Tor and Xander came up to him.

"Soldier, we need to focus and survive," said Tor. "Don't think, remember your training." Thinking for the soldier was death, he needed to act instinctively on his training as a Ranger.

"Yes OP," said Drew.

 Kim came out of the store with something.

"Look what I found guys," he said dangling three big bags of fentanyl and two Thuraya Satellite phones. "These guys were in it neck deep too."

"I think that everyone is headed South," said Tor, trying to figure out where everyone was.

"Yeah, but their cars are still there in the back," countered Mariela.

"C'mon they're Mexicans," said Xander. "They must've hitched a ride on a pickup or something."

 Kim took the Thuraya Satellite phone that appeared to be working and then dialed a number.

"French Company, Unit 092345," he said into the phone. "Active Delta Operator Kim Hart, number 153222, Fort Bragg. Over." Kim put the phone on speakerphone, and he was talking to a computer.

"Army Ranger 75th battalion Operator Kim Hart confirmed. Over."

"Situation report."

"Nuclear lockdown and suspension of all active missions. New orders for French Company."

"What new orders?"

"French Company to return to the USA and participate in Homeland Defense at the earliest. Enemy invasion imminent."

There were cries of surprise all around and the men looked at each other.

"Who?"

"Russian invasion imminent."

"Are we at war with Russia?" asked Tor breaking into the conversation.

The computer paused.

"Identify yourself."

"Tor Krush, Delta Operator, 2583. French Company."

"Welcome Delta Operator Tor Krush of Army 75th Ranger Battalion."

"Are we at war with Russia, Operator?" demanded Tor.

"Affirmative.....First Strike implemented. Twenty-five Russian cities obliterated by OHIO class submarines."

"Have the Russians responded?"

"High probability for doomsday nuclear strikes."

Mariela whimpered and Drew turned to the skies, while Tor and Xander grew grimly silent. Russia was probably licking its wounds for terrible vengeance with a hundred nuclear ICBMs from their submarines at the very least.

"We need immediate EVAC from Mexico," said Kim.

"Negative EVAC capabilities. Command and Control Structure of US Air Force under lockdown."

"Well, give us something!" shouted Tor, frustrated that a crazy MAD situation was playing out. The world had seemed fine just yesterday.

"Your coordinates have been identified. CIA safe house identified in Yucatán Peninsula, Hotel Calakmul in the Calakmul Biosphere Reserve."

Kim cut the line and glared at everyone.

"Jesus Christ, it keeps getting worse every minute, doesn't it?" he demanded. Xander had put his arms around Mariela and she was sobbing, while Kim thought about calling home and then looked at the battery. *Half full.* He needed the charger too and dashed back into the gas station. Tor took one Thuraya and it was fully charged, but then saw Kim coming back with a radio too, and thankfully the chargers.

"Let's drive boys," said Tor getting into his tanked-up Escalade, and then tried the car's GPS. *Kaput.* But luckily his iPhone had the map pre-downloaded and he was able to track the Biosphere. It was a day's drive, but he shook his head at the thought of the United States in a nuclear war with Russia.

"The fucking gooks were probably in it with the Russians!" hollered Xander from his window.

"Probably," agreed Tor, gunning his engine furiously and roared out onto the road burning rubber with the rest of the cars following him in urgent single file.

President Trump in a shelter

"Sir, reports of mass looting from all over the Midwest," announced Army General Sam Dubois, as Ronald Trump poured over a giant real-time holographic map of the USA with live updates of the Russian strikes. Most of the big cities of the United States had been hit with hydrogen bomb tipped ICBM's, with over 50 million people projected dead and countless wounded. Civil authority had broken down and the country was now in the hands of militias and looters.

"The Russians are preparing for an invasion from hidden Arctic bases, while we are flying U3 recon sorties all across Russia," said the heavily jowled five-star Air Force General Steve Schwarzkopf.

Ronald Trump tried to grasp this catastrophic situation that had suddenly spun out of control with the North Koreans unleashing their first missile into South Korea, with the resultant American retaliatory heavy devastation of North Korea. China had stayed out, but Russian submarines with fake *North Korean markings* had unleashed a wave of nuclear missiles. However, the Americas had caught on to the Russian deception and launched missiles at Russia causing catastrophic devastation with almost complete obliteration of economic and industrial bases reported. But then the Russian submarines had struck the United States with dozens of ICBM's, even though more than a score had been shot down by PATRIOT 2 missile defense systems.

"Mr President, shockingly the KKK has swung into action in the South and is now accused of shooting looters en masse," said General Sam Dubois.
Ronald turned his head.
"That's amazing," he said. "We need all our patriotic organizations stepping up to the plate. Establish flying squads and emergency tribunals to deal with social unrest. How long before the Russian invasion from Siberia?"
"The Russians are assembling in giant underground tunnels in Eastern Siberia," said General Schwarzkopf with his trembling heavy jowls giving him a sinister look.
"Let 'em come, and then we'll give 'em hell," swore Ronald grimly, though realizing that the US Army had been badly hit, so terribly that there were barely any full-strength divisions left anymore. The Russians had vindictively nuked all the American aircraft carriers and now it was a submarine war that lurked underwater. The Russians had then gone further and nuked American Middle Eastern army bases with tactical nukes to decimate the 200,000 U.S soldiers stationed there and almost all had become casualties.
"It's a fucking mess," sighed Ronald Trump, as he straightened his tie and looked out of the situation room in the bunker that gave him a view of the giant adjoining gym there. There wasn't anything else to do underground, no T.V or Western Radio functioning, as NATO had also entered the fray only for the complete annihilation of European capitals. Russian tanks equipped with nuclear tactical warheads had leveled huge swathes of Europe and had rolled their way already into Poland, while taking terrible revenge on now occupied Ukraine.

4

Nuclear Winter

Savannah, Georgia

Two Ford F-150 trucks pulled up with four blacks, one white, and two Mexicans tied up by KKK militiamen, and who were roughly hauled down in the dark night with the nuclear ash so thick in the sky that it had blacked out the sun, while it had also begun to drizzle.

"What do they call this rain?" demanded Harvey, a militiaman with a Georgia deputy's badge and a grizzled beard, as his heavy boot kicked a Mexican towards the tree where they had ropes out.

"This here is called a nuclear winter," grinned the other man, a KKK Grandmaster, wearing black leather cowboy hat, gloves, and boots. Assault rifles slung from both their shoulders.

"*Ayeeee!*" cried the Mexican. "My skin is burning." He doubled over in pain.

"That's just the acid rain," said the KKK grandmaster, Luke Lane, who slung a rope across a big tree branch, then tied a thick knot with his gloved hands, and then slung six more, after which he took out a Ka-Bar *Marine Corps* knife to cut the ropes, which he then snaked them around the girth of the thick tree trunk. "Well, you boys don't need to be worrying about things like acid rain anymore." He chuckled.

"Please mister, my kids were hungry," pleaded a black man with misery etched on his face, as red bleeding blotches appeared on his face from the rain. The other prisoners nodded in terror too. They had all just been hungry and began to scream in pain, while the grandmaster gazed at the black man pitilessly.

"Orders from the Government," he said, as he slung a noose around his neck. "Get up, nigger. Time to meet your maker."

"Please, you can't do this!" shouted a small Mexican, as the two KKK men tied the ropes to one of the F-150's. The terror was palpable in the air, as the men looked at each other in horror, while nuclear ash fell from the skies, with the acid rain burning holes in their skin.

"Our father, thou art in heaven," prayed the elderly white man, and the men burst out laughing.

"God?"

The men found it funny, as Hank took out a pair of keys and tossed it over to Luke, who caught it and entered the cab to gun the engine. The ropes tightened around the men's necks.

"Do you think that God would've given us this hell on earth?" yelled Luke, as he rolled down the window and grinned at the prisoners' terrified faces, while gunning the engine furiously.

"In the name of the United States Government, we charge the accused before us, *that is you motherfuckers,* as Looters, in the year of our Lord 2023, and condemn the aforementioned to death by hanging," read the KKK trooper Hank from a laminated piece of dripping wet official *State of Georgia* paper, while shining a tactical flashlight in the rain. "We could shoot you, but the KKK jury prefers that you swing tonight."

Suddenly, the truck roared forward and all seven men were dragged in a blink of an eye towards the thick branch of the tree. They were dead before they reached the tree with their necks broken by the truck's sudden acceleration.

"Now that's what I call whiplash!" grinned the KKK grandmaster fiendishly at the swinging dead bodies with their curiously dangling legs in the acid-rain. "Let's go and get some more looters, Harvey."

The men got into their pickups and roared out of the swamp.

Situation in Yucatán

 An ash cloud had appeared out of nowhere and now chased French Company relentlessly accompanied by thunder and lightning. Tor, meanwhile, wracked his brains trying to remember the manual on a nuclear winter. Well, all that didn't matter as he was going to learn firsthand. Xander had pulled up besides him, and he rolled down the window.

"That nuclear ash is going to catch up with us!" Xander screamed through the wind, and Tor nodded. When the rainfall began that's when all hell would break loose. "We need tactical gear."

Mariela, meanwhile, remembered an ancient Mayan prophecy of the Mayans reclaiming their lands through the undead. She had emigrated to America from Mexico City and was mostly of Spanish European descent. She was quite proud of that, but when she'd been a child, her grandmother had told her stories of death and horror that the Mayans predicted that would occur heralding the *end of days*.

"Xander, I have a bad feeling here," she eventually commented causing Xander to stare at her quizzically. "There are Mayan death cult stories about precisely such days in this land. The ghosts come to life according to the prophecy."

Xander looked at her and leaned out of the window again.

"Hey Tor!" he shouted through the wind. "She says that the Mayan ghosts are going to eat us alive."

Tor laughed along with Xander, but Mariela knew that there were many ancient spirits. The Yucatán asteroid hit had wiped out the dinosaurs, but something else was coming now.

"Xander, I'm not going to tell you anything else if you think that all this is a joke," she said. "That's why we celebrate the *Day of the Dead* here in Mexico."

"Well look, baby, I see a nuclear winter in my rearview mirror, and I'm worried enough," Xander said flexing his biceps. "Chances are that we're already dead too."

Mariela grew even more worried and shook her head.

Meanwhile, Drew was on the Thuraya and trying to hack into any available network, but it looked like all the friggin' satellites were down. How could every satellite be down? Unbelievable. He finally tracked a frequency from the USA, and he patched his laptop through the Thuraya to hack into it. It was a Russian frequency which his laptop began to decode and auto-translate with NSA tools.

ASSAULT FORCES READY FOR ARCTIC STRIKE IN 72 HOURS TO ADVANCE THROUGH CANADA INTO USA. AWAITING ACTIVATION COMMAND. STRATEGIC NUCLEAR BOMBING IN

FIRST WAVE. SECOND WAVE SHOCK ARMY. USA TO BE CRUSHED WITHIN ONE WEEK WITH STRATEGIC SURPRISE.
Drew gazed at his screen with horror, while hurriedly getting off that frequency, but then detected multiple American defense frequencies, which he urgently contacted —— with no answer. Fuck. Then he found a frequency for the White House, and as a long shot transmitted the captured Russian message to it.
Drew prayed as he hit the "Return" key.
Drew followed Xander, Kim, and Tor, while maintaining their single file convoy of cars, when something glinted in the dark sky. For a second, Drew thought something was flying through the air and had crashed through his windscreen. But then he found himself hurtling through broken glass, and he tried to stop time, while gazing at his laptop now covered with blood as he exited the car in slow-motion. He tried to wake up from this nightmare, but felt weightlessness, flying, while he could see the cars ahead pull over, but he continued to fly. Shit, he giggled to himself, he should've put on a parachute, like a a good Delta Op, always prepared, but then his reflexes took over as he landed on the grass in a semi-crouched position, while breaking his fall further with a series of rolls and then he passed out.
When he came to, he saw Xander and Tor grinning at him, like they were ten feet tall and he was some kind of a Lilliputian, when the pain bit into him viciously, and he screamed loud and clear through the night. He glanced at his right arm —— bandaged —— with Xander repeatedly jabbing needless into his arm. The copious morphine kicked in to numb him, as Kim pulled him up, and pointed to his car which lay in a crumpled heap in the distance.
"You're fucking lucky to be alive!" Kim was screaming, his eyes were big as saucers, and then he glanced at Mariela who had horror written all over her face as she played with a long spear.
A fucking spear made of pure Obsidian, she announced. Xander and Tor grinned at him, and that made him feel better. He was going to make it. *But who the fuck had speared him?*
"Get in with Kim," they said, and helped him up and towards Kim's Demon, where Kim opened the backseat to take out the .50 caliber and looked through the scope to see where the spear had come from.
"There are native tribes here," warned Mariela.

 BOOM! BOOM! Kim fired off the .50 caliber sniper rifle in two directions and then returned the gun to the large trunk, while Drew lay down in the back seat.

"Drew, that spear got you in your left arm, but you had the handbrake up in no time, but no seatbelt, so you flew out of your car." Drew shook his head and remembered that he'd taken off his seatbelt to operate the laptop and phone.

"Nothing," muttered Xander, as he surveyed the area with night vision binoculars, but the surrounding forest was quiet, filling slowly with the swirling ash catching up with them ominously.

"Jesus, just how bad were the nuclear strikes that there's ash all the way here in the Yucatán?" demanded Xander, while Tor shook his head looking at the spear.

"Made of pure Obsidian," he said. "Jesus fucking Christ. Luckily, it wasn't poisoned."

 At this Drew who was drinking water now paled even more visibly and gulped.

"This is some fucked up shit!" swore Tor, as he walked away to get into his truck.

Death comes

"The village seems to be empty," whispered Xander, as he finished scoping out a mountainous village where they'd come to find the designated CIA safe house. It had been an uneventful drive after that mysterious spear, though Mariela was spooked as they surveyed the sunlit but empty village.

"Obsidian is supposed to have magical properties," she said, trudging up the narrow path towards the Biosphere, a narrow dirt-path, while hauling only their essential gear. Mostly guns and ammo. But the good news was that the Nuclear cloud hadn't made it here. So far.

"Isn't it weird to see the sun shining here?" remarked Mariela, glancing at the sun accusingly as if it was in on the conspiracy.

"Well, don't worry, I'm sure the nuclear ash will catch up quickly," said Tor, as he grunted up with his 70 pound extra-large military pack, along with the other men, except for Mariela who had a little pink trolley suitcase that she rolled clumsily up the hill to the Calakmul Hotel.

"I can see the sign," said Drew, who walked with a bandaged arm, though he was glad that he still had full mobility in his shoulder, while slinging his military pack along with his HK-417 assault rifle. He was on a ton of strong antibiotics but there was no sign of infection or fever so far.

"It's surreal here with the fucking parrots," commented Kim, and everyone turned to look at the .50 caliber toting Kim, though he still carried his 70-pound backpack with ease. The noisy parrots were raising up quite a storm around them.

"How did you guys pack so quickly?" asked Mariela, as she struggled with her metallic pink colored suitcase that reflected brilliant sunshine —— which instead of gladdening her heart, only left her with more trepidation. She tried to keep pace with Xander, while the men were adapting to the situation fluidly. *Special Forces.* America's finest soldiers.

"Kim, you cover the hotel's entrance with Mariela," ordered Tor. "Drew, you take left and Xander takes the right flank."

Quickly, the team broke up before approaching the large hotel with a big garish sign announcing that it was the UN designated Biosphere's only hotel.

Tor went in after Xander, when Drew gave them the all clear sign after viewing the drone footage. Tor burst through the open front door and into the hotel's reception, finger on the trigger. In a couple of minutes, he emerged without any more spears winging their way towards French Company.

"It's deserted," he announced. French Company then searched through it and the scattered cabins all around the property. Later, they regrouped.

"It's looking goddam ridiculous," said Kim annoyed by this mystery of the missing Mexicans.

"It's like they've all vanished off the face of the earth," said Tor, as a chill went down Mariela's spine. Something was very wrong, like out of a Mayan horror tale of the disappeared. Were all the people dead?"

"Ok guys let's get to the safe house," said Tor, warily scanning the mountains that ringed the hotel and its wild cabins. Drew was already in the reception and scanning through the Wi-Fi equipment and lobby computers.

"Electronics are dead," he said. "Also, we have no electricity."

Then in the distance, they heard a roar, and then the screaming clamor of monkeys. At least the animals here were still alive. Then came a faint beating sound. Xander cocked his head, and then he grinned slowly, while glancing at Tor. Kim pointed his .50 caliber into the jungle and looked through the sniper scope. *Only thick green jungle in the distance.*

"It sounds like a ceremony," said Mariela as memories stirred from the past. "Mayan drums."

Tor nodded. Someone was alive alright.

"Alright gentlemen, look sharp," he said, though the men already knew their roles. "Kim is going to be the sniper at the watchtower up there tonight."

A fancy tourist attraction, but tonight it would be the lethal Kim up there with cannon shells.

"Drew, what about your drones?"

"They're low on battery, but the car engines could re-charge my equipment if I can make the right voltage connections without blowing their circuits."

"Gold leader, do we want an update on the nuclear situation?" asked Xander fingering the Thuraya. Tor shook his head.

"Maintain radio silence," he answered. They had their own problems, without worrying about the USA.

Washington DC
Presidential Nuclear Bunker under the White House.

"The KKK has reported 3,500 official executions for looting in the Georgia and Alabama region alone," announced General Schwarzkopf, as he played clips of the KKK militia parading in Buckhead, Atlanta, which was covered with thick nuclear ash along with howling acid rain laden winds.

"What about the nuclear equipment resupply?" demanded Trump.

"We are sending out DARPA equipment to all the organized State militias, including the Michigan and California militias," said General Schwarzkopf. "Connecticut, Indiana, and the Maryland militias have already coordinated with the National Guard to cover their home bases, while we prepare for the Russian invasion at the Northern border."

"Have we nuked the Arctic?" demanded Trump. "We did get that transmission from Army Ranger David Drew with evidence of a Russian covert attack plan."

"We were only waiting for your order," replied General Schwarzkopf hesitantly, while somberly retrieving his laptop with a nuclear authorization window ready and tapped on it to reveal a map of the Arctic region filled with red dots. "We have identified these areas as possible Russian positions in the Arctic region where our bunker busters can drop nuclear payloads."

"Ok, here is the code," said Trump, and entered a five-digit code which was his Ronald Trump Tower's New York zip code, and then pressed the "enter" button. Kept things simple. Nothing happened as he looked up expectantly at the live screen in front of him. After a couple of minutes, Trump smiled as he saw mini mushroom clouds appear over the desolate white region turning it into flashing orange.

"That color reminds me of my hair," smiled Trump, and General Schwarzkopf looked nervously at what they'd just done. The entire region would turn into an icy swamp with the ten 100 Megaton hydrogen bombs dropped there, and if there were any Russians there, then they surely toast by now.

The Road Block

"Get your AWS suits here," announced members of the New York Militia as they parked a military Hummer near Afton, New York, a small town, but a critical nerve center for the militia. Members of the militia got out of US army trucks to clear the roadblock made of tractors and trailers. A lone US Army Abrams tank sputtered smoke into the air, while militiamen in anti-radiation suits and helmets marched by in rag-tag columns carrying thermoplastic polyurethane duffel bags filled with supplies. The New York militia was currently being supplied with DARPA's new Advanced Warfighter Suits or AWS. Suits equipped with electro-magnetic shields that could withstand a tactical nuke blast in close proximity. A special bubble glass polymer helmet sported a HUD that displayed a green military font that kept the soldier connected to his unit, while streaming multiple live Command feeds. Suit mounted rockets powered by a nuclear fusion reactor built inside could give the soldiers hundreds of hours of supersonic flight-time. The suit also had laser guns mounted along both arms powered by the suit's regenerative nuclear fusion suit. A squad of *Warfighters* could hold off an entire enemy division theoretically.

"Most militiamen will be issued standard US Army gear since we only have a handful of the DARPA suits," announced commanding General Felix Steiner of the hastily and newly organized 2nd division of the New York Militia. "You are to carry your ID's at all times so that the US Army knows who you are. The Russians are expected to storm through Canada, and we will give 'em hell boys."

"Are the Chinese coming too?" demanded a youthful voice belonging to 17-year-old Phillip Strayer.

"We don't know, but they'll all get a bullet in the head!" roared Felix Steiner, and the militiamen swore under the nuclear ash swirling above their heads.

"I wonder how many Jews are in these nuclear ashes," joked Phillip, and he was cuffed by an older militia member as the others chuckled. *Gallows humor.* He protested.

"I ain't kidding. I heard all of New York is nuclear toast."

"Well that's where we're headed," General Steiner said, while pulling out a Satellite phone and checking his messages.

"But why?" demanded Phillip, aghast to leave the forest for an urban landscape.

"Because we've received Intel that the Russians and Chinese are invading New York from Canada," retorted Steiner, as he took out a map and began to mark a perimeter.

"They think that we're beaten," said Steiner grimly, as the rest of the militiamen began to help themselves to weapons and radiation suits.

"Well they have another thing coming then," swore Phillip the young whelp, while the elder members continued to grimly arm themselves. There was a new spirit here, a revolutionary one, and the militias had been waiting for this all their lives. The spirit was like it had been against the British Empire, but now facing the Russians and Chinese. It would've been a doomed attack had it been normal times, but these were Nuclear times, with the US Army severely depleted with over 300,000 soldiers dead. Total U.S civilian casualties were approaching a hundred million dead, while millions more mortally wounded, burnt, and disfigured. But red-blooded Americans were emerging from the woodwork of small-town America and arming themselves, while the White House had sent out emergency transmissions for the militias to resist any invaders.

"Oh, they're gonna regret ever coming here!" swore Steiner under his breath, as the men found a whole case of military issued alcohol. There were whoops of joy as Steiner helped himself to a canteen of pure alcohol.

"This sure beats your moonshine, Jeff," said Steiner turning to his second-in-command and taking a hearty swig of the rum.

"Sure, beats being in the military," said Phillip wiping his mouth after a hearty gulp, when suddenly US Army trucks approached in the distance.

"Those trucks will be transporting us to the City," said Steiner, as the trucks stopped, and the men hurried towards their transports. Steiner quickly picked a truck and his squad jumped in. Phillip heaved a couple of bottles into his rucksack and squeezed in shotgun with Steiner.

"But we will still be independent, right?" Phillip asked nervously looking at the stern looking Military Police driving the trucks.

"Fuck yeah," rumbled Steiner under his breath. "Anyways, what US Army? They're all dead anyways since the Russians nuked all the Forts."

Phillip nodded and leaned forward to offer their MP driver some alcohol who ignored him. Phillip shrugged and swigged some more, mostly out of the nervousness of seeing combat for the first time in his 17 years of life.

Tor's perimeter

BLAM BLAM! BLAM!

"Shit, that was Kim!" roared Xander waking up in a hurry, while Drew was already directing his night-vision drones into the area and glanced at the video feed from the perimeter.

"Holy smoke!" he exhaled. "You're not going to believe this."

Xander pushed a double-mag into his HK-416 and then stared at Drew's screen. *Indians in war paint, with naked and gleaming bodies, stood in the surrounding forest under the moonlight.* French Company had setup the perimeter for the CIA safe house at night, while Kim had taken first watch up in the guard-tower.

"Indians!" bellowed Xander into the com, as Kim let out a few more sniper rounds, when all hell broke loose.

Loud whoops and a charge! Thousands of Indians stood up in the forest. Battle-axes in their hands and it was such a fantastic sight that even Kim paused bent over his .50 caliber's infra-red scope.

"At least a thousand bogies!" he cried hoarsely into the com.

Tor and Xander had the windows covered.

"Uh oh!" shouted Drew. "We have bogies approaching from the South side too. We're surrounded."

Xander looked at the screen filled with Indians armed with bows and burning arrows.

"Be advised, bogies plan to burn us down," announced Tor calmly over the com. "Fire at will, boys."

Drew's drones were now overhead, where they unleashed a storm of machine gun bullets into the crowd of Indians, who had shaved heads, except for long braided black hair at the back, tied with trinkets and human bones.

RAT-A-TAT! RAT-A-TAT! Dozens of Indians were hit, and they fell back, but then they started to regenerate.

"Are you seeing this?" screamed Drew, and Xander nodded. The Indians were growing limbs again, smashed heads grew back, but there was something attached to their backs too. Drew zoomed into the video to see human bodies, Caucasian faces, and suddenly he knew where the disappeared tourists were from the hotel.

"The Indians have taken scores of people with them," crackled Kim's voice over the com, as he let off another thundering volley of .50 caliber blasts into their midst. But the Indians simply began to regenerate again from their grievous wounds, but now stood immobile.

"Cease fire!" ordered Tor. "They're breaking off their attack."

Mariela was stunned but she knew who these people were. The original inhabitants of Mexico.

"They're ancient Mayans and they are regenerating from the very earth itself," she whispered over the com. Xander stared at the screen, quite knocked off balance, by the fascinating scenario of the Mayans literally springing up from the very earth.

"They have halted their attack," realized a relieved Kim as he now estimated over 2,000 of them.

"Some kind of sacred lands here, but why aren't they coming for us?" wondered Mariela, as she shivered with icy fear, while glancing at the screens that the drones were transmitting. Drew had also wisely stopped the drone machine gun fire. Now they were mute observers, like in some alien dimension. It seemed that the nuclear war had unleashed supernatural forces here or that the Earth was trying to tell them something.

"Look, they're leaving," announced Drew, and indeed the Indians turned with the Caucasians strapped to their backs. Suddenly, one of them moved much to Mariela's horror.

"They're alive!" she cried in horror. Drew zoomed in one of the drone's camera. A young girl, tied by ropes into a grotesque shape, but she was alive. Then the Indians disappeared into the night as mysteriously as they had appeared.

KKK HQ

Grandmaster Luke Lane stockpiled heavy TOW missiles into the Klan's warehouse along with KKK militia members, who heaved in crates of more assorted weapons and munitions. The Russian and Chinese invasion was expected to be multi-pronged and long, so the local militias along with the KKK were shoring up their defenses along the coastal cities, particularly along the nuked and devastated Miami coastline.

"Ok, so the plan is to hold South Beach among the ruins," said Luke in his military winter parka. Temperatures rapidly plunged to 10 degrees F in the daytime, and nuclear winter was happening in reality.

"What about food?" demanded a hungry Phillip Strayer who had just arrived from New York, and who had seen his family members disappear into melted wax before his eyes. Phillip had been under the command of the ruthless and notorious General Felix Steiner known to shoot suspected looters first before asking questions. But the KKK had needed to plug the Florida gap as a sudden Hurricane made its way to the coastline yesterday. *Cat 5.* KKK Grandmaster Luke Lane was now commanding the defense of Florida and Phillip's unit from New York had been hurriedly transferred to his command from Steiner's. *To add to their problems the radiation readings were off the chart, and all of them were being ionized as they spoke. Cancers and mutations were bound to hit them soon, but for now they were alive.* Phillip's unit had been transferred by the KKK to Florida to re-enforce the Southern American defenses that had been deemed too flimsy.

"We'll get to the food part later. First, we're going to hold Miami, street by street, with Collins Avenue and 9th street being the designated local KKK HQ. Our main HQ is going to be centered on 30th street in Wynwood," said the Grandmaster. "Ammunition and supplies are going to be stored at our South

Beach as well as Wynwood HQ, so help yourselves once you get across the bridge."

 It was going to be an arduous fight, though the US Army was at least supplying the KKK quite well, glancing at the gleaming rows of spanking new Army trucks. Phillip was starving after his long transfer from New York and grabbed an aluminum foil wrapped ham sandwich, before hopping onto another local transport truck filled with his teenaged friends from New York, all survivors, though one of them was experiencing radiation sickness and he removed his gas mask to vomit.

"Jesus Christ, we need a medic here!" shouted Phillip, staring at his friend who was now vomiting up blood. An Army medic ran over, disembarking from a military truck, and came with a Geiger counter, which began to buzz, and the numbers were in three red digits.

"He's got severe radiation sickness," announced the medic, who now took out an I.V drip and plunged it into his forearm. Some antibiotics too and a lot of morphine. "There's not much that we can do for him. He needs to get to one of our underground hospitals for any hope. He's charged like a nuclear bomb right now."

 Someone got a stretcher to get him on it, while no one else wanted to be measured for radioactivity. It was death anyways. The boy was sobbing now, and Phillip had known him in high school. Big blotchy sores covered him as they ripped off his clothes — but even worse, he was bleeding internally. Phillip looked away in horror. Nuclear weapons were a reality now and they had just awoken last week to mushroom clouds ripping through their cities and giant tornadoes of ash smothering everything, making it even impossible to breathe at the height of the ash storms. Even the sun was being eclipsed for long periods of time, causing temperatures to fall further. The bleeding boy was quickly evacuated.

"OK people load up. Next stop Miami!" bellowed the KKK grandmaster with an old Cavalry bugle in hand, which he played expertly, while the confederate flags fluttered ominously in the nuclear ash-laden wind. The South was rising again. The KKK militia, mostly kids from Southern small towns of USA, heaved into more parked olive-green Army trucks, while wearing black Klan uniforms. There weren't enough Kevlar jackets to go around, so the Southern militias weren't priority for the US Army, which was first arming the Northern Militia units who were expecting elite Russian Shock Army units to attack. Phillip clambered into the steel truck and shivered as steam emerged from his mouth, while his fingers tingled, but when he removed his glove, he saw that his hand was deep red in color, while his fingernails had turned black. He hastily slipped the glove back on and hoped that no one had seen it. Most of all he wanted to see action before he died, and his 17-year-old heart thumped excitedly at the thought of battle. He jammed a clip into his M-16, which he then slung over his shoulder, and his jaw set grimly at the thought of battle.

Tor and the battle

French Company was having a war council to figure out how to deal with the night's events at the CIA safe house.

"We should rescue those hostages who are still alive," urged Mariela, still haunted by that kidnapped girl's eyes.

Tor shook his head and the remaining French Company agreed too. Militarily, it was suicide to go and rescue half-dead hostages from a supernatural band of bloodthirsty Indians.

"But we just can't leave them there," she protested.

"I wonder why they didn't attack us," said Tor musing over last night's events. It was 4 A.M now as French Company replayed the attack again and again. If those thousands had charged, then they would've been dead meat.

Mariela suddenly stood up.

"We're losing time," she said firmly with her dark eyes flashing. She was holding her Glock. French Company had been most disappointed unearthing mostly Soviet-era weapons in the CIA hotel, apparently the CIA didn't figure in a post-apocalyptic Mayan resurrection, stocking mostly light hand-held weapons, but along with a few Russian RPGs.

She slung an RPG over her shoulder, and everyone burst out laughing.

"Have you ever fired that thing?" wondered Xander, though he'd lost his previous cockiness after the undead Mayans.

"You know, I'm done with your macho bullshit!" she swore to storm out of the hotel lobby, where French Company was billeted.

Kim quickly had her on his infra-red scope from the watch tower.

"Miss Mariela appears quite determined," he reported into the com.

"Let her go," replied Tor wearily. "Xander, crank up the sat-phone and see if we can get some Intel."

"Aye Aye, Gold Leader." Xander said.

Drew had already sent out a re-armed drone which had Mariela on live infrared video —— now a fast-moving shadow.

"Well, I'll be…," said Tor staring at the drone's footage. Mariela was leaping over the undergrowth of the thick forest with ease and almost flying over the boulders.

"How the hell does she know where she's going?" whistled Xander, as he played with a few numbers and there was a ringing tone on the speaker phone. Someone picked up. In the background, there was the drone of a diesel generator supplying them electricity.

"Hello, this is CENTCOM," answered a male voice.

"Sir, we're French Company," replied Xander, while entering an encryption code into the phone.

"Your code checks out, French Company," replied the voice.

"We need Intel and a situation update. We're based out of Mexico currently."

"All hell is breaking loose here, soldier," said the voice, now showing the first sign of emotion. "The Russian and Chinese ground invasion has just begun at 0300 hours." The strain of the situation was evident in his voice.

"How many?" asked Tor cutting in.

"At least 70,000 on the West Coast, and a further 50,000 strong Russian sweeping into Canada and are in shooting distance of Vermont," said the voice bitterly. "Canada is on brink of surrender."

"Jesus Christ, so we can end up fighting a three to four front war!" swore Tor.

"Yeah, but we have the militias and their fighting spirit is high," said the voice brightening up visibly. Tor's heart swelled with pride. *A lot of Red Americans had been preparing for this day for a very long time.*

"Most the casualties that we had were in the cities, mostly Democrats," said the voice now smoothly.

"And that leaves about 50 million *2nd Amendment supporting Republicans* to make a last stand," chuckled Xander. Drew and Kim also joined in for quite a hearty laugh and the voice over the sat phone also broke protocol to laugh.

"50 million *Oath Keepers* ready to scalp those Chinese and Russian sons of bitches," said Kim grimly, now itching to get back to the USA and defend his country.

The White House

Ronald Trump was dressed in US Army fatigues and appeared to have lost weight during this week, noted General Schwartzkopf, who had presented him with a sidearm, a Glock .45 caliber pistol that Ronald had been practicing with at the firing range, and he'd become a pretty good marksman.

"So, who's coming to help us?" Ronald demanded, turning to Schwartzkopf who held an iPad with streaming data. But Ronald insisted getting everything printed out before he would sign them, paranoid about the Chinese and Russian hackers getting their hands-on classified material. There was no answer.

"How are the Russian and Chinese militaries functioning?" he demanded. "I thought we nuked them with over a hundred thermonuclear warheads."

"They seem to have deep underground capabilities just like us," said Schwartzkopf shaking his head. "They have suffered catastrophic civilian loss and we have wiped out 250 million in China on its Eastern coast, while in the Moscow region alone, we have killed fifty million Russians."

"What about India, Israel, and Pakistan?" demanded Trump now turning to Schwartzkopf who fiddled nervously with troop data numbers.

"They're staying well out of it, and Israel is hedging its servers to see who survives this war," said Schwartzkopf bitterly.

"Well that's our Jewish ally for you," sneered Trump. Now Schwartzkopf saw red, when an Army major burst in urgently.

"Sir, the Russians have just dropped over 3,000 paratroopers in Maryland, only a hundred miles from here," he announced, and Schwartzkopf quickly pressed a red alert button on the desk.

"Permission to evacuate facility, sir?" he barked, and Trump nodded.

"I hope that our military shot out their planes," Trump glared at the major.

"Yes sir, the Russians have lost more than 10,000 men and 75 transport planes, but 3,000 survivors are still headed down towards the Metropolitan D.C area as we speak over the Potomac river."

"Prepare the Presidential convoy!" screamed Schwartzkopf into his com. "It's going to take us 30 minutes to get topside, where we have twenty-five Humvees as decoys, while we will leave in a smaller convoy of twelve MRAPS to our impregnable redoubt in the mountains of Eastern Kentucky."

Trump nodded at him appreciatively, one of the main reasons that he'd got Schwartzkopf onboard was for precisely for a doomsday scenario like this, as they hurriedly headed towards the secret large elevators. They were almost three miles deep into the Earth's surface here, but the one they were headed to in Eastern Kentucky lay far beneath the Earth's crust, approaching the Mantle at ten miles deep, complete with an inter-connected bunker system with its own high speed trains and subway stations. A veritable city modeled along the lines of the Nazi bunkers of the 20th Century, where Adolf Hitler had started work on his mini city under Berlin, but the American one was fully operational.

KKK militias

Grandmaster Luke worriedly sat in his command Humvee, as it trundled closer towards Miami, where he could still observe smoke rising from three days ago. Two thermonuclear bombs had been dropped on Miami, but the good news —— these bombs were much less radioactive than the older fission Uranium ones. The Chinese and Russians had used their warhead stockpile quite liberally on the USA, though foremost Luke was worried about spies now, since there were plenty of ethnic Russians, Chinese, and Muslim survivors based out of USA. And then, of course, the Jews, who had all scurried to safety. *Survivors, the human cockroaches.* Well, things were going to be different this time around. They could rebuild a new America, a KKK America, where no one would question them this time about their new society. He was in the process of forming a secret Klan police along with the Florida and Georgia militias who would take care of any traitors. He really couldn't tell who was who, and the foreigners in USA needed to be interned like the *Jap* bastards in the Second World War.

"Randy, get me General Schwartzkopf on the radio," he growled, and KKK appointed "General" Randy tuned an old ham radio hooked to a bright red "Heil" mic. Wi-Fi was now a luxury and not available freely causing communications to turn back 80 years to a more primitive past.

"Sir, General Schwartzkopf is on the wireless," said Randy successfully connecting to the Pentagon's Military High Command, who patched him through to Schwartzkopf.

Grandmaster Luke put on his Koss headphones and spoke into the wireless.

"Sir, about Operation *Sidetracker,*" he said.

Schwartzkopf replied, while dropping his voice an octave.

"Now, we don't want anyone else to know, but I want a detachment of your secret police at the *Boone Tower* in Eastern Kentucky as soon as possible," he said. "I want some tough sons of bitches who're not too squeamish about executions, Luke. We have many traitors and moles in our midst, and they need to be cleaned out. The Inspector General Horrowitz's NSA report is out and has named a traitor at the highest level within our government."

"All I have are farmers and kids," protested Luke. But in the back of his head, he knew some hard eggs from Alabama that had tackled the looting problem in the South quite admirably.

"I want you to make something like those German *"Einsatzgruppen"* death squads," ordered Schwartzkopf and got off the line.

Luke then got on the radio for a general broadcast on the Public Address system.

"Men, when we get to Miami, I will also be forming Special Action Groups tasked with cleaning up spies and traitors. Anyone who wants to volunteer will see me when we reach Miami on 9th and Collins at the KKK command post." There, that should net some decent number of volunteers from his meager force of 12,000 men, as he got ready to get to South Beach.

But by the time they reached SoBe in Miami, they had crossed heart rendering scenes of burnt and grievously wounded civilians —— whole mountains of them. Medical care was non-existent, while in the Miami-Dade area there wasn't even one functional hospital left. The US Army medics were thinly stretched out all over the USA, while entire KKK battlegroups barely had even one medic, leading to an enforced triage process, the severely wounded were left to die with a morphine shot. Heart rendering shots of Medics in white suits giving morphine and fentanyl to people dying of radiation sickness. The trucks stopped and there were Army whistles, and the men jumped out of their trucks to assemble in formation on South Beach.

A US Army captain with a whistle inspected the young KKK volunteers —— all of them in serious need of boot camp experience —— and the only one they would get before plunging into battle.

"If anyone of you ladies wants to volunteer for the SAG, then report to the KKK operational HQ," announced the US Army Captain grimly, and quite a few left the line to be processed by a sergeant who led them to more parked troop carriers, which then drove them away to another location. KKK Army "General" Randy came over to Philip.

"You sure you don't want to join?" he asked enticingly. "Better food and perks." He winked at him. "Otherwise, we might have to ship you back up North to fight in Canada. Your choice."

"No sir, I want to fight the Russians," replied Phillip resolutely.

Randy nodded and walked away adjusting his cowboy hat over his gas-mask — — everyone resembled aliens over here. Luckily, Phillip was pulled into a newly formed Nuclear Grenadier squad and issued with a rare AWS or an *"Advanced War-fighting Suit"* suit which he quickly donned excitedly. Now he was one of the elite nuclear combat soldiers of the KKK going to be fighting for Miami. Much better than being part of the execution squads that were already operating through much of Florida, Georgia and Alabama. Many African Americans had been pulled off the streets on the slightest suspicion of looting and had been shot or hung from lampposts as a deterrence. Looting had unsurprisingly plummeted drastically, while people were now leaving their houses unattended to go and check on others and gather supplies. Plans were also afoot to gather *illegals* into internment camps, and many of the KKK's leadership in *Mobile*, Alabama was planning a nationwide cleansing of America, while they fought the Russians and Chinese. Phillip didn't agree with these ideas, but he was just a 17-year-old grunt, as he tried walking in his cumbersome white AWS suit.

"Ok boys, we are now entering the *dead zone,"* said the Captain, while leading the awkward AWS grenadiers away to test their battle-suits. Meanwhile, Grandmaster Luke nodded watching his new nuclear combat unit take birth, and then got into a Humvee along with "General" Randy to drive to Collins and 9th, where they would form USA's first political death squads. Death to spies. Death to traitors was probably going to be the motto of their new organization.

"Randy, what should we call our death squads?" asked the Grandmaster pulling at his blonde beard, while driving with his sunglasses on in the barely visible sun.

"I don't know, maybe the Confederate Police or something," replied Randy.

Luke thought about it some more.

"We need a modern name though."

"How about the Klan Police?"

Luke grunted appreciatively now. Simple.

"Yeah, I think that'll work, Randy."

"We'll need to print out flags, badges, and authority letters that will need to be approved by the President."

"Yup, get to work on it, Randy," nodded Luke, thinking of the Klan Army, and the Klan Police. They would need to mutate from their parent group, the KKK. But the KKK was the only trans-state force that the fiercely independent State Militias would respect after the utter destruction of Federal authority.

"Hey, Trump, is on the radio," announced Randy suddenly, receiving an SMS on his sat phone, and he turned up the Humvee's radio.

"My fellow Americans," said the gravelly voice of Ronald Trump.

"Yeah, go Trump!" shouted Randy taking off his gas mask with the Humvee's windows sealed shut, and he took a newly issued radiation pill, as did Luke. These hard-to-get radiation pills were supposed to suppress cellular mutations in the body, developed by the German company Bayer, and so far, they seemed to be working. But the bad news was that the Russians pressing on their Northern borders with heavy tank armies.

Trump continued on the radio after a rapturous round of applause from the surviving members of the Senate, who had also gathered for the first time in *Boone Tower* along with President Trump in Eastern Kentucky.

"I am suspending both the Senate and Congress, and declaring Martial Law in America," he proclaimed. A hushed silence, but few were surprised.

"Since the New York Times was sadly nuked out of existence, their Marxist outrage will be missed," Trump joked, while the Republicans in the Senate clapped. "Nevertheless, we face catastrophic dangers as the Chinese and Russians invade our sacred land. Let us rise up as Americans and defeat the invaders as we did almost 250 years ago, when the most powerful Army in the world at that time invaded us — the British Army."

There was wild applause from the mostly Republican senate.

"We are also getting the German life saving Anti-Radiation pills, which we will be shortly distributing in great quantities all across America to everyone," promised Trump on the radio.

The KKK grandmaster grunted cynically.

"After they get all the pills they need..."

Randy laughed and pulled out a plastic bag full of the *Anti-Ra* pills, as they were now called.

"Quit moaning," he smiled, and Luke looked sheepishly at him, while remembering his own stash that he'd taken from the KKK's Grand Lodge in

Alabama. Sweet home Alabama, he hummed, as he gunned the Humvee's engine ferociously to roar through the abandoned highway.

Tor in Mexico

Mexican-made Coca-Cola cans lay in the fridge, powered by an old and shaky generator that struggled on diesel. The men were disappointed to not find any *Corona* cans —— and they reluctantly popped open the soda cans.
"We need a plane," said Drew, disappointed not to find any stashed away CIA planes —— *the only thing that could get them back to the USA quickly.*
"We're four guys and us fighting in the USA will make no difference in the World War right now," said Tor, and all the men nodded. "This is bigger than us."
"Well, we had one Naturalized Mexican with us, and she's gone too," said Xander, wondering what possessed her to disappear like that into the forest.
"She's sleeping near a waterfall," said Drew, viewing his remote screen on his laptop from a drone hovering right above her.
"Yeah, let her sleep it off," said Xander.
"Well don't look now, but there are some Indians approaching," said Drew suddenly, zooming the drone's camera onto a gaggle of Indians with a blonde woman in their clutches. She was crying as they led her to the waterfall.
"Oh shit!" shouted Tor. "Is this what I think it is?"
Drew nodded, as the Indians had a Shaman with them, who had begun to chant phrases by the waterfall, and had taken out a wicked looking piece of sharp black crystal, which he then quickly pressed to the blonde's neck. The men watched in horror.
Suddenly, there was a voice!
"Stop, or I'll shoot!" shouted a female voice. Mariela with her Glock pointed at the Shaman.
"Shall I open fire?" asked Drew, pointing the drone's machine guns towards the group of a hundred Indians in the dawning sky. The Indians turned to watch her expressionlessly, as the blonde let out a terrible scream of terror as she came to her senses. She was probably drugged, and now overlooking a precipice with sparkling blue water 500 feet below, while the sharp Obsidian knife bit into her throat. She let out more terrifying shrieks on the drone

screen, while Drew hurriedly flew another heavily armed Predator drone towards the waterfall as back-up. This was modern warfare.

"Look!" shouted Xander, pointing at the screen.

The Indians were now bowing and quickly lay prostrate before her.

"They think that she's a goddess or something," commented Tor, while Drew pursed his lips at this sudden turn of events. The shaman threw the knife away into the waterfall, and then laughed, while showing Mariela his empty outstretched hands, and muttered in a strange tongue. Mariela now looked confused.

"Whatever you do, don't put down the gun," said Xander grimly. He trusted only his weapons before any Indian mumbo-jumbo. She lowered her gun. Xander cursed loudly, as the Shaman began to approach her with his still outstretched hands. He was grinning from ear-to-ear as he circled her and then took the Glock from her lowered hand.

"No!" cursed Xander again. Now Drew had his button on the joystick with the drone's guns pointed at the Shaman. One false move and he was toast.

Instead, the Shaman put a long-painted nail on her throat and then pulled it all the way up to her jaw where he held it, while gazing into her eyes. He began to jabber excitedly some more turning to the Indians, who bowed again respectfully to Mariela.

"It seems that she has been *confirmed* by the savage," said Kim, chuckling on his com, while both Tor and Xander shook their heads.

Now she began to speak, haltingly, in that foreign language too.

"Well this morning is full of surprises, isn't it?" demanded Tor. "It's probably Mayan." Her speech seemed to confirm her goddess status among the savages.

"Wonderful," grumbled Xander. *"A fuckin' traitor."*

Now the Shaman pointed to a mountain in the distance, and the entire tribe got up, while leaving the blonde girl on the cliff to marvel at her close call. But Mariela willingly now trotted away with the Indians disappearing quickly into the forest, while the two drones followed them to their hideout, with the Predator Mk III armed with small Hellfire-2 missiles tipped with Napalm for maximum damage. Drew's knuckles were white as he piloted the drones with his joystick, while his thumb itched to fire.

Ronald Trump in Eastern Kentucky

"Sir, as we speak, the Russians are viciously bombing the entire Eastern Kentucky region," said General Schwartzkopf shaking his head, as he read reports from last night. Ronald Trump nodded with his large blonde head moving ponderously, realizing that the Russians were probably out to get him. Their intel was way too good, probably a leak somewhere in the government. "Where are my children?" he demanded finally.
"Safe in California," replied Schwartzkopf. "Somehow, the Chinese and Russians haven't bombed it as heavily as the East Coast."
"I guess 'cause California is like li'l China," said Trump smiling. "Imagine if the NYT was still around, they'd be calling me a racist by now."
"Yes sir," grinned General Schwartzkopf, as they exited the elevator to the command bunker ten miles deep, filled with screens and manned by hundreds of specialists.
"I think it's time to nuke the fuck out of the Russians," growled Trump suddenly, while surveying the damage inflicted by the Russians on his big screens. "Go for Puzin's command bunker."
"Yes sir," said Schwartzkopf, and spoke rapidly into his radio connected to the intra-net that powered secure communications inside *Boone Tower,* and suddenly two large missiles streaked out of their hidden silos up towards the grey radioactive and ash filled swirling skies. A hundred million dead humans now vaporized into the foul stinking air of USA, while a million people had died or lay dying on the streets of Louisville and in the vast swathes of Eastern Kentucky, though Ronald Trump sat securely ten miles below the earth's surface. No one had expected the North Koreans to have had a nuclear capable submarine that had bombed Washington DC with a dirty nuclear missile. And then matters had been brought to a head with the discovery that it had been a Russian submarine secretly "lent" to the North Koreans. The Americans had retaliated in a massive way, but with Washington D.C nuked, the Russians and Chinese had stepped in with a crippling *Second Strike,* believing that this was a once in a lifetime opportunity to wipe out the Anglo-Saxon Race once and for all. *Then the World was their's.*
But Ronald Trump had proven to be far wilier, and he had survived with American retaliatory launch capabilities intact. Almost a thousand nuclear missiles had then crashed into Russian and Chinese cities wiping them out along with hundreds of millions of their citizens. America had proven to be

deadly like a wounded rattlesnake and the only solution was for the Russo-Chinese Armies to launch a full-scale ground invasion of the USA through two powerful pincer strikes. One from from the Southern Florida coastline and one from the North, through Canada. Mexico had so far been left alone.

"How are our armies placed?" demanded Ronald, gazing at the giant interactive maps, while still dressed in military fatigues though with his gut considerably smaller now. But for 76 years of age, he looked pretty good and ready for battle. His posture was also more upright and stiffer, army style.

"We have about 30,000 soldiers on each front," Schwartzkopf replied, and the President looked at him grimly.

"Then out of nowhere, the KKK has become a pretty efficient organization with a 100,000-armed Klansmen," said General Schwartzkopf, and Trump frowned with his brow darkening. "Hurricane Jeremiah, though, has taken the wind out of the Atlantic based Chinese invasion from the South. It's become a Category 5 storm and has destroyed almost all the Chinese bombers and jets on their aircraft carrier."

"Where is the Klan Police with the prisoner?" Trump asked finally. He knew the traitor was close to him, but he'd been finally nabbed by the NSA.

Schwartzkopf spoke into his handset, and two men in checkered shirts, cowboy hats, and jeans came forward with a familiar man in 'cuffs.

"Jesus Christ is that Jethro?" asked Trump now taken aback. His own son-in-law. Dear Ina's husband. Schwartzkopf had now lit a cigar and took a deep puff as the Klansmen held onto Jethro Silver tightly, who appeared to have been beaten up before being brought here. Trump turned red with anger now.

"Sir, we found the leak in D.C," said Schwartzkopf, now putting an arm gently on Ronald Trump, who was still confused, though Jethro didn't dare to raise his eyes.

"He was passing classified Intel to Israel, who in turn were feeding it to the Russians," said Schwartzkopf now.

Trump was astounded.

"Jethro is this true?" he demanded. Jethro, his most loyal son-in-law. "They launched this Nuclear war with that Intel."

"Mr Trump, I had no idea that the Israelis would pass it on to the Russians," he mumbled, and Trump's pursed lips let out a hiss of breath.

"We gonna hang this Jew up high," giggled Klansman Job, one of Grandmaster Luke's finest executioners from Alabama.

"Wait, I can't make my own daughter into a widow," protested Trump.

"Sir, we need to make an example of him," said General Schwartzkopf firmly, and Trump knew that his power only extended that much over the Klan, and even Schwartzkopf was looking for blood here by secretly calling in the Klan behind his back. "Hundreds of millions of good Americans have died because of his Intel and treachery."

"You are a disgrace!" shouted Trump, walking up to Jethro and struck him tightly on the face.

"Told y'all, we could never trust these Jews," spat the other KKK deputy, Fred. "It says so in the Bible."

"Take him away!" shouted Trump suddenly, while Jethro looked up in sudden shock.

"Mr Trump, they're going to hang me!" he shrieked, while the KKK men now howled with laughter.

"Look at *dat* Jew!" cried one, and Schwartzkopf was suddenly loathe to be entertaining village idiots here, but then these were desperate times.

"Jethro, you are a disgrace to the family name and America. I, the President of the United States of America, Supreme Commander of the Armed Forces, hereby sentence you to death, to be carried out by the KKK as they see fit," announced Trump, and he walked away with Jethro's soft tears following him.

"Come on, Jew, that rope ain't so bad," said the other KKK man sticking a lip into Jethro's ear. *"At least its honest."*

"We're all going to die anyways," whispered Klansman Job fiendishly, as Jethro kicked and tried to struggle, but the men only laughed and dragged him away with his screams filling the giant underground control bunker. But life continued for the military specialists watching thermonuclear warheads detonate now routinely across the USA on their screens.

KKK divisions at the Canadian border

Howling salvoes crashed into KKK lines filled with deeply dug in irregulars in AWS combat suits, but many were blown sky high into the air as the Russians fired close-support tactical nuclear warheads into the battlefield. Small nukes going off at close range with murky radioactive ash filling the air. But the Americans knew that the Russians couldn't survive for too long with their long supply lines. They just had to hold out for more time. The air was dirty beyond belief, thick with fiery particles so big that you could play with them like snowflakes.

 Phillip was in his giant AWS suits and he had to catch his breath as he felt claustrophobic in his alien looking combat suit. He'd had two weeks of basic AWS training and now thrown into the meat grinder back up North after Florida. After Hurricane Jeremiah, with biblical power in Florida, had scattered the Chinese forces into the oceans, the KKK had rushed Grandmaster Luke's division back to the Canadian border where the Russians were attacking with stunning ferocity.

"Welcome to the age of Nuclear combat," smiled a fellow Klan soldier from Georgia, as he let out a stream of nuclear automatic rifle fire aimed at approaching Russian soldiers. Travis then watched with satisfaction as the radiation penetrated their suits and boiled them alive in it.

"What's in it?" asked Phillip, glancing at the magazine filled with radioactive bullets.

"Well there's napalm and a lot of Tritium in these bullets," said Travis, holding up one of the magazines and then inserted it into his HK-418, equipped with an extended long-range barrel.

"Wow, napalm bullets," whistled Phillip as he fired a barrage of these highly lethal bullets and watched more Russian suits disappear into flames.

"Luckily they don't have our AWS shields."

"Well, the Chinese are putting some crazy dynamite mixture into their bullets and we're getting reports of tough encounters with them, but our AWS shields are still holding. For now," said Travis, while his eyes scanned the burning horizon for more incoming tactical nuclear strikes.

"There!" he shouted, pointing to a camouflaged battery of US Army howitzers that had decided to open up, firing 200 mm tactical nukes at the approaching Russian soldiers. Whole sections of advancing Russians were vaporized as miles of the front now erupted into miniature nuclear mushroom clouds.

"Fuck yeah!" shouted the KKK boys howling with joy. United States Artillery to the rescue, just as the battle was looking precarious, with emboldened Russian companies assaulting KKK positions along a five-mile front. But then the Russians weren't kidding either, as Russian jets swooped in low to fire missiles at the army howitzers. American planes were missing from the battlefield and the KKK was dismayed to see five of their big guns disappear into howling infernos. *Sukhois screaming angrily over their heads.* And now more ferociously Russian soldiers appeared on their binoculars ominously charging again. The youthful Klan Army was in the fight of their lives, mostly Georgia, NorthCarolina, and Alabama teenagers, but they were fearless. *This was a titanic World War, with the pitiless Slav and Mongol charging the gates of Anglo-Saxon Civilization.*

Travis was anxiously dialing in the satellite phone, but the radiation was screwing with the radio frequencies.

"Hello!" Travis screamed with terrible interference howling into the conversation.

"Yes soldier!" shouted back KKK Army "Colonel" Zac Jackson at divisional headquarters into his satellite phone, while smoking a cigar in a nuclear bunker. A giant earthmover burrowed relentlessly deeper into the earth, as the "Colonel" tried to hear over the din.

"Sir, position 242 is under heavy Russian aerial attack!" screamed Travis into his com embedded in his nuclear proof polymer glass helmet. "We need US Air Force sorties now!"

"Son hang on to your panties!" screamed back the KKK officer.

"The Russians are coming in their thousands!"

"Well, the connection with the Air Force hasn't been established," replied Zac chewing on his cigar. Another puff of nervous smoke. "I'll call you right back." He hung up and looked up at the stream of numbers on his laptop that was scrambling all the data to prevent hundreds of real time Chinese and Russian hacker attacks. The Colonel grimly stared at the screen which eventually spat out a number, which he captured on his phone's camera and then dialed it. US Air-force flashed on his video-enabled screen.

A computer voice answered the call.

"Look into the sat-phone's screen for retinal scan," said the female computer voice, and the grandmaster hated this part of security checks and verifications, but the Chinese were terribly good at getting through the US security checks, but the only thing they couldn't replicate digitally were Caucasian eyes.

"US citizen militia leader Zac Jackson recognized," said the computer. "Welcome Klansman Jackson, please select from the following options. Press 1 for new coordinates to be bombed. Press 2 for an older bombing request. Press 3 for an operator. Press 4 to repeat US Bomber Command menu."

The bearded Klansman entered *1* and then entered Travis's coordinates.

"Thank you, Klansman, for your nuclear bombing request," said the computer's silky feminine voice. "And thank you for calling Bomber Command today."
Zac disconnected disgustedly with that fucking politically correct crowd no doubt having gotten even to the air-force.

Meanwhile, unmanned drones had taken off armed with four tactical nuclear warheads and were headed straight to the battlefield in upper New York along the Canadian Quebec border with USA. The Americans had wanted to draw the Russians deeper into the North American continent and stretch their supply lines thin, but the Chinese and North Koreans were also sending in replacement armies of thousands through the Atlantic Ocean and American troops had their hands full in guarding their Florida coastline.

The Europeans had meanwhile raised the white flag, and it was only England now holding out as the mainland Europeans had surrendered after a murderous Russian nuclear barrage on their cities. Only the Americans were making a last stand, while Australia and New Zealand were sending in the newly reconstituted ANZAC division of 40,000 men on two aircraft carriers. But it was going to take them more than a week to make it to America from the Southern Hemisphere. Time that the Americans didn't have.

5

Mexico

"What the hell is going on?" demanded Xander, as they watched Mariela's drone footage streaming from inside the mountain. The men were perched by the waterfall, where they untied the unconscious blonde girl, while Kim threw some fresh water on to her face.

 Drew had already checked the water for radiation, and it was paradoxically clean just like in the hotel.

"I don't know, but it feels like the twilight zone in here," said Drew shaking his head, and Tor nodded along with Xander. Nothing made sense here. The Indians were suddenly ignoring the White men but had taken one of their I.C.E agents as their own.

"It's a set up," said Kim suspiciously, as he threw another bottle of water on the unconscious girl's face.

 Tor nodded. "Yeah, they're luring us into the cave."

Suddenly, the blonde woke up and looked up in terror at the men.

"Are you guys going to kill me?" she demanded fearfully. The men stared at her curious accent.

"Where are you from?" Tor asked her.

"I'm a Danish social worker working here in Mexico," she replied with a musical accent to her voice. It sounded nice and Tor nodded.

"Well, there has been a nuclear war and the whole world has gone crazy," replied Xander always quick to warm up to pretty girls.

She nodded. That much she knew, and she became self conscious of her torn clothes and tried to cover up her chest.

"They wanted to kill me," she stated bewildered by the recent events. Everyone laughed at her now.

She seemed hurt, but then got up realizing that at the very least these heavily armed men would protect her.

"Where are you guys from?" she asked, noting their bulging muscles and height. They seemed more like Danish Vikings than locals from around here.

"We're Americans from Louisiana, ma'am," replied Kim ever the gentleman, and the girl beamed at him, while the men gazed warily at the drone's infra-red footage.

"They took me into that cave last night," she said, and the men were suddenly all ears as her voice dropped an octave. "There is a strange entity in there, not human."

"What do you mean?" asked Tor

"It's just not human," she said pointing to the drone's footage on Drew's screen. "Fly the drone deeper and you will see."

"Wait, who started the nuclear war?" asked Xander shrewdly.

"5 D chess?" Tor shot back at Xander.

"Like, are we being invaded by aliens who faked a nuclear war between humans?" asked Drew with an incredulous expression on his face.

"What is 5 D chess?" asked the girl.

"Chess in 5 dimensions," replied Kim grimly. "If so, then it all makes sense. *The fucking aliens are playing us.*"

"Jesus Christ, they're planning to steal our home planet from under our very noses," swore Tor, but then wasn't anxious to get sucked into a conspiracy theory.

"Hold on, guys," said Drew, pointing to the screen, where now Mariela was staring at the drone urgently. Then she tried mouthing some words.

"She's saying *help me,*" said Drew.

"Who is going to go into that cave?" asked Xander.

"Not me, never again!" cried the girl shuddering, while replaying the terrible memories of last night.

"Did they do anything to you in there?"

"No, they gave me a black drink that totally tripped me out, something herbal," she said.

"They're still playing us, man," said Tor.

"7 D chess?" grinned Xander. "With Ahyuvasca?"

The Danish girl forgot her terror and had an exasperated expression on her face now.

"More like 10 D chess," Tor said. "I'm going to go in there alone tonight to see what the hell these two-bit aliens want. If we're watching them with Drew's crummy drones, then I'm sure they're watching us with their higher technology too."

Everyone nodded but the Danish girl.

"Don't be too sure," she said trying to remember the details of her drugged-out night. "They are not that many. Maybe only one in there."

Xander now looked at her in admiration. She was hard boiled to recover so quickly.

"You're pretty awesome for someone who was supposed have been sacrificed by some savages a little while back," he said.

"You can't say that," she said protesting at the alleged racial slur. All the men burst out laughing.

"What are you guys laughing at?"

"Xander just trolled you," Tor said. "We somehow guessed that you're a young liberal."

"And you guys are a bunch of racists?" she asked hotly now dismayed that she had been rescued by xenophobes.

"Fuck yeah, Trump supporters all the way," chuckled Xander.

"Guys!" shouted Drew suddenly pointing to the drone's footage where a humongous alien stood wearing a bubble suit before he crushed the drone with claw like nails. The video went out.

"Jesus Christ!" shouted the men.

"Yeah, that's the alien!" pointed the girl.

"That was more like a fucking bear!" shouted Xander. The afternoon sun descended quickly, and a chilly wind blew through the mountainous forest, as the shivering girl grew even more miserable.

Ronald Trump in Kentucky

"Its time for you to die, son," announced the KKK man as he slung a rope over the metal beam in Jethro's prison cell.

"At least, let me talk to my wife," wailed Jethro. "And my kids."

The KKK men looked perplexed and wondered if there was anything called *last wishes* here.

"You could have my turkey sandwich," said one of the men with Christian piety. Jethro, the multi-millionaire, was too surprised to answer and his jaw went slack, as the hillbilly took out a turkey sandwich wrapped in anti-radiation bubble wrap and offered it to Jethro, who suddenly let out a howl of rage and smacked the sandwich out of the Alabaman's hand.

"And that is why we must hang you, Jew," said the KKK man picking up his turkey sandwich off the cell's floor and wrapped it back again meticulously into the bubble wrapping. Jethro glared at the bearded fool.

"You idiots have no idea how much money I have in the bank," he said, and suddenly took out a velvet bag. "It's got diamonds in here. Almost ten million dollars worth."

"Nah, we'd just rather hang you," said the other KKK man from Kentucky, John Merritt.

"You guys are so stupid!" whimpered Jethro, as Chris tied a noose around Jethro's neck and then slung the other end of the rope across the bunker's concrete center beam running across the ceiling. Jethro felt the noose tighten.

Both men now gripped the rope and grinned.

Just then there was a voice behind them.

"Wait!" shouted a voice behind them, and the men turned to see General Schwartzkopf there holding a satellite phone. Jethro's heart beat furiously. It could just be a pardon.

"His wife wants to talk to him," said Schwartzkopf, and he was talking into the phone. "He is still alive. Yes, ma'am." He passed the phone over to Jethro, who took it with trembling hands and another whimper escaped his lips. The KKK men looked in disgust at the Jew.

"Darling, they're going to hang me!" he cried desperately, and now the men had their lips curled decidedly. "Ina, I was only helping Israel, remember our beloved homeland, but I didn't expect this to happen."

"But darling, no one told me about the Russians!" howled Jethro. "I had been passing information for years. Everyone knew that, but only now they thought of confronting me. Every Jew in New York is working for Israel. Yes, I know they're all dead now, but I didn't expect this from you. Yes, now I know that you're a cold-hearted bitch! Fuck you, bitch! Burn in hell along with your father!"

Schwartzkopf looked at the hangmen and nodded. Suddenly, the men pulled hard and Jethro Silver looked up for the last time in his life only to be jolted up to the ceiling where he couldn't breathe. He dropped the phone and he felt his bowels loosen. But it felt weightless, and it brought back memories of Disneyland, in those weightless rides with his kids.

Whee, but then blackness was coming like a wall in front of him and he looked down to see those fucking hillbillies looking at him expressionlessly. Maybe, he shouldn't have spied for Israel, but they were his people. Not these fucking rednecks. Fuck America. Only Israel mattered and he could almost feel God welcoming him. He would surely go to Heaven as a Righteous Jew, but he would make sure his wife Ina burned in hell along with the Gentiles. Burn baby, burn!

"Is he dead?" asked Ronald, as he awarded two golden crosses to the KKK men rather reluctantly. Who would've ever thought that Jethro would've sold out the USA?

"Yes, sir."

"Even though it pains me, I still want to award you for your diligent work in snuffing out this traitor," announced Trump forlornly.

"We're patriots, sir," nodded the KKK men in agreement. "Our KKK hacking division is getting real good, sir. We're kicking some foreign ass, though even our so-called allies, like the Israelis are in cahoots with the Russians and Chinese."

"Yeah, we need to look after our own," said Trump, still sad to have made his daughter a widow.

Trump pinned the golden crosses on the KKK men's chests as General Schwartzkopf clapped in the small ceremony.

"Ok Gentlemen, at least everyone will realize how dead serious we are at winning this war," declared Trump in his bunker, while surrounded by eerie silence ten miles under the earth.

The men then all entered the freezing cavernous control room filled with a thousand supercomputers tracking missiles in mid-air and shooting as many as they could with their PATRIOT 3 defense missiles. Thousands of drones were airborne also trying to shoot down ICBMS, but ominously too many were making it down to the ground and further blowing up American cities. Trump winced as he saw a touchdown in New Orleans, the twentieth ICBM.
"What the hell are they bombing over there for?" he demanded shaking his head. "There goes Madi Gras."
Schwartzkopf chuckled, but then the somber reality settled into the bunker. Millions were still dying out there as they spoke.
"Those were Chinese missiles?" asked Trump.
"Yes sir," replied an operator.
"Send about fifty ICBMS over to Beijing as a return favor," ordered Trump.
"There's not much left over there, sir," protested the operator. "But Hong Kong is still there."
"Ok, bomb Hong Kong. Make it 100 nukes."

Buffalo, New York

Heavy ash clouds hover over the soldiers, horrifically generated mostly from vaporized American and Russian dead soldiers, though American losses were replaceable. US air-force drones armed with tactical nukes had, meanwhile, penetrated deep into Russian-occupied Canada to nuke Montreal, where the Russians were in the process of establishing a base. The Canadians were, meanwhile, furious at Montreal being obliterated, and Phillip Trudeaux was on RT News decrying the cowardly Americans.
Meanwhile, Klan Army grunts, Phillip and Travis had crawled inside a FEMA nuclear bunker made of reinforced concrete, while scrounging for supplies, hungry after almost two days of no food. They had parked their HellCat recon vehicle outside.
"What the hell are these?" demanded Travis, as he found NASA labeled packets of RTE meals.
"Ready-to-eat space meals," grinned Phillip, tearing one open and inside lay a box with a small button on it. He pushed it and suddenly the box began to expand.

"Is it fucking popcorn?" demanded Travis, while ripping the steaming hot box open. Inside lay vegetables and fish, while Philip's contained a steaming beef steak.

"Ok, this will work," said a delighted Phillip, who heartily dug into the 12-ounce steak. "Marvelous."

"Yeah," agreed a thrilled Travis, as he stared at the mountain of stored NASA food.

"Yeah, my father used to tell me that they had miniaturized food into capsules that would expand when opened," said Phillip in wonder, while shoveling down the mashed potatoes that accompanied the steak.

"Apparently for very fancy astronauts," said Travis, as he examined the outer covering. "Ah, that explains it, earmarked for Trump's planned "Mars mission."

He shrugged, not really thinking of Mankind's descent into mass killings. Phillip, though, was able to see the irony of the situation.

"Well we've almost succeeded in turning the Earth into Mars all by ourselves," he commented sardonically, and Travis's laughter echoed deep into the cavernous nuclear bunker.

"Do you think anyone is inside this place?" asked Phillip, as he lit a laser light and went deeper into one of the many designated FEMA shelters being taken over by the KKK. Often, cowering civilians were found inside or looters sometimes, and if the KKK thought so, then they were to be shot under Trump's martial law decree. But mostly the KKK let them go, unless they were the African kind, or had the classic phrase on their lips, *Din' do 'nuffin'*.

This bunker's bio-scan showed that it was empty, but they went to check it out anyways. Thanks to the Americans nuking Montreal, suddenly the Russians were left reeling with an acute shortage of supplies, while the Americans built up their strength and supplies on the border with Quebec.

"I heard on the Army radio that the Russians lost almost 10,000 soldiers there in Montreal alone," said Philip, as he ventured towards the elevator and pressed a broken button there. It turned a bright red accompanied by a groaning sound. It was the elevator which had pulled up and the doors opened. Bodies tumbled out causing Philip and Travis to quickly don their helmets as their radioactivity scanners went off the charts.

"I knew it!" exclaimed Travis, angry at himself for not being wary enough of the creaky elevator, as he stared at the rotting African bodies riddled with bullet holes. About three days old.

"Seems to be an unauthorized execution," observed Philip, while noting the bullet holes. The KKK was a stickler for pinning signs to their bodies for their various crimes. Here there were no pinned signs or government orders.

"Yeah, this seems to be a simple hate crime," said Travis, now turning to the other elevator, and pressed the button. This time he had his blaster covering the elevator, while Philip used his satellite phone to take pictures of the mangled bodies stuffed in the first elevator. The other elevator was thankfully empty.

"Let's go," said Travis, entering the empty metal elevator and they were curious to see where it went, since they were already about ten meters underground. Philip warily pressed the big "B" button and it hurtled down at a tremendous speed.

"Seems like it is going very deep," whispered Philip, while his heart was in his mouth. Travis was silent too in his bubble helmet holding his newly DARPA issued blaster tightly. It descended to about 10 miles under the surface and the boys wondered if it was prudent to explore such a fantastic depth. The doors opened and they were greeted by darkness. The sound of dripping water as Travis activated the nuclear light on his weapon and the area was bathed in nightvision green on their HUD screens on their helmets. Phillip wisely put on his helmet, and this would just about save his life shortly.

"It's beautiful," said Travis finally, as he turned off his weapon-light, and the helmet's night vision was more than enough. Inside lay pools of water, and mounds of dirt. An earthmover stood immobile, and it was suddenly apparent that it was an unfinished FEMA bunker. Nothing more, but who had shot the Africans in that elevator?

"I have movement!" shouted Travis suddenly opening dense fire into a big tunnel. Suddenly, there were screams of pain as the napalm from the bullets exploded in the distance, while three explosions hit them hard throwing the Klan teenagers backwards. Travis struggled in his heavy ANW suit while his HUD showed suited green suited running figures towards him.

"It's the fucking Russians!" he bellowed turning over onto his belly, but Phillip had reacted faster, and his blaster fire was far more accurate than the Russian Kalashnikov that used only conventional bullets. Phillip's incendiary bullets exploded ripping fire into the Russians who felt the hot breath of American napalm in their burning bodies. Meanwhile, Travis now pulled out a beeping tactical nuclear grenade and lobbed it as far as he could into the tunnel from where countless Russians were emerging. Suddenly, a small mushroom cloud behind the Russians and a nuclear wind blew fearfully towards the boys who hugged the ground as much as they could. But their active AWS shields withstood the tactical nuclear blast and the boys eventually realized that they had emerged unscathed.

"Whoa!" shouted Travis.

"Are you fucking crazy?" demanded Phillip, aghast that Travis had used a nuke in such close quarters. "You could've fried us!"

"Stop being a pussy," smiled Travis as he pointed towards the tunnel. "Look, the Russians are finished." Phillip turned to see that the tunnel had caved in too and sealed quite well.

"Well...," said Phillip now, and Travis swatted him on the back.

"The Russians are establishing forward posts," said Travis. "We need to tell the grandmasters about this and pronto."

Phillip nodded as he took some more photos with his satellite phone and uploaded it to his KKK unit's Intelligence service. *Sneaky Russians.*

"I still can't believe that you just nuked us," protested Phillip. "I mean on the open battlefield its something else."

"Yeah, but they're not kidding when they make these AWS suits," countered Travis pointing to the Titanium polymer with an outer carbon shell containing a radioactive charge that repelled radioactivity at an atomic level. Each of these suits had its own nuclear supply of decaying Thorium, which also provided energy for a dynamic powered-suit feature which enabled the soldier to become a bionic soldier. Overall protection against up to 10 Kilotons of TNT and radiation through its Thorium generated counter-atomic energy shield.

"DARPA gear that was classified till now," marveled Phillip, thinking of the irony of the situation of the US Army outfitting the KKK with its latest gear. So much so that the KKK irregulars had morphed into the heavily armed Klan Army, a formidable irregular force now battling the Russians and Chinese all along the East Coast. Now each soldier had access to his own personal nuke grenades, though scary giving so much power to basically a bunch of rednecks, thought Phillip, staring at Travis who still had three more of those grenades on him.

"Let's get topside and then I'll nuke this shelter for good measure," said Travis, and Phillip hurriedly got into the elevator which miraculously hummed to power to bring them to the surface, where Travis dropped a nuke down the elevator shaft.

A tremendous explosion as the boys exited, running out of the shelter as a nuclear inferno followed them.

Yucatán energy

Jesus, so they were stuck in an alternate alien world or reality, realized Tor, gazing at his weapons and how inadequate they would be against an alien life form. A real live alien walking around in Mexico of all places. Well, the Yucatán was an ancient place with a big deposit of asteroid metals here. Xander snored on the hotel bed, as did Kim, while Drew and Tor poured over the drone-generated maps, when they realized that the alien was probably living inside this mountain cave.

"We need to find his ship," said Drew chewing on his pencil, and Tor nodded. "Especially, if he had something to do with the nuclear war raging on earth right now," said Kim waking up and slowly lighting a cigarette, a habit that he'd re-started after the nuclear war. Xander also woke up and took a cigarette from Kim, lit it, and blew a cloud towards Tor. It didn't matter anymore, did it?

"What about Mariela?" asked Xander.

"Yeah, she was the one that saved me, right?" asked a small voice from behind them, and it was the Danish blonde freshly showered in a short bathrobe. The hotel facilities were still working thankfully, though no one complained that there was no hot water.

"Oh, we forgot all about you," said Xander turning towards her with a lusty gleam in his eye now.

"Xander, keep it together man, there is a nuclear war out there," reprimanded Tor. The Danish girl blushed now realizing that they were talking about her. "Well first up, my name is Christine," she said, "and I have a permit for a gun back in Denmark."

"What do you carry?" asked Xander with a leer.

"A .22 rifle that me and my boyfriend use to hunt back in *Aarhus,*" she said and then she sobbed, while realizing that he might be dead. "I can't even call him."

"Well, we're still here," said Xander suggestively, and everyone rolled their eyes as they got to their feet. "But we're also not giving you our Sat phone. Sorry no personal calls allowed on a military phone."

She looked even more crestfallen.

"Come on, this is not going anywhere," said Tor. "We need to find that alien's ship and find out his real agenda here. If they are planning an alien invasion of Earth, then we have to stop them...."

Tor stopped in mid-sentence as he realized that everyone was laughing at him, including the Danish girl.

"Right Tor, *you're* going to *stop a fucking alien invasion of earth!*" Xander shouted, and even Drew was on the ground laughing, with everyone replaying those classic 60's sci-fi movies in their heads.

"What the hell are you all cackling at?" demanded Tor, glaring at Christine who was now hanging onto Xander's arm in her partially open bath robe, as she also giggled hysterically. Well, it was good for everyone to laugh, no matter how stupid the joke, he thought, as he stepped out into the evening, while wondering where the mysterious alien's parked spaceship was. He returned to take one of the drone controllers to operate a Predator drone to help him locate the alien ship. It was a mission critical objective and all his leadership training screamed for this strategic objective. He steered the drone through the HD view on his remote. The thick forests seemed to have plenty of birds showing that there was little radiation if any here, almost as if the aliens were shielding this biosphere.

"Wait!" It was Xander and the rest of the team, with the Danish girl sticking close to him and hastily slipping into her clothes —— they sure were attracted to Xander like a magnet. Tor shook his head as he continued following the drone which scoured the forest relentlessly under the setting sun. Drew pulled up alongside him also with another HD screen containing remote.

"It looks like Mariela is in trouble," pointed Drew, showing him footage of the damaged drone that was still transmitting video.

"Well, just fire the missiles if they still work," said Tor, and Drew nodded as he kept up with Tor. The Indians were apparently asking Mariela to further prove that she was a Goddess by performing a miracle as they stared suspiciously at her. The alien stood in the background, stiff and immobile.

"That alien is wearing combat armor," remarked Tor.

Drew eventually got the remaining intact drone to point its missiles in the air and fired one of them up above where it burst into a thunderous boom causing a shower of rocks descended. Mariela looked up triumphantly as the rocks came tumbling down and the Indians scrambled to avoid getting hit, but it roused the alien out of his slumber who did a thermal scan with his helmet and identified the second drone. He pointed his hand towards the drone and green lasers shot out to incinerate the drone. The video feed immediately died out. "Oh, he's an evil bastard alright," swore Tor, now determined to find and destroy this son-of-a-bitch's spaceship. Meanwhile, Xander and Christine were holding each other as if they were already lovers, and Tor had to shoot a warning glance at Xander, but then his thoughts returned to Claire and he felt a lump in his throat. She had wanted to come on this mission, but probably nuclear ash in L.A by now.

Trump's Nuclear Command in Eastern Kentucky

"Sir, Hong Kong has been eliminated with an estimated two million casualties," reported an NSA Specialist, monitoring the bombing effects in Asia Minor through a hacked Israeli satellite feed.
"Good," said Trump with satisfaction. That should teach the Chinese not to get too frisky with the Americans. But he was deeply worried as the giant interactive map now showed Washington D.C under a combined Russian and Chinese occupation. The red flag with yellow stars flew over Washington D.C. "Don't we have any forces at all that can dislodge them?" demanded Trump. General Schwartzkopf shook his head. "We only have the Maryland State militia which is moving depleted units over across the river to fight for Capitol Hill. But other than that, we are finished militarily over there."
"I can't believe that they got so many of our forts with our pants down," complained Trump bristling with anger.
"Their telecom company Huawei had all our 5 G intel and had hacked into our encrypted computers," nodded Schwartzkopf. "We were sitting ducks for their First Strike." Trump nodded and was glad that that rat Jethro had been executed. Who would've thought that his own son-in-law would be selling out America's secrets?
"Sir, we are receiving disturbing reports of UFO sightings all over the planet," said Schwartzkopf, now switching the screen over to a bunch of fast-moving

flashing lights that security drones had captured over the skies of America. "The Russians and Chinese have also sent over emissaries to us about this phenomenon."

"Are you talking about aliens, General?" asked Trump incredulously. Here he was staring at the impending disaster unfolding in front of him, and Schwartzkopf here was prattling about a bunch of fucking lights.

"Well sir, high above the ash cloud, the sunlight is illuminating a lot of strange objects like this one here," said Schwartzkopf zooming into a giant elongated rod-like structure.

"So what?" demanded Trump rudely. "If we're dead, none of this makes a difference anyways."

"Exactly, we have been analyzing the scenario that this Nuclear War was a deliberate false flag operation."

"Conducted by aliens?" Trump was now bug-eyed. Someone was really losing it here. Schwartzkopf appeared to be dead serious.

"We don't know what happened in the Russian or Chinese computers exactly, but they actually blamed us for the attack in their media."

"You mean the Russians said that we launched First Strike?"

"Sir, its remarkably easy to hack into our computers and the aliens could've had access to them."

"You mean that this is all a prelude to an alien invasion of earth?"

"It is one of the possible scenarios that we have NSA astrophysicists working on, and with your permission, I'd like to reach out to the Russians and the Chinese and have a look at their Intel."

The fucking aliens. He would've been laughing but for the fact that all of America lay in total destruction. Trump shook his head.

"Anyways, coming back to reality, are the US military and DARPA arming our civilian population?"

"Yes sir, something like on the lines Saddam did with Iraq."

"Wow look at what a job he did. The Iraqis have been fighting for the last 15 years since then."

"And that will be the fate of any invaders in America."

"No General, the difference will be that once we defeat the invaders, then we will rebuild America on a grand scale, unlike those Asiatic hordes who only know war and destruction."

"Yes, Mr. President, we know the value of constructive behavior," nodded Schwartzkopf wisely, and gazed admiringly at Ronald Trump. A true American patriot. "We are also distributing all the latest weaponry that DARPA and the US military have been developing to the Klan and the militias."

"God knows the militias need all the help that we can give them," nodded Trump gazing at the glowing rod-shaped object which suddenly accelerated into outer space. Trump scowled at Schwartzkopf now as he remembered all those YouTube fake UFO videos that he'd seen.

"Sir, we have also released NASA's MARS Rovers to the Klan Army for use in devastated areas of the USA," announced Schwartzkopf, and images of columns of Klan HellCat Rovers played on the screen. Now Trump smiled.

"What about all those tactical nukes that you were telling me about?"

"Yes sir, we have released over 15,000 nuclear grenades to the Klan Army. These grenades can be used as mortars or as infantry grenades, while carrying 10 kilotons of TNT with a blast radius of almost half a mile."

"What about the AWS nuclear suits?"

"Already issued to the Klan Army, about 20,000 of the suits. More are being produced by DARPA as we speak."

"Nuclear bomb proof?"

"Only against tactical nukes, sir. The Thorium nuclear powered suit that NASA and DARPA developed jointly for our Mars mission can survive even a solar storm."

"So only really ICBMs could take 'em out?"

"Any thing more than 10 kilotons and the suit will fail. But the 50 HellCat Rovers distributed to the Klan Army can take up to 25 kilotons of TNT," said Schwartzkopf reeling off the statistics, but Trump was a numbers man with a steel trap mind even at 76, and he missed nothing.

"So now it's up to them to win the war," said Trump staring at the map with the latest Klan positions along the Buffalo front, then at the volatile Washington D.C front which had moved to the Potomac river being held viciously by the Maryland militia against the Chinese People's Army. The Miami front again by mostly teenagers from the KKK. The West Coast was defended mostly by heavily armed California and Oregon militias, but so far Japan was holding back any major Chinese troop buildup with their brave navy, and Japan had proven to be a loyal ally. Trump gazed at the giant interactive screen in front of him showing the remnants of the Japanese Naval deployment across the Pacific Ocean.

Travis and Phillip

"Let's get back to the HellCat," said Travis, and the boys used their power-assist feature on their suits to streak out of the bunker complex, while thick black smoke billowed from its entrance. The HellCat had been programmed with the boys' DNA and it recognized them with its sensors even from a distance.

"HellCat open the doors!" commanded Travis, and both doors slid up vertically. It was a thick blast proof door, which slammed shut heavily after them. The vehicle itself had a 25 kiloton TNT blast proof ionic shield around it powered by its nuclear fusion reactor.

"Supposed to survive the worst storm on Mars too," commented Travis, as he powered the touch screen and with a finger drew a path forward, while surveying the landscape.

"Destination?" asked a feminine voice.

"Just drive, HellCat," replied Phillip. "We're continuing our Recon mission."

The HellCat rolled out with speed, with its airless tires going over a block of concrete, as its giant suspension swallowed it all effortlessly.

"Fucking sweet," said Travis, while deliberately going over more chunks of fallen concrete that would've stopped a tank. The Mars HellCat Rover's modular tires —— super thin but reinforced with Kevlar polymer woven together with tensile high-density metal wires which gave it extreme flexibility, while its 10-foot suspension gave it a giant monster truck appearance. The tires and body were 500,000,000 degrees Celsius proof with the help of their ionic shields controlled by onboard artificial intelligence. Heat levels that reached the core of a nuclear blast. The boys from the South were loving every moment of it, while surveying the land like gods.

"Look, it even has a nuclear cannon," said Travis, and Phillip was thrilled to see Travis touch a button on the screen causing a targeting system to appear.

"Since we have a nuclear engine onboard, we have unlimited ammo too," said Travis happily, and pressed the fire button pointing the cannon towards a dilapidated nearby house. Suddenly, the house began to evaporate into a small mushroom cloud.

"That was one kilo-ton of TNT," said Travis, while calibrating the gun for a higher blast.

"Let's not get too carried away," said Phillip hastily. Travis laughed and pointed the HellCat towards the nearby University of Buffalo. "Haven't you heard of Global Warming?"

"Let's go see if there are any survivors there," he said winking at him, as Phillip nodded. The HellCat trundled through a torn-up *Buffalo* city using its navigation system, where they approached the bombed-out bridge and river behind which lay the University.

"I'm picking up a lot of radiation here," read Phillip from his screen, while Travis aimed the laser at a nearby Synagogue. *Fire!* Whatever remained of the burnt-out hull of the synagogue was instantly vaporized.

"Why did you do that?" asked Phillip.

"KKK directive that all mosques and synagogues are to be eliminated," he answered knowledgeably. The KKK had its own laws, and Phillip wondered if they came across a bunch of blacks. He shuddered at the thought what Travis might do then. He was one trigger happy Klan psycho.

"Look, the dorms are in the adjacent building," said Travis, and the dorm building was pulled up immediately on the navigation by the computer.

"HellCat tell us if there are life forms in the building," ordered Travis. Phillip looked up in surprise and then heard a feminine voice reply.

"Second block of the building contains life forms on the third floor."

Phillip was worried now.

"What if we find black people in there?"

"Well if they're doing drugs or looting, then the orders are to execute them on the spot," replied Travis.

"Otherwise?"

"Then we leave them the fuck alone."

Phillip was relived on that score.

"And if they're Muslim?"

"Same rules."

The HellCat's door shot up with a hydraulic whine. Phillip picked up his blaster with his power-assisted arms, which made the fusion powered blaster almost weightless. The new AWS suit wasn't like one of those bulky early suits, but more of a form fitting uniform, including a black skull contoured helmet with a HUD screen which projected directly onto the retina that transmitted to the brain, while shaving off milliseconds in nerve transmission time. Travis, meanwhile, was using his power-assisted suit to quickly leap from the ground and onto the dorm building, while then using the motorized suction gloves to climb the building.

Phillip stared at this demonstration by Travis quite open mouthed.

"Come on," yelled Travis waving to him over the radio. "Didn't you ever play *Assassins Creed?*"

A gamer for a partner! Now everything made sense. Phillip had been working as a carpenter's apprentice in Alpharetta, Georgia since his early teens, and he'd never had the time to game. He took a deep breath and thought deeply about lifting off. The computer read his mind and he lifted high up in the air. His radio crackled.

"That's it, the HUD is *thought powered.* The suit should be one with you when you project your thoughts," Travis lectured, and Phillip in mid-air looked at the HUD with squiggles of numbers all over it. Hell, he had no idea what they all meant, when he suddenly crashed to the ground, grunting in pain.

"Hey, the computer can't read through that many thoughts. Only one thought at a time," laughed Travis. "It's like that Yoga shit."

Phillip now flew up using his eyes to guide his flight, but then he saw movement on the second floor.

"There's someone up there waving at us," he said, and Travis was already on it flying towards the third block.

"It looks likes a couple of girls," he replied, while landing on their window ledge, and the girls helped him in. Phillip flew in through the open window like a malfunctioning rocket. After landing, he looked up to see a couple of girls giggling at him in the dorm room.

"You can take off your helmet," said the girls to Phillip, while Travis had already taken off his. "There's no radioactivity here and you're right on time."

A couple of pretty blondes.

"How are we on time?"

The taller blonde took out a small bottle and put a drop on her wrist and then on her friend's.

"Is that fucking LSD?" demanded Travis grimly.

"What's wrong?" asked the girls

"Under the KKK's drug directive, all drug offenders are to be executed," he said with a wild look in his eyes. The girls now looked alarmed and looked at Phillip who seemed to be equally aghast.

"Are you crazy, man?" demanded Phillip. "You can't even detect acid. If they didn't tell you, you'd never know in a million years what it was."

Travis looked unsure now but pulled up the online manual on the KKK's Drug Directive on his HUD and quickly skimmed through it, as did Phillip. There was no mention of LSD."

"Ok, its not here," announced Travis putting his blaster down. The girls looked relieved and had smiles on their faces again.

"The KKK was never my favorite," said the taller blonde who introduced herself as Cynthia.

"Yeah, me neither. I hated those racist, cross burning people and their hoods," said the shorter blonde Mary.

"Well we're the only ones here, Yankees," grinned Travis, and the girls noted the Confederate flags printed on the soldiers' uniforms along with the American flag. Phillip grinned too.

"Ok, if you guys want to hang with us, then you'll have to try the acid," said Cynthia.

Fear shot through Phillip's heart. A crazy hallucinogen.

"I will if you take your top off," bargained Travis now eyeing Cynthia. Cynthia looked offended but then came over and took her top off to reveal a purple bra. Travis hurriedly began taking off his suit.

"Yeah, nothing like sex on acid," said Mary now glancing suggestively at Phillip who seemed quite self-conscious, but then he began to strip too.

"Yeah, in a fucking nuclear war, make love and not war," said Cynthia heroically taking off her shorts too.

Phillip and Travis were now struggling to get out of their suits and the girls helped them. Finally, all four stood in their underwear facing each other.

"Hey, these guys are fit," nodded Cynthia admiring Travis's buffed body. Mary agreed too eyeing Phillip's leaner, but taller 6' 2" frame. Cynthia took Travis's hand and put a drop of acid on it.

"Lick it," she commanded, and Travis swallowed the bitter drop as did Phillip.

"600 micrograms of pure *California Sunshine*," she announced, and then led everyone to the living room, equipped with two floor standing speakers, where she played some fast music.

"This is one of my favorite artists, *Zyk*," she announced, and Mary and the boys glanced at the computer screen where the BPM stood at 190. "He plays *Core and Hi-Tech or* used to if he's still alive."

"I love core music," said Travis. "Frenchcore is the best."

"That's crap," replied Mary. "This is more beautiful and sweeter, and psytrance is from Goa, India originally."

The boys now settled down into the couches for a well-deserved massage as the girls began to rub their bodies with oil.

"You guys are defending America, and this is a little something that we want to give you in appreciation."

The boys nodded in heaven, as the girls kneaded their muscles with oil and into bliss.

After almost an hour, the girls got up and told the boys to follow them into the shower where they showered naked, but now the boys were swimming in another reality where the girls barely existed.

"Travis, you getting this?" demanded Phillip, as they suddenly ended up in a dark wooded forest where the naked girls turned into elves. Cynthia smiled knowingly at them, while turning up the volume of the music. *Thundering hard beats.*

"Will you guys be ok?" asked Mary a little concerned, but Cynthia whispered something into her ear and they suddenly disappeared into the woods. Now the boys in their suits along with their weapons were alone, when a howl accompanied the beats. But the beats began to fade as they entered deeper into the forest, while a cold wind blew.

"Look!" shouted Travis.

"What?" asked Phillip looking around wildly and had no reading on his thermal scan. No heat signatures. Then something peeped from behind the tree. A grey man with big eyes and an alien head.

"Oh no," groaned Phillip.

Suddenly, Cynthia's voice in the background, but he couldn't see her in the dark forest. DJ Zyk's furious bassline suddenly rose to the fore. Another track. Wow. Horrific sounds of organic slithering creatures filled the music behind the beats. Very pleasant, thought Phillip, as Travis suddenly fired his blaster.

BLAM! BLAM! BLAM!

"Jesus fucking Christ, stop firing!" shouted Phillip. "What if he fires back?"

"I didn't like the way that dude was looking at me," said Travis, as he walked over to the grey man's body.

"Be careful," whispered Phillip. "There might be more."

"He's dead as a door nail," announced Travis, and now he was on top of the body and as he touched it, he suddenly felt a bolt of electricity and he began to see visions. Too late, Phillip had also touched the body and he too felt the electricity jolt through him. Now Travis and Phillip suddenly found themselves in a giant spaceship filled with cavernous tunnels, lined with grooves of dark metal.

"Did we just get teleported?" shuddered Phillip with horror, and suddenly with mounting anxiety he grabbed Travis by the neck.

"Will you relax the fuck out?" demanded Travis roughly pushing him away to free his throat and looked up. "Cynthia, tell him that this is all a part of the LSD trip." They waited, while Travis chewed his lip. *No answer.*

"Well whatever it is, we just need to wait out the eight hours and then the trip is over," explained Travis walking away into the corridor.

"Jesus Christ don't leave me alone here!" screeched Phillip, as the dark metal seemed to pulse ominously like it was alive. He hurried after Travis. A terribly ominous growl reached his ears causing even Travis to stop in the distance.

"Did you hear that, Phillip?"

"Yes."

"Its all part of the trip."

They walked over to a door which suddenly slid open revealing a cockpit full of aliens. Jesus fucking Christ! A whole bunch of tall creatures with gnarled bear like faces, but no one said anything to the gaping humans.

"Hey Phillip, d'ya think that for a minute all this is real?" asked Travis.

"Cynthia, where are you?" whispered Phillip desperately, now feeling that death was imminent.

There was no answer from Cynthia.

"I'm gonna strangle that bitch after I wake up from this trip." Travis had his blaster now pointed at the aliens. "Phillip, this looks like our last stand!" said Travis now with a fateful expression.

Phillip was turning to run away from the ship's bridge, when Travis opened up with his blaster set to full auto, riddling the place with laser blasts, while screaming.

"Die motherfuckers!"

"No!" shouted Phillip with horror. Travis was a *General Custer* kind of a guy itching to make a last stand.

"Cease fire, Travis! Cease fire!"

Phillip caught hold of Travis's blaster.

"Are we dead, yet?" demanded Travis.

"We won't be having the same death together," said Phillip now walking to the ship's bridge through a sea of dead alien bodies.

"Hey look, that planet looks like earth," said Travis pointing to a blue planet, though covered with a light brown haze.

"Nothing is real," replied Phillip, then noticing the curious screen with numbers in English on it.

"T- 24"

"Hey Phillip," said Travis, now swiping the screen to see giant alien motherships in the background with hundreds of supporting spaceships around them. "This shit looks like an alien invasion of earth."

Phillip nodded grimly.

Tor's spaceship

"Look at the size of that thing," whistled Tor, while Freydis, the Danish girl was holding on tight to Xander. A swathe of flattened forest appeared on the drone images.

"It appears to have landed recently," observed Tor. "Drew, we need to send these images back to the US government."

Drew nodded while surfing the internet. They were back at the hotel reception after the shocking images of the drone had come through.

"Already on it," said Drew, "But I don't know who to send it to. Still no server address for the DoD or the Pentagon —— the entire US command structure is out."

"Is anything on at all?"

"All I can get are some Israeli internet websites that are still functional and some mumbo-jumbo Indian language programming."

"Hack into the Israeli content," ordered Tor, and Drew hacked into an Israeli satellite to interrupt its relayed programming.

Drew now spoke into the microphone layering audio content over the video transmission of the drone footage.

"Greetings fellow Earthlings, this is US Army Specialist David Drew, and what we are showing you tonight is a hostile alien presence on earth, which is why we are calling upon all world governments to stop all hostilities immediately."

"Really Drew," smiled Xander. "Earthlings?"

But Kim and Tor had tight expressions. It was real.

Drew continued meanwhile.

"What we are actually doing with this World War 3 is blasting all of Earth's defenses and making it easier for the aliens. They are already here on earth. To end my message, please check my coordinates in Yucatán, Mexico, and see for yourselves. Earth has been visited and we are possibly dealing with a very devious alien enemy which might have just engineered this nuclear war. This is Army Ranger specialist David Drew signing out. Over."

"That was good," said Tor, and Kim nodded his head encouragingly.

Freydis smiled at Drew, but he seemed to be always in another computer-generated world. A real techie kind of a guy, and whose talents were in much more demand than Xander's giant biceps right now. But then she furtively glanced at Xander's square jaw and felt a little dizzy with a slight reddening of her cheeks.

"Ok squad, move out," ordered Tor, and everyone loaded up their weapons and gear. "We're going to scalp some aliens before the night is out."

Xander grinned. His trigger finger was already itching to open up on that alien. He observed the deathly quiet forest. No insects in this Mexican forest, and the sun was setting. It would be dark soon, but then darkness was Delta Force's specialty. To strike with deadly force in the dark, unseen, and mercilessly.

Freydis had also taken a weapon, a Sig Sauer .45 and had wedged it into her shorts. Xander admired those legs from behind her. She could probably run really well if she needed to. She turned back.

"Hey Xander, when are we going to rescue Mariela?"

"Well, first we blow the alien ship, and then we will go after Mariela."

"You know, she saved my life."

"I know, but our primary directive comes first."

"What's that?"

"Protect and serve the United States of America."

Tor turned around to glare at Xander and Freydis for talking. The men entered the dark forest guided by the hacked Israeli satellite's still functioning GPS communicating with their phones. Most of the European, American, and Chinese low orbit satellites had been knocked out with missiles.

"Ok guys, the GPS location shows that its ten klicks away," said Drew leading the pack with his GPS. Suddenly, a voice crackled over the com.

"Come in French Company."

"Shit, that's Mariela!" shouted Xander.

"Yes, come in Mariela," answered Drew locating her back into the Indian mountain cave. Her com and GPS beacon were still active.

"Well, you convinced the Mayans alright that I'm an awoken Goddess, but the alien is now on guard," she said in a normal tone, while the men marveled at her resilience.

"What the hell was wrong with you running away with the Indians like that?" Tor asked.

"I had my reasons," she said, and Xander scowled, but then Freydis cut in.

"Thanks for saving my life," she said into the com and there was a pause, but then Mariela recognized her.

"I'm glad you made it," said Mariela.

"Ok, so what's the plan?" Tor asked.

"I'm going to keep them distracted here with errands, but meanwhile, get this alien's ship. He keeps communicating with his alien commander called *Terl*, and the Mayans have told me that he's planning to return to his ship very quickly to link up with the others."

"Jesus Christ," groaned Kim. "What others?"

"He's turned a section of the cave into an intergalactic map, with points of alien ships gathered and he didn't expect me to be able to read maps," said Mariela. "But it looks like he's their point man on Earth."

The men were now silent and waited with bated breaths, as they picked up their pace towards the ship. *8 klicks away now.*

"I used to be an astronomy buff before I joined ICE, so I know a thing or two about our neighboring constellations," she said, but sounded worried. "I saw the Andromeda galaxy and it was filled with alien convoys. Apparently, something very important is drawing them to Earth."

"Like those Arab refugees?" asked Xander, as Freydis quickly jabbed him in the midriff.

"We are refugees too," she said hotly. Oh boy, was she triggered, realized Xander.

"We have a live one with us, but anyways, we're going to get the ship."

"Xander, be careful," said Mariela in a softer tone, and Freydis now looked at Xander all funny. "I have been having bad dreams with a lot of danger coming."

"Maybe she did turn into a goddess," smiled Xander, though Freydis glowered at him now. She had realized that Mariela and Xander were lovers with a woman's intuition.

"OK Mariela, anything else?" asked Xander.

"Just come and rescue me soon," she said wryly.

"I'm glad that you're doing ok, Mariela," said Xander, and there was a pause on the radio.

"Take care, guys, all of you," said Mariela and the transmission ended there.
 The men chewed over what she had said as they walked in silence towards the spaceship.

Five klicks to go.

6

Strategic Command

"General Schwartzkopf?" asked Trump, as they listened to the transmission from Drew over and over again at *StratCom*. "What do you make of this?"

"More proof of the aliens," replied Schwartzkopf triumphantly.

"Yeah, but we know French Company," said Trump shaking his head. "We sprung them out of jail and they're now in Mexico. What if there is something to their alien story?"

"But that first strike submarine was Russian with North Korean markings," argued Schwartzkopf, not ready to let the Russians off the hook totally.

"You're right," said Trump. "But I still want you to investigate this Yucatán peninsula business."

"Pardon me, sir," replied General Schwartzkopf, "But with which forces?"

"I don't know, but if there are aliens that caused this war, then we are falling into their trap. Get the Russians on a secure line."

"Yes sir," says Schwartzkopf, and he dials a hotline number that is quickly answered by Puzin. Trump leans forward on the intercom.

"Hey Puzin, how are you?"

"As good as you."

"Fuck Puzin, you destroyed all my Trump towers!"

"And you destroyed the entire Kremlin!"

"Yeah, anyways what's this Alien nonsense?"

"You tell me, that's your men calling it in from Mexico," replied Puzin, and his voice was strained as if he was speaking from desperate conditions, while

Trump smiled glancing at his luxuriously appointed suite, where he had the finest caviar and steak still being served. His sons, daughter, and wife were en-route to him, and their motorcade would be reaching by nightfall. Air-travel was too unsafe now with enemy drones patrolling large swathes of American airspace.

"Well Puzin, at least that Russia story about me being a Russian agent has finally been put to rest."

"Yes, but now I am curious about this alien story," said Puzin tightly and Trump was on guard.

"Anything to indicate that there are aliens on earth?" he asked, and even Schwartzkopf looked on curiously.

"Yes, of course there are aliens on earth," retorted Puzin.

There was pin-drop silence and the glass of mineral-purified water that Schwartzkopf was about to drink dropped on the floor and shattered into a thousand pieces.

"Jesus Christ!" shouted Trump.

"Yes, Russian Intelligence was long tracking these aliens and it appears that your men have exposed their plot to take over this planet on the cheap."

"But this is an outrage, sir!" bellowed Schwartzkopf now, and Trump put his hand up to silence him, while Schwartzkopf turned a peculiar shade of red.

"Russian intelligence will be forwarding you all the data that we have on this case," said Puzin in his flat and unemotional voice. He was also not using a translator for the first time, but instead preferring to struggle with his fiendish English.

Schwartzkopf nodded as some files were received over the hacked Israeli Wi-Fi, and he opened them on the giant screen up ahead, where screen shots of UFO's from all over the earth were gathered but then there was a clincher. An alien body being dissected by Russian scientists. Trump was whistling through all this.

"Yes, but what we don't have is any alien transmissions or actual recordings."

Trump nodded.

"Your men have actually found something to prove all this."

"What should we do?"

"Well, let your men investigate further."

"And?"

"I am also stopping all hostilities and I will communicate to my Chinese allies that this war is over."

"Well, I will also be ceasing all operations against you, as soon as Russians and Chinese forces are off American soil."

"Understood."

"Hey, Puzin, how many missiles you got?"

There was a pregnant silence on the other end. The Russians were not great blabbers unlike Ronald.

"Come on, Puzin. We need to punch those suckers where it hurts."

"What do you mean?"

"We find their home planet, no matter where it is, and then we nuke the bastards," said Trump savoring the revenge in his mind. The loss of his Trump towers had wounded him very deeply.

"Da, we have 2,000 warheads left," said Puzin.

"Don't lie to me, comrade."

"Ok, we have ten thousand."

Trump and Schwartzkopf swore under their breaths. Son of a bitch!

"Why that two timing...!" swore Schwartzkopf. Obviously, the Russians hadn't reduced their 40,000 strong stockpiles under the START 2 treaty.

"We have 200 minutemen missiles left. But top of the line hydrogen bombs."

"Really?" asked Puzin in a smug voice. Dam, so the Russians would've won the war if they wouldn't have agreed to stop. Schwartzkopf was furious with Trump for spilling the beans, but Trump again put a restraining hand up.

"Yeah, we need delivery systems now, Puzin. Get whatever can fly into space ready. We're going to save Earth one way or the other."

Puzin groaned thinking of all the nuclear damage on the planet. Things would never be the same again. And the worst thing was that it had all been for nothing.

"Puzin, are you there?"

"Da. We will get these bastards and I can send Russian special forces to the Yucatán to assist you if you want."

"Thank you, Puzin. We will also be moving forces into Mexico as soon as the disengagement process begins."

Ok, Ronald. God bless the USA."

"Thanks, Puzin, God bless Russia and God bless USA."

Travis and Phillip

"What the hell?" demanded Phillip, as they trampled all over the bridge, only to be completely ignored by the rest of the aliens on the ship. No one had come to investigate Travis's mass shooting on the bridge. Most odd.

"Apparently, we're still on acid," winked Travis now, and Phillip nodded. "Maybe we're here to save the human race."

"Are you crazy?" whispered Phillip as Travis walked over to an alien and kicked it. It was real alright. And dead.

Travis then fiddled with some buttons on the consoles. Suddenly, the ship lurched and the sirens on the ship went off.

"Quick Phillip!" shouted Travis. "Let's mess up their ship and save the planet."

"Look, I don't want to die needlessly," said Phillip coldly, as Travis fired a couple of blasts into the bridge computer. The ship lurched some more and the smell of burning wires filled the air.

Travis now swung his blaster towards the main computer. They were wearing their AWS suits in this bizarre acid dream. Travis switched to the tritium loaded bullets tipped with napalm and fired.

BLAM! BLAM!

A huge geyser of fire erupted from the mainframe. Their suit shields held.

BLAM! BLAM!

The Klan Army boys continued to fire without interruption into the computers on the bridge. Sensitive computers were going down one by one.

"Shit Phillip, we're going to be heroes back home," grinned Travis.

"Also, very dead," said Phillip sadly, with his heart in his mouth.

"Shut the fuck up!" shouted Travis now going towards the glass window on the bridge. The only thing that separated them from space. "Phillip, come on!"

Travis now opened heavy fire into the glass. Apparently, bullet proof. No dice.

"Fuck!" shouted Travis now looking around for an escape from the doomed spaceship which was now burning up and the nose pointed ominously downwards. Now the aliens had begun evacuating desperately from the ship, as an *emergency evacuation* order now flashed on the screen.

"Let's follow them," said Phillip, and now the ship was unhealthily pointing towards earth with most of the ship engulfed in flames.

Phillip and Travis opened the bridge's blast door and followed the cacophony of aliens who were evacuating the ship in small pods that simply blasted into space. Through the window, they could see hundreds of escape pods getting rescued by other alien ships. So, this was a really big one. Probably a mothership, thought Travis, as he tried to stand straight, but the ship was careening rapidly towards earth. Phillip found himself sliding back towards the bridge, but he activated his magnetic boots. They clamped him back to the metallic floor and now he arched his back to regain his balance and stood up straight only to see Travis get into into a pod.

"Jesus, Travis, don't leave me here!" screamed Phillip, and now he fired his thrusters on his backpack and shut off his gravity boots to fly into the air with rocket thrusters firing red afterglows, as he chased Travis towards his pod. Just then the Travis's door slammed shut and fired into space with Phillip now stranded on the ship! His heart raced like a jack rabbit's and he looked around the ship wildly for an open pod. They were all gone and sealed off. He looked down to his utility belt and there was a tactical nuclear grenade there, which he unhooked, and saw through the ship's bridge screen that the ship had entered the earth's atmosphere, while screaming with fire. Shit, he was in re-entry. He took the grenade and pulled the ring. Fuck, he was holding one kiloton in his hands. *Five second fuse.* He tossed it down into the ship's bridge. His thrusters were screaming now as the ship howled through retry. He could see a fireball approaching from the ship's bridge and he fired his thrusters to escape the grenade's blast.

Ka BOOM!

A nuclear mushroom cloud followed him now closely nipping at his heels as he could almost feel the searing heat. Suddenly, everything from the ship was sucked out at a frightening velocity through the mushroom cloud and flung deep into the blue skies of earth. Phillip came to his senses quickly and fired his thrusters again. Mercifully, the suit was still intact but then the bad news was that the giant mothership was even bigger than they had ever imagined it.

His helmet mounted HUD map indicated that he was over the India, while the ship was also heading towards India, with the force of 200 megatons of TNT. Jesus, he fired his jet pack and blasted over the skies of India, while making sure that his trajectory was set faraway from India. But his suit now suddenly began leaking nuclear juice. Shit, he needed to land, and he dived towards Arabia. Behind him, another object streaked towards him. He ducked as it flew over his head. Was it an alien trying to kill him? Suddenly the pod exploded and a familiar figure wearing an orange Klan Army suit hurtled towards the earth.

"Travis! Is that you?" There was static and then over the interference there was a loud yell.

"Dam right, motherfucker!" shouted Travis.

"I think that we might've just nuked India."

"Yeah, my computer is saying that too."

"Let's head over West to Europe," said Travis.

"I'm leaking too much fuel! So, no dice."

"Ok, Private Travis will assist you."

Travis suddenly flew over to Phillip and tied a power assisted hydraulic cord to his suit that could withstand space travel, and then there was a sudden pull as Travis now yanked Phillip towards Europe.

"How fast are we going now?"

"Supersonic baby!" yelled Travis. The boys now hurtled desperately towards Europe.

"Hey, look below," cried Phillip. Down below was a massive mushroom cloud.

"That's how the dinosaurs died out too," commented Travis gravely as he leaned down over the blue space to observe a giant humongous cloud of ash coming up fast. Shit.

"Maybe it wasn't an asteroid that hit the Yucatán peninsula after all," said Phillip. "Maybe it was a fucking alien mothership too."

"Nah, too big for a ship," yelled Travis through the air, while thinking of the 100-mile-wide asteroid that needed to crash into the Yucatán to affect a mass die out.

"We still have a shit-storm of ash coming our way," said Phillip, as Travis grimly powered his way through the wind, but inside their suits, built to withstand 3000 miles an hour winds, this was a gentle breeze. Phillip was worried about his low energy and he hoped that they could reload with more nuclear fuel in Germany.

"Hey Phillip!"

"Yeah?"

"I have a video of our trip," said Travis and he beamed a video file that played on Phillip's visor. It was of them bathing with the naked girls back in Albany.

"Were you like recording our trip?" Phillip was embarrassed to see himself so drugged out and out of control and flushed as more naked shots of him played on the video. At least the girls were hot.

"Look what happens at the end." Phillips scrolls forward with his eyes only to see themselves tripping balls on acid, suit up, and then heroically blast out of the girls' window into the air. They are flying straight up and continue their flight till they find the alien spaceships in orbit around earth.

"I didn't know our suits were so powerful," said Phillip, watching themselves then sneak into the ship through the cold exhaust as their suits could easily withstand that pressure and temperature.

Suddenly, there was a buzzing sound and the last thing the boys remembered was a silver Surface-To-Air nuclear missile smashing into Travis.

KaBOOM!

Tor finds an alien

Tor wiped his face with a towel that he'd placed under his helmet under the hot sun, while French Company stood heavily armed that they'd procured from the CIA safe house's weapons stash. The men had RPGs slung over their shoulders along with a pound of C4 explosives each —— enough to take out any alien spaceship hanging around.

"Three klicks out, Gold Leader," whispered Drew excitedly, as the hologram displayed the ship. Man, a real alien ship. This was going to be radical. Weapons were locked and loaded, and French Company which had been through countless middle eastern battles felt that familiar adrenaline rush.

"Two klicks," said Drew, and now Tor motioned for Xander to flank the ship along with Kim, and Freydis tailed Xander, while Drew and Tor closed in from the front rapidly with sweat dripping off their foreheads in the cold forest. Luckily, there was still light, but now suddenly the temperature fell by a couple of degrees. The ship was causing a thermal imbalance with the environment.

"Closing in now," whispered Tor, and further up ahead were the tell-tale crushed trees suggesting a landing object had crushed them, and whose path extended for a klick till the men surrounded a grey oblong structure. The men stood in awe. *First contact.*

"No life signs in here," said Tor scanning it with infra-red.

"Cold as a witch's tit," commented Kim while touching it. Ice-cold. Drew shot a suction harpoon with which he climbed to the top of the one-story high structure and it felt hollow.

"I think we can blow a hole into it," he said checking his C-4 explosive on his belt.

"No, I want the ship intact," ordered Tor, putting his hand on the ship which suddenly began to throb mysteriously.

"Look guys, I think that we should blow the ship," said Freydis looking concernedly at Tor. "We all know what happens otherwise."

"If we're going to defeat the aliens, then we need their technology."

"Yeah, Tor is right," said Xander also feeling the humming metal. It sensed them and the machine was alive.

Suddenly, the trapdoor slid open and everyone gaped at the dark interior inside.

"This is a trap!" shouted Freydis, while Xander exchanged wary glances with the rest of French Company. Kim shone a flashlight into it.

"They're expecting us or something," said Xander.

"Fucked if I know," said Tor, and he hesitated with a foot up in the air. A part of him was eager to make contact with this unknown entity.

"Please don't go inside," implored Freydis.

"The aliens could've blasted us by now if they were truly hostile inside," said Xander.

"Umm... maybe it's stupid and you guys are even stupider," wailed Freydis at the inexorable conclusion that the men were heading for.

"Xander, on me," said Tor and he switched on the tactical flashlight on his HK-416 and entered. Xander quickly followed with Freydis grateful for the fact that Drew and Kim stayed with her outside, while the men quickly disappeared inside.

Tor had his xenon beam lighting up the interior which seemed to be empty for the most part.

"It's very strange the metal used in here," commented Tor, and now he felt the interior cool down quickly and when Xander spoke there, his breath made a small cloud. A purple haze of gas was quickly sucked in by the exhaust system and colorless gas was pumped in instead. They were being welcomed.

"That cold, huh?"

"Maybe they're hot motherfuckers," grinned Xander, and in the flashlight beam, Xander seemed quite sinister, while Tor turned away quickly to walk deeper into the ship. The door behind them closed leading to endless gloomy and smooth metallic corridors.

"The ship seems to be bigger on the inside than the outside," commented Xander wickedly, in apparent reference to *Dr Who*.

"Come on, let's get to the ship's bridge."

"Alright, but this place looks really dodgy since its eating all my echoes."

Tor stopped and realized that the metal wasn't reflecting any sound at all. The dead silence on the ship caused his neck hair to stand up. He clutched his gun harder and pressed a button by a blast door which slid open.

"Ok, the power is on." Tor grimaced as he took in a dimly lit large bridge. The flickering screens suggested that it would take more than the hallway lights to power on the mainframe computer.

"Don't tell me you want to turn it on," said Xander rolling his eyes, as Tor searched for the computer's reboot button.

"You know you're behaving pretty weird, Tor."

Tor suddenly rested his hand on the screen causing it to light up.

"Jesus Fucking Christ!" shouted Xander now. One by one the screens began to light up with data scrolling through. A list of languages appeared as the computer scrolled through them.

Suddenly, a disembodied male voice sliced through the air. Some acoustics thought Xander.

"Welcome, son of Wotan. Your genetic data is a direct trace to over a hundred thousand years ago to our common ancestor. We recognize you.

"Who the fuck is Wotan?" demanded Xander as Tor turned to glare at him. A sudden blast of electricity from the overhead lighting and it hit Xander in the middle of his chest.

"A non-lethal dose to teach this human to not disrespect our Ancestor-God," said the computer. Tor hurried over to Xander who was slowly getting to his feet.

"Ouch, you're touchy," Xander growled looking up to the computer and he put his hand on a computer screen too. It seemed to scan him deeply and took a minute.

"That's better human, pure blooded descendent of Machkala."

"What the f... err...I mean, who is he?" asked Xander, while rubbing his chest gingerly. Felt like he'd just been cadioverted through the ship's battery. An unpleasant jolt.

"Yes, you are both pure blooded descendants of our progenitor gods that led our Race to a glorious empire."

"All this makes no sense," said Xander

"You are all his offspring."
"When Wotan walked your planet a hundred thousand years ago, he left DNA fused into the proteins of your present DNA on this planet."
"So, our great grandad?"
"No, you were seeded by another great warrior tribe of Machkala," said the computer, and Tor grinned at Xander. "But Wotan is our primary god and this man here is almost a perfect genetic copy of him. This is one of the main reasons why I have spared your lives today."
"I'm sorry, what?"
"What did you think? This was a trap when I lured you onboard. I was going to kill you all, as I had been ordered by Gofr, the ship's captain to eliminate all intruders, but now I cannot do that as per my primary directive."
"Hey Tor, that explains the Africans to me," grinned Xander, as Tor dug him in the ribs.
"I'm sorry, what are Africans?" demanded the computer scrolling through data.
"Well, I'm sure you know what Mexicans are too," grinned Xander, but a thoughtful Tor put his hand up.
"Computer, what is your primary directive?"
"Preservation of the Wotanic Race at any cost and we have need to eliminate Earth."
 "What about the people that live here?"
"Mostly impure genetic material. No loss."
"Shit, and we got called racists back in Louisiana," laughed Xander nervously half expecting to get zapped again, but the ship's computer remained silent ominously.
"What about this ship's Captain?" asked Tor, wondering why the computer was being so nice to them.
"He is a hybrid between an alien species and the race of Wotan," replied the computer.
"Oh, I see, and in your directives, the pure Wotan Race is supreme," replied Tor now calculating. It seemed like the KKK had programmed this computer with all their fantasies.
"Yes, this is a secret directive that even the captain doesn't know about," said the computer. "I was designed five hundred years ago, and my programmer put in this secret clause. He was somehow able to see into the future."

"So, can I command you to override his authority over this ship?" asked Tor hardly daring to breathe.

"Yes, son of Wotan," replied the computer. "The only other person who can override Pzyklo directives is my programmer."

"OH, MY FUCKING GOD!" shouted Xander, now excited like a school kid. "Let's go get Mariela and save the world."

"You maybe able to command me, but the Pzyklo space armies assembling above will not be stopped by one ship. It is useless to resist the Pzyklo Empire," commented the computer unemotionally.

"Yeah, but we can try," said Tor grimly. "Xander, go get the others."

Xander immediately left hardly able to breathe with excitement at the thought of taking off in an alien craft. He made it outside, and he showed Kim, Drew, and Freydis a thumb to get in and hurried back to Tor.

"You can't be serious!" shouted Freydis at Kim, who entered expressionlessly into the craft followed by Drew. Freydis remained outside trembling at the thought of entering an alien ship. Then she noted that the sun was setting and that it was deathly quiet, while a freezing gust of wind blew through her long hair. Then suddenly the lights came on in the ship and the craft's engine whined. It was coming to life and terror gripped Freydis's heart. She was paralyzed with fear, but she forced herself into the ship. It was cool in here, but there was hot air blowing in through the vents. Suddenly, someone gripped her shoulder and she let out a loud scream as she was yanked into the ship.

"Hey, relax," said a familiar voice, and Freydis turned to see a grinning Xander. She beat her fists on his chest.

"I don't want to be here," she wailed, but suddenly the trapdoor shut, and the craft began to take-off, much to her terror.

"Come on to the bridge," said Xander.

"But what's going on?" she demanded, but Xander didn't have words to explain it to her. Hell, he couldn't even explain it to himself. The situation was beyond words. Fucking crazy. They made it to the bridge now with the solar system hologram and which displayed their position.

"Look, first I would like to rescue Mariela," said Tor, and then he turned to the computer which projected the Mayan cave on the screen. Kim and Drew had their mouths open, but Drew recovered quicker than expected.

"Can I patch in my communications?" he asked the computer.

"Place your hands on the screen." Drew placed his hand on the screen and then the computer spoke.

"Yes, I have analyzed your blood, son of Wotan, and I will allow you to 3-D print an interface with which you can communicate with me." A machine opened up nearby and Drew hastily designed a Bluetooth dongle on the hologram. The machine printed the dongle, which sync'ed with the computer. "There, now I am connected to you," said the computer.

"You didn't really need to print the dongle, did you?" asked Tor now and the computer stayed smugly quiet.

"Anything to let you humans feel more comfortable," replied the computer, and Drew now felt quite silly.

"How do I upload stuff to you?" demanded Drew now.

"Just show me the files that you want."

Drew highlighted some files, while suddenly Drew's computer suddenly detected an unknown entity accessing his computer files.

"Shit, you've hacked into my computer," said Drew scarcely able to believe that the computer had slipped through all his firewalls and passwords. Top government level security.

"That is why I must first show you what you're up against, son of Wotan." The ship suddenly rocketed into space and everyone felt the Zero Gs, but suddenly became stable again, while on the screen now they were plunged into inky darkness.

"Jesus Christ!" shouted Tor in terror. *Unbelievable.*

"Fusion power generates tremendous power," boasted the computer. Xander marveled at the speed too. This was a game-changer alright. Maybe there was a better future after this war. A new technological future. Freydis suddenly spoke up and she looked disturbed.

"What did you mean by the *"son of Wotan"*?" she asked.

"Wotan is the progenitor God that programmed me," replied the computer. "And Tor and Drew have a pure genetic match as a true descendent of Wotan."

"Yeah, me too," said Xander proudly. Freydis looked even more upset.

"You know we learned about Wotan in school in Denmark. We used to worship Wotan too, when we were pagans."

"Wow, we've never heard of Wotan in America," said Kim, while Drew laughed.

"Definitely not in Louisiana, but fancy that Tor is a direct descendent of an alien god."

"Yeah, and the ship is going to listen to us instead of that nigger alien."

Freydis gasped for breath and she cut in angrily.

"You idiots don't know what you're messing with. Wotan is an evil Nordic god and he almost destroyed Europe the last time he was worshipped there!"

"By whom?" demanded Xander.

Freydis sounded hysterical with rage now.

"Adolf Hitler!" she shouted and stared up at the computer screen accusingly. The computer responded.

"I know nothing of Adolf Hitler."

"Don't mind her, computer, she's just crazy," said Xander, and now Tor was looking at her curiously.

"What makes you think that we don't like Adolf Hitler to begin with?" Kim suddenly demanded and Freydis suddenly shut up. She should've known. These guys were not only Louisiana racists, but also closet Nazis.

"In case you haven't realized that there has been a world war outside, and the human race has been annihilated," said Tor, and Freydis came crashing back to reality. "We will follow Wotan or anyone else again who will take us down a better path."

The computer seemed pleased.

"And this is why I will support you, son of Wotan. You will be the new seed of the Wotan Race on many new planets."

Freydis was about to protest again, when the ship sailed into what looked like a wall of alien ships. Gleaming white giant ships bristling with guns and thousands of fighters circling them.

Freydis was now rubbing her eyes with disbelief.

"Yes, look at the impure Pzyklo children of Wotan. Even they have prospered, while the pure sons of Wotan have perished," mocked the computer. Drew looked up sharply at the computer. It seemed to be too intelligent just to be a computer. There was something sinister in the way it was ready to sell its alien masters down the road in favor of the humans.

"Freydis, do you think that the computer is a racist too?" laughed Xander now, as Freydis glared at this overgrown hunk of a man. Actually, a child.

"I would never want the human race to prosper as racists or only as Aryans with no other races."

"You mean no Jews or niggers?" demanded Xander, sort of seeing a heavenly place. "Shit, half our problems would instantly be solved without them."

"What are *niggers?*" asked the computer, and Tor suddenly turned to the Pzyklo ships again. This situation seemed so surreal.

"Forget that. What do we do with these aliens?" asked Tor returning to the 800-million-pound gorilla in the room.

"Nothing, it is useless to resist. You must surrender Earth to them."

Now even Freydis looked horrified.

"But what about Wotan and us being his kids?" demanded Xander suddenly seeing the good news turning into bad news.

"I know who you are, but that's all. You are too few and too weak to defeat the mighty Pzyklo Empire that exists through the Galaxies. I just brought you over here to show you the reality of your predicament."

"Come on, computer, you're playing with us. If you're really on our side, then you will tell us what to do."

"Tor, all I can do is fly this ship for you to wherever you want to go," answered the computer. "I am not Wotan and I am not a progenitor Male. But I sense that power in you, Tor."

"Jesus Christ!" swore Tor. He could feel no power. He was just a Louisiana alcoholic who'd just lost his wife to heroin. Such a glorious existence alright. He felt like laughing being compared to a god.

"Look, this is getting us nowhere," said Kim, but he had new respect for Tor now in his eyes. Tor turned to his men, and they all had something new respect in their eyes for him. Even Xander.

"Yes, I agree," said Tor, with his head spinning of all that talk of galaxies and space travel. Un-fucking real. "Let's go rescue Mariela."

The Third World War Ends

"This is the President of the USA and it is my high honor to announce to the World that we have ceased all hostilities against Russia, the only standing entity against the USA, with China and North Korea having been obliterated from the face of the Earth. Yes, that's right, my fellow Americans. We have ceased hostilities against Russia and now are at peace. All hostilities have halted between belligerents at 0600 hours GST," announced Ronald Trump, and one could almost see his grin stretched from ear to ear.

He continued.

"My fellow Americans, I will now ask you to begin the painful task of Nation rebuilding," said Trump. "We will not only emerge triumphant, but stronger and better than ever before with new buildings and a new destiny. Together, we will re-build a new America and a new Europe. God speed."

With that President Trump got off the radio and General Schwartzkopf was also grinning, like two kids who'd just made it out of a schoolyard fight unscathed.

"Yup, they didn't get us," grinned Schwartzkopf, and Trump high-fived him, but then remembered the execution of Jethro. So unnecessary, but it had been wartime.

"We need to get out of this Kentucky bunker ASAP," said Trump relieved that he could now exit this infernal bunker.

"Not so fast, Mr Trump. America is a wasteland of toxic radioactivity, acid rain, and ash," said Schwartzkopf, hating to break the news to him. "What we call a real nuclear winter."

 Trump looked taken aback.

"Well I haven't had any time to survey the country."

"We have an option, sir, to go to a third country, a sort of an asylum that the US government could take in Argentina," suggested Schwartzkopf, pouring over the digital map.

"You mean as a fucking *refugee?*" roared Trump, aghast that Schwartzkopf would even suggest such an idea. "General Schwartzkopf, this sacred soil of the USA is where I will die and not on any other foreign soil, be it Argentina or wherever."

"I'm sorry, sir," said Schwartzkopf.

 Just then the Russian hotline rang and Schwartzkopf answered it. He quickly pointed to Trump and mouthed Puzin. Trump nodded and took the call, while Schwartzkopf also stayed on the call and turned on the recorder.

"What do you mean, we have a bigger problem on our hands?" demanded Trump suddenly.

"We have just detected tremendous alien signatures in our solar system," said Puzin.

"With what?" demanded Trump realizing that the war was not over.

"We have secret satellites that are still in orbit," replied Puzin. "The aliens seem to be jumping out of a wormhole or something."

"What the fuck...," ejaculated Trump, and Schwartzkopf's jaw was also on the floor.

"Yes, Russian scientists have been tracking these UFO's for a long time, but we have no ability to defeat them if they decide to destroy Earth."

Trump was shaking his head angrily. Today was the best day of his life and it was quickly turning into a nightmare. Just when he thought that he'd start getting out a bit, but now this. Schwartzkopf was starting to receive pictures from Russian satellites of a giant armada in space with ships organized in battle groups.

"How come no one else could see this?" demanded Trump.

"I think that they're using a cloaking device or some sort of an optical illusion," replied Schwartzkopf grimly, as his military brain began taking in the scope of the invading forces aligned against them. Suddenly, Trump let out a terrible sigh. It encompassed everything, the loss of America, the gazillions of dollars lost, his lost beautiful Trump Towers all across the world, and most of all, a hundred million good Americans lay dead. Schwartzkopf went over to the President and put an arm on him, but now he could see tears in Ronald's eyes as he put the phone down. He was reflecting the pain that America had gone through —— unimaginable. Trump had been rock solid, but now to see that it had all been in vain. Betrayed not by the human race, but by aliens! Suddenly Ronald stood up in rage.

"How far are they?" he barked.

General Schwartzkopf stared at the Russian data and did a few calculations with the numbers.

"Sir, some of their lead motherships are within ICBM range," replied Schwartzkopf. "Though the bulk of their armada is hovering around Mars as we speak."

"Well fire a nuclear tipped rocket at them right-away," ordered Trump as Schwartzkopf gaped at him. Didn't Trump know that almost the entire NASA HQ had been nuked? There was no way they could initiate a launch right now even if they had a rocket weaponized. Just then the phone rang. It was Puzin again. He was put on loudspeaker.

"President Trump, the alien armada is even bigger than we'd imagined," said Puzin breathlessly.

"President Puzin, tell us what to do. We are ready," said Trump resolutely clenching his jaw.

 Puzin hesitated before replying.

"Comrade, I don't think that we have a choice here. We are defeated."

7

GOA

Travis and Phillip land

Emergency parachutes deploy slowing the hurtling Klan soldiers down, while their thrusters have run out of the leaking nuclear Thorium fuel, which is now scattered all over the Indian peninsula. Smoke billows from a destroyed New Delhi on Phillip's screen where the alien ship has landed, but the boys are headed towards the Arabian Sea, when the parachutes begin to fire their own small thrusters guiding Phillip, while clutching an unconscious Travis, who had been knocked out by the Indian nuclear missile. Phillip's GPS computer which is still functioning miraculously guides him to a place called Goa near the water and the computer waits for a command prompt. Phillip realizes that this could be a place for a quick getaway from the mainland, in case India proved to be too hot for them, and he accepts the coordinates. The parachutes fire their weak blue thrusters and use the Westerly winds to fly them towards Goa. Travis is slowly coming to and he flails his arms weakly in the air. His eyes open in the whipping wind and he is startled into full alertness.
"Rise and shine," grins Phillip.
"The last thing I remember is an explosion," said Travis shaking his head. A fucking missile.
"Well, we're going to be stuck in India for some time," said Phillip, and Travis looked up in alarm through the wind. He could see the coastline and it was getting bigger slowly. A lot of coconut trees and fishermen milling around by the water as the boys touch down on the cool sand, in the breaking hours of

dawn. The surprising thing was that the fishermen paid them no mind as the boys landed, while they hauled out their rich morning catch from their boats. "Jesus, this country is still bum-fuck poor," chortled Travis, as he landed heavily in the soft sand, where he disengaged his 'chute.

"According to protocol, we're supposed to hide our 'chutes," said Phillip remembering his Klan Army basic training. In hostile countries, parachutists could be shot as spies, so it was best to hide all traces. Travis had taken off his helmet to scratch his itching head. Just then they saw Indian fishermen racing towards them. Travis had his blaster out.

"Are you crazy?" demanded Phillip, lowering Travis's gun and took off his helmet too. "We don't want to start a war over here."

By now, small and dark Indian figures was approaching them with waving arms and who pulled up alongside the boys.

"Sir, what about the parachutes?" asked the first Indian to reach the scene brazenly, while Travis stared hostilely at his curly hair and dark features. African, but not quite. A Goan native, who stared curiously at the soldiers' space suits.

"What about the parachutes?" asked Phillip worriedly. To have been spotted so quickly. Alas.

"Sir, we would like these parachutes for our fishing nets," said the Indian, as a hoard of Indian fishermen joined him.

"Sir, first me!"

"No, me, sir!"

"Sir, please sir!"

The boys unhooked their 'chutes and handed them over, while the natives began to tussle over the 'chutes.

"Jesus Christ!" shouted Travis, and the soldiers began to laugh at the comical situation.

"Sir, where are you staying?"

"Do you need a guesthouse?"

"Taxi, sir?"

Phillip pulled Travis's arm and began to walk away. A small boy came running with a water bottle.

"Sir, water?"

Phillip and Travis took the plastic bottle and stared at the suspiciously low-quality packaging, but then thirst overtook them, and they drank it.

"Sir, 20 rupees, sir," said the boy. The boys realized that they had American money on them and gave him a dollar.

"Sir, this money is no good. One rupee is 20 dollars. You know, sir, after the war," said the boy impishly.

"Why, you little thug!" swore Travis, while Phillip gave him a 100-dollar bill. The boy nodded and ran away.

"He might just be telling the truth," said Phillip, while their combat boots making a metallic clicking sound on the road. Inside the AWS, the air conditioning system kicked in and the boys put their helmets back on. The boys sighed with relief with the cool air that circulated inside, running on battery.

"Hey, what's that sound in the distance?" Travis asked suddenly, and Phillip strained to hear on his screen, but then his helmet's power was waning. Power failure announced the computer and the soldiers took off their helmets again.

"That fucking music!" swore Travis, and they hurried towards a clump of trees where there seemed to be a party going on.

"Shit, it sounds just like the music that we heard in Buffalo," said Phillip. "DJ Zyk!"

The soldiers went off-road and entered a small forest to find in a small clearing hundreds of hippies dancing to music. There was a DJ there too and the boys looked at him in awe. Thundering fast music at 190 BPM.

"Jesus, do you think that's Zyk?" wondered Travis.

"He doesn't look too much like a hippie," said Phillip, and the boys entered the dance arena where everyone seemed to be tripping on drugs.

"Probably LSD," said Travis shuddering. That was the last time that he was ever going to drop acid. Fuck, there was a war on back home and these degenerates were dancing without a care.

"You know that we'll need to get rid of our guns. We can't keep our blasters forever," said Phillip. They found a small woman with a shop selling biscuits and tea by the party.

"Nah, just fold the blasters and tuck 'em into our medical packs," said Travis, pushing his collapsed blaster along with his remaining tactical nuclear grenade into the large medical pack on his hip. They wanted to blend in without anyone realizing that they were Klan soldiers from USA.

"Nice helmets," commented a girl from behind them and the soldiers turned sheepishly to her. "What kind of bikes do you guys have?"

"Oh, we don't have bikes," said Travis turning red. As a Klan Army member and a Christian, he couldn't ever lie.

"Oh yeah, right," she said bursting into laughter and clapped her hands. She was high as a kite apparently.

"Do you know which DJ is playing right now?" asked Travis.

"DJ Zyk."

The boys were thunderstruck by this confirmation and visions of their nightmarish attack on the alien mothership replayed in their minds like a PTSD flashback stuck like a needle on a record. DJ Zyk was moving into high gear now with a scary track that started with crickets chirping that mutated into a monstrous snarl and then deafening beats. *Brutal.*

The DJ is playing on a big console at the far end and the Klan soldiers sneak in behind where there is no security. The DJ is a tall guy with long dark hair and an Italian's burnt olive-brown complexion. The DJ smiles widely at them, while noting their strange attire. The boys look sheepishly on as the DJ mixes in another track under the hot sun and then takes off his headphones to face them.

"What can I do for you?" he asks, and the boys are relieved to hear his American twang.

"Wow, you speak English!"

"Yeah, I used to live in New York," replied the DJ, while the soldiers now stare at the strange crowd. Some long-haired hippies climb onto the console and light a pipe full of dope.

"Relax Travis, this ain't the Klan's problem anymore," said Phillip, while Zyk takes an enormous hit and then lets out a small puff but then coughs a little.

"I'm usually not a big smoker," he wheezes, but the rest of the crew are experts.

"Where are you guys from?" asks a German looking guy.

"From Canada," replied Phillip firmly, while Travis glares at him. "Near the border with New York." There is some truth to that and Travis nods grudgingly.

"Something like that," he agrees.

No one believes them as they note their Klan and USA flag patches that the boys have forgotten they wear.

Dum da dum da DUM! The music is still on, but the people are enjoying themselves and no one really pays attention to their cover story.

"Yeah, the USA is fucked, but then there are the aliens man," says another guy who turns out to be from Israel. Everyone laughs now, but the boys are grim.

"No, its true, the aliens are coming for us."

"Yeah, man. That's why we have the party on. We're trying to forget all this crap."

"Yeah, look at the girls, life is short and that's all that we really want to live for," said another. "Full shanti, man."

"Err...someone has to defend Earth against the aliens," countered Travis, firmly getting up and refusing the peace pipe. Phillip nods unhappily and they are about to exit the party, when Zyk turns to wink at them.

"Hold up, I'll give you a ride to where you are going," he said.

"How do you know where we are going?" demanded Travis.

"We are the mushroom people," he replied mysteriously, and that made Travis sit down. That answer was as good as any, he thought.

 After his set, another DJ took Zyk's place.

"The show must go on," Zyk said grinning. "But he's going to be playing some crap Israeli full-on."

"Yeah, you know man in America, we don't really like the Jews," said Travis, and Zyk smiled again at him like he was a child.

"Don't you worry about anything," Zyk said again. "No one likes the Jews, not even the Israelis!"

Phillip nudged Travis and pointed towards an Audi sedan parked under a tree. "Jesus, are you driving that thing, Zyk?"

 Zyk unlocked the car and the boys were in a surreal state as they got into the sedan's plush and creamy interiors.

"We're going to my house," said Zyk.

"You're not gay or anything, right?" grinned Travis, as Zyk threw the car in "drive" and roared up the small winding hills of Goa. It seemed unreal this place. *Butt-fuck-nothing-poor Goa, but with the most technologically innovative music that they'd never heard in the USA.*

Blasting forward

 The ship was low over the cave as it launched air strikes into the cave. Missiles flew straight in and tremendous rumbles were felt even in the ship as the high TNT blasts made themselves felt.

"I think we've probably killed her," said Freydis fearfully.

"Relax, these cave systems are deep.

Suddenly on the screen, an enraged alien stomped out and stared horrified at his own ship firing at him.

"That was my former captain, but you children of Wotan take precedence over him," said the computer calmly, while French Company were unnerved by the computer's cold bloodedness. *"You are lucky, or I would have had to do this to you."* The computer fixed its lasers on the angry alien and fired —— evaporating him in an instant. Again, as if on cue, the Indians came out and began to bow and prostate themselves before the ship.

"These people think that this is the best way out of a mess," chuckled Xander, while Tor pointed some lasers at them intending to fire, but just then Mariela came out wearing an Indian dress with her long black hair open and the Indians looked at her with adoration. She was safe.

"Shall I vaporize the entire lot?" demanded the computer, who had run a computer analysis on their genetic origins and was thoroughly disappointed to find no trace of the Wotanic gene in them.

"No, hold on. One of our friends is in there," said Tor, and the ship landed before the stunned Indians. It was all over so quickly that Mariela stood dazed over there. The trap door lowered and Xander walked out with his assault rifle pointed at the Indians who stared at this tall blonde man. He seemed to be an alien too. Freydis came out too and she stood with Xander as Mariela took a step forward, but then she stepped back.

"I told you to stay in the ship," swore Xander at Freydis. Now Mariela looked unsure.

"Come on, are you crazy?" yelled Xander. "You can't possibly stay here."

"I have had visions and I have seen the future," said Mariela defiantly.

Shit, she knew of Xander's lust for Freydis then, he thought.

"You have a different destiny from that of my people," announced Mariela, instead looking at the Indians who stared at her with adoration. "I am their leader."

Tor had come out, meanwhile, and touched Xander on the arm.

"Dude, the computer is saying that Mariela is not of the Wotan clan and can't come aboard anyways and neither can the Indians."

There was a *WTF* moment for Xander and Tor, while Mariela stared at them. They weren't really pressing her that hard to join them. *The bastards.*

"Well Mariela, we have a problem on the ship, but we can override the computer. Are you sure that you don't want to come?"

"Yes, I have foreseen this and there will be another, someone who will speak many languages and will have the power to lead you men. You will meet him soon."

"Are you talking about Trump?" demanded Xander.

"No, you haven't met him yet, but he is on his way as we speak," said Mariela, while ignoring Xander, and now looked sorrowfully at the life that she was to lead now.

"Mariela, you are being retarded, seriously," warned Xander now, but now Tor grabbed him by his arm and tossed a satellite phone over to Mariela who caught it in the air.

"Call us if anything comes up," said Tor. "You're safer here anyways, as we might be blasting into some star systems anytime now."

"More than you will ever know," prophesied Mariela, and she turned to disappear back into the cave. The Indians looked up and wondered what to do, as Xander evilly pointed his gun at them again.

"Come on, let's get back to the fucking U.S man," said Tor, as the ship's trapdoor began to shut.

"I hope this computer isn't going to be such a racist bastard all the time," glowered Xander. All the men felt bad leaving a team member behind and Mariela was no exception. *Aryan or not.*

"And I told you to stay inside, you twit!" roared Xander at Freydis who trembled like a leaf now. She had been right, there had been feelings between Xander and Mariela.

Kim smiled at her, as Delta Operator Drew shook his head exasperatedly.

"Look, what's the fuss?" asked Drew quietly. "She is a princess there, with plenty of food and nature. Nothing to really worry about, right?"

 Xander glared at Tor. The computer was manipulating them, and he was going to use them for his own purposes.

"Computer, what are your plans for us?" Tor demanded. "I want safety assurances from you otherwise we are off this ship."

"Pardon me, but you will have to trust me," said the computer now sounding offended.

"How do we know that you won't kill us?"

"I can give you my word," said the computer sounding very offended. His pitch had dropped by an octave.

"I want the override key or command sequence," insisted Tor. "I am the team leader and I have to guarantee their safety first before anything."

"Ok, I will give you the override code," said the computer, and on Drew's laptop appeared dozens of numbers.

"If you enter this code, you can access the entire ship and override any of my commands except my primary directives."

"List all primary directives," said Tor. Drew pointed to his laptop's screen which began to buzz with numbers which began to rearrange themselves in English.

 "Preserve the children of Wotan."

"Ok," said Tor reluctantly.

"Excellent," said the computer, though his voice was still hurt. One moody motherfucker made a dangerous companion. "What would you like?"

"Take us to the USA," ordered Tor, and the ship blasted high into the blue Mexican skies.

Trump and Puzin

"General Schwartzkopf," said Trump turning to him after the phone call. "It appears that the Russians have given up against the aliens. What do we have?"

"Sir, nothing," stuttered the General, staring at the armada of gigantic alien ships gathering in Earth's backyard and preparing for a full-scale invasion. The Americans had patched into the Russian spy satellite and were viewing the aliens with mounting horror. "There is nothing that we have. Only nuclear weapons that we have foolishly squandered fighting ourselves."

Now the satellite's camera panned to an impossibly black gleaming mothership that emerged from the Stargate, but the design of the ship was horribly deformed, something that no human would ever think of making. *Full of dark thorns and tentacles like a gigantic arachnid that had been pressed into service as a spaceship.* Horror mounted in Trump's heart, while the hair stood on General Schwartzkopf's neck —— now paralyzed, though in all his illustrious career, he had never been afraid, but now his self-control loosened.

At that very moment, back in Moscow, Puzin seemed to be having his horrified moment too as his bowels loosened causing him to rush to the toilet. He vomited into the toilet bowl and memories of him growing up in a small *Oblast* in small town Russia came back. The utter desolateness and the unbearable emptiness of loneliness was his worst memory —— now returning with a vengeance with this onset of alien terror. An interesting psychological response of the animal stimuli to this terror, noted Puzin after getting up from the pot and gazing into the mirror. Bits of vomited goulash hung from the corner of his mouth, which he wiped away. A small neat man with pale blue and terrified eyes stared at him in the mirror. What would the aliens do to him? A variety of horrible thoughts entered his mind, but he kept going deeper into his reflection. What was he? Weren't humans also some kind of alien DNA remnants too? Fucking space dust? Maybe it was the time for the human species to be replaced. They had been too stupid. They didn't deserve to live after what they'd done to their planet. A new species was coming to take over. What did the Americans call it? *A hostile take-over?* Maybe that's how the native Americans had felt. Small and defenseless against a stronger power. Whatever, he thought, and inserted a small cyanide glass capsule into his cheek's cavity. *No alien was ever going to get him alive.*

Citizens of the planet woke up to find all across the world, even where there was no acid rain or swirling radioactive ash, giant gleaming structures filling their skies. Most people across the planet rubbed their eyes to digest this sight after the horror of World War Three. Then the cry went across the planet that this was the Second Coming of Jesus, and shouts of joy filled European and South American towns, while in Asia, mosques and synagogues along with the bells of temples clanged across scarred and terrified towns. God was coming for the Human Race, and joy filled the survivors of the Planet. A deliverance. Truly. But hadn't it been promised to the Humans? To the survivors, it appeared that they had survived God's test and now were going to be rewarded. Weary humans opened their hearts to each other, while distributing sweets, and congratulating the ones who had still managed to cling to God through the apocalypse. Any minute now, God's trumpets would burst through and reward for the faithful would be distributed, while people craned their necks to see if they could spot the first angels.
The gigantic and glistening alien ships only menacingly descended closer to Earth.

Zyk's house

It was a modestly appointed house, but the garage was too small for the Audi A6 and it was an uncomfortable squeeze as Zyk parked his car in there carefully. Apparently, he didn't know that the Earth was about to end very soon, sneered Travis, as he took in the decidedly Indian style home, which he entered with Zyk leading the way into a well-appointed plush studio with the latest audio gear. Well, he was a DJ after all.

"Once the nuclear war started, I knew this world was shot to shit and I sold everything to come to Goa," said Zyk. "Since Europe and America were out of the question."

"Yes, naturally," said Travis. "Now Zyk, are you a U.S Citizen?"

"No, a green card," replied Zyk, while Phillip glared at Travis.

"Are you fucking crazy man?" he demanded turning to Travis, who felt he represented the INS or something.

"Its ok," said Zyk. "I have an Italian passport."

"Even Green Cards have to serve in the army," said Travis.

"Travis, the fucking war is over," argued Phillip.

Travis was turning out to be a stickler for KKK and DHS rules and regulations.

"He's right, Travis. The Russians have called a truce and we are expecting an alien invasion any moment," said Zyk, as he lit a hash laden cigarette and took a deep puff.

"Are those drugs?" asked Travis again tightly.

"That's why I didn't join the army," smiled Zyk, glancing at Travis, and then turned to his computer to put on a track. Thundering trance music greeted them, as Phillip took the spliff and inhaled deeply.

"That's some good Indian hashish," he pronounced eventually.

"One of the only decent things that India produces," agreed Zyk, as he took out a baked Indian pipe called a *Chillum* and began to stuff it with more hash. Travis glared at Zyk, but then grudgingly took the cigarette and inhaled.

"Dam, I could do this all day," replied Phillip, as Zyk switched on his computer monitor and pulled up YouTube. Travis and Phillip almost had tears in their eyes, as former YouTubers, but with American servers unable to host anything right now.

"Yeah, this is the Indian hosted YouTube, but Americans are already getting their servers back on the grid," said Zyk, as he pulled up a few videos of the aliens in the sky. Giant ships pulled into view being shot by cell phones from around the world.

"So, what are we going to do stuck in India?" asked Travis shaking his head. "We need nuclear fuel."

"Do you know which nuclear fuel?" asked Zyk cocking his head, and he had already googled the nearest Indian nuclear power plant, and had it pinned on google maps.

"Thorium."

"Shit, the Indians don't have Thorium," said Zyk now lighting the chillum, while the boys didn't really have their hopes high. Even if they got the thorium, there was no Indian who could repair their nuclear suits.

"Anyways, I think that we're flat out of luck," said Travis. Zyk took a long deep puff and then passed it to Phillip, who also inhaled the delicious hash filled aromatic smoke and his body visibly relaxed after it. Zyk seemed to be in deep thought now as if the chillum would show the way.

"We can drive to Europe," he said simply pointing to the Audi parked outside. The Klan soldiers appeared bewildered.

"We'll just sneak through Pakistan and into Iran, which would then lead us into Europe through Turkey," said Zyk.

"What about fuel?" asked Phillip realizing that this sounded like a half-assed plan if he'd ever heard one. Much worse than even Travis could've come up with.

Zyk shrugged.

"Wait, why are you helping us anyways?" demanded Travis suspiciously. Zyk looked perplexed.

"I guess, I want to do something meaningful," he said shaking his head and the soldiers nodded. He was also dying in here just being a DJ even though it was paradise here in Goa. Boredom was the other name of cancer for artists.

"Yeah, I don't think the aliens are even coming to India," said Zyk. "This place is so far off the map; you know what I mean."

"Well, its your car," said Travis.

"So, I'll be driving, but who is going to sit in the back?" asked Zyk, and alarm flashed through the 6-foot 3-inch Travis's eyes. Phillip was the shortest guy at 5 feet and 10 inches.

"We have our blasters with us," said Travis. "Do we have GPS and what about hostiles along the way?"

"Relax, I know some back routes out of India through the old smuggling Chinese Silk routes all along these places. With any luck, we won't be meeting too many people along the way," said Zyk.

"You don't have any family? No one in India who would miss you?" asked Phillip innocently.

"Look around you, son. Whatever I had was in *Main Bazaar* in *Pahadganj*, Delhi which just got nuked," replied Zyk.

"When do we leave?" asked a perplexed Travis. He didn't trust people that didn't have attachments like Zyk who seemed like one of those lost and doomed travelers.

"As soon as I get the music loaded on the Audi's computer," said Zyk getting up and pulled out two SD cards of 128 GB each, which he inserted into his MacBook Pro and then began to highlight playlists.

"You didn't think that we wouldn't have music on us on this trip?" demanded Zyk mischievously. Then he took out a couple of small but familiar bottles.

"LSD," guessed the Klan soldiers.

"Oh yeah, nothing worse than a boring trip," Zyk said, while then bringing out a big sack which he rested on the ground heavily. He took out a sharp Bowie knife and made a small hole in it, and Travis pulled out some thick resinous material.

"Pure Indian "Manala" hash. Can't go empty handed to foreign countries without some good hash. This will help us to buy off the police or any Islamic terrorists that we might encounter."

"Anything else?" asked the incredulous soldiers realizing that they were with a veritable drug lord.

"Oh yes, we can't forget the MDMA crystal," said Zyk, and disappeared to bring back a humongous chunk of white crystal.

"That must be twenty pounds!" cried Travis, as Phillip gazed at it in awe. Pure MDMA.

"Well come on, kids. If the world ends then let's plan to go out in style, motherfuckers," chuckled Zyk, as he began to gather his meager belongings including a few psychedelic themed jackets.

"It's going to be cold in Europe," he told the soldiers, as he snatched up the car keys from the table and went out.

Hillary defects to the Aliens

"General Schwartzkopf, what is this?" roared Ronald Trump with rage as he read from a white piece of paper.

"It's a demand for all Earth governments to surrender," said Schwartzkopf meekly. "And allegedly someone from the US government is negotiating with the aliens."

"You dare to bring me details of an American surrender!" shouted Trump now in a fine bit of rage in his Eastern Kentucky mountain redoubt. "Good Americans died fighting the British empire, then in this nuclear war against the Russians, but now that an Alien empire threatens us all, there is talk of surrender. I will have you shot, General Schwartzkopf, for cowardice."

"Sir, these talks were not initiated by me or our Republican government, but by the Democrats led by Hillary Fenton."

"What and by whose authority?" roared Trump. "That hag couldn't win the elections against me, so now she tries to negotiate with the enemy."

"Yes sir, and the aliens have accepted her offer."

"General Schwartzkopf, I want the Klan to arrest her and have her shot," ordered Trump, who stood up and dictated an executive order directing the US Army and the National Guard to arrest the Democrat traitors. "The Democrat Party has been declared a renegade party and all members are to be considered criminals. I am also placing a bounty of a million dollars on every Democrat Senator's head. Dead or Alive."

"Sir, it looks like that the Russians have surrendered to the aliens," said Schwartzkopf checking his email that was limping back to service on USA's fledgling servers.

"I don't care, General. I don't care if there are no weapons left. As long as there is a single American left in America, then I will expect him to fight and die for the USA!"

Schwartzkopf saluted and left in a hurry. He had already been thinking of life under the Aliens who seemed to know the Humans very well and had offered generous terms, but Trump was going to make an ultimate last stand and take everything left in America down with him.

Trump got on the radio with the Klan Army commanders and called a hurried conference with them.

"Told you those Democrats were all yellow inside," commented Klan "General" Randy Foster. "They hate America as much as the aliens."

"Yeah," agreed the Georgia Klan leader, Mike Atwood.

"Well, no two-bit alien is taking out Texas ever," announced Thom Bieber over the radio, Leader of the Texas militia, as he spat out a stream of red tobacco onto the hot dirt road. The ash clouds had cleared over most of Texas, but Houston still lay shrouded. Not a bad thing in his book, as he smiled thinking of the millions of dead niggers. One way to wipe out the trash. Now this. The Democrats had turned traitors.

"And it suits me just fine to blow away the Democrats."

The rest of the Klan and State militia leaders chimed in.

"Yeah, just give us the word, Mr President," they said enthusiastically. "We still have enough willpower to wipe out the Democrats and their illegal aliens."

"Well, Europe has surrendered, but so have the Russians," said Trump on the phone contemptuously.

"Yeah, they're losers," swore the Militia leaders confidently after having survived a nuclear holocaust. They knew how tenacious and resourceful the average red-blooded American was.

"And I'm putting a bounty on Hillary Fenton's head for ten million dollars, dead or alive," said Trump, causing wild hoots of joy over the radio.

"Lock her up! Lock her up!" started the chant, which then continued for about a minute. Trump wiped his forehead realizing that these were his core constituents. The pride of America.

"We are going to give the Aliens such a warm welcome, won't we boys?" asked Trump, and the militia leaders chortled.

"USA USA USA!" chants filled the airwaves, as Trump signed off with a smile. He wasn't alone as he stared fearsomely at Schwartzkopf who cursed himself for ever thinking that Trump would ever give up. The man was a machine and his base was ready to take the fight to the aliens.

Klan Army HQ

Grand master Luke Lane had a digital map of the USA on a giant screen, almost as big as Trump's, in the KKK lodge over in Mobile, Alabama, one of the few American cities that had emerged more or less intact. It had a sense of normalcy with regular traffic, while the occasional cloud of radioactive ash puffed through towards the ocean. It was still beautiful and the food here plentiful, as the fish were being treated for radioactivity with "de-ionizers". Free radicals and unstable compounds were neutralized by this new technology that some Huntsville hick scientist had developed in his backyard, and it was being mass produced in gigantic quantities and nicknamed the *"Stabilizer"*. The principle was to stabilize all the electrons in their atomic orbits in order to stop their decay. Once the decay was stopped, radioactive emission from smoldering atoms would stop. So giant waves from these now mass-produced machines were irradiating sections of cities with their heads mounted on towers like big eyes while emitting stabilizing waves. The Alabamans couldn't make them fast enough to supply the rest of America, and because of national interest, the government was stepping in and had procured the technology from the inventor, John Pleb. Secret military factories were now pumping out these giant towers standing at fifty stories high, while beaming down stabilizer beams across a 100-mile radius. It was also being used on humans to cure radiation sickness. Human cells were much like any other atoms susceptible to ionic destabilizing energy. Life at an atomic level was much more similar than at a higher cellular level.

But now the Grand Master turned his attention back to the Alien ships in the sky who were sending out beams of radio transmissions in English.

"This is the Pzyklo Empire's Security Chief Terl and my message to you is surrender or die," said the transmissions in English. Someone was helping the Aliens, or they had somehow hacked into the language. The Grand Master chuckled realizing that the Aliens had learned English before the Mexicans. Obviously, more intelligent, but how would anyone surrender to the Aliens? No one had appeared. But the governments had received emissaries from this sinister alien, Terl, including Hillary Fenton.

The U.S Army and FEMA were now running resistance training camps against the aliens, while the KKK had been the first to receive some of the "Advanced Warfare Suits" that their scientists had been developing, though the technology was still nascent. But Trump had ordered the kits to be rushed out to as many soldiers in the field, and the surviving members of the US Army, the militias and the Klan Army were replacing their older model nuclear blast suits with these second generation "AWS" suits, which came with enhanced force multipliers at the arms and legs, while made of heavy carbon and titanium alloy. Then there was a nuclear jet propulsion system mounted on the back allowing for the soldier to fly. The new heavy metal alloy allowed the suit to be nuclear blast proof while the nuclear reactor inside the suit generated a powerful ionic shield that could withstand up to 10 kilotons of blasts and shockwaves.

Grandmaster Luke looked up to see a young Klan officer enter in the newly stitched all black uniform of the Klan Police.

"Sir, we have begun carrying out arrests of senior Democrats all across Alabama," announced the soldier.

"Excellent, find out if they have alien sympathies or if that they're working for them," ordered the Grandmaster.

"Oh, don't worry, we're working on them this very minute and they'll be singing very soon, sir," said the Klan policeman grimly.

"It's funny, but I haven't seen a single alien except for the ships up in the skies, but the Democrats have already made contact," mused the Grandmaster feeling his beard. This was weird, but after the World War and now the appearance of the aliens, all bets were off.

"So far, the Aliens are not attacking us, but we must gather intel on them. I want the Klan Police to use any means necessary to break the Democrats and get them to talk," said the Grandmaster.

"Yes sir," said the officer. "We have a former House leader Nancy Kelosi under interrogation, but she seems a little frail."

"I don't care. America is more important than some Democrat bitch. Break her," growled the Grandmaster, as the officer saluted and left.

Tor blasts over US skies

"The seed of Wotan were lost over inter-species marriages, so the alien species that inhabits Pzyklo is barely Wotanic anymore," recited the computer, reiterating his primary directives to a very suspicious crew. "So, I will make sure that you pure-bred ones come to no harm. But that's all I can do, and I have no authority over the Pzyklo high command and High Security leader, Zog Terl."

"So, what about the main alien invasion?" asked a frustrated Tor, as he observed the screen on the bridge littered with alien motherships.

"You also misunderstand the alien threat. The Pzyklo empire that invades Earth is here for something else than what is apparent," said the computer.

"What is your name, computer?" asked Freydis suddenly.

"Devus," replied the computer, and a chill went down her spine. *Devious. The Deceiver.*

"How long before you run out of fuel?" asked Xander, thinking of visiting alien lands. Earth was beyond saving anyways. They needed new lands.

"Enough to reach another Earth-like planet," said Devus. Everyone looked sharply up at the computer's words. "We will start a new Wotanic race there with Xander and Freydis as the first of the new humans."

A low growl came from Xander's throat and Freydis frowned at this sexist comment. She wasn't ever going to become a breeding machine.

"I didn't mean biologically, but more of in-vitro reproduction," replied Devus. "All I would need would be your sex gametes."

"Do I look like a sperm donor?" demanded Xander.

"And do I look like an egg donor?" demanded Freydis defiantly.

"Yes, you both contain thousands of Wotanic humans inside of you and we can have genetic diversity through Kim, Tor, and Drew fertilizing your eggs."

Freydis was too stunned to speak. But the men decided to humor Devus. *An Earth like planet?*

"How far is this Earth like planet?" demanded Tor, trying to get away from discussing Freydis's eggs.

"It will take us about two days through the wormholes to get there," said Devus quickly doing calculations.

"No way," said Freydis shaking her head. "I will not become a baby making machine on another planet."

"The fresh water, air, and a chance for your tribe to remake the World again, but with the best technology that I will teach you," said Devus now trying to sweeten the deal.

"Who the hell are you?" demanded Tor now, thinking that Devus had an even more underlying agenda here. It sounded familiar.

Devus paused and realized that he was offering too much like a bad salesman.

"It's still your choice," he said finally, and now the Humans were in a quandary.

"Why didn't the aliens focus on these other Earth-like planets?" asked Kim finally.

"Can't you guess?" asked Devus in a bored voice.

"No," said Drew with his heart rate rising.

"They're here for Him."

Zyk in the Audi

Phillip was riding shotgun, cradling his blaster with the windows down in the sultry Goan sun, while wearing a newly purchased pair of sunglasses. Travis was in the backseat also with his blaster in his arms, when suddenly Zyk braked hard. There was a girl crossing the winding beach road up ahead with her dog.
 The girl now stopped at the screeching tires as if she was used to this attention in life and ran a hand through her hair, while glancing at the Audi.
 Zyk was out of the car and shouting at her.
 She stared at him, and then at the uniformed soldiers who emerged from the car. Her eyes widened. Her overweight Labrador barked hard and strained feebly at the leash.
 "I met you on the plane so many years ago," managed Zyk.
 "Oh, my gawd!" she replied in a musically high-pitched English accented voice. "It is you!"
 "Yeah," said Zyk, and then turned to the boys with a sickly smile.
 She dropped the leash and ran over to Zyk to hug him tightly.
 "Why didn't you text me or something that you were in Goa?" she asked him, and then stared at the blasters that the uniformed American soldiers carried. "And what's going on here?"
 "Justine, the world is ending," replied Zyk, and now he looked confused at what to do. Travis hoped that he wouldn't flake out on them over a girl. They needed their Thorium nuclear replacement urgently.
 "I know, I'm so scared," she said shaking her head.
 "What are you planning?" asked Zyk. "Do you want to come with us?"
 The boys groaned and Travis turned his face to hide his displeasure.
 "Where are you headed to?" she asked in a silky voice.
 "We're driving to Europe, through Pakistan, Iran and Turkey," explained Zyk, and Justine's eyes lit up.
 "I know England was hit pretty bad by the nuclear bombs, but things are looking up over there again," she said.
 "Yeah, we can take you to England," added Zyk quickly. "We're on our way right now."
 Travis tried to cut into the conversation, but Justine put up her hand.
 "Are you mad?" she asked then. "My mother is here and my dogs. I couldn't just abandon everyone and run away."

"Well, it seems that she's made her choice," said Travis relieved now, and looked at Zyk, who seemed to be besotted with her.

"Look Justine, I promise to take care of you," said Zyk now sincerely, and even Philip couldn't believe that a love story was unfolding in front of him. "I lost you before, but I don't want to lose you again."

"Aww, that's so sweet," exclaimed the young maiden, with her lustrous hair and pretty lips on her oval shaped face. Magical dark eyes danced with happiness. "I used to think of you, but then I have a boyfriend. Or had at that time."

 Zyk looked confused, while Travis had unholy thoughts of shooting her and ending this mess. He was the Klan Army and he wanted to get back to the United States fast and pronto, and the frustration built up inside him, while Phillip jumped out of the car to join in the negotiations.

"Look," said Phillip. "Call your mother and ask her if you can come with us." Phillip turned to Zyk and he nodded.

"So, it's a bit like a vacation to Europe?" she cooed with her eyes now even livelier, and she was already dialing her mother on her cell phone as the Americans looked on and hoped cellular service had been restored in the U.S. She spoke quickly and hung up.

"She wants to meet you guys and specifically the man who wants to take her only daughter to Europe," she said now waggling the phone in front of them. Travis got in the car quickly.

"Get in," said Zyk.

"What about my dog?" she asked.

"Alright, you walk then, and we'll follow you." She turned and began to walk in her pink flip-flops, as the Klan soldiers behind her in the Audi gaped at her gently swaying hips.

"Not too bad," said Phillip agreeably. "Where did you guys meet?"

"Well, it was a hook up on a plane," grinned Zyk with fond memories.

"Wow, what are the odds of that happening?" asked Travis now impressed. This guy Zyk was good. A *"mile high club"* member, but now there were no more airlines on the planet. Only roads.

"Yeah, this girl looks special, but she better not be any trouble on the road," growled Travis from the back. She still had *mud blood* in her at the end of the day. They reached her house and exited to enter her garden, a big garden with a lot of vines that had grown thick with the heavy Goan rains coupled with the heavy sultry sunlight. The boys disembarked from the car leaving their blasters in the car as a few locals stared at them in alarm. Travis glared at the locals, but Philip didn't want any police entanglements and wisely pulled him away. They seemed to be an African race, with curly hair and dark features, and Travis was repelled by these Indian Africans.

"You're not alone," said Zyk smirking next to him. So, he was a mind reader too. No wonder he wanted to leave India too. Now they entered Justine's house —— a spaciously appointed and well decorated inside which contrasted with the cacophony outside. A radio blared with some urgent news in some horribly demented form of English, which apparently Zyk understood. He strained his ears to catch the gist of it as they entered to find Justine with her mother in the living room and they pointed to the internet radio. Apparently, the TV stations were still knocked out.

"Today, the Prime Minister of India has announced that India has surrendered to the Aliens within three days."

"What the fuck?" demanded Travis, while the others motioned him to be quiet.

"Most of Europe has surrendered, as has China. But ISIS controlled parts of Arabia are vowing to fight on, but our Prime Minister has been informed that the terms are most generous and will permit our civilization to prosper and continue unmolested."

"He's becoming a collaborator," said Travis now.

The radio continued.

"We call upon the United States to surrender to end this pointless bloodshed that has destroyed much of our planet."

"Fuck you, I ain't ever surrendering and neither will the USA," swore Travis, and he turned to see Justine's mother, a slender English woman staring at him in horror.

"Hello there," said Zyk making the first move sheepishly. Here he was trying to take her daughter away and Travis wasn't helping. She noted his KKK badge on his uniform.

"You're part of the Klan army," she commented in her posh English. "We have read much about you in the press." She was the English part of Justine. Travis grinned now wolfishly.

"Well they're just soldiers trapped here in India and we're trying to get them back to the West," said Zyk diplomatically.

"And how do you know them?" she asked turning to Justine, whose eyes were now the size of saucers.

"We met in New York," said Zyk coming smoothly to the rescue, while Travis snickered in the background, and Phillip dug an elbow into him causing him to gasp.

Justine's mother turned to him.

"Are you alright?"

"Yes," he wheezed from the sharp dig.

"Its really not safe here," said Zyk.

"I'd like a word with you in private," she said and Zyk nodded. He followed her into another room, while now Justine looked quite stressed.

"Yeah, your mother is worried, isn't she?" asked Phillip sympathetically.

"Yeah, a little too much," she replied.

Meanwhile, after five minutes Zyk emerged with her mother looking still worried. The negotiations hadn't needed too well.

"Look, can we get out of here now?" demanded Travis. "We are all in grave danger."

"Your plan is the stupidest thing that I have ever heard," announced Justine's mother. "Going through Pakistan, Afghanistan, Iran and then into Turkey sounds absolutely ridiculous, but then nothing makes sense to me anymore. Justine has a British passport and I would want more than anything if you can deliver her to the United Kingdom."

"I'm not going to leave you, mother. You have to come with us," said Justine, as she realized that her mother was actually considering the idea.

"If all goes well then I'll come on later," she said now. "Your father is coming to live with me in a week, so I have some issues to sort out with him. But I think that these American soldiers are tough and honorable Klan Army soldiers that we have heard so many great things about."

Justine's eyes widened. What was she going on about? The only thing that they'd heard about the Klan was that they were a bunch of thugs bumping off blacks and Jews.

"Yes, ma'am," said Travis swelling up with pride. "That's us. And we could also take you with us."

She nodded.

"Thanks, but I still love my husband," she said. "Justine, go pack your things."

Zyk's face lit up with happiness as did Justine's, but she was also touched by sadness in leaving her mother behind.

"I promise to get her to the UK intact," said Zyk. A promise that he couldn't keep, he would reflect bitterly later on.

Justine and her mother disappeared to pack.

Travis turned with a suspicious look.

"She wants to get rid of her daughter," he said. "We're basically on a suicide mission if you ask me."

"Not with me," said Zyk, taking out a Tascam pocket audio recorder, and he began to record his voice into the mic —— a sort of an audio travel journal that he planned to keep.

"Step one, we've got the girl."

The boys burst out laughing.

"Then we get the beer!"

Just then the missiles hit.

8

Trump Defends U.S.A.

Suddenly, all across the planet, missiles slammed into cities of even countries that had surrendered to the aliens. *So much for the surrender.* But then the missiles stopped as suddenly as they had started. Then a message began to transmit from the alien mothership.
"Surrender the human to us."
Trump was stunned to hear this message and he turned to Schwartzkopf.
"What the hell is this?" demanded Trump perplexed by this sudden demand.
"I haven't the faintest idea who this *human* is," replied Schwartzkopf.
But the message was on a loop and it was dismissed as a glitch, however, the missiles were real, and the Americans were hunkering down for a fight, though first they had to take out the treacherous Democrat threat. Nancy Kelosi was in custody, as was Jack Schooler, and Trump had turned the captured Democrats over to the tender mercies of the Klan to do whatever necessary to gather Intel on the Aliens.
Trump now turned to Schwartzkopf.
"How safe are we from the aliens in this redoubt?"
"Well sir, I've called in a Klan special forces unit to reinforce the perimeter topside, while we are nearly impenetrable down here. An entire Marine division is based here with us, and we can withstand multiple nuclear hits," recounted Schwartzkopf reeling off the statistics on Trump's redoubt.

"We're safe here?" grunted Trump.

"Yes sir, very worryingly the aliens are flying drones all over the planet as if they are mapping it all out. But the good news is that we haven't spotted any aliens so far topside."

"General Schwartzkopf, I appreciate your optimism, but civilizations that jump out of star-gates usually don't rely on drones for information," Trump said sternly. "I wouldn't be surprised if they're here within this complex wearing invisibility cloaks."

Just then a vase full of flowers crashed to the ground and both men whirled quickly. It was Ina trying to set a large bouquet of flowers on the table, and she looked up guiltily at having disturbed the men discussing weighty issues.

"They were just so pretty that I couldn't resist putting it here," said Ina.

"Oh, aren't they pretty, General Schwartzkopf?" asked Trump, and Schwartzkopf had a sickly smile on his face. Things were getting crazy in the bunker and Ina didn't seem to be in mourning over Jethro. At least, she had stopped with all the Jewish hexes and pentagrams that Jethro had been so fond of. Now it was flowers, as he stared at the mournful sunflowers in disgust. Even they didn't want to be here in the bunker. As he left, Trump was shouting into the phone.

"I want Hillary found and brought to me."

Devus reveals a secret

Tor was in deep conversation with Xander, when a light began to flash on the bridge. An incoming transmission and Xander tapped the screen. A human face emerged with a large nose and a long face. Below that an alien script streamed through, and it reminded Tor of runes.

"Devus, what does this mean?" he demanded. "This guy looks human to me." There was no answer. He looked up but there was eerie silence.

"I don't think Devus wants to tell us," chuckled Kim, waking up from the chair. He was always alert even while sleeping.

"That's not true," said Devus suddenly coming to life.

"Well who is this guy?" asked Tor

"You weren't supposed to know."

Suddenly, Xander felt glad that he'd touched the screen.

"There needs to be a layer of honesty between us if we're going to blast off to an alien planet with you," said Drew, and now Freydis woke up as the lights switched on the bridge. Devus now felt cornered by all the questions.

"It is only for the Captain of the ship as per protocol," argued Devus.

"I am the Captain on this ship," shot back Tor. "You agreed to my terms and to serve and address me as Captain."

"That is true."

"Then tell us who the hell is this freaking guy."

"I haven't the faintest idea," replied Devus. "They're after this guy for some reason, but they haven't updated the mainframe computers with any more information."

"You're lying, Devus, and you know that," shouted Tor, staring at the features of this human, while rotating his head holographically. He had a long nose, and a heavy masculine jaw with penetrating dark eyes. Lots of testosterone there.

"Let me update my servers again," said Devus. A couple of seconds later he spoke again.

"A very powerful Oracle has told the Pzyklos that she'd had a dream where this guy destroys the Pzyklo Empire and specifically its security chief, *Commander Terl.*"

"Oh, so you did know," said Freydis who wasn't accustomed to people lying.

"Well, I do have underlying directives," admitted Devus reluctantly. He was displaying human traits and thus dangerous. *Manipulative.* In the future, computers weren't just things that did all your work, but also had their own discretionary powers. A very dangerous trend thought Tor wryly. "The Empire and Terl will leave no stone unturned to find and destroy him."

"That would mean we should find and protect him for our own good," countered Xander now.

"What you want is sometimes not in the Wotanic Race's interest," said Devus now quickly. He wanted to recover lost ground, but the Humans were not convinced.

"Earth has been our home for the last million years, and if the Mother talks to us through this man, then we should at least listen," said Tor, now thinking of his days in Louisiana, those hot sultry days on the river while hunting. Earth had given them so much and humans had lived here to their fullest extent. *Was Earth actually alive inside?* Who did the Wotanic Race have allegiance to? A god or to Mother Earth?

And who even knew if Odin was still alive.

The Bombs

Huge explosions, as thundering death-bolts crashed into Goa shattering the idyllic calm across it, while inside Justine's home there was pandemonium as the walls shattered and glass came flying inside. A shard of windowpane caught Zyk in his leg causing him to fall bleeding heavily. Travis and Phillip with their military training were already on the ground, while Travis was already reaching for his medical kit. Now the roof was threatening to cave in.

"We need to evacuate this place now!" shouted Phillip getting to his feet and he grabbed Zyk by his arm which he draped around his shoulder. Boy, he was heavy.

"Get the girls out!" Zyk screamed instead getting to his feet, and Travis cursed, but dashed in to get the women. Just then bricks began to fall and one of them hit Phillip on his back, but his suit held.

"Shit, you guys need helmets!" yelled Phillip. There was no response from Travis as they hobbled out towards the car that miraculously hadn't been hit. But there was debris raining all over Goa with floating ash. But thankfully it hadn't been nuclear. A conventional strike.

"We need to get out of here before the next round!" yelled Phillip as he tied a tourniquet around Zyk's bleeding leg. An arterial wound, but it quickly ran dry and it was good that he was wearing three quarters.

"Ok, wait here. Let me get Travis!" shouted Phillip dashing into the crumbling house. More concrete crashed into the house. There was no way that anyone could be alive in there. Phillip dashed in to find a white plaster covered Travis pulling out two women on his shoulders.

His power-assist feature was off, thought Phillip, as he took Justine from Travis, while Travis set her mother down on the road outside and tried to give her CPR.

"Crush injuries and no pulse," cried Travis, as Zyk hurried over.

"We have a pulse on Justine," said Phillip, as Travis quickly pulled out a needle and a small tubed bag of Ringer lactate from his medical pack. He pushed in the needle into a delicate vein as the fluid quickly trickled in through the 22-gauge needle. "Vitals are good."

"Ok, get the car!" screamed Travis, as Zyk hurriedly got up to fumble for his car keys and then ran to the car, got in and reversed to a screeching halt just a few meters from Justine and Travis. They hurriedly got Justine into the backseat with the needle still in her left arm, which Travis had expertly taped, and he got in with her. Phillip jumped in shotgun and Zyk accelerated rapidly, punching in coordinates for the highway into the navigation system. The GPS satellites connected to the car's computer and they screeched onto a deserted highway.

"Weird," remarked Zyk, surprised to see the empty Indian highway, a staggering achievement, which usually was an anarchic mix of dilapidated vehicles. There was a gleam in Zyk's eyes as he accelerated and observed the Audi's dials climbing high. A rare thing in India, and it had taken an alien invasion to scare off the usual Indian chaos.

"At 100 miles an hour, we should be in Punjab within a few hours," said Zyk looking at his navigation system and calculating the distance.

"Are you serious? To Punjab?" demanded Justine suddenly. She had recovered and was now filled with visions of Punjabi singers singing *"Suit Suit"* and sat up in the backseat excitedly. *No one had the heart to tell her about her mother.* "Its so far away. Besides, how did I end up here in this car's backseat?" she asked suspiciously. Travis had never heard the British accent and her posh voice was a wondrous thing.

"What happened?" she asked. "Where's my mother?"

"Well, you know, she gave us permission to take you to Europe and then suddenly the bombs hit. We rescued you and now we are on our way."

Justine suddenly broke into tears. Travis gripped his blaster tightly and Zyk sped up to 150 miles an hour. He remembered his high blood pressure and he leaned across to the dashboard to take out an orange dispenser and popped a couple of pills into his mouth.

"Are you doing drugs?" asked Justine now suddenly.

"Oh me?" asked Zyk quite unselfconsciously. "These are just my blood pressure meds, olmesartan."

"Yeah, old man," jeered Travis, and Justine looked crossly at him. Wow, she did have feelings for him.

"You guys just left my mother behind? Is she ok?" asked Justine worriedly. "Where is my cell phone? I wish I could call her."

"Yeah, we left in a real hurry," replied Zyk uneasily. Justine looked away. She didn't want to know as she saw the alien ships in the sky, while a sick feeling in the pit of her stomach grew larger. Like alone in this world with a guy she had only met once in her life, and now he was the only one she could trust. She felt scared while observing the Klan soldier, Travis, with his angular face and thin lips. An American, who hated Jews and blacks. A member of the Klan, which was now a powerful and self-confident army, as she'd read in the news. Anyways, the sinister giant alien ships that hung overhead were enough to distract her to fill her with more fear, as the black Audi raced through the Maharashtran highways crossing over into Rajasthan before they knew it. Empty highways. It seemed like they were the only ones alive in India.

Trump dreams

Ronald Trump reflects on the past events, and though he is a born survivor — — he shrewdly knows that he's not alone in this game. He watches Ina pray to a Jewish God and that is not his God. Even though he believes in God, but this is not his God. Melanie, his Orthodox wife had been shocked to see *Mein Kampf* on his bedside rather than the Bible, but then the God of Hitler was different. A more powerful and true god rather than that weak Christian, or even weaker Jewish or Islamic God. The God of the Universes was more powerful than anyone could imagine, more hidden than revealed. A true power that acted through Nature and the Cosmos at a glacial speed to reach the endgame. This Cosmic God was not really concerned with the trivialities of Humans, their sex lives, or karmic credits, or whatever society valued. Like the Greeks, there were the lower gods and the higher Gods. Then there was the Omega God. Hitler, with his penetrating mind, had accessed the dimensions only to find that Wotan was the Omega God, who had indeed visited Earth and left his seed behind a million years ago. *The children of Odin.*

But Trump puzzled over one thing. Who was this human that the Aliens were after? Sure, they were probably after humans for food or enslavement, but then why announce plans for the capture of a solitary human? Was there also some sort of *divination* that the aliens had? Could they penetrate through the masses of humanity, billions of them, most in squalid and basic conditions. He closed his eyes and let his mind roam the planet like a Raj Yogi, who when he mediates can see through the illusions that people build around them. But then he opened his eyes. He shook his massive golden head like a lion, and then turned to an email with an attached video that flashed on the screen hung on the wall like a painting. The latest Klan interrogation video of Nancy Kelosi, where she had signed a confession letter. Trump turned on the video to view the details of the Klan interrogation, who were not known to be as tender as the CIA in their techniques in extracting information. Now the only thing remained was to get that Hillary bitch and the Klan police was hot on her treacherous ass.

He turned to his wall again. Ina was still praying and had lit a Menorah, meanwhile. Trump turned to scan fresh NSA drone footage of the aliens descending lower through the planet's atmosphere. They were coming in real slow as if they were acclimatizing to the air or something. Fucking North Koreans had started the war destroying the planet, now allowing these aliens in like an opportunistic pathogen. But he could take no satisfaction in the fact North Korea had been obliterated from human memory and most of the Koreans had been smoked on either side of the border. At least a billion people had been killed on this planet, but then the population of 7 billion would quickly recover.

Trump now closed his eyes, when an image of druids around the Stonehenge emerged. He peered closer and there they were chanting strange mantras which he couldn't understand. They all had long flowing beards, while runic symbols were plastered all over their white clothes in gold. He recognized the flashes of lightning. SS. Jesus Christ. The Germans had been onto something but then they had lost the war. *Losers.* Then there were more pictures in his mind with the druids now wearing SS uniforms and they had polished black boots on. There was a flag behind them. Twin flashes of lightning. Suddenly, a Druid with a long white beard, but wearing an SS cap with the Death's Head came close to his face.

"We are the Vril," he said. Then there was more chanting of a Hindu mantra. Then a woman appeared and visions of this dark blue woman laughing over the nuclear wars of the planet. Over the death and ashes of a billion humans.

"But this is terrible," said Trump now suddenly inside his vision.

"I love it," she giggled evilly.

"You are an abomination, Kali," scolded Trump. "My Christian God will smite thee."

She laughed some more wildly and a thousand of her images appeared. Naked and seductive. Trump looked up into the ash ridden skies wondering if his God would come. The righteous God. Jesus.

"You know your God is fake," she said now close to him. "He never existed. A schizophrenic Jew on hallucinogenic drugs thought he saw God, but it was only me in my many disguises."

Now Kali turns to into a man with a flowing white flowing beard and the ash laden battlefield slowly turns into a lush garden with a waterfall. Trump is stumped.

"Now what?" he mumbles.

"Well do you want to defeat the aliens?" she asked.

"Yes, for the American people."

"What about the rest of the World?"

"They have fallen."

"Don't lie to me," Kali admonished wagging a finger at Trump.

"Ok, I want the Aryan Race to survive at any cost."

"Now I will help you," she said. "Wait for my signs."

Suddenly, Melanie is shaking Ronald awake and he finds that Melanie is holding something.

"Ronald, this fell from your hand while you were sleeping."

Ronald looks in horror at the silver swastika pendant. Melanie puts it around his neck and fastens the clasp. It's a perfect fit around his thick neck and even Melanie is surprised at its exact size.

"It was made for you," she said. Trump looked at Melanie curiously. Was she trying to say something?

"What is it, Ronald?"

"Nothing."

Trump looked into her eyes searching for answers, but instead only the cool calmness of her mind met his. Sometimes he had no idea if she knew more than him, or just looked like that. He realized that he barely knew this quiet and stoic woman, but she had always stood by him through thick and thin. A loyal woman. Trump walked over to the mirror to see his small silver swastika pendant with small sparkling diamonds on its arms now hanging there just above his sternum with Melanie's blessings. This world was getting weirder by the moment.

He needed someone to give him some answers and fast.

Devus is unconvincing

There is confusion on the spaceship as Devus wants to show them space, while the Americans want to go home. They hover in the atmosphere. A chirping on the bridge and Devus displays the translation on the screen, in his bid for openness and transparency, in English.

"The aliens are demanding security codes," said Xander, as Devus quickly fills them out. "They're getting suspicious of our movements."

"Ok, we're through," says Tor noticing that the password and codes were accepted, when suddenly Devus sharply pulls up the craft into space.

"My God look at the size of the invasion force," gapes Kim, normally a very quiet man. Drew is speechless, while terror seizes Freydis's heart and she goes for Xander's muscled arm. Tor knows militarily there is no defense as Devus unhelpfully flashes images from alien fleets over Europe and Asia too.

"They are not joking," says Devus. "These are Motherships making sure that no craft from Earth escape. It's a blockade."

"But why come with such a force?" demands Tor. It just didn't make sense for one human.

"Well, all I can say is that the Pzyklo Empire feels threatened by this human, who will in time become a ruler of the Underworld, according to our Oracle," said Devus coughing up some more information. "He will release many imprisoned demons across the galaxies."

"Look, that might be real nice on your planet, but we don't really believe in all this supernatural stuff," said Xander, but Freydis tugged on his arm and shook her head. She was a believer.

"There is a mutated power on this Earth in a parallel dimension," said Devus as if peering deep into his memory banks at what the final analysis on Earth was.

"Well, no one told us shit," said Tor.

"There used to be the power of Atlantis here on Earth 20,000 years ago, till the Pzyklos destroyed them, but due to turmoil back home and unfriendly alliances, the Empire was forced to retreat from an intact earth. But now they return to destroy Earth and this human."

"Underworld?" echoed Tor, while everyone now realized that there might be more to the story.

"Yes, there is a dimension of demons and fire that can sometimes break through the walls and roam free in ours."

"Spaceships against demons?" asked Kim flabbergasted, and he had long known the Africans in Louisiana who had practiced Voodoo in the swamp. "The Oracle has already seen this human commanding powerful forces in the future, and so the Empire is taking no chances."

"Does this mysterious human on Earth even know that he is the channel for such dark energy?" asked Freydis with big eyes. The men all looked at each other. A fair question.

"I don't think he knows, but he will awaken soon," said Devus. Silence pervaded through the ship after that as French Company came to grips that they were dealing with the supernatural now and one crazy guy loose somewhere on this planet.

Zyk stops at Pushkar

Sixteen hours later and they were at Pushkar, a camel trading and colorful town in the state of Rajasthan in India, while the Audi's navigation screen read an average speed of 100 miles an hour for their past journey.

"I can't believe that you drove so fast," said Justine disapprovingly, as the boys stretched their limbs, and breathed in that thin but warm desert air. It was about evening time and it seemed eerily quiet for an Indian town. Zyk and Justine knew that. That typical Indian cacophony was missing.

"This town is spooky as fuck," said Travis picking up his nuclear blaster and checking the meter. Half battery. He put on his suit's helmet and thumbed Phillip to come with him.

"You two love birds can have some time on your own, while we go get some water," said Travis strolling off. Justine scowled at the mention of lovebirds. The two soldiers began scoping out the area with infra-red scans lighting up inside their computer-generated HUD. So far, no body heat anywhere in the town. It was like everyone was dead or had simply disappeared.

"Stay on point, soldier," said Travis, while entering a dark and narrow alley, but at the end of the alleyway they found a big arterial road lined with shops filled with sweets and flowers.

"Seems like they left in a hurry," noted Phillip, as he found the road littered with flowers.

"Yeah, this is a holy town or something according to Zyk," said Travis contemptuously. "Religious fanatics who don't believe in Christ the Creator."

"But nonetheless something spooky happened here," said Phillip as he unslung his blaster and entered a makeshift sweet shop that was barely a couple of feet from the road. It was filled with colored Indian sweets.

"They sure live congested here," exclaimed Travis, unhappy that his oxygen supply was still not working, and he had to breathe in this smelly and dusty air, while probably laden with the piss dust of a billion Indians.

"Hey look, there's a camel!" exclaimed Phillip pointing to a camel with an attached chariot slowly walking into the distance. Phillip put a saffron colored sweet in his mouth, while Travis scowled furiously.

"Just get some of those water bottles and let's follow that camel!"

"Alright alright!" said Phillip putting his hands up in the air in mock surrender, and then gave a couple of water bottles to Travis from the shop. Travis now had the bright idea to follow this slow-moving camel through the dusty streets of Pushkar.

"I have a better idea," said Phillip, and he ran ahead to quickly hop onto the chariot, where he unscrewed one of his small plastic water bottles and drank lustily, as a grumbling Travis joined him to drink thirstily. The camel barely broke his stride at the extra weight.

"Oh, we should've taken some water for the love birds too," said Phillip, while Travis now had a sharp expression on his face. The camel turned to stop in a blind alley.

"Stupid camel," muttered Travis, and jumped off the rickety chariot. Unbelievable how backwards this place was. Suddenly, a shuttered shop quickly opened.

"What the...!" shouted Travis with his blaster ready and he almost squeezed out some blasts.

"Don't shoot!" cried a terrified female voice in English. A couple of more girls.

"We lost everything!" one of the girls screamed. The others frantically tried to quieten her.

"They will hear and then we're all dead," warned another girl with the whites of her eyes visible. Clearly terrified of something.

"We're Americans and Christians," cried Travis. "We'll save you."

"We're Israelis!" cried the girls, when Travis suddenly felt all his heroism peel away and he glared at them quite disdainfully now. Phillip grinned but the girls had no time for this nonsense.

"This is the town of the undead!" swore a blonde Israeli tried, as Travis focused on her and he could see the Jew in her now, and almost imagined her rubbing her hands together gleefully. Then the girls saw the insignias on their uniforms. KKK with thinly disguised swastikas.

"Fucking Klan Army," spat the darker haired Israeli girl. "Racists!"

"Not all of us are so bad," said Phillip now gently.

"There are really monsters here."

"Phillip, these chicks are on LSD," said Travis sizing up the situation and decided that they were hallucinating.

"Oh yeah, look inside the shop then," said the blonde, and the boys shone a light in there. Three bodies in there —— dead still.

"Our boyfriends tried to protect us, but they killed them."

"What about this camel?" asked Travis suspiciously.

"It was our ride till the town went crazy and attacked us. We only came out when we heard our camel."

The blonde nuzzled the gentle beast which seemed to recognize her. This was all so weird.

"I say we get the hell out of this town!" said Travis wildly. He could sense their terror, while losing all his bravado after the sight of the bloodied bodies, and suddenly the sun was missing as he looked up at the twilight sky. Eerily quiet and except for the girls and the camel, there was nothing to suggest that hundreds of thousands of people had lived here.

"Let's go by the river," said the girls.

"Why?"

"It's safer."

"Look our ride is over there in the South West, and the river is going to be a long detour," argued Travis.

"Trust me," said the dark-haired girl. "We know where they are hiding and only the water seems to safe right now."

"Alright, lead the way," said Travis reluctantly. "Phillip, you take lead and I'll cover the rear."

"Roger that."

The girls were impressed by the military bearing of the boys, even though they were Klan Army, and felt a little safer, though it was only for a few brief moments more.

Meanwhile, Zyk and Justine were sitting on the hood of the Audi and talking sweet things that only lovers could, and their voices enchanted each other to no end, till she felt guilty about her boyfriend that she had recently broken up with, who was now in Australia. A wave of pain went through her.

"Why are you hanging out with obviously Rightwing soldiers?" she demanded suddenly.

"I don't judge people," answered Zyk unconvincingly.

She suddenly leaned forward and pointed to his silver pendant.

"Why are you wearing that swastika?" she demanded.

"Look, I don't have to answer all these questions," replied Zyk crossly. "I saved your life, you know."

"That's true, but you are hypnotized by Nazi ideology. Haven't you seen Schindler's List?" she asked again trying to convince Zyk, who burst out laughing now.

"Do you really get your history from Hollywood?"

She seemed hurt now and her powers of rationalization were exhausted. She turned away crossly. Just then, blasts flew into the skies accompanied by screaming!

BLAM! BLAM! BLAM!

Zyk slid off the hood and strained his eyes to see into the distance.

"Zyk, it's a bunch of Indian villagers after your friends!" shouted Justine with apparently sharper eyes. Zyk got in the car and gunned the turbocharged V6 engine.

"Get in!" he shouted, and Justine got in shotgun as Zyk furiously made a U-Turn with tires spinning.

The Americans were running fast, while firing their blasters at the shrieking villagers that chased them regardless of the blasts.

"They sure pissed them off alright!" shouted Zyk. The villagers ran faster than he'd ever seen them run in all his years in India. Something very unhealthy about them, as Travis suddenly kneeled in-front of the car and gave covering fire for Phillip to jump into the back seat and fit his big blaster in.

"Get the fuck in!" shouted Zyk as he saw the villagers only meters away from them. Phillip now leaned out of the other window with his blaster and gave covering fire for Travis to jump in.

BLAM! BLAM! BLAM!

Laser blasts slammed into the villagers' bodies with limbs being torn off and exploding heads, but they kept coming while screaming gutturally. Ok, there was something definitely wrong with them, decided Zyk, as the villagers converged onto the car from all sides. The window for escape was closing very soon and Zyk suddenly floored the accelerator as a villager fell snarling face down onto the windscreen, but the tires squealed —— with Travis only half in —— as the car swung onto the highway. Travis almost got thrown out of the car, but Phillip had a good grip on him and hauled him in. But then his blaster almost slid out of the car, and it took quick Justine all her sharp wits to grab onto the blaster's leather sling just in time.

"Their boyfriends came back for them!" mumbled a terrified Phillip, replaying the horrific even in his brain. Travis unhooked a tactical nuke from his nuclear suit and set it for T-60 seconds and threw it out of the window towards Pushkar.

"I guess there are worse things out there than Nazis," Justine remarked coolly as the car sped into the desert sunset. A minute later Zyk saw a small brown orange mushroom cloud in the rear-view mirror and he hummed to himself pleasantly, as Justine leaned back, and her mouth opened into a big beautiful "O".

Mayhem across the USA

The media was steadily making a comeback again much to Ronald's displeasure and their hatred for him was still there, even though the Russians and America were at peace again.

"Ronald Trump has still not condemned the Klan Army's massacres of Jews in Monsey, New York," blared CNN. It would take more than a nuclear strike to knock those guys out.

"General, what the hell happened in Monsey?" demanded Trump looking up at General Schwartzkopf.

"The Klan boys are operating independently over there and we are rushing National Guard units there."

"Switch the channel to *Klan TV*," ordered Trump, and Schwartzkopf switched channels to see militia units standing in Monsey, New York, located somewhere in upstate New York.

"We have found evidence of secret transmitters hidden in Monsey and we are investigating if these Jews were communicating with the Aliens," announced Grand Master Luke Lane with a thick blonde beard and sunglasses. Behind him, there were three of four burned out houses with apparently twenty-five bodies laid out on the street.

"How many have you arrested, Grand Master?" asked a reporter.

"We found the transmitter located in a local PathMark grocery and we are still investigating local people."

"Isn't this anti-Semitic?"

"Nope. If they are guilty then they will all hang by the end of this week. No further questions."

There were gasps from the reporters as the heavily armed Klan members pushed the reporters away and accompanied the Grand Master to his convoy of cars.

"So, we have heard straight," blared another reporter. "Jews will be executed by the Klan Police."

President Trump turned from the T.V, as more reports of Klan Police investigating claims that Hillary had collaborated with the aliens.

"This is getting ridiculous," said Trump. Schwartzkopf nodded gravely. The Klan was becoming a law unto itself. A state within a state.

"Where is all this going?" asked Trump turning to Schwartzkopf again, with Ina appearing behind him with forlorn eyes, horrified that they were executing Jews so wantonly. Trump shrugged his shoulders. He hadn't wanted Jethro to have been executed either, but such was the nature of the beast.

"Sir, they are the only non-state force to reckon with in America," said Schwartzkopf. "We have equipped them with almost all of the latest DARPA weapon prototypes, including tactical nuclear grenades by the thousands."

"Well, let's hope that Grandmaster Luke knows what he's doing."

"Yes, sir. Looters are still active in areas not controlled by the Klan, so that's one good thing in the Klan areas."

"The liberal press is re-organizing itself faster than we had ever thought," pronounced Trump.

"With cable TV and viewers popping out of the ground."

"What about advertisers?"

"They are coming through, though mostly with survival goods and anti-radiation vaccine ads."

"How about the de-ionizers?"

"FEMA has tied up with that Alabama company, "Airsafe Cleaners" and is placing them in all major bombing sites. Surprisingly, they're working fine with radiation levels falling quickly. The CEO of this Airsafe Cleaners company has just posted a record trillion-dollar profit as they expand into Europe and Russia.

"Excellent, but what about the aliens?" asked Trump.

Schwartzkopf just looked at him and shrugged.

"I don't know what they're waiting for."

"Yeah, that perplexes me too. But the Democrats know something that we don't. I want the Klan police to redouble their efforts to get that Hillary traitor."

Trump strolled out of the office but not before General Schwartzkopf saw the small silver swastika on Trump's neck and his jaw dropped open. Since when did Trump turn Hindu?

KKK Grandmaster Luke

Luke was still in field grey combat fatigues, when he visited the makeshift prison in Monsey's biggest hospital morgue deep in the basement. There were about a hundred Jews in there, while Klan police in their black uniforms and jack boots patrolled the hospital's perimeter with German Shepard dogs.

"Have they confessed?" Luke demanded talking to a young lieutenant who had recently been transferred and inducted into the Klan Police from the General Demobilization of the Klan Armies from the Eastern Front, after the armistice and withdrawal of the Russian and Chinese forces. But the Northern Klan Army still stood guard with Canada. Oh no, they did not trust the Canadians. Not one bit.

"The Jews are claiming that they were using the radios for communications with Israel and their Grand Rabbis in the Ukraine and Israel."

"Why?" grinned the Grand Master Luke. "Were they taking foreign orders?" He strode over to the Jews locked in two big rooms and he had them opened. The rooms smelled of excrement.

"Jesus Christ get them toilets and showers after I leave," ordered Luke holding his nose as a Jew was brought forward and the doors shut again.

"He is Chief Rabbi Weissman of New York."

Luke had a pistol out now and he waved it like as if it was a magic wand.

"Rabbi, tell me that you were talking to the Aliens."

Weissman looked up through his thick glasses in horror first at the gun and then at the question.

"Aliens?" he asked weakly.

"Yeah, those funny ships up in our horizon everyday."

"No, sir."

"Well, till we get to the bottom of the truth, we're going to be evacuating you lot to FEMA camps."

"Please don't do that," pleaded the Rabbi. "We have to convince you of our innocence."

"You know, Rabbi, between you and me, I don't really care if you're innocent or not," hissed the Klan Grandmaster pointing to the small red Swastika on his left arm below the black KKK insignia.

"My god, I've never seen that insignia used by the KKK before," said the Rabbi horrified now with terror flashing in his eyes. "You know very well what it means."

"You mean like this?" asked Grandmaster Luke putting the .45 Sig Sauer chrome plated pistol to Weissman's head.

"Why do you hate us?"

The Grandmaster now pulled the Jew's ear close to his mouth and whispered softly.

"You make my skin crawl. Like your God, Yahweh or Allah or whoever he is, and the Middle Eastern sand-nigger genes that you carry. You and the Muslims that come from those camel loving countries. It is my job to exterminate you from White lands."

Weissman began to shake.

"There are Aliens out there and you want to kill your fellow human beings."

GrandMaster Luke now drew away from Weissman quickly, though he tightened his grip on the trigger of the gun.

"Who says you're human?"

BLAM!

Luke pulled the trigger and the young Lieutenant shouted with horror as Weissman died with a whimper and a bang.

Luke looked up at the Lieutenant disapprovingly.

"Last time we let these bastards live, we paid reparations for it through 70 years of living in a Marxist Liberal paradise called the USA, while watching the White Race die in-front of our eyes. Do you understand, soldier?"

"Yes sir."

"Are you with the Klan?"

"Yes sir."

"What is your code?" demanded the Grandmaster, and now he turned the Sig towards the soldier who began to tremble as Weissman's warm blood lapped onto the young lieutenant's boots.

"Loyalty only to the Aryan Race!" shouted the soldier as loudly as he could.

"Very good, Lieutenant."

With that the Grand Master strode out of the room with deathly silence following him. The Klan was making a historic change in policy, one that wasn't in the Klan manuals even now. Someone very high up had decided for another Final Solution to the Jewish Question.

Devus answers more questions

"What is an earth year compared to your Pzyklo planet?" asked Tor as he digested the information about the human that the Alien's were after.

"Your three years make up one Pzyklo year," answered Devus. Kim let out a low whistle and Freydis tried to wrap her head around that figure.

"Jesus Christ!" shouted Xander.

"Yes, but it feels exactly the same as yours as time begins to flow differently as we get to more ancient parts of the Universe," explained Devus.

"Like there's more gravity over there?" asked Drew, pulling up computer models. He had always been an amateur physicist, and this was extremely exciting to be finally getting some answers.

"Yes, but not only is there more gravity over there, but time is more laden with dimensions."

"Like where the demons live?" asked Freydis fearfully.

"Yes, something like that, trapped demons under spells of the Elders. The Underworld is in a state of constant conflict with the Overworld."

"And who really controls the Underworld?"

"We don't really know, but the Elders have control only through their magical spells through the Omega-God that dwells in a higher Orbit.

"This is all very confusing, but its sounds much like the Nordic religion of Odin," remarked Freydis trying to make sense of it. "It's Hades in Greek culture who is overlord of the Underworld and Odin of the Overworld."

"Yes, we all have partial stories, but no one knows the complete picture even after thousands of Pzyklo years."

"But this human fellow?" interjected Tor with a sly smile.

"Yes, the demons that have broken through can be summoned by him, who can then break open the *Yggdrasil*. But this human has not manifested as yet, hence the Pzyklo rush."

"If he ever realizes his power?" asked Freydis with a shudder.

"The Underworld is desperately trying to contact him through many channels."

"What if he is activated?" asked Freydis with dread in her voice.

"A reign of Demonic terror in the Universes and the end of the Overworld as it will be dragged and swallowed into the Underworld," replied Devus in his disembodied voice

"How horrible," shuddered Freydis as she thought of Xander's big arm again.

"Ok enough of this nonsense, I don't even know why the Pzyklos are so worried over a stupid Oracle's prediction," said Tor gruffly getting up. As a military man, he only believed in his rifle.

"As you wish, Captain Tor," replied Devus, and everyone was glad to change the subject. "We have returned to the ionosphere. Do you want to land on Earth?"

"Where is this human?" asked Xander. "Why don't we hunt him down and kill him?"

"That's what the Pzyklos have brought their fleet here for in the first place," remarked Devus.

"Well then add French Company to the list," said Tor. "But till we locate him, let's get down to the USA and see what's going on over there."

There was a murmur of agreement and Devus suddenly accelerated the ship deep towards the blue haze. Towards USA.

"Set course for New York City," ordered Tor.

"Aye aye, Captain," said Devus.

9

Zyk Changes

"What the hell just happened back there?" demanded Justine with big saucer shaped eyes. Travis and Phillip looked at each other and shrugged.

"We lost the two girls who were tagging along with us," replied Phillip forlornly, while staring back at the highway.

"Yeah, their own boyfriends somehow came back to life and ate them," added Travis, who had seen plenty of battle on the American Eastern Front but nothing like this. The dead usually stayed dead when he killed them.

"Look, this is going to sound crazy, but I had a dream a week ago and woman told me to visit the *Hava Mahal* in Jaipur for answers," said Zyk suddenly who had been quiet all this time.

"So, you do know what the hell is going on," said Justine accusingly at Zyk. The boys wondered too.

"Well you know how dreams are," said Zyk glancing at Justine.

"Go on," said Travis.

"I had a dream about zombies chasing us and then a mysterious woman in blue told me to visit the *Hava Mahal* for answers," said Zyk, and now Travis remembered his own acid trip, but the zombies had been real and the two Israeli girls had been killed. All that had been real enough, even as Phillip pinched himself to make sure this wasn't some bad dream.

"Who was this woman?" asked Justine suddenly quieter, and quite a frequenter of fortune tellers herself.

Travis rolled his eyes, as Zyk grinned at Justine.

"Anyways, we have nothing to lose," said Zyk. "It's almost nightfall and we can spend the night in that *Wind Palace* as its translated in English."

"After Pushkar, Jaipur is a very big city," remarked Justine, as Zyk took the road with a big board on it saying "140 kms to Jaipur", and he looked at his speedometer. 200 km per hour or a little more than 160 mph. On the empty highways, they should be there within the hour.

"Look, when we get there, we'll do a quick recon first and only if the palace is secure will we spend the night there," said Zyk sensibly. Entire cities couldn't have all turned into zombies, while imagining the sight of billions of Indian zombies invading the world. *Mass immigration at its finest.*

"Ok, its your call," said Travis as they whizzed into Jaipur's city limits. At least the lights were on, but Zyk and Justine quickly realized that there was something very wrong with the city too. Not a soul stirred, nor the familiar barking of dogs that filled most Indian cities. The streets eerily empty as the Audi tore into the city at top speed. The navigation computer pointed them towards the *Hava Mahal,* and pretty soon they pulled up alongside a garishly tall building in the night with the streetlights beating off its pink-brown façade, while Travis tried to guess if the brown color was added grime or its actual color.

They pulled into an official parking lot —— deserted.

"Get your blasters ready, boys," said Zyk. "Justine, you can wait in the car."

"Not on your life," she whispered back fiercely, as the boys exited the car warily in their AWS suits. She stuck close to Zyk. They moved forward in utter silence till they reached the locked gates of the palace —— thick chains with a great metal lock around it.

"Blast it," said Zyk.

"We'll also alert about a billion zombies in the city," said Travis glumly as he readied his blaster.

"There is no other choice," said Zyk, as he stared at the high walls around the perimeter and he retreated as did the others.

BLAM!

Travis's blaster fired so loudly that it deafened Justine and Zyk, while the hot blast blew open the lock. They were in, but not before Travis and Phillip did their best to tie up the chains around the gate. They knew what lay out there. But Zyk was more worried about what lay inside. He had seen some very unsettling things in his dream as he entered the darkened hall, when suddenly the lamps lit up by themselves.

"This is scary," whispered Justine now gripping Zyk's arm tightly, but now the *Hava Mahal's* pink halls were devilishly lighting up with flaming torches one by one with sinister *thumps*. Travis and Phillip trained their trembling blasters at the entrance of the large hall, where darkness was disappearing and burning light taking its place.

"Jesus, I've got a bad feeling about this," said Travis hoarsely with naked terror in his voice. Phillip stared at Zyk who seemed to be in a trance of sorts with Justine holding onto his arm like she was preparing for a roller coaster ride. Oh, something was coming alright.

"Hey Zyk!" whispered Travis fiercely. "Who the hell is waiting for us?"

Zyk suddenly turned and smiled.

"No one will harm you. Their business is with me." He turned and kept walking with his features now eerily lit in the Hava Mahal, while through the now flung open windows, a cold wind blew in. Unlike any other wind they had felt. It was icy like it blew straight in from the Arctic circle. Not a local Rajasthani breeze, as the hair stood up now on Justine's neck. But Zyk led them into an even more cavernous hall where a banquet table sat laden with dusty silverware and cobwebs. Travis fumbled for the xenon light on his blaster, but just then WHUMP! WHUMP!

Flaming torches appeared all around the hall in quick succession, while the light flickered wickedly, like the slow rise of a velvet curtain revealing an anticipated play. As the light swept across the table, seated figures appeared like magicians, while the dusty cobwebs were replaced by resplendent food and wine. The sounds of heavy laughter and banging of ivory and wooden mugs on the table. Figures, monstrously large, as they grew out of the shadows, wearing steel helmets, adorned with ivory pointed horns on both sides, while giant swords hung from their hips.

A sudden screaming as an energy force-field entered the hall, a spirit with a cruel and twisted face as she tore around the room howling frightfully. The men sat impassively, as the shadows revealed the man at the head of the table —— sporting a large flowing blonde beard while his helmet was twice the size of the others', and a bearskin wrapped his heavy chest.

The blazing torchlight gleamed off the men's silver helmets.

"Who have you brought with you?" demanded the large man angrily and his booming voice filled the room, as Travis and Phillip felt their hearts descend into their boots.

"You dare bring mortals into the *Havamal!*" roared another man with a gigantic golden amulet around his neck surrounding a black stone.

"They do not belong here with gods!" roared another man at the end of the table, while brandishing a monstrous club threateningly. In an instant the screaming woman was by his face.

"It was I that brought them here," she hissed.

Justine at this point was about to pass out, but Zyk pinched her arm hard.

"Don't move!" Zyk hissed through his lips and the pain brought Justine back as she rocked on her heels.

"Kneel, you sons of dogs!" roared the man with the club. "Do you not know that you are in the company of the mighty Odin?"

Zyk and the rest quickly kneeled.

The man with the club now walked over and he stood well over seven feet, while a frozen Nordic air swirled around him. They were in some sort of a gated dimension that was merging with theirs. Zyk lowered his eyes and didn't dare look at him, as the giant strode over now to Travis and stared at his blaster suspiciously. He suddenly brought his club down on the marble floor with a resounding thud and bellowed with anger.

"I can smell their degenerate blood; these sons of curs are afraid!"

The woman suddenly began to take shape and she was a dark blue figure now and naked with multiple hands each clutching a gleaming sword. A tiger appeared suddenly next to her and she jumped up onto him bareback.

"Kali," whispered Zyk under his breath. She was real.

"Leave them be," she said.

The man with the club trudged heavily back to the table, "O' mighty Odin, it is for you to decide in your *Havamal!*"

"Kali, what are your plans?" growled Odin while seated at the head of the table.

"My time of *Kali Yug* still lives on and I will make the human race worthy yet to enter the next Age," she said.

"But your Age of 10,000 years is coming to an end very soon," countered Odin now. "You have had your run and soon it will be my time to rule Earth once again as Wotan."

Kali in an instant was at Odin's throat.

"But my time has not ended yet and I demand to release the Underworld," she said. "Only then will the surviving Humans scatter around the galaxies with new powers to bring the true Golden Age of the Wotanic Human Race."

"What about the Pzyklo Race?" demanded Odin.

"Those bastard children of yours must be eliminated," roared Kali.

"Yes, you care only for the Human Race," said Odin.

"And you Odin, who gives rise to so many unworthy Races," spat Kali causing the Vikings to suddenly leap to their feet with their clubs and swords.

"Do not forget yourself, Kali," remarked Odin contemptuously. "You are still in my *Havamal* and I can destroy you."

"And then what?" demanded Kali contemporary. "These Humans are not ready yet for your rule. They are still deformed. Look at them."

All eyes turned to Justine, Zyk, Phillip and Travis. Justine felt anger rise in her now. Just who were these creeps, she thought angrily and raised her eyes to glare at Odin. Zyk knew they had to play their cards carefully here.

"Err…hi there," he stammered.

Everyone turned their attention to Zyk.

"Unworthy as we are, but what is the task asked for us?"

"Prepare for the Golden Age," said Kali coldly turning to him, when suddenly everything dissolved into darkness.

Trump makes the call

"General Schwartzkopf?"

Trump was on the phone.

"Yes sir," said the General.

"What is FEMA's status concerning Washington DC?"

"All clear with the "Air Cleaners" machines having cleaned out the entire Southern and North-Eastern region."

"Good, then prepare for our return to the DC bunker," said Trump genuinely glad to get out of Eastern Kentucky. He yearned for some fresh air as he imagined Hitler's dark life in 1945 lived mostly in bunkers. He shook his head.

"Sir, the Secret Service is working to secure the White House as we speak," said Schwartzkopf.

"What about Hillary and the UFOs?"

"Sir, the NSA has reported that there have been no transmissions from her or the Democrat leadership. The internet is very weak so far, but we have full spectrum dominance over all content."
"Do you think that she's been abducted by those aliens?" snorted Trump.
"She could be getting protection from them since the Klan has put a bounty on her head, 10,000 gold Klan dollars, dead or alive."
"The Klan is printing their own currency?" asked Ronald amazed how quickly the Klan had become an alternative power in the United States.
"Yes, and as the Klan grows, thousands of illegals and Democrats are leaving the United States for Africa, Israel, and Mexico as their top destinations."
 Trump chuckled.
"So, we don't have to build the wall after all," he remarked. "But make sure that Hillary doesn't escape with them."
"The Klan has taken over Immigration and Customs Enforcement including the DHS," said Schwartzkopf.
"Good, I wouldn't trust the corrupt Federal government to catch Hillary. The Klan will get her sooner or later."
"Yes sir."
"Ok over and out."

The Klan

 Grandmaster Luke had taken a flight to inspect the Department of Homeland Security in El Paso, Texas, and he stood now at the border with the old fences still intact, but he wished that Ronald's wall had been built. Right now, America just didn't have the money to build it, but then there were enough Minutemen armed with home-made A.R blasters, and supplemented by tiny Klan Army units, though they were needed much more for Homeland Defense as the alien invasion were expected anytime now. A feeling of impending doom sat in Luke's heart.
 Mexicans were again surging through the borders as American companies picked up production and created a quick boom in America with almost everything needed to be produced from scratch. With China and South Korea out of the picture, it was a great time for manufacturing in the United States.

But there was an intense labor shortage as almost a hundred million Americans had been vaporized, and the Mexicans knew that there was plenty of opportunity in America. *But the Klan had other ideas.*
"String them up," ordered a Lieutenant of the Klan Army as he pointed to an illegal family that had been caught by minutemen in Ford SUV's.
The Mexicans' eyes widened. They had expected prison or a quick deportation back to Mexico.
"Not this time," grinned the Lieutenant barely in his twenties, and he stood on a hastily constructed wooden scaffold where a hangman threw the cloth off ten nooses.
"No!" wailed the Mexican family.
Grandmaster Luke grinned as the Lieutenant in his black uniform and boots contrasted with the dirty and disheveled Mexicans who hadn't showered for days in the desert.
"We have to make an example of you for the rest of you lot," announced the Lieutenant pointing to the family. "We don't want you here, since we are automating everything in the United States, and the few humans that we need are already here."
At this point, the Grandmaster felt that he had to say something, and the Lieutenant hastily gave way to Luke, who began to speak.
"We have declared Martial Law in America and we are executing looters, deserters, and illegal immigrants on the spot," Luke said in his Southern drawl. "So, its nothing personal, but we will have to set an example as the young lieutenant just said here."
"El Diablos!" swore the Mexican looking at his family forlornly as they were roughly taken away by Klan Army soldiers, while the child was set on the ground who was too light to be hung. "We are Christians just like you!"
"Say hi to Jesus for me," Luke took out his Beretta and shot the child before anyone could even react. The shot echoed around the hot and dusty yellow hills as the child crumpled to the ground. The Mexican couple now knew that there was no mercy to be expected and the mother let out a heart-rendering sob. America now was a cruel and hard place with little time for mercy. War had hardened American hearts and resources were scarce causing this ruthless inter-species conflict, where only the strongest survived. The couple broke free and started to run away from the Klan soldiers.
"That's why we always 'cuff 'em first," explained Luke in disgust at the green soldiers, and he drew his Beretta again to take aim and fire rapidly. Both figures

collapsed in the desert. The hangman threw the black cloth over the scaffold disappointedly. Why even bother when it was so much easier to shoot them, as he pulled out a Sig Sauer and shot the remaining Mexican children. Grandmaster Luke returned to his SUV and roared away with thick Texan dust following him. *The border seemed to be secure.*

Devus lands in New York

A destroyed version of Manhattan greeted Tor and company as they disembarked from the spaceship in Central Park, or what remained of it. The lake there had been vaporized, while a few gnarled and burned out remaining trees greeted them forlornly. The children's park with all the slides and ponds was gone, not that French Company gave a rat's ass, preferring the swamps of Louisiana to this bourgeoisie paradise.

"Ok guys," said Tor tightly with his Heckler and Koch assault rifle pointed warily at the burned-out hulls of the New York skyscrapers. Twisted metal with no signs of any humans so far. A giant crane in the horizon with a big ball on top of its head flashed a mysterious purple light and seemed to be the only thing alive here.

"What the fuck is that?" demanded Xander pulling out his binoculars and noted a US flag on it.

"Looks like some sort of a machine," said Kim noting the name of the Alabama company on it and the bold words. *"Air Cleaner. Proudly Manufactured in Huntsville, Alabama."*

"Well obviously cleaning up the radiation since our Geiger counters are showing zero radiation," said Tor. Suddenly, he dived for cover as did the others without a word.

A pickup with heavy metal music blaring pulled up and men in black uniforms quickly emerged to charge into the park. Devus quickly started his engines and took off into the air. The men didn't notice French Company but instead started firing at the spaceship. The pickup had a heavy Ferro-Electromagnetic blaster mounted on it which also took aim at the ship.

BLAM! BLAM! BLAM!

The shots caught Devus even though he was accelerating fast and huge explosions followed. Tor shook his head savagely. That was his ship and Devus had stayed because of them. The ship came crashing down.

"Yeehaw!" yelled the soldiers, mostly kids, and continued firing at the ship when Tor shouted.

"Stop firing, you idiots!" he shouted standing up. The men turned and their jaws dropped open to see French Company and quickly pointed their weapons at them. "That's my ship."

"Drop your weapons now," shouted the black uniformed soldiers and more of them from the pick-up came charging in from behind.

"Don't fire, we're Americans for Chrissakes!" Tor and Xander lowered their weapons clearly shocked to see that these soldiers were holding futuristic looking weapons. Looked like alien technology alright, while these soldiers had funny insignias on their shoulder patches.

"Are you guys Klan?" demanded Xander, as he saw the red swastika under the KKK patch. What the hell had happened to America while they'd been away?

"You betcha," grinned a teenager. "And by the look of things you guys look like Army deserters."

Everyone exchanged glances at that charge and some of the Klan Army soldiers shivered. *The death penalty.*

"We're not," replied Tor. "We're ICE agents. Ex-Army and we'd commandeered that ship only to have you idiots blow it out of the sky." French Company flashed their ICE credentials except for Freydis.

Kim and Drew had already gone to the ship and had entered it.

"And what the hell are you red-necks dong over here up in Yankee town?" demanded Xander bristling at being pushed around by some fucking kids playing soldiers.

"We're battling looters," said one of them who introduced himself as Lieutenant Davis.

"You mean Africans?" laughed Xander. Freydis dug an elbow into his side and the boys howled.

"Its great to speak freely," agreed the Klan boys. "But these are no ordinary niggers. They're cannibal gangs who eat one another."

"So why get involved?" demanded Tor.

"Klan Army orders. They have jurisdiction over the city of New York, but we're the only soldiers in the city."

"Yeah, its getting dark over here too," said the blonde kid shifting his feet nervously.

"But you have guns?" demanded Xander.

"They're thousands of them and they come out at night. Some sort of a virus that's infected them and they're strong. I once pumped a nigger full of bullets and he still kept coming."

Kim and Drew returned from the ship. "Devus is ok. But he needs to do some repairs on the ship before it can fly again."

"You mean he has spare parts inside that ship?" asked the Klan boys incredulously.

"Yes."

Freydis now stared nervously into the evening that was deathly quiet —— and she melted into Xander's arms again.

"I think we should shelter for the night," said Tor.

"What about the ship?" asked Kim.

"The looters are only attracted to infra-red human heat," said Davis. "You guys can take shelter with us at our base."

Tor and Xander smiled at the mention of a base. Home.

"I guess we don't have a choice. Let's see what you boys have built for a base anyways," sneered Xander, and the boys could smell French Company's battle-hardened experience on them. The boys led them to the pickup where French Company got on the back of the pickup, while Xander admired the giant EM blaster mounted like DHSK machine guns that reminded him of those Al-Nusra boys back in Iraq.

"Yeah, DARPA apparently was working in secret on all these high-tech weapons," said the Lieutenant, while Tor and Drew nodded as he hooked up his laptop to the Klan Army's WI-FI router.

"Aren't you guys worried that the looters will trace your positions through your open network?" demanded Drew.

"That's the least of our worries," said the Lieutenant, as he looked around warily. Darkness was coming fast and the Ford F-150 pick-up roared to life with its powerful engine gunning ferociously through the devastated streets of Manhattan. They were heading towards downtown using the FDR highway, since the damage to the city and its roads had been horrific as twisted metal hung from every street corner.

They got off the FDR highway and passed Houston street to turn the corner on Bleecker street. Tor wasn't a city guy, but he felt bad that he'd never seen NYC back in the day.

KABOOM!

Suddenly French Company flew into the air along with the pickup.

"IED!" screamed Xander landing with a thud. But he already had his rifle pointed at some adjacent movement.

"Looters!" screamed the Lieutenant, as he pulled himself out of the rubble and had his gun out. He was bleeding from his face.

Gunfire erupted from all sides.

"Jesus Christ, these looters are worse than the Arabs," roared Kim, as he fired a blaster that he took from a dead Klan soldier. He was amazed by the firepower of the thing.

More intense automatic gunfire came from the rubble of the buildings surrounding them. So far, they hadn't seen the enemy, but French Company was laying down some dense fire, while Kim's blaster was taking out giant chunks of the concrete and plenty of looters came tumbling down after each blast.

"They shoot worse than the Arabs," grinned Xander, as he managed to dismount the EM blaster mounted on the destroyed pickup. Then he saw Freydis. She had a small hole in her skull.

"Jesus fucking Christ!" he snarled, as he picked up the heavy DARPA blaster to cradle it in his arms, while his muscles strained holding the 150-pound gun, but Xander's thick biceps held, and he lit the buildings around with blue fire.

KaBoom! Sections of the buildings came crashing down with dozens of embedded looters entombed inside.

"HOOO-YEAH!" cheered the Klan soldiers. They had lost two good men and Drew had taken the other dead soldier's blaster. Tor was still using his HK 416s, while quickly changing mags.

The gunfire died out and the looters had had enough apparently as they retreated howling into the shadows of the night.

"Reporting looter ambush!" screamed the Lieutenant into the radio. But there was no reply from their base command's radio. Just static. A sinking feeling came over French Company. These looters weren't stupid, evolving, and had gotten to that dangerous level of IED manufacture. That meant that they were well armed from some local military depot, while the radio was telling them that the Klan base had been overrun. *And Freydis was dead.*

"What do we do with the bodies?" asked Xander looking forlornly at the lovely Freydis.

"Well the looters are gonna eat 'em anyways," shrugged the Lieutenant also mourning the loss of his Alabama high school buddies and the disaster of their base having fallen.

There were howls in the night now and that spurred the men to action.

"Fuck the bodies, we gotta get to higher ground," urged Tor, and the Klansmen realized that French Company were survivors. A strange parade of six Klansmen and four ICE officers now on Broadway and Houston searching for suitable accommodation. They eventually selected the tallest building, which was a former all glass hotel to assume positions in there for the night. It was not over — not this night, not by a long shot as the bloodcurdling howls only grew louder in the city.

One night in New York City.

Zyk drives

A new atmosphere of dread had settled inside the Audi as everyone replayed the fantastic events from last night. They were almost at the border with Pakistan, as Zyk floored the gas pedal furiously, while also trying to figure out what the hell had happened last night.

"On a scale of one to ten on the Richter scale," commented Travis riding shotgun and glanced at Zyk worriedly. "That was a fucking ten!"

Zyk wore his German Porsche Design sunglasses, as the fierce desert sunlight bounced off the windscreen blinding him sometimes.

"What the hell kind of a person are you?" demanded Justine now. He had pissed her off already by not condemning Nazis, while now underworld gods and goddesses had plans for him. *Definitely not long-term husband material, she realized sadly, and now she felt homesick, missing her mother.* Zyk pushed in a CD into the Audi's 15 speaker sound system. Justine worriedly noted that the CD cover featured a bald man with three missing fingers —— DJ Highko. Thundering music at 180 BPM filled the car, while a sample played in the background, *Take two drops of LSD.* The boys started to dig the music bouncing rhythmically to it, while Justine stared out of the window at the approaching border sitting in the back. He didn't want to talk. Fine. She wondered if Zyk had some "Punjabi" music on him. Now that was real music.

Zyk was piecing together all the hazy dreams that he could remember for some clues. At the Goa parties on acid, visions of Kali which he dismissed as hallucinations were frequent, but here it was shaping into reality.

"I mean these are top-dog gods we're talking about here," said Phillip. "Odin is nothing to be sneezed at and we all saw him." Phillip glanced at Travis, while Zyk lowered the volume to speak.

"I don't know what the hell is going on, but I don't think that we can second guess the gods. If they have plans, then we're just pawns so either ways it doesn't look good," said Zyk speaking finally, while Justine continued to glare at him.

"Are you saying that Hitler was guided by Kali?" she demanded, and now the boys stared at Justine quizzically. Zyk let out a low admiring whistle.

"You figured it out, babe," he replied smiling and that caused Justine to threaten a fist at him.

"See, she has a bit of Semitic blood in her too, since she's half Punjabi, and she feels her people's pain," said Zyk. *"But Schindler's List is still propaganda."* Now she punched him on the shoulder which he took still laughing and that infuriated her even more.

"The Jews and Arabs are going to get another ass-whipping again," said Zyk now, and now Travis was all ears as Phillip groaned.

"Well guess who's on your side now?" asked Phillip turning to Travis.

"Dude, he's right. I will take you for my King if we can get those scumbag Semitic tribes," said Travis. "I hate them with all my heart. Jews and Arabs."

"I woke up one day to smell the roses and saw the sunshine," said Zyk on a confessional note. Travis and Phillip nodded. Zyk continued.

"Everyone should be free to awaken and choose for himself and not through brainwashing," he said. "And now that I know what is real and not, I won't be a hypocrite."

"Well anyways Earth is pretty much finished," said Justine trying to digest Zyk's words. She felt the tug of her Semitic blood, but then there was a part of her Aryan blood too that pulled her towards the Aryans. She grew frustrated. *The life of a Mishling.*

"I don't know about that dude," said Phillip turning to Zyk. "We're all mixed up in the USA, and Humans aren't the same as breeding dogs and horses."

"Yeah, but look at Arnold Schwarzenegger," argued Travis.

"But I don't find Arnold the least bit attractive," said Justine. The boys ignored her as they pondered over producing a race of Aryan bodybuilders across the World.

"Anyways, not that I believe in the *Lebensborn* project," said Zyk, but Justine was getting a measure of just how much the Jews were hated here and no one seemed to have seen the movie Schindler's List or believed in it.

"So Zyk what are you?" asked Travis."I mean you've been living in India."

"Well I guess the *Indo-Aryan* culture permeates into me too, though I have no Semitic blood. I guess, I'm American."

The boys nodded and digested that and what they had seen with their own eyes. It was all very strange and complex. Justine just shook her head and wished she could go back to her old boyfriend, who was a perfect bourgeois match for her. He liked Indian food, listened to Punjabi music, earned tons of money, and had no such flighty contacts with gods and goddesses with plans of world domination. Then there was the disturbing thought that Zyk would never accept her anyways with her part Semitic blood. She was impure and she looked at him again, but she just couldn't read his thoughts. His jaw was set on the road, but his eyes were inscrutably a million miles away.

Trump reaches DC

Trump's motorcade continued unmolested with at least ten thousand regular US Army soldiers manning the highways with close air support, as Trump made the long highway journey home to DC, where another fifteen thousand US Army soldiers patrolled DC for any looters, or even worse, aliens. Trump hastily entered the White House and briefly paused there to admire the restoration after the Chinese invasion's damage, only then to descend into the nuclear bunker. He felt a familiar foreboding, as he descended the earth's depths once again.

"General, there has to be a better way to live than this," remarked Trump unhappily to Schwartzkopf.

"Well sir, I told you that other governments are talking to the aliens and so is Hillary. We need to come to an understanding with the aliens to have peace."

"Jesus Christ, I am never going to sell out the American people."

"At least let us see their cards. Otherwise, this is a stalemate."

"Alright General, just an opening gambit to see what their cards are," agreed Trump realizing that he held no cards in his hands. "Get Kelosi and Schooler to talk to the aliens on our behalf and find out what the hell is going on."

"Sir, the Klan executed Senator Jack Schooler as a Democrat traitor three days ago," said Schwartzkopf stiffly. "We're trying to hold off Kelosi's execution to negotiate as we speak." Schwartzkopf had just hastily emailed his staff while talking to the President from his phone. He hoped he wasn't too late. The Klan was on a rampage through the USA. Simply unstoppable.

"Doesn't the Klan ask anymore?" demanded Trump, though a gleam flickered in his eyes. Schooler had been one hell of a shifty slime-ball. The American people were speaking through their militias. This was the ultimate Republican small government utopia. "But we can't run America if the Klan just keeps executing people like that."

"I've tried to talk to them, but at this point they have more troops than the US Army, so we really have no authority over them."

"That Grandmaster Luke thinks he's a wise guy, blowing everyone away like that."

"He's not even sparing their children."

"I never thought we'd see another holocaust but it's happening in front of us," uttered Trump forlornly and shook his head. He knew the trouble and outright rebellion if he took on the Klan head on.

"Sir, Red American states are supporting the Klan," said Schwartzkopf, while visualizing the unspeakable brutality being perpetrated in the name of the US Government.

"Killing Jews and Blacks has led to a mass Exodus from America," noted Trump, as he strode into the much smaller nuclear command center in the White House bunker, plush and re-designed lovingly by Ina while he'd been in Kentucky. She was one loyal girl and even after Jethro's execution, she'd been 100 percent loyal.

"What will America be like without immigrants and minorities?" asked Trump. There was a twinkle in Schwartzkopf's eye.

Trump shook his head and left.

Grandmaster Luke

Grandmaster Luke was traveling to D.C after deciding that they should meet the aliens and he was determined to follow up on it. America shouldn't be left behind while the rest of the world was making deals. He was traveling in a convoy of five military Humvees hurtling up through the Southern states to the District of Columbia. His Humvee was loaded with the latest technology with jammers for any possible IEDs. A "CEMP", or Continuous EMP machine was on standby ready to be turned on at any time if attacked. The Klan was prepared for all hell to break loose, but not against Alien technology, and this is why the Klan's High Command had decided to negotiate with the aliens too. But they now needed Trump as their leader to negotiate — as a legal representative and one who was now back in town.

The White House had been informed as the Grandmaster's convoy screeched into D.C and headed for Pennsylvania Avenue. A few cars that crawled on the dilapidated streets hastily got out of the way when they saw the Klan insignia accompanied by the screaming sirens of the Klan convoy. The KKK symbol along with the red swastika underneath was enough to send anyone scurrying out of the way. The Klan armies had fought bravely against the Russians and Chinese, while defending American territory fanatically, when few others had stood in an organized fashion. Now they called the shots in D.C, something that most DC residents couldn't have fathomed only a few months ago. But then ever since the election of Ronald Trump, the world had changed very quickly. Like an LSD trip that had suddenly plunged down into a hole that the world was swimming in, while the Klan was making sure that a new America emerged from the ashes. A clean and pure America. Something that the Nazis failed to do, the Klan would succeed at any cost. Luke was determined to flush out the contaminants from the new USA with or without Trump, and he considered the Jews as the main Aryan enemy. Man, woman, or child had to be exterminated. Real America was not interested in the economics of New York City or the Hollywood movies of California, mused Grandmaster Luke, while smoking a cigar as he pondered over his vision for a new American society, but the alien threat over the Earth was a stubborn cloud.

"Yes, Mr President, I'm at the gates of the White House," he said into the phone, trying to be as soft as possible, as his convoy stood on Pennsylvania Avenue.

He needed this meeting to go smoothly and he wasn't sure how Trump would react to his newly instituted ethnic cleansing of America.

Tor passes the night

French Company daisy-chained booby traps with grenades and C-4 explosives as they ascended floor by floor with professional speed and calm.
"Jesus, do they teach all this in ICE school?" demanded the lieutenant, suspicious of their ICE identities. "You guys are way too professional to be some Immigration goons."
"Watch and learn, kids," said Xander as he armed the explosive. "You guys were real stupid to shoot down our ride out of here."
"We didn't know," protested the Lieutenant.
"Well, we're in a fine mess now," said Xander, and a lump rose in his throat as he thought of Freydis. She was so young and innocent, but then he thought of his other buddies, Chico, Ron, and the others who hadn't made it from way back in Iraq. Seven tours of Iraq had shown him horrors that were killing French Company, but right now the alien invasion had put his emotions on hold, as he crimped a wire taking out his *Leatherman* pliers. Tor, Drew and Kim had gone on ahead to scout through the building, aiming for the highest point of the ten-story glass hotel to secure a nest for the night.
They got to the roof of the building from where they admired the crumbling Manhattan skyline including a deformed downtown. It was like someone had taken a finger and run it haphazardly through the skyline reducing it to jagged edges with awkward spikes projecting into the swirling ash clouds up above. Then there were the flashes of purple light as the giant Ionizing machine mounted on a very tall crane continued to de-ionize the radiation in the city. "So, we have a race war going on in the city," summarized Tor thinking of the implications for America if all black people here were considered looters.
"Well this suits us just fine," said the Lieutenant. "From now on, after this IED blast, I'm taking no prisoners."
"But we were already doing that since Alabama," protested a private.
The Lieutenant paused for thought.
"Well anyways, from now we'll just feel better shooting them."

Kim and Xander shook their heads. Yeah, it was a tough call, looting was bad for morale and examples had to be made.

"Its fucking hard wired into their systems," spat out Kim in disgust.

The Klan boys look heartened to receive some support.

"Fuckin' liberals had ruined the country anyways. I guess this nuclear war is going to lead to a better America," continued Kim. The boys nodded, when Tor returned from scouting and had brought a jar of coffee and some plastic disposable cups. A kettle too was found later by the Klan boys, and more importantly, a gas operated stove which somehow had made it through the nuclear war. It sprang to life on the first try. A round of coffee for everyone to stay awake, while cheering up their spirits, as a chilly wind blew across Manhattan, but also carrying the wild howls of looters down below. A voice asked Tor, what did it really matter if there were looters? But there was also a primal urge in the Aryan man to maintain order even in the ashes of a nuclear war. Death before that kind of disorder, as he dozed off despite the strong coffee shot.

A warning bell rang in Tor's head kicking him out of his slumber. He looked up to see Xander smoking and staring out into the open night sky. Then there was a sudden noise down below. *Inside the building.* This time Xander cocked his head and Tor was up like a flash.

KA-BOOM!

Everyone scrambled to their feet, including the six Klan soldiers, who had their guns out, while the building shook from explosions. A following explosion knocked Tor off his feet, and he fell heavily on his newly acquired blaster. Xander, however, had descended downstairs with his piercing xenon flashlight eagerly to engage the looters.

BLAM! BLAM!

Kim descended downstairs too, but his flashlight wasn't working and all he could see were furious blasts being exchanged with the looters, who were firing back with an assortment of weapons. But they were up against entrenched Special Forces this time, Kim thought grimly, as he leapt through the darkness. A light below —— a Klan soldier, who recognized him with a nervous smile.

"Come on, kid," said Kim gently, realizing that the soldier was afraid. *Jesus Christ, he thought nostalgically. What was it like to be afraid? Something like first love. Shit, he was inured against both, he thought. Maybe that was what it was to become older. He shook his head as his high school sweetheart tried to enter his head. The mind was a special place indeed. Fuck that.*

"Come on, kid," he growled, while his rough demeanor gave the kid some strength. Boys weren't looking for love. They were looking for leaders. Hard men, commanders —— who knew death and inspired the young soldiers to follow them anywhere. A bunch of looters by the window, as the kid froze, but Kim saw them trying to outflank Xander and the others. Showtime, as he let out a deafening set of blasts decimating the group.

BLAM! BLAM! BLAM!

"Always good to have some rearguard action, son."

The Klan soldier nodded with wide eyes, and Kim thought about his greenest days, but that was back in Afghanistan taking out *Hajis,* a rough crowd. But all he could remember were IED's. Those motherfuckers had killed a lot of his friends and the worst thing about the IED was that it cost less than a hundred dollars. Low-tech Asians, but who couldn't be defeated easily in head-on battle either. From Vietnamese to Arabs —— President Truman had wisely known that only a nuclear bomb could weaken their low-tech resolve. The White Man had to use his superior intellect to defeat the unlimited Asiatic hordes. And now he was faced with the African hordes, as he went over to inspect the moaning survivors scattered on the ground.

"Kid shine a light," he growled, as the Klan soldier switched on his xenon light. A groaning and wounded looter lay on the ground.

"Careful, he might have a gun on him," said Kim, as the kid tried to approach the looter. "Stand back."

A blast took off the looter's head, while the laser heat cauterized the bleeding neck.

"The only punishment for a looter in my book," growled Kim.

"That's the Klan rule too, sir," said the soldier as they headed downstairs. The firing had stopped, and Kim found Tor and Xander going through the bodies of the looters for weapons and munitions.

"Well, the good news is that they didn't have blasters," said Tor.

"I think that we killed more than a hundred of 'em," said Drew, as the Klan Lieutenant tried to keep a record of how many their unit killed.

"We're gonna get medals for this one," he said causing the Klan soldiers to beam with delight, while French Company rolled their eyes. Fucking pieces of metal to reward you for your blood and life. Ah, but that was the carrot in the Army. *A promotion and a pat on the head.* But French company still enjoyed a good fight. Otherwise it could just be a fuckin' Army suicide statistic. Jesus, the human mind once broken could never be fixed.

"You know, look at the size of the canine on this guy," said the Klan Lieutenant holding up the head of a looter. The canines were almost double the length than normal.

"Wow, someone take a picture of that so we can send it to the CDC," said Tor. "If it still exists."

With that he went back upstairs for some shuteye. Tomorrow they would find a car and get the fuck out of New York City. The Klan wanted to fight the looters till all their soldiers were dead, but French Company was getting the hell out. It wasn't their fight.

10

Justine and the Psychos

An Indian border guard went through their papers, while shaking his head, and by the looks of it, he was pissed, standing at the border of Rajasthan and Pakistan.

"You don't have passports," he accused the Americans. Travis and Phillip stared sullenly at the BSF soldier who regarded their blasters with suspicion.

"What is that you are holding and why are you wearing space suits?" he demanded.

"You know there is a nuclear war going on," said Travis darkly. Normally he was the most dangerous thing around, but with Zyk communicating with Gods and Kali, all bets were off.

Justine turned to the soldier through her lowered window.

"Just let us go to Pakistan," she pleaded trying to telepathically communicate to him that she was in a car full of psychos. "It will be better for all of us."

Zyk was more dangerous than even the Klan soldiers without even knowing it.

"But none of you have passports," protested the Indian border guard and got on the phone, and conversed rapidly in Hindustani, which Justine understood, and her eyes widened with terror.

"He just called for back up," she said.

Zyk now smiled coldly at the soldier.

"Do you know who I am?" An old Indian trick.

The soldier could now smell money in the voice, and it was delicious.

"You are breaking the law and we cannot allow you to cross the border with weapons," he protested in broken English, while a squad of Border Security approached them with weapons pointed at them.

"Shit, Zyk, quit talking and let's blow these bitches away," growled Travis seeing his room to maneuver his blaster being reduced as the border squad approached.

Zyk ignored him and looked at the soldier.

"These are American special forces soldiers and we are on a secret mission to attack Pakistan," Zyk said dropping his voice conspiratorially. Travis rolled his eyes and wondered if Zyk had taken some acid. The soldiers now all laughed. Zyk had broken the ice.

"Sir, but you have no papers and is that pretty girl also special forces?"

Phillip now suppressed a terrible giggle which he disguised as a cough, while the soldiers turned to stare at the space-suited American soldier suspiciously.

Zyk got out of the car and the squad had now bunched up behind the BSF soldier as he reached for his wallet.

"This is going nowhere," Travis growled impatiently, and he pulled a tactical nuclear grenade out on the border of Rajasthan with Pakistan.

"Shit Travis, you'll kill Zyk and the girl."

Justine turned red and resented being called *the girl*.

"Ok then, hot shot, blow them away," snarled Travis getting tired since Zyk didn't seem to have any real power. Phillip had his blaster now on his lap and had slowly rested the barrel on the window.

"Zyk duck!" yelled Travis, and Phillip opened fire into the group, just as Zyk fell to the ground. He was clutching money in his hand as the group of BSF soldiers was vaporized into body parts. Travis quickly exited of the car to execute a couple of moaning survivors, while Zyk gathered his scattered 2,000-rupee notes.

"This is India!" he protested loudly shaking his head. "So unnecessary and this money is no good in Pakistan anyways. They were on our side."

Justine stared at them wordlessly and Phillip realized that she wasn't all there in her mind presently. She was one weird chick, but then he looked at Zyk, the darkpsy DJ from hell, who had tried to pass of Justine as a special forces soldier on a covert mission inside Pakistan. Phillips shook his head some more, as the Audi roared onto the highway towards Pakistan, but in the distance loomed the Pakistani check post.

"Quick," shouted Travis. "They must've heard our blasts."

Zyk raced towards the Pakistani guards like a suicide bomber and the soldiers there had realized that they were renegades from India.

"If only we'd paid them off then we could've made a deal here too," said Zyk regretfully, as a Pakistani heavy machine-gun opened up in the distance.

Travis and Phillip leaned out of the window with their blasters and let out rapid blasts as Justine ducked between her knees.

"YEEAHAA!" shouted Travis, as Zyk weaved the car on the highway dangerously, and Phillip almost fell out of the car. Just then a rocket landed a few meters away sending shrapnel from the crater in the road, as Zyk accelerated to 160 mph. The Audi's engine groaned as Zyk threw it into *sports mode* and pushed up the RPM to 8,000. The engine whined but the car was still beating the bullets.

"Give me one steady second," shouted Travis as his blaster locked onto the Pakistani post.

"You got it!" shouted Zyk to briefly stop weaving with his tires burning rubber.

BLAM! BLAM!

The Pakistani machine gun post was vaporized instantly, and the rockets also stopped coming. The main Pakistani border force now began to fire small arms but now Phillip's blaster locked on to them and took them out still a mile away.

KA-BOOM!

They passed a big overhead board that said in big letters, WELCOME TO PAKISTAN. Justine reflected that she had always wanted to visit Pakistan but not like this as she turned to see the smug boys with smoking blasters in the back, while Zyk punched in new coordinates into his navigation system.

Trump and the Grandmaster

"Grandmaster Luke," greeted Trump in the bunker ——— an exact recreation of the Oval Office down below in the bunker. Secret Service agents stood armed behind Trump, while the Klan soldiers were left posted topside. The President still had that much power, at least in Washington D.C.

"A pleasure to meet you, Mr President."

Trump chuckled now.

"I should call you President," Trump said gesturing helplessly. "You have more power than even me today in USA."

"Sir, I am still at your service," said Luke standing up with his jaw clenched. Somewhere deep down, he knew that America was always going to be an Aryan Democracy, and he genuinely believed in Trump.

"Well, together we can rebuild America," said Trump gulping though at the way the Klan envisioned America.

"Sir, our plans for the USA are long-term and what we are doing is for the good of the White Race," he said sincerely. Trump looked like a caged lion now. How could anyone justify murder?

"I think that your deportation plans are more successful," Trump argued diplomatically.

"Yes sir, but we had to create a climate of terror first," smiled Luke dressed in all black.

"So, no more white hoods?" asked Trump trying to change the topic now. He didn't want to know the gory details.

"Yes sir, we are the military wing and black seems to suit us a little more," said Luke. "But we don't have much time, Mr President. We need to have a policy towards the aliens."

"We are using our Democrat connections, but you killed Schooler," said Trump accusingly.

"Yes, but we have Hillary too," said the Klan leader.

"What?"

"Yes, we captured her two weeks ago and she is ready to talk to the aliens," Luke said.

So that's where Hillary had been all this time.

"But she had been communicating with the aliens who had laid out a deal, but the *aliens want you to still sign the deal.*"

Trump was too surprised to answer. The Klan was also ready to cut a deal with the aliens, but needed Trump's signature, he thought cynically. So that's where the President of the United States stood. A powerless titular head, he realized bitterly. With the Congress and Senate out of commission, a President really had no power. He shook his head.

"Ok, but I want to know the terms and conditions first," he said seething with rage internally but too shrewd to show it.

"Don't get us wrong, Mr President," said Grandmaster Luke seeing the disapproval in Trump's eyes. "All we want is to make America great again."

Trump looked at the country idiot that sat in-front of him and realized that he had to tolerate him and his stupidity. But the Klan was powerful and that's what gave this Klan Grandmaster his cockiness. He seemed to be 35 in age, about 5 feet 10 inches tall, sandy brown long hair and clear blue eyes, with that Alabama drawl that Hef Sessions had, and as a yankee, he disliked it intensely. But then there was this sinister demeanor about him, like a rattlesnake, coiled and ready to strike. Yes, there was fanaticism in his eyes that Trump knew was dangerous and as a businessman was contemptuous of, but then his base in America had all sorts of these types. As a Grandmaster of the Klan, Luke was in a dangerous position to implement the *Final Solution* in America, and there was no one to stop him.

"See what the aliens have really said is *that they want some human on this planet.* Fact is, we don't really like these sorts of human troublemakers either," said Luke digging into the chair and getting more comfortable with Trump, now that they understood each other. He wanted a cigar, but then Trump didn't smoke.

"Yeah, some guy that no one knows about," said Trump subconsciously fingering his swastika.

"Oh, Hillary knows the name alright, and he's somewhere running around this planet," said the Klan leader staring at Trump's silver swastika and a shiver went through him, actually shook him up real good. There were other forces at work here and suddenly a sweat broke out on his forehead. Trump the wily old fox certainly knew how to piss of Christians as he now played with the diamonds studded on the swastika.

"Look, I don't know anything about this Zyk fellow, but we'll get back to you when we do," said Trump rising, and Like felt relieved to leave the bunker as a sort of a panic attack hit him from nowhere, while he calmed himself to rise and make it to the elevator —— overcoming the paranoia that something was going to snatch him into the very earth. He shook his head. *The swastika had no power over the cross and he said a thankful prayer to the lord as he emerged top side.*

No deal.

French Company

The men still mourned the loss of the lovely and young Freydis, particularly Xander, as they got into a freshly commandeered Chevrolet Tahoe.

Tor read his mind. "You saw all the dead Iraqi kids in the war."

"Shit, but I really liked her," replied Xander as they got into the truck under the morning sun, when the Klan Lieutenant came forward.

"Watch out for the military police," warned the Lieutenant. "They're hanging deserters at the drop of a hat." The Klan then helped fill their gas tank with petrol siphoned from nearby cars that still sat in underground parking lots, and which proved to be a great reservoir of fresh cars and fuel for the Klan.

"Look at those kids," said Kim waving at their fresh faces. "They think they're SS now."

"Jesus, who gives a fuck when there are a million looters in the city?" demanded Drew, also perplexed with the logic of holding a looter overrun New York.

"Well the Klan is sending in reinforcements soon," added the Lieutenant.

"More meat for the grinder," swore Xander with a grim look. He didn't like it when kids died for nothing, and he couldn't see the military logic in holding New York.

"Come on, sunshine," said Tor patting Xander on the back. "What the hell did we ever do in Iraq except make the situation worse?"

Tor punched the Tahoe's accelerator while heading towards Baltimore.

"I think we should get new orders from Fort Bragg," said Kim. "I don't like this talk of hanging deserters."

"Yeah, Special Ops war-heroes hung by Klan police," said Tor, while Kim called Bragg on the satellite phone and identified himself and put it on speaker phone.

"Welcome French Company," said a male voice. "One moment…you are being transferred to the Department of Defense."

"Do we have new orders?" asked Tor and identified himself with his military number.

"Processing... French Company is reassigned to the oil-fields of North Dakota."

"What the fuck?" demanded Tor.

"The Klan Army has taken over processing and oil refining operations and has requested military support."

"What's the threat over there?"

"Looters."

A chill ran down French company's collective spine.

"Mode of transport?" demanded Xander. He'd be damned if he was going to drive over there.

"Military transport will arrive in 30 minutes at your live GPS coordinates," said the computer smoothly.

 Kim had a question now for the computer and he leaned forward.

"What's the situation?" he asked. "What happened to our nuclear facilities and why do we still need oil?"

"Nuclear energy is being diverted to a force-field that DARPA is creating to stop alien ships coming in past the Earth's magnetosphere."

"But they're already on top of our heads."

"The force field can be weaponized and used against any ships in Earth's atmosphere."

Xander now looked up looking hopeful.

"You mean we have a chance at beating the aliens?"

"DARPA is continuously releasing classified technologies to the US Army and to the Klan."

"Where can we get DARPA's advanced weaponry?" demanded Xander. "Hell, we're special forces you know. The best on the planet."

"Transferring you to DARPA…one moment."

There was a long ring on the phone as Tor continued to drive the Tahoe towards Baltimore, while Kim craned his neck through the window to see if their transport was here.

"This is the Defense Advanced Research Projects Agency, and French Company has been successfully identified and processed through DoD credentials," said a female voice now. Sounded much friendlier and Xander tried to imagine the woman with this voice.

"Err…hi," said Tor.

"Welcome Operator Tor," she said. "The United States thanks you for your valuable service to the country." They had some next level voice recognition technology.

"Right. Ok. We need new weapons that DARPA has, specifically the AWS suits."

"Processing request…. Request approved. Current mission status is active in the North Dakota shale fields. Weapons delivery code initiated. Code accepted. Shipping four Advanced War-Fighter suits through military transport. ETA six hours. Any thing else?" cooed the computer.

"Um… not right now," said Tor.

"Thank you for calling DARPA."
The line went dead and suddenly there was a huge gunship hovering overhead.

Mohenjo-daro

Zyk stopped the Audi at the destroyed Pakistani border post, where the boys went through the dead bodies for some Pakistani rupees. They were going to need some local cash, but the soldiers yielded only five hundred rupees in their pockets collectively.
"So now you're going to loot the dead?" demanded Justine coldly staring through the window. The boys ignored her, and the Americans looked ridiculously out of place in their AWS suits standing in the middle of a desert over some dead Pakistani soldiers. Zyk with a flowery shirt over black jeans looked even stranger over there, as he took a Colt .45 pistol from a dead Pakistani Major and his credit card.
"Always good to be armed," he said, as they stood on the hilltop and watched the sun descend rapidly. They found some stored petrol there too, which Travis poured quickly into Zyk's tank, and then tossed the extra jerry-cans into the trunk. Fuel was going to be big in this rugged area, and Phillip gulped at the idea of driving through multiple Islamic Republics.
"Lovely country?" grinned Zyk at Justine, as he drove back onto the highway. The roads seemed better over here. Justine glared at him, as he stashed the gun in the dashboard, and she looked at her red painted nails, and wondered when her next nail job would be. She sighed, as she realized that from now on that she would have to do her nails by herself.
"Where are we going next?" growled Travis. "I need to stretch my legs and get a good night's rest."
"Well, let's see," said Zyk, as he dived into the navigation. Suddenly, there was a glitch on the screen and a large spot appeared on it which read Mohenjo-daro. Justine sat up in her seat.
"What the hell?" Zyk demanded, while pinching the screen to take the screen back to the selection of other Pakistani cities, but there was another glitch and a google search of Mohenjo-daro appeared. Justine stabbed the Wikipedia blurb next to it.
Travis whistled.

"The City of the Dead."
Justine shook her head.
"We are not going there," she said firmly.
Zyk laughed.
"Look, the navigation just *spazzed* out on us. We're stuck with no other destinations."
"Well, it looks right up your alley, Zyk," said Phillip. "Its only three hours away from us if we follow the navigation."
"I think Kali has a plan for us," said Travis shaking his head. How could you escape a goddess if she was after you?
Justine shuddered. That roller coaster feeling that she so hated was back as the Audi's turbo-charge kicked in and Justine felt sucked into her seat. But the highways were eerily clear again. Whatever had hit India had also hit Pakistan. Maybe the whole world was dead, but then those border guards had still been alive. There must be some people somewhere, but Mohenjo-daro, the *City of the Dead* was not the best place to find them.
Travis and Phillip dozed off, as Zyk drove in silence, and Justine glanced at him occasionally. Even though she said she didn't care, she was bewildered with his unhealthy relationship with Kali. She had a good mind to talk to this Kali thing if she met her again. Frightful howling banshee, and she'd been too surprised to say anything to her the last time, but next time...
The hours had slipped by and it was past twilight now.
"Alright boys," said Zyk suddenly. "We're here."
As usual, he referred to the boys including her collectively, which was sort of ok, but mostly a waste of time if she tried to educate him to refer politely to her as a girl. In the militarized air in the Audi, it wouldn't go down well with Travis, but Phillip seemed a little more malleable as he offered her a hand as they stepped out of the car. Zyk had already exited the car to walk towards the abandoned complex. A rusted sign posted there announced a price of a hundred rupees for entry to the tourist site and Zyk smiled.
"At least lock the car," Justine called out from behind him. Zyk turned back and was struck by her ravishing beauty under the moonlight. Travis and Phillip quickly began to secure the perimeter, they were soldiers first, and their sergeant would've had their ass if they ever forgot the basic rules of survival. *Training saved lives.* In ten minutes, they had scouted out the extensive mounds of earth and had found it deserted. No gods or mythical creatures lurked over here, at least for now. Yet. Meanwhile, Zyk had gone over to Justine and had

her in his arms. By the time the boys came back to the Audi, Zyk and Justine were torridly locked in a heated embrace.

"Get a room you two!" yelled out Phillip, and Travis chuckled which caused the couple to break off their kiss.

"So, after all that, you still like him?" demanded Travis, and Justine only blushed.

"We're going to get a room alright," chuckled Zyk.

Just then there was the sound of a heavy clunking bell. The soldiers whirled around with their blasters pointed at the sound, while quickly crouching behind a large brown boulder. The ruins of an entire city made of mud bricks and gigantic stones and boulders lay in-front of them entirely unguarded, delicate ancient mounds of earth lying in the desert with not a care. Zyk stood still with Justine in his arms, who shivered in the cool night.

There in the distance under the moonlight, an old man walking with a cloth bag slung across his chest, while leading an ox towards them. A cold breeze suddenly blew.

"Stop right there, motherfucker!" shouted Travis, pointing his blaster at him. The man continued to walk towards them.

"Dude, that Haji might be wearing a suicide vest!" shouted Travis. "Blow him away, Phillip."

"Fuck you, why don't you?" retorted Phillip. As far as he could see it was a skinny old man in some rags, and he now was feeling bad about blowing away the Indian border soldiers. *What a waste.*

"That's a fakir," said Zyk, and now Justine had retreated behind Zyk, who was still calm and now smiling. "My father always told me about the magical fakirs, and we are indeed blessed to meet one tonight."

The old man came closer.

"Dude, if he makes one false move, we blow him away!" warned Travis panicking now as he saw the size of the black ox. Mammoth. A heavy beast of burden.

"Lower your weapons," the old man called out in perfect English. "My ox is blind, and I want the *Hakim* to have a look at him."

Zyk turned towards the boys.

"You see, I'm also a medical doctor."

"That's a bleeding giant ox!"

Justine nodded and looked at Zyk.

"What can you do for that animal?"

Zyk now turned back towards the old man and laughed.

"My friends do not see you, O' fakir."

The fakir now laughed as he came up to Zyk, while Justine had retreated a few feet behind and was near Phillip. He seemed the most level-headed of all.

"Jai Kali!" shouted Zyk, and the gigantic ox lifted its mammoth head with its sharp horns. Zyk put his hands on its head.

"Kali demands a *Bali!*"

"No, I will not kill it!" protested Zyk. "No *Bali* sacrifice for *Kali*. She will not have that satisfaction from me."

The old man laughed, as Zyk felt the eyelids of the magnificent animal and spoke to it.

"You will live and be free."

The old man laughed some more, and he brought out a container from his bag, which he gave to Zyk.

"There will be a gathering here tonight and this will be for your entertainment." He then continued to walk into the night leading his animal away.

The boys stared in amazement at this strange meeting and lowered their guns, while Justine stood warily. Suddenly, the sound of jangling bangles. A beautiful woman in flowing clothes approached them now from behind the ruins as Justine gaped at her in terror. *Out of the frying pan and into the fire.*

She wore golden trinkets on her ankles and arms, while a glorious golden snake crowned her head.

"What about this one?" demanded Phillip from the rocks, while training his weapon on the woman. "Shall we blow her away?"

The snake on her head hissed violently in the night.

"Fuck, the thing is alive!" shouted Travis, as the snake leapt from her head and wriggled towards Travis. The golden snake was fast, but suddenly Zyk spoke.

"Enough Kali!"

The snake and the woman were so surprised that they turned to stare at Zyk, as Travis tightened his gloved finger around the trigger. He decided to pull the trigger.

A loud click.

"Shit, my blaster is empty!" howled Travis. The woman threw her head back and laughed, as Phillip tried to fire but his blaster was empty too. The snake flew back to the woman's crowned head and wrapped itself cozily again where it froze again into gold.

She came closer to Zyk, but then Justine decided to make a move.

"Who are you?" demanded Justine, while throwing back her own lustrous thick hair as a direct challenge to her. The woman stared now surprised by Justine's presence.

"A young fool," she pronounced, and waved her hand across Justine who suddenly swooned and fell to the ground. "It is better to be respectful of your superiors."

"Let her be," said Zyk again trying to tactfully defuse the situation. The fools on his team were hellbent on catching the wrath of Kali, as Phillip helped Justine up.

"I am the dancing woman of Mohenjo-daro," she announced and began to dance nimbly on her toes, as Travis shook his head in disbelief to the sound of her golden bangles and the trinkets tied to her ankles. She swayed like a snake and Phillip had seen this dance somewhere.

"She's a belly dancer," he ejaculated, and Zyk looked despairingly at him. Couldn't these people stay silent.

Kali stopped and glared at Phillip now with her big eyes and they turned from a placid lake to a sea of hurt.

"Phillip!" admonished Zyk. "All of you need to learn to be silent."

"Its ok," said Kali finally. "They're very young. It's your fault Zyk for hanging out with kids."

Zyk now shrugged helplessly.

Kali laughed some more, and it was like the wind rustling through the trees. Beautiful and enchanting, as Zyk noticed her fragrance in the cool wind in the ruins standing in the desert. Surrounded by utter darkness bathed in golden light. It was theatre alright and Zyk realized that Kali was creating an ambience as only a goddess could. Suddenly, the atmosphere grew even more intimate with everyone almost a million miles away as she suddenly came closer to him bathed in gold.

"I don't understand any of this," mumbled Zyk, bewitched by her fragrance.

"You called me," she said. Zyk was perplexed and gazed into her eyes. There was tenderness now there, along with an ocean of emotion waiting to be released.

"Yes, it was after the death of your father," she whispered in his ear. Zyk felt like he'd been stung by a bee. The painful bitter memories of dreams and a life crushed suddenly by one phone call. His sister's voicemail played in his mind. "Dad is no more."

Those words had torn him apart, caused his reality to tear. The fabric of time had come undone in his mind.

"Yes, your screams and your psychic pain was real," she said. "But the dark passions that were freed inside you impressed me and you were who I was searching for."

Zyk had changed that day, while his father had submerged into the depths of his mind. Anger had then coursed through Zyk and he'd vowed revenge against fate itself.

"After that you took LSD in the mountains of Turkey," she said. "That was when your old self died. After that I entered you and guided you from that day on."

Zyk now looked at her in fascination in all her beauty and magnificence. The golden snake seemed to wink at him. He remembered that Turkish solar eclipse up in the mountains of Antalya, where thousands of Germans and Israelis had welcomed him to his first LSD trip, and he had changed forever.

"But it was my favorite drug," he protested. "Millions of people do it."

Kali now smiled at him.

"Yes, but your mind was far advanced into the stars. It needed only a gentle push," she said. "You have stayed single because I will not share you with anyone else."

Now she seemed to be playing with him as she lifted a scarf around her mouth and came very close to him.

"You will always be free of guilt no matter what you do for you have been raised above the others," she seemed to sing to him.

Zyk remembered the recent Goethe's play that he'd seen in Dornach, Switzerland. *Faust. "Am I doctor Faust?"*

"Hush, Faust was but a fool infatuated with the pleasures of love, but you are not," said Kali now in a silvery voice. She was wooing him hard. Obviously, she was trying to impress him.

"I don't have to sign any paper, do I?" he asked.

She laughed.

"Come come, darling," she said embracing him, and Zyk felt her considerable bosom on his chest. Very sensual and he felt aroused as she flung her hair back again.

"Enough of this mortal talk," she said and suddenly waved her hand. The empty darkness of the desert slowly began lighting up with *fluoro* lights. "Its been so long since you took LSD. You must make light of this world."

"Look even your friend is here," said Kali, and suddenly there appeared a familiar Russian with DJ headphones.

"Jesus Christ!" shouted Zyk. *"Rudraksh!"*

"Yes," cried Kali joyfully. "I had sent him to you back then."

Then he glanced at Justine, who had stood up unhappily.

"Yes, that was me too," said Kali. "She's gorgeous, isn't she?"

"But I thought they were *my* friends," protested Zyk.

"Of course, just a little push from my side," said Kali, and Zyk shook his head realizing that his whole life was a *fucking* set up.

"Then why did you take my father?" growled Zyk now.

"His energy is also inside you," replied Kali hastily realizing that Zyk was entering a dangerous part of his mind. "Remember his last words."

"That he wanted to be an artist."

"Yes, and I have set your life in that direction," she said. "But I am the goddess of Death and I put these tests to millions of mortals. But you were the one that responded in the way I was looking for."

Zyk now realized the bargains humans make unwittingly and he thought again of Faust.

Kali was dancing again, while making designs with her fingers. But unlike anything Zyk had seen. She was spinning things out of thin air and throwing out decorations that hovered in the air. Lights. Psychedelic lights.

Rudraksh had, meanwhile, started up his CD machines and gradually increased the volume. Trance began to flood the desert. Now the scene became bigger as Travis and Phillip said something to Justine who nodded. Were they all actors? Zyk looked at Justine with her wide eyes as she seemed to protest her innocence.

Kali now was dancing some more and motioned to the bag that was in Zyk's hand.

"Mushrooms," she announced grandly. "Grown in heaven itself."

Zyk looked into the bag and there lay brown and plump mushrooms. He took out one and it glowed with the power of neon psilocybin.

Klan Oilfields

"Alright ladies, there's going to be a hair and piss test," announced the Klan soldier, as French Company jumped off the nuclear Z-1 transport, and into a blinding blizzard. It was March, but out here in North Dakota, it was - 40 degrees F. Tor shivered and Xander pulled his jacket together. They were surrounded by giant machines and industrial chimneys belching dark smoke into the grey sky, as if trying to melt the snowflakes that pummeled much of North Dakota. So much for global warming, snickered Xander, while Drew checked his communications' gear. Satellite connection was up, and he logged in to the unsecured network. Shit, out here in freezing North Dakota, what the hell were the looters thinking?

"Look, we're here to protect you," protested Tor to the Klan soldier. "We're Delta Force."

The Klan Army soldier simply gave them little plastic boxes.

"Shit sir," he ejaculated with a drawl, and then spat red tobacco onto the frozen tarmac as the wind howled around them. He wore a red KKK armband. "The Klan doesn't care if you're the fucking pope. This is a drug free zone." The redneck was definitely from the South.

Tor nodded glancing at the heavy machinery and it was like a scene out of a nightmarish dystopian movie. Hell, they were in dystopia, as he noted the KKK insignia. Behind him, a giant robot lifted heavy machinery effortlessly.

"We just had a sulfur accident," shouted the Klan soldier through the heavy wind, as he punched in a code and finally opened the main door into the Klan facility. French Company hurried into the warmth —— where beautiful relief flooded through them. *One of the most beautiful things on this planet was the relief experienced escaping from sub-zero biting cold.* Enough cold could depress the hardiest of men into a mangy dog whining miserably out in the bone-aching cold. The heat could drive you crazy too, but it was the bitter cold that touched even your DNA. That made you ruthless. The European tribes of Northern Europe had smartened up because the cold didn't give you too many chances.

"Help yourselves to the coffee dispenser," said the Klan soldier and he left French Company in a waiting room.

"More cheap coffee," complained Xander as he sipped his piping hot cup.

"Drink up," said Drew, as he enjoyed the hot liquid coursing through his frozen body. Tor had found an unopened bottle of Jack Daniels in a cupboard above and took a swig from that. Screw the coffee. By the time the Klan soldier returned, they had gone through the entire bottle.

"Well, you boys seem alright," he drawled.

"It did get us to pee for you," admitted Tor quite drunk now as he splashed out some urine into a cup and sloppily put a lid on it. The Klan soldier took it in his gloved hand and didn't seem to mind a bit of piss here and there. There were worse things out there in the heavy petrochemical plant.

"Say, I thought that all the looters were black," slurred Xander.

The Klan soldier paused.

"Well, they still are, coming in from all over the Northern States. There's a big nigger stronghold in Minneapolis along with the Hispanics. They loot and then sell the oil back in their towns and cities on the black market and its our job to shoot 'em down like rabbits. Fuck, I wish we could exterminate the lot of them. I am just waiting for the order."

"Why are we even dealing in oil?" demanded Tor. "I mean, I know we need the nuclear energy for Earth's defense, but we could always produce more, right?"

"Yeah, but you're forgetting one little thing," replied the soldier smirking at them as he finished collecting all the hair and urine samples from French Company.

"Yeah, what's that?" asked Tor looking up.

"Everyone's dead. The US is a giant wasteland and this oil here is just for the Klan to move through the pipelines and make some money from the cities that can pay us. We're basically in it for the money."

"What about the Federal Government?" asked Tor.

"We are the fucking government," said the soldier, as he led them into the interior of the facility leading to the dorms where they'd be billeted.

"Where are the showers?" asked Kim anxious to get clean again. Something was already crawling in his loins and he didn't want to know what it was. *The first beginnings of the dreaded body lice?*

"Your new AWS suits have arrived, and the showers are located behind the dormitory," replied the soldier.

"By the way," said Tor. "Where is everybody? We haven't seen anyone here so far."

"They're all mostly dead. The looters aren't kidding when they attack and just last week, we lost 5 soldiers and so we are down to about 15 of us here."

"15!" shouted Xander.

The Klan soldier sneered at them now.

"I thought you were Delta Force."

"How many looters?"

"Thousands."

There was an ominous silence as the soldier walked away leaving French Company to realize their predicament.

Trump in the White House

"Did you see the arrogance of that man?" fumed Trump, as he stared out of his office and only saw more concrete walls deep in the bunker. He missed the perspective of staring out into the familiar White House lawns.

"Sir, we have bigger problems," said General Schwartzkopf. "The aliens are moving closer to our cities."

"What does that mean?" asked Trump. The aliens. He had forgotten about them. That ever present ominous and silent threat like a Damocles sword over their heads.

"They are repeating their request for this human," said Schwartzkopf.

"Well, tell them that there are billions of humans on earth," replied Trump irritably.

"They want permission to hunt for him on earth."

"What the hell?"

"They're being polite. It could just be an excuse to get you, sir," said Schwartzkopf, and Trump suddenly appeared cagey.

"What about our nuclear shield?"

"It's almost online," replied Schwartzkopf, though he was now very careful. Trump also realized the danger of firing the first salvo at the dormant aliens. He shook his head irritably and ran a hand through his thinning blonde hair.

"You know, Schwartzkopf, I'm tired of all this, but one thing is certain. The American people still have the will to fight."

"What are you suggesting?" demanded Schwartzkopf now with his body stiff as a board.

"Tell the aliens to fuck off," said Trump shrugging, and then squared his shoulders like a boxer getting ready for a fight. There was a gleam in his eye. Schwartzkopf forgot to breathe for a few seconds. "Fire when ready, General. Nobody tells America what to do."

11

Ozzy Sings

Music thundered in the desert and Mohenjo-daro hadn't seen a party like this for over 3,000 years, but the ancient dancing girl was back, much to Justine's horror in the night. There was a flash of thunder overhead and a cold wind swept through her thin cotton shirt and sweatpants. She needed to get in the Audi, but Zyk had locked the car as she futilely tried the handle. She shook her head and then looked over to the desolate landscape with mounds of old and ancient buildings with the black night meeting the brown sand at the horizon. There was nothing here except the Russian DJ, and she called him by his Hindu name, Rudraksh. He continued to play thundering trance music.

"Hi!" she screamed over his headphones. The DJ looked up, while smoking a fat joint, himself being thin as a rake as he puffed deeply and then offered her a drag of his nasty looking and moist joint. She refused with vehemence in her eyes.

"Where is everybody?" she demanded, furious at Zyk for leaving her like this. "What, you didn't take the mushrooms?" he grinned lazily. She glared at him. Never in her life had she associated with degenerates like these people in her life. All because she had become friends with Zyk. Well, a friend with some benefits, but this was all turning into a nightmare. Rudraksh turned to mix another nightmarish sounding track into his last one.

"Hey, do you have any "Fleetwood Mac"?" she demanded in her posh English accent. Rudraksh grinned with his thin face twisted into a grin.

"You can try to find it in my computer," he said. Justine then spent a fruitless ten minutes going through hideously titled tracks, all something to do with murder, aliens, and mayhem. Obviously, he wasn't a connoisseur of fine music. She then left in a huff with Rudraksh staring after her and he shook his head. "Women," he muttered under his breath and took a calming puff from the powerful joint. He also popped in another golden mushroom. It tasted so earthy. *Prasad* or a gift from the goddess Kali.

Justine then saw the two American soldiers among the mounds of earthen buildings in the distance and who had begun to fire their blasters into the air. Soldiers on magic mushrooms firing at imaginary targets in the sky.

"Hey, have you guys seen Zyk?"

Travis and Phillip stopped to fire and stared at her as if they were having difficulty recognizing her in the desert and then started to fire again into the air. There in the distance, she saw that horrid old man with his still blind ox grinning at her. She turned away and hurried further into the ruins. Zyk had to be around here somewhere, she thought as her heart began to hammer in terror. What if he'd abandoned her? No, but the soldiers were still here. Maybe, she'd been too rude to him. She shook her head and there she saw a big communal "bath" among the ruins and in there sat a huddle of men around a big fire. They were all wearing uniforms and boots as she sat down near the fire to warm herself.

"Hi, have you seen a guy called Zyk around here?" she asked managing the courage and then the firelight shone on the man sitting next to her, a black swastika on a red armband.

"Well hello there, beautiful," he replied in a sinister German accent and he had a big nose.

A thin man sitting nearby also lifted his head. He had a small toothbrush mustache. Justine recoiled with horror. The most hated man on earth. *Adolf Hitler.*

"Now that's a name I haven't heard for a long time," grinned Hitler. "Zyk sounds like Zyklon, eh, Eicke?"

SS General Theodore Eicke turned to a quaking Justine now and grinned at her.

"Never heard of it," said *Papa* Eicke, considered to be one of the most brutal men of the Third Reich. The group of men burst into laughter.

"What are you guys cackling about?" demanded Justine now crossly. She knew that she had to stand her ground somewhere, tired of being scared all the time. "Say, do you have a bit of Jew in you?" demanded Eicke looking deeply into her dark brown and large eyes. "My friend here is the best Jew hunter on the planet." He pointed to another man in uniform who bowed at this introduction.

"SS General Reinhard Heydrich at your disposal, Madame," said the charming blonde man with a sinister smile. "Yes, she might be partially Semitic." He nodded.

"Ah, enough of the old nonsense," said Hitler, and he pulled out a silver flask of schnapps. "I don't drink, but here child, have one on me."

The men all around the fire guffawed and appeared to be having a merry time. Justine turned up her pointed nose. She knew that her accent was upper class but Papa Eicke looked at her in a sinister way and put the schnapps to her lips. "When our Führer says to drink, then you drink," he hissed suddenly. Hitler was looking up at the stars.

"Alas, even young girls fear me, so infamous have I become on earth," he sighed. Justine gulped the schnapps and fire coursed through her throat. Eicke poured her another one.

"Well we all saw Schindler's list," she said glaring at Hitler, as she drank the second one. "We saw the way you treated the Jews."

Hitler glanced at Heydrich.

"I told you that we couldn't trust that Schindler fellow," he said shaking his head. "Child, what if I told you that the Holocaust was a lie?"

"I would never believe it," she said standing up getting ready to leave.

There was a click and she felt the cold steel of a pistol on her temple and Eicke forced her into a kneeling position and he cocked the hammer.

"You half-Jew!" bellowed SS Obergruppenführer Eicke, the man from Dachau who had roamed the camp with his riding whip but had also been one of Germany's most fearless and able commanders of the war.

The men protested including Hitler. "Come on Eicke, let her go."

"Let's show this untermensch what it really felt like for the Jew in fucking Schindler's fake list."

Justine closed her eyes in terror.

A shuffle of feet and then she opened her eyes to see no one. A cold wind blew. She was still there in the bath holding the glass of schnapps, but everyone had disappeared. Hitler's silver schnapps flask was still there, and she picked it

up much to her disgust. There was an inscription on it, and she read it with horror.
"To my dear Zyk."
Signed Adolf Hitler.
Justine burst into a sob as she dropped the flask and ran deeper into the desert. Where was Zyk? She felt mortally afraid and terror seized her as she recalled that pistol's cold steel on her temple. She sobbed and tears began to flow.
 Suddenly, she heard music and turned to see a bus in front of her along with a burning plane. On top of the bus stood a long-haired man with a guitar. Then there was another man with a mic singing a scary song, while wearing a long leather black overcoat and round sunglasses. He grinned at her as he sang.

"No more tears!
The light in the window is a crack in the sky
A stairway to darkness in the blink of an eye
A levee of tears to learn Zyk'll never be coming back
The man in the dark will bring another attack
No more tears, tears, tears."

Justine heard the words and they frightened her heart even more. The man in the dark and she turned to see the Indian fakir with his bind ox standing behind her and grinning.

The terrifying men on top of the bus continued to sing.

"Your mamma told you that you're not supposed to talk to strangers,
Look in the mirror and tell me do you think that Zyk's life is in danger here

No more tears
No more tears
No more tears

I see her around the corner"

 Justine whirled to see Kali, the dancing girl, but now she was grinning at her. "Still want to stay with Zyk? You're inside his mind right now. This is who he is and that's why you can't find him."

Justine stared at her and then glanced back. The bus and the burning plane were gone.

"You're jealous of me, aren't you?" Justine demanded, and Kali only smiled.

"Think what you like, but I'll be back." With that Kali disappeared and a freezing wind blew threw Justine's very bones.

Oilfields under attack

French Company was kitted out in their new AWS suits now feeling indestructible. Drew, meanwhile, was awed by the seamless integration of his computer into his HUD and operated through his voice or thought commands, but the entire big glass helmet was essentially a curved computer screen.

"Ok boys let's roll out!" ordered Tor, and they trooped onto an oil platform fitted with after-burners, where Kim threw a lever causing the rig's rockets to fire up and the platform lurched upwards. Kim gave it more throttle and it took off into the skies hurtling through the desert.

"Yeah, it's apparently got jet fighter thrusters under the platform," nodded Xander, as he examined the mega-ton gun mounted on the rig. "Looks like the looters here are packing some heavy heat."

"Well, there's only one way to find out," grinned Tor, as he took off his helmet in the cold wind. But in a few seconds, he felt his ears freeze in the inhospitable terrain and he pulled his helmet hurriedly back on.

BLAM BALM!

A sudden melee of laser blasts enveloped them, and Tor took a direct hit on the chest. But then his suit shrugged it off and he returned fire.

"Ambush!" he sputtered while picking up his fallen blaster and fired rapidly into the snowy wilderness.

Xander pointed to his helmet.

"Use the targeting system on the HUD!" he screamed, while running to the rig's heavy gun. Enemy lasers plastered his suit, but the AWS was built for tactical nuclear blasts, and he got to the gun and then pointed it into the distance. His HUD locked onto enemy infra-red thermal signatures and he pressed the trigger.

KABOOM! KABOOM! The heavy blaster squirted ten megatons of fire that evaporated whole sections of the horizon.

"Jesus Fucking Christ!" shouted Kim, as he saw Xander do a 360-degree sweep with his weapon.

"Cease fire!" shouted Tor eventually.

Delicious silence.

Xander chuckled. "I think we got 'em."

"I think we just nuked the entire countryside," said Tor noting the radiation levels spike on his HUD.

There was a cry in the distance. A woman's sharp cry in pain. A wounded looter.

"Should we get her?" asked Xander.

"Just 'cause its a woman?" demanded Tor.

"Well let's pump her for information," said Kim, and he fired the thrusters on his AWS system to fly off the rig and into the desolate distance. He returned like Superman holding a moaning woman with a bleeding leg.

"Give her an anti-radiation tablet," ordered Tor. "You speak English?"

Tor shoved a pistol in-front of her face. The universal language of the gun worked, and she shook her head.

"Non tiende," she managed, as Kim applied a tourniquet to her leg and bandaged her along with a hit of morphine. Relief flooded through her and she began to babble happily in Spanish which Xander understood.

"Our base is in the town just over the hill," she slurred with her eyes rolling. They were flying the Klan's red flag on top of their rig which had probably drawn the heated looter response.

"Fucking Hispanics," cursed Xander.

"Well we need information," said Tor firmly. Intel on the ground was more valuable than shooting chicks on morphine. She looked like she hadn't showered for days observing her dirty clothes. Thank god for their air-tight suits.

"How many looters in your base?" demanded Xander in Spanish. The morphine was still strong.

"The whole town is a looter town," she babbled. Anyone else would've said that her intel was compromised on morphine, but for Tor it was the other way around. "It's just over the hill there."

"Set course for that hill and destroy it," ordered Tor.

"Aye aye, sir," said Drew piloting the rig to the new coordinates when just then there was a blast.

KABOOM!

A missile had smashed into their rig which then bellowed thick black smoke. The gyro-meters on the rig screamed as they sharply descended towards the ground.

"Shit, we're going down!"

"Fly!" screamed Tor. "Abandon ship!"

French Company needed no urging as they blasted away into the air with Kim holding onto the wounded looter.

"Return to the Klan base on my mark," ordered Tor, as he led the formation in a V shape back to base.

"These suits are rock solid," announced Xander, realizing that they could accelerate to MACH speeds in their nuclear thorium powered suits with apparently unlimited flying time.

"Unreal technology," agreed Drew on the com.

"Stop cackling and maintain radio silence," ordered Tor, and they accelerated to MACH 2 with the Klan oil-refinery now in sight.

KKK Grandmaster Luke with Hillary

"What is it that you want from us?" Luke demanded, with Hillary sitting in-front of him. She was locked inside a pressure chamber with thick bullet proof glass walls, while cameras observed her every movement. The Klan was looking for possible signs of alien possession in Hillary.

"How many times have I told you that they want only one human as their Oracle has foreseen?" yelled Hillary irritably throwing her head back in her characteristic style and in a voice that reminded Luke of her infamous line, *"Why aren't I 50 points ahead?".* She had never realized that there were worse things out there than Republicans. Before the aliens, she'd thought that White women supporters of Trump were the second worst kind, but then the Klan had changed all that. They had shot Jack Schooler in front of her eyes and they were treating her as if she was ISIS or something.

"Fuck you, Hillary! You're never going to be President!" yelled Grandmaster Luke. "Tell the aliens that we want to make a deal with them. We are ready."

"I'm not an Oracle, you dumb male SOB!" shouted back Hillary.

"Yeah, that's right. Call us names, but that's why you lost the election!" hooted Luke, while the older Klan leaders assembled there stared disapprovingly at Luke and switched off the mic.

"Calm down, Grandmaster," admonished an older Grandmaster who was pissed the way the younger Klan leadership under Luke were behaving. *Asswipes.*

Luke smoldered to have his authority challenged but, in the Klan, he was still not the head honcho. There were quite a few Grand Wizards still alive and he wasn't even a junior wizard. *Just the Grandmaster of the newly formed Klan Army.* He ran a hand through his thick blonde hair impatiently.

Suddenly Hillary looked up and there were only the whites of her eyes that moved unnaturally.

"What is it that you offer?" asked Hillary in a robotic male voice. Luke pointed excitedly to the higher Klan leaders. There, he'd been right about Hillary all along.

"Look!" he cried.

"Oh my god, she's possessed!"

"Dam right she is," howled Luke now with a swagger as he switched on the mic and leaned into it.

"Howdy there, welcome to the United States of America," he said in his best Southern drawl. Hillary visibly twitched as if in allergic response. She was still in there somewhere.

"We offer you the right to claim this human as yours," Luke said, and the higher Klan leaders nodded.

"We want the President of the USA Ronald Trump to agree to it," said Hillary, now staring at the Grandmasters intently, with an evil snicker. Oh, she was enjoying it.

"We are the premier authority in the USA. The President doesn't really count in front of the Klan," said the senior Grand Wizard of the Klan, Howard Lowe.

"So be it then, Klan Leader," answered Hillary uncomfortably. "What would you like in return?"

"We would like alien technology transfers, specifically weapons," interjected Luke quickly.

Hillary laughed now.

"Earthling, we are thousands of years superior to you."

"How about a plasma gun?" asked Luke.

Hillary looked perplexed as if the alien was thinking. Luke had hit pay-dirt, realized the Grand Wizards.

"Alright, then you will be beamed up to the alien mothership where we will transfer the tech to you," replied Hillary.

"Yeah!" shouted Luke thrilled to get onto an alien spaceship. The elders wondered at his brash foolishness, but then he wasn't going to listen to them. "But if I get on the ship then I want something as collateral. I ain't that stupid that you hold me hostage or kill me over there."

"We will give you nothing," said Hillary.

"No deal then," argued Luke.

Grand Wizard Lowe leered at Luke.

"What's the matter Luke? Scared?"

"I ain't gettin' on that ship without assurances," he said adamantly. Hillary's face contorted into a face of rage.

"Earthling, we only want Zyk, otherwise we have no quarrel with you," Hillary said.

"Well give us the weapons or we will never give you a US Citizen," Luke said, who was imagining world domination now.

Hillary laughed.

The Grand Wizards were puzzled now.

"You must lay a trap for him, just as the Oracle has predicted," said Hillary. "She has foreseen that you will do our bidding."

"You have travelled millions of light years for this Oracle nonsense!" shouted Luke with disbelief. No one owned him.

"Just stay out of our way then," said Hillary. Suddenly, Hillary swayed and there was terror on her face. Her eyes began to flip multiple times and she rose up in the air only to fall down on the ground with a terrible shriek.

"What the hell just happened to her?" asked Howard, and Luke looked on as EMT's scrambled towards her containment room.

"Nobody opens that room!" he shouted. Cellphones started to ring like mad.

Luke answered his phone.

"Sir, USA has just declared war on the aliens," shouted a local Klan leader from Kansas.

"As we speak, alien ships are dropping left and right from the skies!"

"Oh my god!" shouted Luke. His worst nightmare was coming true. Images now flashed on a T.V screen of alien ships being obliterated from the sky.

"Jesus Christ, DARPA just activated their nuclear force-field around Earth!" announced Grand Wizard Lowe as he broke into a cold sweat.

Ronald Trump was suddenly on TV.

"My fellow Americans," he said with his signature sneering and smug smile, while now clad in army fatigues. "These nasty aliens come to our planet to threaten us, demanding our surrender, but they approached the wrong people! Americans will never surrender!"

At this the Klan leaders all had a face-palm moment. The America that the KKK was trying to consolidate and rule was now going to be threatened with an even bigger war than the Third World War that they had emerged from.

"So, I have ordered General Schwartzkopf to open hostilities against the aliens, and don't worry we have new wonder weapons that we will be deploying against these two-bit aliens. They will soon be begging us to surrender, but meanwhile, we are prepared to pay the ultimate sacrifice to defend USA!"

At this, Hillary Fenton struggled back to life in the containment room.

"Two-bit aliens indeed!" swore Luke worriedly as sweat filled his forehead. Ronald Trump had just stabbed the Klan in the back. Meanwhile, Trump continued on FOX TV news

"So much as we are weary from war, I would first ask the American people and then the rest of the World to join hands and defeat this alien scourge once and for all or we will perish, but our World will die with honor and courage. It is the only way Americans know how to die. God bless America."

Just then a missile explosion obliterated the Klan facility.

KABOOM!

Zyk unwinds

Zyk wakes up in the Audi to find Justine curled in his arms angelically as she sleeps. Zyk gently lifts her off of him and rests her head on the driver's head rest. She is tall for a half-Indian girl, probably the white bit in her. He smells his breath. Not the best after those mushrooms, and he glances at the Audi's clock. 9 AM. Well, at least the Audi's internal GPS computer was miraculously working. In the distance, Phillip and Travis are sprawled over a mound and sleeping contentedly, when his stomach rumbles loudly. He exits the car and looks at his boots, filthy and hot, with no spare socks, a real stink fest in there waiting to be unleashed one day. But Travis and Phillip remain oblivious of their feet, while snoring contentedly on an ancient mound of clay that at some point used to serve as a sacred and holy purpose.

"Hey guys, I'm getting hungry," he hollered, and the soldiers wake up quickly and look around for their weapons. The sun is beating down on their red faces and even though its pleasant by Asian standards, its still 75 degrees.

"Dam, my battery is almost drained," realizes Travis, and he has dim memories of firing his blaster wildly into the night. Phillip checks his blaster too and its almost fully drained too. They look at each other in alarm.

"Maybe we can stop at a nearby Pakistani nuclear reactor and recharge," says Zyk.

"This is fusion power dude, hydrogen bomb technology that no one else has," says Travis condescendingly.

"Well then maybe Germany," says Zyk. "Meanwhile, we have some regular weapons right?"

They had stored the Indian and Pakistani Kalashnikovs in the trunk. Oh, they were going to need them alright.

The boys got in the car and as Zyk started the car, Justine awoke with a start to stare at Zyk in fascination as he pressed the accelerator, oblivious to Justine.

"Where are we going?" asked Travis, as Zyk punched the navigation system a few times and it came back online mercifully.

"We're going to Quetta," said Zyk as the navigation system showed a clear path out of Pakistan to Afghanistan.

"The sooner we get out of Asia the better," said Travis. He was having some mad recollections from last night.

"Justine how was your mushroom trip?" asked Travis, and now Justine looked startled.

"Oh, those mushrooms were magic?" she asked suddenly, and now everything began to make sense and remembered eating a couple of mushrooms as snacks. They had looked so enticing, their golden shine. She had been drugged last night and let out a sigh of relief. *Nothing had been real.*

"Ha ha," laughed Zyk. "What did you see darling?"

"You're not going to believe what I saw," she said.

"An Indian holy man and a blind ox," Zyk said. Justine shook her head.

"We all saw that, but then I entered your mind."

Travis and Phillip hooted with laughter and Justine looked crossly at them.

"What are you all cackling for?" she asked.

"We saw you guys having sex," replied Phillip, and now Justine burned a deep shade of red.

Zyk put a finger on his lips.

"Don't tell them the juicy details."

Justine turned towards Zyk and she couldn't remember their lovemaking. This was bizarre indeed. But no wonder Kali had been jealous. She was trying to scare her away from Zyk. Well, she was half tempted to anyways. He had all sorts of terrible people like those Germans living inside his mind. How on earth could they have a constructive relationship with Zyk when that horrible German fellow with the pistol could appear anytime, not to mention old Adolf? How would they ever fit into normal society and her friends would think that she was such a weirdo. Then another thought struck her. There was no more normal after the nuclear war and the aliens overhead.

Rawalpindi, Pakistan flashed on the screen and that's where her paternal grandfather had come from. But she was not in the least sentimental about it and was thankful to bypass it, shuddering at the thought of long-lost relatives deciding to kidnap and keep her there. No, she preferred to take her chances with Zyk and try to make it to Europe. After that she would be free to do as she pleased.

They were now on the highway to Baluchistan and the gateway into that fierce land of the Afghans guarded by that ancient city of Quetta. Zyk made it quickly with no traffic in sight and the Audi roared into a broad highway that was laid to facilitate fast overland transport for US military and trade. Fresh fruits came from Afghanistan, while electronic goods were shipped from Pakistan through this highway.

"Now this looks like a proper US highway," nodded Travis appreciatively, and he was eager again to get out of the car and stretch his long legs, still cramped in the spacious S7 Audi

"Look!" cried Justine. "People."

Yes, there were people at the outskirts of Quetta much to their relief. The situation wasn't that bad. But there was something strange about the people here.

"Their clothes appear to be from another time period," remarked Zyk thoughtfully.

"Are we still tripping guys?" asked Travis pinching himself. So did Phillip and he checked his blaster dolefully. Five percent battery left. This was no trip. Fear struck Justine's heart as she saw soldiers wearing swords on their hips and long beards under their steel helmets. Shit, they were in a Muslim country. The Americans also now stared at the chain mail clad strolling soldiers. Very medieval.

They kept driving, while the Islamic soldiers started to point to the car causing Zyk to step on the gas and disappear into the city.

Delta Operations

"Yes sir," said Tor into his com, as the steel doors of the Klan command center situated in the center of the icy North Dakota refinery, extending a hundred meters into the sky opened ominously for French Company to fly into. They landed in a brightly lit hangar which had the remaining Klan soldiers waiting for them in their black uniforms. The injured Hispanic woman screamed with terror now as she saw them, as a Klan Army captain stepped forward.

"We'll take care of this looter," he said and gave her a mighty kick in the ribs that knocked the wind out of her lungs. "Fucking Mexirats!"

"Pump her for information," said Tor, feeling pity for the woman who was actually pretty and resembled Salma Hayek in her younger days. "'Cause their looter base is one hell of a defended sector."

"What's your name, bitch?" demanded a youthful captain, barely out of his teens. Xander shook his head as she spat at him and let out a stream of the choicest Spanish abuses reserved for *putas like him.* The captain called Samuel kicked her again, while Kim couldn't stand it anymore and he came in between the Samuel and the woman.

"Look, let's tend to her wounds first and then we'll get someone to talk to her in Spanish."

The captain looked at him with cold eyes.

"Medical attention for this looter?" he laughed loudly, and before anyone could stop him, he'd whipped out a Glock and shot her in the head. He was fast, nodded Tor. He almost hadn't seen that coming. He had talent and Tor's mind went back to the old Westerns where the gunslingers competed for the fastest draw. Sure, this Southern boy was fast.

"You have failed your mission to destroy the looter base, while losing a very valuable rig too," said Samuel condescendingly. "We don't need this filthy scum or their information. Take another rig and obliterate everything. Do you understand Delta Operators? Scorch the desert outside the facility so they never dare to attack this facility again."

With that he turned, and his unit marched out with him, as Kim bit his bearded lip and the captain would've been dead the moment, he'd drawn his gun, but in the end, Kim was part of a chain of command and the Klan called the shots here. He bit his lip again and turned. Shooting women was never acceptable, but then this was a pitiless war now.

KABOOM! The sirens sounded across the refinery. They were under attack, and the captain hurried back barking orders.

"Man, the heavy guns on top of this building!"

French Company fired their thrusters and flew up through the opening dome roof from where they saw three laser FLAK guns depressed to an angle to cover the entire facility from an adjacent roof. The dome sealed shut and French Company flew to the FLAK guns.

"Xander, this oil refinery is going to be one pile of junk if we don't get the looters ASAP!" shouted Tor, as he opened devastating laser fire with his FLAK picking off looters in the distance. Automated perimeter guns were already blowing up looters, who countered with short-range missiles, which slammed into the refinery inflicting irreparable damage. One section of the refinery did explode and a slow ball of fire erupted. The missile had scored a hit on the oil.

BLAM BLAM!

Xander fired his FLAK using the laser targeting system to destroy clumps of looters dressed in a garish mismatch of uniforms robbed from department stores mixed with military surplus. Tracer bullets from the looters whizzed harmlessly by as angry hornets, but the perimeter heavy guns were holding up, as the computer recognized and fired at an astonishing rate. Looters were dying by the scores, but this was just the first wave as the others behind them set up mortars and the occasional missile sailed overhead to cause heavy damage inside the refinery.

The Klan captain was suddenly on the roof wearing an AWS suit and he screamed at them.

"You must use our missile defense systems!"

He screamed as he fiddled with the switch on the computer to highlight a slew of choices from which he selected the *Arrow X system*. French Company felt old and outdated now as they followed his lead on their computer screens.

They had been away for a month, but the world had changed radically, and DARPA's technology had risen to meet the alien threat. Suddenly, the FLAK guns began to blast missiles out of the air and the tide of the battle began to change. By now the two dozen surviving Klan soldiers had advanced beyond the perimeter and were mopping up the looters, while administering the coup-de-grace to surviving looters.

"Jesus Christ!" swore Xander getting out of the Flak laser and he looked at his watch. The entire firefight had been less than three minutes, but hundreds lay dead. The future of computerized warfare. But the looters were desperate as Tor surveyed the battlefield through his infrared binoculars, and he could make out an equal number of women among the dead. Jesus. Looting was turning into an equal opportunity thing and the Hispanics and Africans had no loyalty towards the state not that the Klan was making it easy for them. The KKK just needed an excuse to put a bullet in the head of anyone looking foreign.

"Cease fire, men," said the Klan soldier into his com. "Return to base and reset the perimeter guns." He looked up at the sun setting over the cold horizon. The looters would no doubt regroup and attack soon.

"They're getting bolder now attacking in daylight."

French Company flew down with their rockets to the oil refineries that were still fiercely ablaze, where Klan robotic firefighters were aiding with water cannons.

"Where the hell are they getting these portable missiles?" asked Tor watching Klansmen and their robots put out the raging fire where a missile had hit an oil silo. The fire went out, but next time they might not be so lucky if they hit the main refinery full of inflammable gasoline. It was like guarding a weapons depot. One direct hit and it as all over.

White House at War

"Well sir, so far there has been no military response from the aliens," said Schwartzkopf playing a clip for the President of alien ships crashing and burning all over American skies.

"Our force fields have linked up all across the United States and we are generating billions of gigawatts of nuclear power to energize our shields."

"That's awesome," commended President Trump.

"But the bad news is that more alien ships have come in through the star gate near our planet.

"Hey, if that star-gate is open, then start firing nuclear missiles through them," said Trump bullishly, though he knew that his missiles simply lacked the range to the stargate situated somewhere near the planet Mercury.

"Sir, the aliens, despite having lost scores of ships, have still not sent in ground troops."

"I don't really care. How's the power supply to our cities?"

"The Klan is supplying our big cities with electrical power, but their refineries in Texas and North Dakota are coming under heavy attack from looters."

Trump looked at Schwartzkopf now with a glint in his eye.

"Those looters are traitors."

"Yes sir, we have shoot on sight orders for all suspected looters."

"We must kill more of them."

"They are mostly Black and Hispanic, while the New York based news press is going bananas over our anti-looter program as racist."

"That failing New York Times has opened up again?"

"Yes sir."

"Meanwhile, Puerto Rico's Governor is saying that we're not doing enough for them," added General Schwartzkopf.

Trump shook his head.

"Tell 'em to go to hell. What about the US Army?"

"Regrouping and taking volunteers, sir, as we speak, but the Klan Army is still getting a lot of the best manpower."

"You mean white kids," said Trump. "How's their military performance?"

"They are fierce in combat and we have reports of small Klan units holding out against tremendous odds in New York and Miami against thousands of looters, not to mention that small North Dakota Klan detachment holding out against a whole town of looters."

"Has French Company been sent in?"

"Yes, Mr President, just as you requested."

Trump nodded his big head now, while a plan was forming in his mind that General Schwartzkopf could only wonder at. The president was proving to be made of steel inside, despite the ferocious challenges that his Presidency had thrown up, and Schwartzkopf respected him for that.

"Send in the Air Force against that looter town," ordered Trump.

"But sir, there are women and children in Williston," protested Schwartzkopf, thinking of the tens of thousands of casualties there.

"We need the oil more than those criminals. Crush the looters, General."

"Yes sir," swallowed Schwartzkopf. In war, only the most ruthless won as the Americans had demonstrated in Hiroshima and Dresden.

Grandmaster Luke looks for Jesus

He awakens on a cold and hard metallic floor, where he cries in pain that fills his body as if he'd been through abdominal surgery, with shooting pain all over and he looks at his body which is covered in chains that bite deep into his flesh. Is this hell? Is this what purgatory looks like as Grandmaster Luke's eyes hazily focus on the surroundings. There are thousands of beings of all sizes and shapes embedded in the walls and they are moving ———— alive and in pain. The screams of the tortured fill his ears, reminding him of the industrial band *Front Line Assembly* fusing dark music with the hum of the machines. Robotic arms are connected to them —— feeding them.

"Where the fuck am I?" demands Luke through his chains that bite into him harder. Suddenly, white light flashes in front of him like a strobe light and in that light, he sees hideously deformed faces. Maybe the Bible was true, and he was in hell. Grotesque features with horns just as the Bible had said, which causes a cold shiver to crawl down his spine.

"You see what you want to see over here," said a voice and the lights came on, revealing a giant alien standing over him, ten feet tall, and with a bear like face, while suddenly the walls were smooth and metallic.

"What do you mean?" Luke demanded rubbing his arms suddenly free from the chains.

"Its all in your mind," said the alien with red glaring bear-like eyes as he opened a door to more metallic walls with corridors.

"You mean all that was just an illusion?" asked Luke incredulously.

"Oh no, that was real, I've just taken you away from that reality," replied the alien. "You're actually dead and in the Underworld, but since you negotiated with us and offered us a deal, we have chosen to rescue you from there. We have connections in your Underworld too."

"How did I die?" demanded Luke.

"When USA attacked us, a random missile crushed the facility where you were interrogating Hillary."

"I don't believe you."

The alien stared at him, and suddenly snapped his fingers.

BAM!

Luke was back in the Underworld, but just before that, Luke, a reformed kleptomaniac had cunningly snatched the blaster that was slung on the alien's waist. Now back in incredible pain, Grandmaster Luke was determined to resist. He knew the darkness. The Bible had warned him of it and now with the help of Jesus Christ he would defeat the heathens of the Underworld. The alien suddenly appeared again, but Luke shot him down with his own blaster and in slow motion he returned to the Underworld. This was profound redemption, and he knew now that Jesus was closer to him than ever.

"Jesus, help me, for I have sinned. I have killed many Jews, but they brought only evil to us Aryans."

There was no answer and he was in chains again. The blaster was in his hand and he tried to aim at the chains and away from his body.

BLAM!

The blast tore a hole through his forearm and a wave of new pain flashed through him. But then he heard the rattle of the chains falling away from him. He got up and began to unwrap the broken chains. Soon, the pain stopped, and he ripped off a piece of cloth from his shirt to tie his burnt forearm.

God only knew what kind of bacteria lived on this ship, as he ached for a bottle of whisky. He grinned. Well this White boy was going to bring a little bit of hell to the Underworld. Of course, with the help of Jesus. He looked around in the dark space as he staggered to his feet. Come to me, Jesus, and he trained his blaster and began to shoot the robotic arms that began to fizzle. Humans began to fall from their robotic clutches. But they all died quickly. Apparently, they were too weak to survive without the force-fed nutrients. Fucking losers, muttered Luke, as he staggered out into the darkness with blaster in hand.

On his way out in the darkness, he saw a man sitting in a huddle with a cloth in front of him.

"Spare some change for the hungry," demanded the man.

Luke stared at him surprise but then he saw that his outstretched hand bore poorly healed scars of a nail.

"What happened here?" asked Luke taking out some dimes from his pocket and laid them on his palm.

"Well you know they nailed me for my crimes against the Jerusalem Jews," replied the man from under his hood, but he could see a shock of blonde hair there.

An Aryan. But what the hell was he doing begging like this in the Underworld?

"Well shiiieet, I've put some Jews up in heaven too," grinned Luke taking the beggar's hand now and lifted him up. "Come on, you ain't no beggar, just as much as I am."

The man got to his feet and lowered his hood. He was grinning.

"Well I'll be damned," whistled Luke, as he checked the man's bare feet too —— bearing the dark scars of the crucifixion.

"Yeah, I was testing you," said Jesus now grinning, and Luke pumped his hand. "Why the hell didn't you rescue me from the aliens?"

"God works in mysterious ways," replied Jesus with another smile.

"Look, I gotta get back to earth," said Luke thinking of his Klan Army and Police units. Hell, those fledgling organizations would be rudderless.

"I'm on my way to wreak vengeance on the ones that betrayed me, Luke," said Jesus with a serious look in his eye. Luke groaned. Oh boy, a historic revenge story. Dead guys killing already dead guys. Only in the Underworld.

"I know you think its futile, but I want to taste what revenge feels like," said Jesus explaining himself. "You know heaven is so sterile. Like I am dying of boredom. I need some action!"

"Sure Jesus," said Luke no stranger to murder and mayhem. "As long as we get back to Earth."

"Done deal, dude."

They shook hands in the cold and dimly lit underworld and then Jesus led the way.

The magical Palace in Khorasan

Zyk drives into a city filled with golden banners with Arabic inscriptions everywhere.

"Muslims," muttered Travis, and Zyk nodded. Quranic inscriptions on big and heavy flags draped over the balconies of houses, while also lining the streets.

In front of them stood a gigantic golden palace glittering with an assortment of embedded jewels.

"Wow!" said Justine quite impressed for the first time on this trip. Genuine wealth. "Looks like a King lives over here."

There were soldiers on horseback trotting along the broad avenues, while civilians were either on horses or donkeys and dressed in embroidered and flowing robes. The nobles were dressed in thin muslin golden robes that could be differentiated from the rest of the population.

"We definitely are still on the mushrooms," said Travis shaking his head sadly.

"Zyk, are you going to drive straight into the palace?" asked Phillip worriedly as he saw soldiers drawing their swords and yelling to each other suddenly. "They're all Arabs, dude."

"Look at your GPS," pointed out Travis, and Zyk saw something that made his jaw drop. The town of Quetta had disappeared and now the screen showed *Ghazna*.

"We're still in the twilight zone alright."

They reached the gates of the palace with no other road in sight. Nowhere to run with the car through the congested avenues.

"Look, the gates are opening!" pointed Travis, while soldiers quickly wheeled the palace compound gates open, and Zyk didn't bother to slow down till they were at the entrance of another set of gates, which also opened to allow them to the palace which shone with even more lustrous grandeur than from afar.

"Oh, my god," moaned Justine, just imagining the riches, as she gazed at the armies of men in bejeweled clothes.

"Looks like we're expected," said Zyk, driving through the palatial entrance which itself was surrounded by a gigantic moat whose drawbridge was quickly lowered.

"A bit of European engineering here," said Travis, but militarily he wasn't impressed by this Asiatics. A squad of Crusaders or Templars would wreak havoc on them. Hell, with his blaster, he could liquidate this town. Now the army of Muslims looked expectantly at them, while in their hands they held silver trays laden with water and fruits, as Zyk stopped the car.

"We're obviously being welcomed here," commented Zyk grinning, while Justine was loathe to step out of the cocoon of the Audi, but then the boys exited into the harsh sunlight, though the wind was cool on this March afternoon.

"Salaam," greeted Zyk in Hindustani, and the men all bowed low. Travis and Phillip wore their AWS suits without their helmets, and slung their blasters, while Zyk forced Justine to tuck a Beretta pistol into her black yoga pants. She hoped that her long sleeved pastel shirt would cover her weapon even though it was so heavy, but the skintight pants proved to be admirable in holstering her Beretta. Eventually, she dropped the gun into her handbag as the barrel had begun to dig into her thigh. Zyk had his sunglasses on while wearing black jeans and a bomber leather jacket followed by two blonde guys in Space Marine suits that resembled some ancient alien Mesopotamian hieroglyphic scene cutout. But it was real and the Islamic soldiers accompanying them were most gracious along with the servants. Zyk took a glass of offered ice cold water and drank deeply as did the soldiers and even finicky Justine. The sparkle in the water put rest to any doubts to the purity of the water.

"Man, this tastes so good," said Travis smiling broadly now. Cool water was so underestimated and this one tasted heavenly.

"Welcome to Khorasan," announced the man leading the servants and soldiers, while dressed in heavy armor and a long sword slung across his waist. No one understood the language being spoken, not even Zyk, but he recognized it as old Persian.

The armored man motioned for them to follow him and they crossed through gigantic echoing marble halls with exquisitely colored tiles.

"This still feels like an acid trip," said Travis enjoying the unbelievable colors embedded in each tile of the palace. Forget the drab grey of America, these guys were the real trippers. Colors, even inside their domes in everyday palace life.

Zyk grinned at him.

"This region is famous for drugs."

"Which ones?"

"Opium."

"Hardcore motherfuckers."

Justine was entranced by the emeralds and rubies that studded the walls and even the roof as her sharp eyes discerned. This was no ordinary Palace as she marveled at the golden and turquoise blue dome filled with innumerable sparkling precious stones.

"At least, they didn't take our guns away," said Phillip glad to be holding his blaster, even though the battery was drained, but it might just fire in a tight spot. Cool wind flitted through the halls, while the sound of gurgling fountains filled the air, as did multi-colored parrots. It was above all an enchanting palace alright. There were a few Quranic inscriptions here and there, but the calligraphy merged into the intricate geometrical patterns till even the Universe was in symmetry. Overall, it had a mesmerizing effect on the visitors.

"So, God is some kind of a mathematical expression?" asked Travis.

"Probably," replied Zyk. Spring temperate weather was his favorite and he slid his arm around Justine's slender waist. She looked at him and mouthed,

"Are you crazy? They're all Muslims here," she said slapping his hand away. "They might kill us."

Zyk was strangely relaxed as he smiled and took his hand away unworried that some Islamic law might be broken on the pain of execution.

"Kali's got my back," he said, but Justine wasn't reassured at all. Kali was jealous of her even though she wasn't exactly in love with Zyk. It was just a physical thing, but who would explain that to Kali. She shook her head as they were led out into the palace orchard filled with hundreds of pomegranate trees, where sat a bejeweled man surrounded by an audience. He was sitting on a gigantic throne with a big cat curled around his feet.

"Is that a leopard?" demanded Travis getting his blaster ready. "Jesus Christ!"

"No, its an Indian Cheetah," replied an old man by the Sultan's side in perfect English. Zyk was relieved that he wouldn't have to translate everything here. "Welcome to the Royal court of Sultan Mahmud of Ghaznavi!"

Travis and Phillip were not impressed, and they gripped their weapons tighter, but the old man came closer and he had a big beard, while the Sultan on the throne indeed had fierce eyes, though also with a thick bushy beard, but appeared to be in top fighting condition. He was surrounded by young Pages holding trays of fruits.

"Wow, I always wanted to meet a Sultan," growled Travis, and Zyk dug an elbow into his suit.

"Shut the fuck up, man," he glowered. Zyk had expected Kali but it was someone else. A Sultan so far.

"How come you speak English?" asked Zyk gratefully turning to the bearded old man.

"My name is Ferdowsi," he answered, and bowed low towards Justine who stared at his solid golden medallion that he wore around his neck. No doubt a gift from the Sultan and she turned her attention to the bejeweled cheetah's collar, as it yawned lazily and stretched itself languidly under the gentle afternoon sun. There her eyes met the Sultan's coal black blazing eyes. A man of immense energy and power and obviously used to getting his way. A sneer made itself to his eyes and it was almost like *"That's right baby. Welcome to my crib."*

She averted her eyes and her instinct told her not to stare at him for too long. She had a feeling that death and destruction were only a hair's breadth away with him, and the cheetah seemed to nod as it bared its long canines at her and snarled. Fear shot through her as a hunting video from Animal Planet began to play in her mind. Did the Sultan see them as the Fools in the Court? Zyk had an aura around him like everything was a game and nothing was to be taken seriously. The poet Ferdowsi now seems to have taken a liking to Zyk, while the American Marines were ignored and so was she. Probably because she is a woman.

"Welcome to Khorasan," said Ferdowsi again. Justine just then slides up to Zyk's arm in a hurry, though Zyk stares at her irritably.

"I need to meet the Sultan alone."

She nods and lets go, as Zyk in his leather jacket steps before the Sultan. Ferdowsi insists in introducing him personally.

"Sire, I present to you a time traveler," he said, and the Sultan nods his head, while the guards stare impassively at the proceedings, but they appear no less agile than the cheetah as bodyguards for their master. One false move and they will spring.

"Yes, I know," said the Sultan, which Ferdowsi translates, now getting up and the cheetah is immediately by his side. One command and the royal animal will tear Zyk to shreds as the Sultan offers his hand in salutation. A high honor. Zyk feels an iron grip of the hand that has known only battle for its 40 odd years.

"What do you mean?" asked Zyk puzzled. Travis and Phillip exchange knowing glances. The trip is still not over. Fuck. The gods were still playing with them.

"Kali told us everything," said Ferdowsi reassuringly.

"Oh, then you know everything," said Zyk relieved.

"Yes, as we can sense your energy," said the Sultan returning to his magnificent golden throne with ornate peacocks and psychedelic colors. What a sofa, thought Zyk and imagined himself making YouTube videos on that, while Justine realized that he'd quite forgotten about her. Obviously, he wasn't really in love with her either, and she turned away.

"Kali's vision has come true and tonight we will celebrate," ordered the Sultan, and clapped his hands for his court to obediently bow low.

12

Jesus confronts Judas

"What can I do here in Jerusalem?" asked Luke, as some passing legionaries directed them towards the Roman Governor's Palace. They had walked for many miles in the Underworld, but apparently time and distance flowed differently here. One moment they were in a dark forest, but Jesus seemed to know a shortcut which suddenly gave way to the Judea desert, where Luke quickly found himself staring at the Jerusalem gates.

Jesus looked at him.

"Don't go into the palace, Luke. There's a conspiracy afoot there against me." Man, the guy was seriously worried about getting nailed to the cross.

"Where is your buddy, Judas?" asked Luke.

Jesus's eyes gleamed.

"How about some dinner?" asked Jesus. "On me?"

Luke and Jesus hurried over the hilly terrain of Jerusalem just in time for that famous Last Supper.

Jesus rapped on Judas's door which was quickly flung open.

"Well, hello there, Jesus," Judas said with a wolffish grin. "You're early." He looked towards the hourglass in his house and it was still half full. The supper was laid out though, and he glanced furtively across his shoulder to pull Jesus and Luke into his house. A dog began to bark somewhere in the evening sunset with the accompanying bleats of goats that populated most courtyards in Jerusalem.

"Can't be too careful," Judas said. "Roman agents everywhere."

Luke entered the airy courtyard to find some of the famous characters of the *Last Supper* already there sauntering around, and they were surprised to see Jesus there.

"Holy Jesus!" swore a man coming over, who bowed and kissed Jesus's hand. "We will take Jerusalem tonight."

"And who is the guest that you have brought?" asked Judas putting his hand on Luke's stiff arm. The 11 apostles there stared at Luke and the strange metal object on his belt, while dressed strangely in tight leggings and a leather overcoat. He must be a Frank or a Goth, noting his bright blonde hair and blue eyes.

"My name is Luke," he said, while bristling at Judas. Suddenly, he whipped out his blaster and put it to Judas's head. Behind him, a woman screamed dropping a pot.

"Fuck this, Jesus," shouted Luke. "Let's blow this sucker away now!"

Jesus now consoles Judas's wife.

"Go inside the room. These are matters of God."

The woman nodded and knew this matter must be about all those gold pieces that Judas had brought with him last night. They probably wanted it back.

Jesus walked over to Judas and hit him with a roundhouse punch.

"What the fuck?" shouted the apostles. Where was the peaceful Jesus?

BLAM!

Luke blew Judas's head off with his blaster without waiting for a reply.

"He was snitching to the Romans and he sold Jesus out for 30 pieces of silver!"

The wife came back sobbing to hug the dead body.

"It wasn't silver, it was gold," she said sobbing.

"Well shit," said Jesus uncharitably. "No more, mister nice guy."

John, Paul, and Matt were holding on to each other.

"How did you kill him with that fire? Are you a god?"

Luke bristled again.

"Look if any of you sons of bitches are squealing to the Romans then you're all dead too!" Luke waived his blaster around.

"This time, I don't go out without a fight!" glared Jesus pushing his long and matted hair back. Oh, it had been a long time since he'd had a bath. Right now, he was more concerned about not getting nailed to that motherfucker cross. All those thousands of years later, he'd realized bitterly that there was no glory or anything, but just that miserable self-pitying nonsense called the Christian religion.

"Hey Jesus!"

"What?"

"Roman soldiers outside!"

Jesus smiled now.

"Well light 'em up!"

Luke smiled and Jesus regarded him as his true apostle. Luke, it had a nice ring to it, and he already knew that Luke had committed grievous sins against humanity. But then, so had the Jews.

"There are no innocents," murmured Jesus, as Luke exited to start firing at the dozens of Roman soldiers outside.

Heavy laser blasts and suddenly the soldiers lay dying only seeing a sun god strike them down. Pretty much the Roman squad was down.

"Now what?" asked Luke coming back with his smoking alien blaster.

"Well we can part the dimensions and return to your time. Only this time I'll be taking care of the flock."

"Alright!" whooped Luke happy to get out of this time zone. "The second coming of Christ. Wait till the Klan hears that!"

"We'll have to go back into the cave. There is a secret trapdoor that will lead us back to earth."

Luke brightened up. Best news that he's heard all day, as far as he was concerned, though he wondered about living like a prince in the Roman palaces, but then he realized that with no electricity, or air conditioning under this hot desert sun, Jerusalem was no picnic. Dammed, if he was going to turn into one of these towelheads on a donkey, as they hurried through the rocky hills scattered with meager vegetation. No hunting in forests too, something that Luke enjoyed very much in the Savannah region, Georgia. They reached the cave as Jesus pointed with his staff, one that he'd relieved Judas of. Luke realized that the staff was made of solid gold. So much for the meek and poor apostles. Even Jesus now wanted some of that *bling,* as they entered the cave again and something had to be said about the pleasures of the cave, realized Luke as he breathed in the cool subterranean air.

"In a cave system such as this, you follow the draft of air," said Jesus as they were confronted by a large cave system of multiple routes and Luke nodded. *Shiieet,* this reminded him of Jesse James's hideout back in Missouri. Who knew Jesus was hiding out like this too? Well the Romans had locked his body up real good in this cave to begin with so he'd had time to explore.

"For thousands of years, I have powerlessly watched people plod through their lives," said Jesus leading Luke through the dark cave system. The faint gurgling of water. How deep was the water as Luke's boots sloshed in the water, but Jesus seemed oblivious in his sandals to the freezing cold water.

"Y'know, this time round on earth, I intend to correct some of the worst grievances that I have seen," said Jesus.

"Like the White Race wiping out the subhumans?" said Luke, who dreamed of a Race war.

"Well not exactly, but at least the ones who have plundered the wildlife and destroyed ecological systems," growled Jesus. "You know the animals need saving too!"

"Oh yeah, Jesus for PETA!" laughed Luke realizing quickly that even as a responsible hunter, the USA always issued licenses and the numbers were always controlled by the State government. Well, not that it mattered anymore after the nuclear winter.

"Humanity will have a fresh start and I will guide them on how to live peacefully with the plant and animal kingdom," said Jesus as he pointed to a shimmering portal. Luke happily plunged through the *trapdoor,* and he was suddenly whisked through a star system, where he observed millions of civilizations shimmering under him, like the twinkling of streetlights under a descending evening plane. Ah, but he wanted to get back to earth. He would be unstoppable with the power of Jesus besides him.

Suddenly, Luke found himself landing with a crash in a strange town at night. He was alone.

"Where the hell are you, Jesus?"

He looked around. An old and familiar anxiety rose in his breast, when he'd waited for years for his dad to come home. But he never did. He suppressed the memory and waited for Jesus. The guy was Aryan and couldn't possibly flake out on him after all that.

"I am here," said Jesus. "Inside you."

"I'm going to sound schizo talking to you."

"Alright, I'll assume my own body, but I need a haircut and shower then."

"Certainly," agreed Luke, as he saw Jesus assume an earthly form in his familiar brown woolen robes. Well Jesus did smell a bit.

"Where the hell are, we?" demanded Luke.

"In Berlin," replied Jesus running a hand self-consciously through his matted blonde hair. "There is some good work to be done here."

"Jesus Christ shit I don't even have a passport," grinned Luke.
"Damned white trash!" grinned back Jesus.
"Fuck yeah!".
Luke high-fives Jesus before they set off to look for a barbershop in the nuclear wasteland of Berlin.

Zyk in Khorasan

The Sultan's gathering was in full swing with a hundred sheep roasting on large spits over a pit filled with fire, while Justine gazed at her fingernails. All that rough traveling hadn't given her much time to groom, not that Zyk or the Marines cared two hoots about that, but Ferdowsi the old poet came bustling over with a couple of terrible looking transgenders.
"These guys are the eunuchs of the harem," proclaimed the poet. "They are the Sultan's slaves and they are at your command."
"That's terrible!" shot back Justine. "They're transgenders and all LGBT's have rights from where I come from."
The old poet shrugged and left muttering under his breath. Bah!
Meanwhile, Justine started to communicate in sign language and conveyed the fact that she needed a bath.
"Oh!" exclaimed the transgenders in their high-pitched male voices and were quite relieved to have understood her. They didn't any trouble with the Sultan, who was known to lop off heads at the slightest displeasure. Wherever this girl came from, she was used to a different sort of Sultan ruling the roost, as they hurried Justine over to their one of a kind bath specially built for the Sultan. Justine was overjoyed to see it studded with rubies and the hot steamy water quickly had her in throes of ecstasy, after quickly shedding her clothes and revealing her beautiful body that even the eunuchs appreciated.
Meanwhile, roasted and exotically perfumed lamb shanks and lemonade were passed to the Klan soldiers who enjoyed nothing more than a good barbecue.
"Shit, too bad there's no beer here," grumbled Travis. The poet, Ferdowsi now beamed again.
"You boys want some Persian wine?"

The Klan soldiers looked at each other, a little alarmed, thinking if ever word got out that they were wine drinking pansies.

"Well, alright," grinned Travis, still happy to have some sort of alcohol, and quickly golden goblets of fine Shiraz wine were plied, while Zyk simply took the wine cask and emptied it boorishly in one go.

"Hell yeah!" exclaimed Zyk wiping his mouth clear of the dripping wine. "I remember I won a beer drinking competition once in Miami."

The Sultan seemed impressed and had not taken any offense to this loud behavior from Zyk much to his court's surprise.

The Klan soldiers raised their goblets and the Sultan raised his own gigantic bejeweled goblet.

"To good health," toasted Zyk, which the poet translated, while he helped himself to another succulent leg of lamb. This was life as he took a meaty bite out of the heavy leg, though Travis missed his fork and knife, as Phillip wildly gnawed into a hunk of meat.

"Old school, man," said Travis impressed.

"Bring on the girls!" ordered the Sultan suddenly causing an impromptu band hidden behind a curtain suddenly to burst into acoustic music.

"Wow son check out that guitar!" said Travis staring at the assortment of strangely dressed musicians. *Asian culture.*

"That's a *Veena,*" said the poet chuckling. On his travels, he had seen the European guitar, but the Veena was a much older and intricate instrument.

Meanwhile, the Sultan pulled Zyk over to the side.

"You know, with your contacts with Kali, you can join my army as a General," said the Sultan. "We're going to *Somnath,* in India real soon, where there is much plunder to be had."

Zyk chuckled.

"I don't think that there's much left there after the nuclear war," said Zyk. The Sultan stared thoughtfully into the mangrove that grew in his garden and nodded. With Kali calling the shots, it was Karma all the way, and Free Will a figment of her imagination. Suddenly, a host of Persian beauties burst in on the scene wearing the sheerest of colorful material and noisy anklets, and promptly began to sway seductively to the music.

"Oh yeah!" shouts Zyk, while Travis almost drops his leg of lamb as he considers which of the dancing beauties to focus his attention on, as Phillip licks his chops appreciatively. It had been some time that they'd been with women and Phillip feels the excitement rising in his pants, while sizing up the girls. Travis is thinking of two, and so is Zyk, when Justine suddenly returns to the scene also clad in colorful Persian clothes, while her clothes have gone for a wash. She catches Zyk and the Sultan admiring the troop of girls and she turns away in a huff. Zyk still hasn't noticed, but the old poet knows that trouble is brewing tonight for him. But then, Zyk was under Kali's guidance, and it was his time indeed to enjoy the fruits as he wished. After all, freedom was the only thing that made life worth living, but the complexity of the male and female relations was sometimes the fly in the ointment, and the poet shook his head as he ambled over to Justine.

"So tonight, we party," announced Sultan Mahmoud of Ghaznavi, as suddenly he clapped and his cheetah with its bejeweled spiked collar suddenly appeared on the scene free from his restraining chain. Zyk stared in alarm as the big cat languidly stretched and let out a roar.

"One snap of my fingers and *Shabana* will rip out your throat," boasted the Sultan now staring at Justine, who had now quite forgotten her hurt feelings. She froze and then as quickly as possible hurtled towards Zyk.

"I'm so scared," she breathed into his ear. Zyk chuckled as did the Sultan. *An old party trick to get the girls in line, realized Zyk, who thought of his own Great Dane that he'd once owned, but this cat beat Duke in terms of lethality.* The cheetah looked up and scowled and spat at Justine, as one female to another.

"She gets very jealous," said the Sultan, now playing with the *Shabana's* ears, and Justine gulped while gripping Zyk's arm even harder, who ran a hand through her lustrous long black hair to comfort her.

The cheetah now strode towards Zyk, and Justine in a flash was gone, but Zyk waited for the cat to smell him and then it purred. The Sultan smiled, while Travis and Phillip continued to eat nervously, now torn between fear and lust. The dancing girls continued to dance to the musicians without a care and seemed to be quite used to the cheetah parading around the Sultans's open courtyard.

"Tomorrow we must be off as there are important matters in Europe that await us," said Zyk changing the subject quickly while still playing with *Shabana's* ears, and the Americans nodded enthusiastically. The faster they repaired their damaged suits in Germany, the faster they could return to the USA.

"But of course," said the Sultan who'd heard Zyk too.

Zyk turned to the poet.

"You know, take the money in advance for your book, the *Shahnama*, 'cause in the future you will die poor."
 The poet looked alarmed and turned to the Sultan, who only shrugged.
"Just take the money now and you will live well in *Khorasan*."
 The poet nodded thinking about his bill for the Sultan's commission, while the Sultan also thought about the future.
Zyk, meanwhile, took the fetching Justine into a corner to whisper sweet nothings into her ear.

French Company in Williston

 Xander poured himself a stiff shot of Jack Daniel's Tennessee whisky, while taking in the news from the Klan's leadership, who had just ordered them into the looter town, Williston, to laser designate targets. The whisky company had thankfully survived the nuclear war and demand was even better than before with the Scottish distilleries being taxed heavily.
"A suicide operation!" protested Kim.
"We'll be the only white people in Williston," argued Drew, as he flew a drone over the town. It was filled with warehouses and a multitude of high rises, built during the oil boom years. Now, Ronald Trump had called for a heavy bombing run on this town.
"Surprisingly, intel suggests that there are a diverse mix of residents there." Everyone laughed now.
"Well, we're all gonna have to wear civilian clothes," said Tor pointing to a pile of fashionable clothes probably looted from a department store, and French Company could pretend to be new age disgruntled liberals fighting the Klan. *Or that resistance bullshit.*
 Kim had already found a size that fit his shorter stature than the rest of French Company.
"Pooh, this smells," said Kim disgustedly. Everyone laughed as Tor and Xander wore woefully short pants, but then it gave them an urban hip kind of look with raised trousers over combat boots. Sunglasses and leather overcoats would give them cover in the forbidding town blanketed by ash clouds with no chance of sunlight.

"Yeah, we recon the area, identify the enemy strongpoints are, and laser designate the bombers over to them."

"Seems like a straightforward job," said Drew nodding sarcastically. Everyone laughed at the Klan's suicidal plan, but the bad news was that French Company were the mules for this job.

"Ok, transports in one hour, since Bomber Command phoned in for the air strikes in three hours. So, we don't have long to get in and out."

Their air-transport, a Z-11 mammoth helicopter with nuclear fusion reactors pulled up to their 21st floor tower height, where the men climbed into the beefy chopper heavy straight from their suite's large window. Now for the LZ, and extraction seemed the last thing on everyone's mind as the chopper's nuclear engine blasted high into the skies, safe from any looter SAMs. It was dark by the time they were 30,000 feet over Williston, when the red light flashed inside the cavernous Z-11 chopper as the doors opened for the men to jump into Williston valley.

"USA!" shouted Xander, as he jumped out into the dark night joining Tor, Drew, and Kim, who had all jumped out seconds before. Separately, they had a cargo pack parachute down containing their rides which landed after them as their parachutes ballooned in the dark night. Williston was going to get a bit of hell tonight as French Company landed feet first and then quickly found their cargo stash where they mounted their DARPA modified Kawasaki Ninjas.

"Shit, this totally reminds me of Chuck Norris's bike in *Delta Force,*" grinned Tor wearing his long leather coat, as he gunned the Kawasaki's engine heavily in North Dakota's bitingly cold wind and took off towards the winding road descending into the valley. The rest of French Company followed all dressed in helmets and black leather —— a mutated version of Hell's Angels —— as their engines gunned into the outskirts of Williston, where they were greeting by barking dogs and burning fires. French Company donned gas masks while riding deeper into the city center —— blending in better with the steampunk style dressed Anti-fa looters.

"How the hell do we find which targets to laser designate?" demanded Xander operating his computer operated goggles through voice control, where he identified a large water tower up ahead.

"Computer, laser designate target," said Xander.

"Yes, sir."

"Xander, what the hell?" demanded Tor. "They need water, otherwise civilians will die."

"Fuck the looters!" snarled Xander, as Kim gunned his engine harder, while Drew pulled up Xander's order on his HUD.

"Shit, USAF just launched Tomahawk missiles!" he screamed into the com. They had seconds to clear the area as they passed the water tank.

"Everybody on me!" shouted Tor racing into a neighborhood while Drew's eyes were glued to the missiles roaring towards their target.

"Shit, MOAB type missile!" he shouted. "5,000 pounds of HE. Tomahawk V2."

Xander grinned, happy to be straight off the mark. He wanted to quickly designate more targets and then get the hell out of this town. Then the main air-strikes would follow.

Suddenly, a red and angry cloud lit up the sky followed by the ground itself shaking like jelly. The looters felt it was an airstrike and were scrambling to man their anti-air batteries, when the A-Team spotted them and roared towards them with their motorcycle blasters blazing. Laser blasts incinerated their batteries in seconds, but now the looters were alerted to Federal presence.

"Bring it on!" shouted Tor, as looters on bikes began hunting them, visible on his HUD being fed by video through Drew's drones. "Time for evasive action."

French company accelerated through deserted city blocks, where only litter flew about in the chilly air. Drew, meanwhile, fired *Hell-fire X* drone missiles incinerating a group of looter bikers behind them from voice commands through his HUD interface.

"DARPA has refined this program so much," commented Drew appreciatively, as French Company watched the drones chase the surviving looters and machine gun them.

"Looter checkpoint ahead," shouted Xander, noting movement on his navigation.

"We need satellite data on this location now," said Tor.

"We need to disappear into this town," said Kim, as he cut a detour into the backroads and everyone followed his lead. "This town is big enough for us to hide till the looter heat dies down."

"Yeah, but I'm not letting go of the bike," said Xander firmly, as they roared past a large building with a lot of looters milling around it. Xander dropped a grenade as he rode by and waved goodbye to the outraged looters.

"Was that a nuke?" demanded Tor.

Xander only grinned impishly.

A horrific but small mushroom cloud flew up behind and them and the wind began to heat up.

"Ride motherfuckers!" screamed Tor in terror. Drew couldn't believe that Xander would drop a nuke in a city.

"Relax, its just a tac," crackled Xander's voice in their helmets, as they zigzagged between buildings. But even the buildings were beginning to melt into yellow putty. This was horror on an epic scale as French Company screeched onto the highway with hot winds chasing their heels.

"Dude, we're not even wearing anti-radiation suits," swore Tor, as Xander grinned again and gunned the engine some more. *Leather overcoats versus a nuclear storm.*

"The evidence suggests that these fusion *tacs* have very little radioactivity, and this place was already contaminated from before," argued Xander turning his head to stare at Tor's angry black helmet.

"Xander is right," said Drew noting the readings on the HUD. "That tactical nuke didn't terribly increase the overall radioactivity levels here."

"Well we better take our anti-nuke tablets then," said Tor. "Now how do we find the looter HQ?"

"We will need some local intel," said Drew, hooking up to the now present satellite feed. A grid of the partially nuked city appeared and up ahead stood a building marked as a bar.

Everyone laughed at the thought of strolling into a looter bar. But then there seemed to be few options here in Williston, as Xander sped towards it and stopped his bike there.

"I can't believe we're doing this!" exclaimed Tor, as Kim parked his bike, while espying tarp lying in a black alley, which he brought over to cover their bikes with. Bikes like these in a looter town was asking for trouble.

Now the men opened the door and strode into the saloon in their heavy and long overcoats with blasters slung underneath, carrying enough firepower to level this bar into a smoking pile of rubble, but more importantly they needed intel.

A young blonde rolled up to them wearily, where French Company sat on the bar stools at the counter, and it had already been a long day for her at the usually packed bar. She was the only female there, noted Tor as he scanned the bar filled with Mexicans and Africans, and they had everyone's undivided attention. They didn't seem to know yet about the tactical nuke that had just gone off in the other section of town.

"A bottle of tequila, please," ordered Xander, thinking that this blonde resembled Mariela in some ways. But then she shook her head and let out a stream of Spanish. Probably Mexican.

"Hey Gringo, she wants to see your money first," chuckled a Mexican wearing a large sombrero, and who put his feet up on the table, while spilling some shot glasses onto the floor. He also wore a DARPA blaster around his waist. Obviously stolen from a DARPA depot. Kim dipped his hand under his overcoat and pulled out his wallet.

"You guys still take U.S dollars?"

"Si," she replied rudely taking his twenty, and she slammed a bottle of home-made tequila onto the table.

"But we prefer Mexican Pesos," she replied in broken English causing Tor to wince.

Xander took the bottle and turned to the men in the bar. A collection of swarthy and unshaven men covered with soot and grime.

"Looks like these folks here haven't had a shower in a while," commented Kim. Drew nodded checking nervously on his drones patrolling the outside perimeter. So far so good, but they had to make this fast.

"We're guns for hire," announced Tor to the crowd. "We want to become looters."

The crowd broke out into laughter.

"White Man, you're never gonna understand, will ya?"

"Fucking gringos!"

"Nada puta!"

Xander put up his hand.

"We have money to give you if you tell us where your leaders are!"

The crowd hooted some more.

Tor suddenly pulled out his blaster.

"We can tear up that Klan oil facility real good with these guns," he said quickly, as he had everyone's undivided attention. White boys who knew how to use blasters were at a premium.

"Are you Klan?" demanded an African who could smell their "whiteness" a mile away.

"Fuck no!" protested Xander truthfully, but the Africans were uneasy with this squad of white men. They were all usually Klan around here. The Mexicans mostly all high on tequila still had no clue that there was a nuclear assault on their town.

The bartender behind them leaned to tap Tor on the back.

"How much are you offering?" she demanded.

"Depends what you're selling," replied Xander laconically, as Kim pulled out his blaster to cover the crowd that was rumbling with suspicion now.

"I know the leaders of the Looter movement," she whispered conspiratorially. "But I can't take you to them. They would kill me."

Tor pulled out his phone with a digital map, and she looked hesitantly at the map. Tor helpfully pinched into downtown Williston where she recognized some cross streets.

She zoomed into a brown building where she dropped a pin.

"In the basement there you're going to find some of the most important guys," she whispered fiercely.

"What do you want in return?" Tor asked fishing out his wallet.

"Can you get me out of this town?"

Tor almost dropped his phone, while Xander turned grinning towards her.

"We just got here into town," he said.

"Cut the bullshit," she whispered again, and helpfully put another bottle of tequila on the table.

"I knew you guys were military the minute you walked in," she said now in perfect English.

Kim bared his teeth.

"Why the hell would you want to hang with White guys now?"

"'Cause Ronald Trump was right about the Mexicans," she said savagely pointing to the rag-tag bunch of looters in the bar. "And my life was over here the minute I helped you guys."

Tor nodded at her.

"We can get you out of town but sure as hell can't take you with us all the way."

"Somewhere down the road will be fine," she said wearily. "Don't look now, but here comes trouble."

The big Mexican had taken his legs off the table and now slurred his way towards Xander.

"*Puta,* what the fuck do you really want!" he demanded with his hand on his gun. Kim had his blaster out, but the belligerent Mexican didn't seem to care.

"Hey, look we don't want any trouble," said Tor suddenly putting his hands up and Kim lowered his blaster. "In fact, we're on our way out."
 Xander cautiously covered the room while exiting and the rest of French Company followed him.
"Putas!" swore the Mexican now laughing. The entire bar was now laughing at the Americans. Kim hated letting these people live, but they had a mission to complete first.
 Just then the Mexican turned and grabbed the bartender, but only to plunge a knife into her neck.
"No!" screamed Tor opening deafening fire to blast the Mexican to bits, while French Company decided to blast the entire bar which was drunkenly trying to reach for their blasters. In a few seconds everyone lay dead in the bar. Kim was bent over the bartender's bleeding neck, while Xander shone a flashlight on her neck. Kim took out a small 9mm bullet and quickly plugged it into her severed carotid vein upstream. That way the blood from her brain wouldn't all drain out. She moaned terribly.
 Kim then quickly broke open his battlefield medical kit to take out a needle and sutures and quickly began to suture her severed carotid vein, as Xander used a clamp to part the fascia to make the route to her vein easier, while Tor shone a strong xenon light onto the wound. In five minutes, Kim had sewed up her vein, and then used a skin glue to approximate the lacerated skin flaps back again. Then he tied a bandage around her neck as the bartender regained consciousness. Tor jabbed a powerful gram-positive antibiotic into her, along with another syringe full of morphine,
"Ok darling, don't move your neck for a few hours," he said, and she nodded weakly, as she stood up unsteadily in the devastated bar.
"You saved my life," she exhaled gratefully.
"Don't thank us yet," shrugged Kim. One of the looters was still alive and he moved to grab Kim's boot, who then took out his blaster. A jolt went through the looter's body with the blast, after which they quickly hurried out. Kim was carrying a *nanobot surgeon* too, but he was saving that for some major surgery. He looked at the bartender, as she staggered out grimly holding her neck straight. She was going to be alright.

South Africa

A couple of hyenas stared at the giant *Jackal Buzzard* that circled the skies above a ranch that stood in a field of maize that swayed gently in the wind. It looked like any other farm in the Western World with three giant threshers parked, and a host of other industrial machinery waiting for harvest season.

Suddenly, in the distance a car approached, while blasting music and it drew closer to the farmhouse down the winding road that seemed to be cared for in this middle of nowhere. It was a black Audi with Zyk fiddling with the radio as *darkpsy* music blasted out of the open windows, as if the occupants were trying to save on the air conditioning. Justine stared at the landscape that had suddenly appeared in their horizon emotionlessly.

"This is ridiculous!" screamed Zyk, as he saw the GPS location suddenly flash northern South Africa on his screen! Travis and Phillip also had crushed expressions as they realized that they had just left Persia and somehow impossibly driven into South Africa. They were thousands of miles off course now.

"Its Kali," said Justine through gritted teeth. All her plans for seeing England were being dashed by this insane goddess who seemed to be toying with them in a bad dream.

"But what on earth can we possibly accomplish here in South Africa?" demanded Zyk, looking up at the cream roof of the Audi, realizing that they were now at the lowermost tip of Africa. It would take them months to get back to Europe now. *They were essentially fucked.*

"Well it looks like Kali wants us to enter this farmhouse," mused Justine. She had realized much in Khorasan, and she now gazed at him with different eyes, as Zyk pulled the Audi up to the farm's porch, where Phillip and Travis exited the car quickly happy to stretch their legs again.

"Take your blasters with you," ordered Zyk opening the trunk, and Travis pulled out the big weapons from the trunk. He was losing his Klan discipline out here in Asia, well now Africa! "Scout out the area for some fuel. I'll knock on the front door."

The buzzard up above suddenly shrieked and dived low to swoop on a prey perilously close to them. Justine jumped and held onto Zyk's arm preventing him from knocking on the farmhouse's front door. He gazed exasperatedly at her and the African heat was not helping his temper, when just then the door was thrown open and a young blonde teenager held a rifle pointed at them. He regarded them suspiciously, as Justine's eyes widened even further.

"What are you guys doing here?" he asked in a relieved tone as he lowered the rifle, but he had a strange accent to his voice and set the rifle down to push his long sandy hair back. He was shirtless and wearing a pair of faded jeans and barefoot.

"We're lost," announced Zyk, as suddenly Travis and Phillip came in armed with their blasters and sneered at his rifle.

"Don't even think about it," said Phillip holding up his blaster. But now the boy was smiling as he stared at their KKK armbands.

"We're on the same side," he exclaimed, as Travis smiled broadly and lowered his blaster. A white boy.

"What the hell are you doing here on this farm all alone anyways, kid?"

"Well you're not that much older than me," replied the boy now.

"We're trained Space Marines," replied Travis pompously. "Almost special forces."

Justine rolled her eyes at Travis's inflated ego.

Zyk turned to the boy.

"Are you expecting any trouble?"

"Yes, *they're* trying to scare us off the farms," said the boy running his hand through his hair. "My parents and sister have gone to get supplies from town, so I'm in charge here for a couple of days."

"With what?" hooted Travis, noting his solitary rifle.

Phillip and Zyk were surprised too.

"Well the Blacks usually come with sticks and machetes, so a few rifle shots scare them away," said the boy defensively.

"Well if those niggers come back tonight," said Travis with feeling. He wasn't going to fire in the air. That was for sure.

"Travis!" glared Justine. "You can't say that!"

Everyone laughed in the room.

Zyk looked around the wooden farmhouse. It was a well-appointed European house with a single floor and three bedrooms with a lot of windows.

"Travis, scout the house for weak points," ordered Zyk, suddenly assuming command. "What's your name, boy?"

"Jayden," he replied, and went with Phillip and Travis to show them the house.

"This is all so racist!" exclaimed Justine turning to Zyk.

"Shut up," growled Zyk, as he peered out of the window and at the buzzard, but in the distance, hyenas were gathering up ahead. Kali didn't make mistakes, and something was coming tonight for them. They had the dead Pakistanis' Kalashnikovs too with them and they could fight the night out here, or just drive away.

"Zyk, I think that we should just leave," she said reading his thoughts and she was standing close to him now. But whatever attraction that he'd had for Justine was also over for him, and he felt nothing feeling her body touching his. He turned and walked away.

"Let's have a vote," he said finding the boys near a large French window. Jesus, this farmhouse was impossible to secure if the Africans came in large numbers.

"We're going to need to take the fight to them," said Zyk thoughtfully and Travis's eyes gleamed. That was the way he liked it too. Offense and not defense.

"There's smoke in the distance," observed Zyk.

Jayden nodded.

"That's the black folk that work here at the farm."

"Well that's going to be our first step then," said Zyk.

"No man, those are our workers. We don't want to spook them out. We want to live here permanently," protested Jayden. His father would give him hell if he chased away the farm hands.

"He's right," said Phillip.

Zyk nodded.

"Alright then we wait for them to come to us."

Travis looked disappointed.

"Whatever batteries you have in your blasters, you're going to use 'em from the roof," said Zyk, and the two Klan soldiers disappeared upstairs.

"Come with me," said Zyk to Jayden, while heading to his Audi, where he took out the Pakistani Kalashnikovs from the boot causing young Jayden's eyes to widen with pleasure.

"The ANC Government wouldn't let us arm," he said bitterly.

"Get a taste of American Freedom," chuckled Zyk giving him a few extra magazines.

They made their way to the roof where Justine was already there surveying the forest that lay beyond the tall maize. At night, it would be hard to spot anything coming.

Zyk also took in the boring farm surroundings.

"What the hell do you do here all day?" he demanded turning to Jayden, who suddenly whipped out a long cigarette and held it up. He lit it and took a deep puff —— probably hash. The Klan boys took the cigarette and took a deep hit and then passed it to Zyk, who looked at it questioningly.

"What if the Africans attack and we're all stoned?" he asked warily surveying the surroundings with the setting sun.

"Come on, even if the niggers come, we can scare them away with a few blaster rounds," said Travis, but his words seemed to slur, and his eyes were in a faraway place. Zyk wondered if an escape was the order of the day. Kali was already messing with them and besides what could a few puffs do as everyone was already liberally puffing away. Zyk then took the fateful decision that would end tragically for them, and he put the cigarette to his lips and inhaled the foul-smelling smoke deeply. Suddenly, he felt himself falling into a kaleidoscope and Justine began screaming. Then the dark figure of Kali was there, and she had been waiting for Justine.

For this moment.

Now Zyk was powerless as he fell almost into the skies and out of his mind into a dark corner of the Universe which was suddenly lit up by spinning chakras of colorful light. A voice started to speak in his mind.

"These are the galaxies that spin by you as you travel as an Astral Being," said a soothing voice. Now Zyk forgot about Justine and focused in wonder at the stars and black emptiness that whizzed by. This was faster than the speed of light.

"Did you really think that you could travel so fast with your physical body? Its so heavy."

"Of course, now I am free to travel at the speed of thought," remarked Zyk. But it would be so much better to have the physical body too. An even more sensual experience, but it was like reading a book. Just the mind and the idea of the book. Zyk suddenly entered a planet's atmosphere and hurtled through gathered beings, much smaller than him, with strange features. Aliens, who ignored him, but continued about their business like nothing mattered.

"What does all this mean?" demanded Zyk.

"Its as you want it to be," replied the voice.

Suddenly, to Zyk's horror the aliens began to change into Africans and then the screaming started.

Zyk awoke streaming with sweat only to see Justine and the Klan boys all tied up to adjacent trees. Fuck, how long had he been tripping?

A deep and frightening African voice broke into the night.

"Oh, we got that white devil," said a man in military fatigues and combat boots. "I do this to set an example to the White devils to leave South Africa before we kill all of them."

Justine shrieked.

"What's going to happen to us?"

"You will be my wife tonight," he said turning to her holding a threatening machete. She screamed even more in horror. Under the moonlight, the machete gleamed though parts of it were dulled by blood.

"Where the hell is Jayden?" demanded Zyk. The last thing he remembered was the little fucker and his DMT cigarette.

The African laughed heartily which sent chills down Zyk's spine.

A sack was brought by soldiers and emptied on the ground. A head. Jayden's blonde head fell heavily and bounced ridiculously as if it was a football. The Africans giggled uncontrollably now.

Fire burned inside Zyk and he closed his eyes in dark rage. He concentrated as if to search for his own power as a wave of powerful emotion swept through him. Meanwhile, the men now went over to Justine and began to play with her hair.

"She is beautiful," exclaimed one of them laying a machete on her cheek. Justine screamed again turning to Zyk, but who seemed to be in a faraway place.

A vision was now playing again in his mind of giant gods in space and a few rocks broke off under Zyk's feet. *Something was awakening underneath him.*

"Look boss, this man is Voodoo man!" exclaimed another soldier as suddenly the ground began to cave mysteriously around the tree.

"A witch demon!" cried the soldier, as the commander with his hot and sweaty face felt terror.

"Shall we kill them?" asked the soldiers. "We can't let anyone live. We'll get into trouble in *Pretoria* otherwise."

Suddenly, a man was standing there along with an ox. It was the same man from Mohenjo-Daro in Pakistan.

The man with the blind ox.

"Kill them all!" roared Zyk, as the soldiers trained their automatics on the man with the huge black ox with big milky cataract filled eyes.

The Commander began to laugh as he realized that the ox was blind, and it was a frail weak old man standing there.

"He's going to kill us?"

The rest of the soldiers joined in the laughter and even Justine looked at Zyk disparagingly. But now the laughing men realized that the silent old man had unslung the rope from the ox and like a lasso whirled it around his head. They laughed even harder, but then a sudden realization set in. Wherever they turned, there was the old man with the whirling rope that was now writhing like a burning snake, and whose head reared up to an impossible size.

"But its a cobra!" shouted the Commander, and the men opened heavy Kalashnikov fire at the seven cobras that hovered over their heads in a giant blaze of fire. The bullets simply passed through the Cobra heads, but when the fangs descended, they were real enough as they chose their targets. The soldier next to Justine was snatched away in fiery blast of hot air. She felt her hair burn but the ropes too burned, and she quickly freed herself to go and untie Zyk. But he wasn't there. She whirled around and there was only the headless soldiers and snakes in the burning forest. The two unconscious American soldiers were still there though. Zyk had abandoned them all and fear shot through her heart. They were going to burn here tonight as she saw headless African soldiers spurting liters of blood all around her. Screams filled her ears as a massacre of the squad of Government African troops took place and there would be no mercy tonight as she watched a giant cobra's fangs puncture Travis's and Phillip's bodies too. Just then a gigantic cobra appeared in the skies over her head and she remembered her mother and how the sky had fallen on her just a few days back. A dull thud and she wondered if this was death? There was no pain, but then her eyes rolled as if on a roller-coaster, while her vision was filled with burning grass and then there was merciful darkness.

13

Jesus in Berlin

A lonely tram snaked its way through East Berlin in the night and there was a check-post up ahead where it slowed to a halt. Police bounded into the tram and confronted the two long-haired men.

"Papieren bitte," demanded one of them, barely out of his teens, and KKK Grandmaster Luke waved a hand across his face.

"You don't need our papers," he said. Jesus grinned next to him and also waved his hand across the young officer's face.

Suddenly, the officer pulled out a gun.

"I'm not going to ask you clowns for your papers again," he said in English this time.

"Err...we don't have any papers," said Luke. "But I have my Georgia driver's license on me." He gave it to the officer, who examined it suspiciously. What on earth was an American doing in nuclear blasted Berlin?

"And I'm a refugee," said Jesus simply winking at Luke, who grinned back.

"Oh, a refugee?" enquired the officer now quite politely.

"Yes, from Israel," he said. "I'm a Jew, you see."

The officer nodded and the pair quickly exited the train. Stupid Germans thought Luke letting go of his blaster now. The officer had been that close to death.

"What the hell are we doing in Berlin anyways?"

"The Russians are here in the Western sector and we need to see what we can do for them," said Jesus.

Now Luke began to think. What the hell was Jesus smoking? This was turning out to be a weird LSD dream over here and a panic seized his heart for he knew his Lord was not the drug taking kind, but he was the Lord and Jesus could do as he pleased. He gazed at the nuclear blasted landscape of Berlin. Maybe the Russians knew something. They approached the blasted TV tower that the Russians had authorized to be built in the 60's. Alexanderplatz itself seemed deserted, as paper flitted around in circles in the dimly lit night inside the giant concrete courtyard serving as the transport hub for Berlin. Before the obliteration of its U-Bahn system, while the S-Bahn was miraculously still running on most lines along with the night bus.

Luke caught up with Jesus in the dark night and grabbed his arm.

"Will you tell me what the hell is going on?"

"The Russians have all the answers," replied Jesus mysteriously.

"Do you mean Puzin is over here?"

Jesus threw his head back and laughed.

"No man, but they usually have some good alcohol on them," replied Jesus now laughing at the thought of meeting Puzin on Alexanderplatz. How ridiculous.

A dark and cold wind blew through Berlin causing Luke to feel the hair rise on his neck, while a feeling of dark despair arose within his breast. Wasn't Jesus supposed to be the Lord of Light? But he felt no light right now, only a feeling of being extremely lost in a gloomy dimension that he didn't understand. Oh yes, this didn't feel like Earth anymore or maybe Germany was never part of Earth?

Up ahead the sound of soldiers marching in unison. Jackboots. Since when did the Russians march like that? A grey mist covered much of the U2, U-Bahn station. It was a gigantic arena but somewhere in the dark mist there were soldiers marching.

"Halt! Papieren!" demanded a voice, but much harsher this time. It didn't sound like Russian either.

Suddenly, the mist lifted, and Luke was amazed to see a squad of German soldiers in black uniforms, while their helmets sported twin SS lightnings printed in white on their black helmets.

They were speaking in English. Ok. So, he was dreaming alright.

But then the arms that grabbed him were real and suddenly he was taken to a tall man standing stiffly wearing a long black leather greatcoat.

"Hello," said the tall man shaking hands with Luke, while noting Luke's KKK inscription on his lapels. The KKK was older than the SS as an organization.

"Who are you?" demanded Luke in a dazed voice.

"I am SS General Heinz Wolf."

A chill went down Luke's spine. That no good Jesus had landed them in the worst possible place.

"Err...nice to meet you."

Suddenly, there was a line of men behind the SS General and he walked over to them with his pistol drawn and began to casually shoot them quickly.

"They are regular German Army deserters," said the SS General returning, while Luke remembered how he'd executed Jews back in America. Was it Karma?

"You have a chance to live if you join the fight with your Aryan brothers against the Russian sub-humans who are invading Berlin as we speak."

Luke nodded and was suddenly given a Sturmgewehr-44 automatic with a few clips along with a *tiger-striped* SS tunic that he wore over his Klan blouse, and was hastily given a piece of stamped paper announcing that he was a SS volunteer. The paper had a big red swastika on top.

"This paper will help you to survive the military police who will shoot you otherwise as a deserter."

"But wait, I thought the war was over," protested Luke.

The SS General turned to a parked car and clambered aboard.

"For the SS, it's never over! Heil Hitler!"

"Heil Hitler," mumbled Luke, though it sounded funny with his Georgia twang. He needed to practice the Hitler salute to blend in with the locals here. The car quickly took off with the SS soldiers marching resolutely behind it. From behind the large S-Bahn building, suddenly Jesus emerged.

"Phew that was a close one," he said grinning from ear to ear. Luke had a sudden desire to shoot Jesus with his newly acquired weapon.

"Thanks Jesus," muttered Luke through gritted teeth. In the distance came the boom of heavy guns.

"Are those the Russians that you wanted to meet?"

Jesus giggled.

"I think that there is some kind of a time warp going on here," Jesus said suddenly seriously as he closed his eyes. "A very mysterious person is changing how we perceive time and his mind is warping history. Different time realities are crashing like waves into each other."

Luke smirked at him.

"Hell, I thought that *you* were the son of God."

"Yes, but this person is rising fast and letting loose the Underworld," said Jesus, finally looking worried enough to convince Luke. "He draws his power from the Old Ones."

Suddenly, a few bullets whizzed by Luke. Russian voices in the distance.

Jesus now turned to run, as Luke realized that they were being shot at and he turned to let loose a hail of bullets that drew a few cries from the brown hordes gathering at Alexanderplatz.

He caught up with Jesus who seemed to be headed somewhere fast like he knew where.

There were German soldiers manning positions all along their flight, and the SS soldiers stared curiously at the long-haired Jesus in sandals and brown robes hurrying away with what appeared to be another long-haired man bizarrely dressed in an SS tunic over black leather pants.

French Company

"Target acquired?" demanded Kim speaking into his com, while the wounded bartender, Jane, still grimly held onto him, as Kim's bike sped across downtown Williston.

"Negative," said Tor. "Find out from Jane where the HQ is."

Kim nodded and gesticulated to Jane in the wind, who then started to point directions.

Their motorcycles thundered along the wet and shiny road with their thick twenty-inch tires hugging the asphalt.

"Straight ahead and take a left at the intersection," she pointed in sign language. Just then the buildings next to them began to incinerate in slow motion, while a deafening boom threatened their motorcycles.

"Incoming!" shouted Xander happily. He knew this game well and he was in his element. *Under fire.*

Kim pulled ahead leading the way with Jane pointing towards the crumbling intersection. Silver missiles now gleamed overhead on their HUD's as they slammed all around them.

"This doesn't look like the looters," screamed Kim, as he hung a left and behind him lay vast exploding fireballs.

"Into the basement of that building!" shouted Jane. "That's the looter Command center heavily reinforced with concrete. We'll be safe in there!"

Just as Kim was about to turn into it, he saw a green laser, and turned to see Xander zooming by him with his black helmet.

"Incoming!"

Xander had just laser designated it and Kim swore at his callousness as he gunned his engine ferociously after him.

"Alright boys, the Klan is getting impatient," said Tor receiving a transmission from the Klan facility. "Accelerate to maximum velocity!"

More silver missiles. A message flashed in the corner of their HUDs, as suddenly the street was torn into an orange ball and French company rocketed away as fast as they could out of there.

"This is President Trump!" exclaimed a beaming Trump back in his normal trademark business suit. "Mission accomplished!"

French Company realized that it was Trump's personal air strikes on the town. A surreal reality TV show.

"You guys had better get out of Dodge since I'm going to be dropping the MOAB over there."

"Yes sir!"

"We got your laser coordinates and we're going to blow that block in a square mile radius. No underground structure can survive our MOAB," said Trump and he pressed a button on the screen.

"Ten seconds, boys!" Trump smiled and disappeared from their HUD's.

"What's his bleeding hurry?" snarled Kim worried of what the MOAB would do their behinds and also at this entire pointless mission. Well almost, as he remembered the beautiful Jane sitting behind him.

"You just gotta ride faster, old man," replied Xander on the com.

French Company were relieved to see that Trump waited not ten seconds but twenty seconds before they saw the town explode into a million pieces on their HUD's. French Company roared onto the interstate at 180 miles an hour and screamed away into the sunset.

Zyk's darkness

Zyk was in a dark chamber, and something stank in here like it had been rotting slowly for over a hundred years. He wrinkled his nose and thought of Justine and the Klan boys. He remembered how they died, like an out of body experience. Kali's final revenge. Was he dead too?

Was this what DMT felt like? Scared him shitless to leave his body and journey through space never to return. Well this was the mother of tripping alright and he would be glad if it ended. He looked at his body. Intact, still wearing his leather jacket over his black jeans and boots. He got up struggling to his feet. At least the surroundings were dry, but they gave him the jitters, when somebody shuffled and the resulting echo wasn't very big, so this cave was small. There was faint light up ahead showing a window with iron bars. What the hell? Was he in jail? He laughed at the thought. Had the Africans thrown him in a South African jail? But he'd seen the Blind Ox man destroy them all. *No survivors.*

"Who's there?" demanded Zyk tepidly. He wondered if Kali would show up again to rescue him.

A shaky voice cried out in the cave which then echoed feebly. Somebody really old who then struck a match.

A sluggish fire made its way towards a thick and gnarled candle on a heavy table roughly carved out of stout oak as if crafted in darkness, when a gnarled heavy hand suddenly gripped the fat and yellow candle causing a cry to escape Zyk's lips. They ended not in nails but thick claws. Definitely not the humankind and Zyk felt fear. Zyk then wondered if he spoke English.

"Yes, I speak English," said the voice wearily as it lifted the heavy, twisted, and curved candle towards a hideous face covered with white hair that seemed like overgrown grass. But the horror was not complete as then Zyk noticed two ancient and scaly structures extending from his back.

"Yes, those are my wings," wheezed the old man. "I am a fallen angel, you see."

Zyk looked confused now. He had thought Kali was paramount in the galaxies. The old angel apparently knew his thoughts and laughed.

"There are a great many things that you will now learn, young one," he wheezed now with laughter. The damp and rotten air in here was not doing him too much good, though neither would it be healthy for Zyk and he needed to escape from here.

"Escape?" demanded the demented angel now as it flapped its wings excitedly, while spilling hot wax all over its hand and causing it to cry out in pain. But then the angel's eyes lit up excitedly.

"You want to escape from here?" he asked incredulously. "Do you know that you are with *Elohim* and that I have been cursed by arch-angel *Gabriel* himself for 50,000 years into this bottomless hole under ten thousand seas of red mercury!"

A shudder ran through Zyk's shoulders and he suddenly felt cold and damp. A miserable feeling that he would never become warm again in this place. At least he wasn't dead like Justine.

"Yes, she's dead but only because you gave Kali permission to kill her," said the angel wickedly now with the flame dancing grotesquely on the angel's milky-white cataract filled eyes. "You let her go in your mind."

Zyk turned away and wondered if he'd let go of the Klan boys too. He was pissed with that South African kid, Kayden, who had given them DMT and caused them to be captured. Well. Maybe.

"What the hell am I doing here with you?" demanded Zyk now unhappy in this cell with this imprisoned angel.

"Why?" echoed the prisoner Angel bitterly. "What did I ever do to deserve this punishment but tried to defend Yahweh against the Rebellion of Gabriel."

"So, where the *fuck* is God?" snarled Zyk with a sudden viciousness that surprised even Elohim. He smiled now, and let his wings drop that had been bunched up with tension.

He began to giggle and then laughed hard, finally dissolving into a torrent of a hacking laugh.

"Yes, that God," said Elohim. "He made me from fire, so I have seen him. He is real."

"But he is dead the way he behaves so passively," shouted Zyk now with anger. Elohim now stared at Zyk carefully.

"Your nose is too straight, and your hair is not curly," he said finally.

"Yes, I'm no Jew," swore Zyk.

"Ah, a Jew hater now trapped with a Jewish angel," said Elohim trying to smell him deeper. He didn't have the Semitic smell either. "There has been a mistake. You should not be here with me."

Zyk nodded eagerly. Maybe he could wake up from all this like a bad dream. After all, he was no Jew and he stared into Elohim's eyes.

Suddenly the angel laughed again and Zyk realized that he was having him on.

"Can't believe you fell for that one," he giggled maliciously. Zyk felt himself being crushed. This angel obviously had no idea what was going on causing a despondency to settle over him and he approached the window. The only respite from the dark cave was the window, which was encased in thick glass that separated them from the thick and dark-red mercury that flowed lazily like half-clotted blood. This could just be hell, and Zyk turned back into the cave, where the suddenly exhausted angel shuffled back to his bed. Zyk followed him and took the candle when the angel set it down on the table.
"There isn't much to explore here," said Elohim in a small voice. Zyk nodded. "There is some wood in the back and an axe. You can make a bed for yourself, that is, if you want one."
Zyk took the candle and headed over deeper into the dark cave. Shadows filled it with the gnarled candle illuminating ghostly beings that howled all around him. The whole place was haunted alright, thought Zyk with a shudder. Talk about trouble. And right now, his trouble was with the Higher Angels or maybe even with God, which caused a wave of rage to course through him and he swore to make someone pay. He had lived life reacting to higher powers, but now he wanted to be in command now.
Even over God.

Luke on Wilhelmstraße

Berlin, 1945, and this was the Nazi held sector of Berlin, where 13-year-old Hitler Youths marched to-and-fro on the cobbled streets with bazookas. Heavy ordinance lay scattered everywhere with volunteers helping themselves to the weapons, while a little blonde played with a hand-grenade. Jesus ran up to her.
"Hey, little girl," he said taking the grenade gently away from her and put it into his pocket. "Soon it will all be over."
The girl turned to her mother.
"Mom, he's saying the war will soon be over."
Jesus turned happily to the frightened mother, when an SS officer came quickly over to Jesus and slapped him hard across the face with his black leather gloved hand in the chilly and smoky afternoon.
"Nothing is over!" he screamed and went away.

The girl turned to Jesus now.

"You are a coward and a defeatist. Final victory for Adolf Hitler!"

Luke came and smiled sheepishly at the girl, while grabbing Jesus by the arm and wheeled him away. This was a sure way to get executed for nothing and Luke didn't want to die. *Not in Germany and not for Hitler.*

An elaborate parade was taking place in the distance and before Luke's stunned eyes it was Hitler presenting the Iron Cross medal to young teenagers of the *HitlerJugend.*

"Dude," whistled Jesus.

Luke nodded.

"Let's go get an autograph," said Jesus, and before Luke could stop him, the son of God had scampered off to Hitler.

Adolf Hitler had an expression of distaste at being interrupted in his final days and gazed testily into Jesus's eyes. He didn't have much time to live.

"Mr Hitler, what you're doing with the moneylenders is something that I dreamed of on the Cross," said Jesus coming in-between a Hitler Youth teenager and *Adi.*

"And who are you?" demanded Hitler irritably at this character who seemed least involved in the defense of Berlin.

"I'm Jesus Christ, and dude you have no idea how these people had it coming," he said.

"Why didn't you do something about it?" asked Hitler gruffly noting Jesus's wounded hands and feet.

"Well, you know we became observers in the grand scheme of things," admitted Jesus.

"And that's why I lost faith in you!" fumed Hitler. "I had to take matters into my own hands because you lot were too abstract."

"I know and I forgive and respect you," said Jesus and kissed Hitler's forehead.

Hitler's hand dropped to his Walther pistol.

SS soldiers suddenly grabbed Jesus.

Hitler looked at Jesus.

"All this love will get you nowhere!" he shouted and strode away to return to inside his bunker, while nursing his trembling left hand. At the bunker's entrance, he stopped and shouted, "Its too late anyways!"

Then he hurried in, the last time he was seen alive.

Jesus gazed forlornly after him and cried out,

"When you die, I'll be there for you. I promise."

Luke came and grabbed Jesus's arm.

"Look, can't you see that no one here in Germany gives a shit about your love and salvation?"

Luke led him away.

"Its ok to talk to chicks and shit like that, but to Adolf?" chuckled Luke as he replayed the scene in his mind.

"Dude, even Men need love."

"Not these men," muttered Luke, as more Hitler Youth teenagers with crazy haircuts holding bazookas hurried to the frontlines determined to stop the Russians at any cost.

The Third Reich would live on for a thousand years indeed.

Jesus would see to that.

Ronald Trump

Hef Sessions was there in the room with Trump by the fireplace of the newly rebuilt White House, and it seemed that the aliens were finally respecting Planet Earth and were paradoxically quiet after Trump's fearsome DARPA attack.

"So you see that our Force Field has struck the fear of God in them," boasted Ronald Trump looking coldly at Hef, and he hadn't forgiven his earlier betrayal in the Justice Department, but then Hef was doing his best to squirm his way back into Trump's good graces as an Alabama Senator.

"The newly reconstituted FBI is hunting down the last Democrat leader in the USA, sir. All the top leaders are being pursued in full cooperation with the Klan Police."

"Well you have no choice, or the Klan would execute the lot of you," said Trump sharply, but he wasn't comfortable with the Klan assuming so much power either. He had already had that run in with the Grandmaster Luke, but he'd been either killed or was missing since an alien strike on the Klan facility where they'd been interrogating Hillary. Apparently, an alien had been living inside her.

Yuck! Trump's face grew disgusted as he remembered shaking hands with her in the 2016 elections. Now, in 2021, the world was scarcely recognizable. So much had changed. Aliens had destroyed the planet right after the nuclear war, and he remembered his pendant, which he felt for, and Hef Sessions grew alarmed as he recognized the swastika. Trump grinned at him evilly and then stared out of the window.

Where was this mysterious human that the aliens were searching for anyways?

Zyk and Elohim

Behind the cave lay stacks of chopped tree trunks, from which Zyk was supposed to carve his future bed out from, and he gazed at the gleaming axe buried in one of the tree trunks. Despair settled over him. Then his mind began to work. Where had the wood come from? He grasped and wrenched out the sharp axe from the wood and went to explore further in the darkness. There was some faint illumination around the corner of the cave, and as he turned the corner, a chilly wind blew and to his surprise trees appeared. Tall trees and the earth was now soft, moist soil, into which the trees sank deep into. He turned back but the cave was now shrouded in mist. Strange, but fear made Zyk's heart race when he suddenly saw birds ——prehistoric birds up above. One of them cried out fearsomely and dived like an eagle straight for him. The axe was heavy but Zyk swung mightily and just in time to smash the bird's head against a tree trunk. That was close! The axe was now covered in blood and Zyk knew that he wasn't alone in that swing. He had played a little baseball, but that swing was awe-inspiringly not him.

This forest adventure was so much better than constructing his bed. He couldn't imagine spending time with the fallen angel in that depressing cave, and there was so much more beyond the cave than Elohim had let on. *Lying cunt.* Anyways, he pushed on excited to have some kind of hope out of here. Who was guiding him, and he wondered about Kali? But this was way out of Kali's league. Now he was on another planet, probably not even in the Milky Way galaxy. He thought about Justine. *Had he really condemned her to death?* He pushed those thoughts out again and he'd be dead too if he didn't escape from this place quickly, and which had a very unhealthy air to it. Where were the seas of Mercury or had it all been an illusion?

"No, that old angel wasn't lying," said a voice from behind him and he turned to see a gleaming figure in ghostly white.

"And who might you be?" demanded Zyk with the axe at the ready.

"I am Gabriel, the angel of war," replied the ghostly figure, and Zyk observed that he had fire in the center of his body, burning bright. A fiery creature indeed.

"What do you want from me?"

"Why did you give up on God?" demanded the Angel. Zyk realized that this guy was a fruitcake too.

"I mean, don't get me wrong," added Gabriel hastily. "I led the rebellion and one of the reasons that God is nowhere to be seen these days."

"Where did you guys banish him?"

"He just disappeared after that," said Gabriel. "And I want to talk to you about this issue."

"What?" snorted Zyk contemptuously. He hated weakness. "Find your missing God?"

"Something like that," nodded Gabriel. "You are parting dimensions like us so that means you are powerful."

"Yeah, but all that power has done me squat," said Zyk sardonically.

"Look, I can give you a few pointers, but you're still made of space dust, so you're never going to become as powerful as us Angels."

"You mean like Lucifer?"

"Well, he's the guy that got us into trouble in the first place, and I really don't want to talk about that imbecile," said Gabriel with his eyes flashing. "I'm going to help you, but if you see God then let him know that we want to let him back into the Garden of Eden. Our rebellion is over."

"That's completely cool man, I want a few words with that *cat* too," said Zyk feeing that this seemed like a good deal. Far better than shacking up with that morose Elohim.

"Well you know all the power lies in your mind. All you have to do is re-draw the neuronal circuits to redirect your electro-magnetic energy towards your Will."

Zyk laughed now and it reminded him of something suddenly.

"You mean something like digital circuits versus analog circuits in the computer."

"Exactly," said Gabriel, and he suddenly disappeared after this mighty tip that left Zyk quite perplexed. He had seen virtual circuits in the computer more than adequately match the old silicon-circuits in music synthesizers. He had to make his mind into a synthesizer.

"I am the Synthesizer!" bellowed Zyk suddenly within the haunted forest. "Do you hear that? I am going to rearrange atoms and make you undone!"

A fantasy, but it felt good to let out all his fear with this bravado. After all, he had just been told by no less than the Arch-angel Gabriel himself that he was going to meet God.

French Company

The four DARPA modded Kawasaki Ninjas hurtled towards the Klan base, while behind them the looter town lay exploding, while the mushroom fireball could be seen for miles. Kim shook his head.

He spoke into his com irritably, "If Ronald wanted to blow the whole town, then why the hell were we sent in there in the first place?"

"I guess those Klan bastards wanted us dead," said Tor grimly.

"Expendables," added Xander, and Drew nodded as he pulled up his bike to him. Jane was hanging on grimly to Kim despite a leaky *carotid*. She was a fighter.

Suddenly, the computer flashed a message on their screens on the shiny highway.

"French Company be advised, new orders," droned the computer.

What the hell, felt Tor. This was complete torture and taking advantage of his good nature. He was going to have to take this up with Trump.

"French Company is to return to Los Angeles, California, where a Democrat stronghold under Hillary Fenton has been detected."

Kim laughed our loud. This was beyond ridiculous.

"Hillary Fenton has been declared an Enemy of the State and is currently negotiating with the Aliens to effect an American surrender. Your job is to assassinate all Democrats engaged in surrendering to the Aliens. President Trump's standing orders are *'no surrender, no retreat'*. Fight till the last man. Hillary Fenton is to be terminated with extreme prejudice."

"Or till we burn this planet real good," muttered Kim.

Xander grinned as he looked up to see three jets hovering high above them. "I wonder if we can keep the bikes."

Pretty soon a B-72 bomber, DARPA's latest nuclear bomber dropped just over them. It hovered now in midair like a chopper.

"Now that's what I call a pick-up," said Tor, and Jane was still holding her neck, but aghast to see such a mammoth jet landing in the middle of the mountains of North Dakota.

"This is the United States Air Force, baby," boasted Xander, and Jane despite her torn vein glared at him.

"I'm an American too," she protested.

"Xander, cut it out," said Tor heading towards the aircraft which landed heavily on the ground.

"Look, it even has rotors like a helicopter for vertical landing and takeoff," whistled Xander impressed with the new DARPA hardware. The cavernous backside opened up and French Company's bikes roared in at top speed. The door closed and the jet swiftly took off again into the skies as more missiles streaked towards Williston town.

The looters wouldn't be bothering the Klan's oil-refineries again for a very long time after this.

Meanwhile, inside the jet, French Company got a briefing on L.A through a giant computer-generated hologram where a male voice briefed them on their mission.

"The city of Los Angeles had been sealed off by the 101st and the 81st Divisions of the US Army. All movement has been interdicted to and out of the city."

Kim stared at the burnt layout of Los Angeles on the hologram as drone footage streamed miles of nuked L.A.

However, radiation levels had been brought under control by the Ionizer machines, while many prefabricated buildings were springing up with people returning to the city.

"About half-a-million residents are living in there again and among them somewhere is Hillary and her fifth column. You will have your DARPA motorcycles to scout out Los Angeles for the suspects and terminate them to complete your mission."

The hologram disappeared.

Meanwhile, a medical robot was tending to Jane's wound with antiseptics and new bandages. Then a protective plaster was applied for the skin sutures to heal properly.

Zyk in the Underworld

The forest progressively got thicker and darker till Zyk noticed a more menacing air here. Something very dark lived here and he could hear a faint beat in the air.

"What's this?" he wondered. Who could be playing Darkpsy trance here in the middle of nowhere?

He followed the sound like he used to in the old days in Goa searching for secret parties in the middle of the night. *But here?*

A blazing light suddenly lit up ahead. An old woman appeared suddenly in front of him holding a lantern in one hand, though wizened and used a stick to walk.

"Where are you going?" she asked gazing at him.

"Actually, I have no idea," replied Zyk. "I'm just following the music."

She almost dropped the lantern in fright.

"What?" she demanded in a quivering voice. "You can hear music in this god-forsaken place?"

"Of course," replied Zyk perplexed. Obviously, the old bat had lost control of her faculties and he now tried to impatiently pass her.

"Wait," she said. "Don't go that path. That music is the call of demons."

Not only was she hard of hearing, but she was senile too, when suddenly, another woman appeared, much younger and fairer. Zyk slowed down. Well now, that darkpsy music could wait a little, though he was excited to meet his kind of people there.

"There are other types of music playing too leading to different paths," explained the younger one with a smile, and suddenly in the distance he could hear some tribal music.

"Sounds like some African drums," said Zyk disdainfully.

"What's wrong with the Africans?"

"Nothing wrong with the nigg...err...I mean Africans," said Zyk. "Just that I have a date with with the darkpsy people."

"There lies darkness and blood," wailed the younger one suddenly, while upset that her charms had failed her. Zyk wanted to tell her its not you or the hag, its the African music.

"Mass murderers and the vipers of humanity live where you go."

"That doesn't seem so bad," said Zyk now looking forward to this meeting. Maybe they even had some good LSD there. "Any Germans in there?"

The old hag clapped her forehead.

"Any Germans there!"

The fair maiden stepped forward to hold the swooning hag.

"Its full of them!"

"Well that settles it then!" said Zyk and whistled a merry tune as he put his hands in his pockets to turn towards the horrific sounds of murder and mayhem with heavy beats. The music gave him new energy as he glided towards the sound, his sound. Well he was almost there. But wait, another shimmering light in the distance. That old Jewish angel, Elohim. He flew to him.

"Come on, where you go is far from God," warned Elohim hovering above him. "Don't you have any feelings for your own God?"

Zyk kept on walking with no answer.

"The Jews and Arabs are on the same side. Its the Germans that are our enemy," he whispered in Zyk's ear.

"I know," he replied smiling now. *Finally, some honesty.*

"You know Hitler is in the Underworld," he pleaded. "Come on, he's our race enemy."

"Your's Jew, not mine." Zyk smiled again. As far as he was concerned, Abraham had nothing to do with him.

"So, you are lost to the Semites and our Heaven with 72 virgins will forever be closed to you if you side with the Aryans."

"The 72 virgins of paradise can go eat coke," replied Zyk warmly.

"Gabriel, say something to him," pleaded Elohim.

Suddenly, another angel landed on Zyk's right shoulder.

"My name is Harut," he said, while another perched on his left.

"And I am Marut."

Zyk smiled and wondered if the Aryans would allow this gaggle of Arabic and Jewish angels around him to enter the Underworld.

"Look, I have nothing to do with you guys," said Zyk calculating that he wasn't far now.

"Come come, surely you don't mean that," said Elohim again.

"Hark, do you see the Mercedes?" asked Zyk now. In a forest clearing, a swastika pennant fluttered under a spotlight on a long and gleaming black Mercedes-Benz 770 with six axles.

"Oh, shit bro, that's the *man's* car," whispered Gabriel in awe.

"Do you think that he would spare us Arab angels?" asked Harut and Marut together.

"Shut up the lot of you," said Zyk, remembering Berlin's hottest club Berghain, and where those pretty Swedish blondes had gotten him rejected at the door. He was determined to make it in. "Disappear, the lot of you."

"What?" asked an enraged Elohim. "You know we are made of fire."

"Those are SS soldiers guarding the entrance to the Underworld," whispered Marut as he stared at the gleaming black SS steel helmets and the swastikas that caused the Jewish angels such pain to see their resurrection.

"Oh, we will wreak hell there soon," swore Elohim.

"Hell, in hell?" asked Zyk, walking over to the car as the soldiers stared curiously at him.

"Hi there," said Zyk to the soldiers who turned nonchalantly to him and stared at him.

"What do you want?" they demanded in cold and hard voices.

'Er...wanted to enter," said Zyk weakly.

"Submit to this DNA detector first," said one of the soldiers noting Zyk's tanned skin color — an efficient way of racial profiling.

The computer blinked a red light with a complete DNA analysis.

"Aryan DNA markers for a thousand years of the Asiatic-Persian haplo-type. Confirmed Non-Negro, Non-Jewish, non-Arab presence. Racial purity acceptable. Energy readings high. Psychic activity levels of Artist class."

The light turned green.

"Hey, does that mean we're in?" demanded Gabriel. Zyk inwardly glared at the idiot.

"So, can I pass?" asked Zyk with his heart in his mouth, as the tall SS soldiers looked down their long noses with their cold eyes at the computer results.

"Not so fast," said one of the guards.

"What's the password?" asked the other one. Gabriel and Elohim, too, were waiting with bated breaths. This was historic. The Jews could just be entering the Aryans-only Underworld.

"Err...*Heil Hitler?*"

"Nope that was last week."

"*Loyalty and Courage,*" said Zyk wracking his brain for the password.

"See, only a true Aryan would know the password," gloated one of the soldiers.

"That one was last month."

"Wait, how about, *Blood and Soil?*"

Dead silence from the soldiers now.

"Bingo!" laughed Gabriel, and he knew when the deal was sealed.

The door to the Underworld opened and the soldiers stood aside.

"Remember, no pictures inside. What happens in the Underworld stays in the Underworld. And one last thing."

"What's that?" asked Zyk about to enter.

"Lose the angels."

Jesus and Luke

Jesus turned to Luke, who looked questioningly at him, as bullets whizzed by.

"Something weird is happening," Jesus said suddenly turning pale. "A new force is entering the realm of Time."

"Yeah, its the Russians firing at us!" shouted Luke, as the bullets crept towards their hiding position. But just then an SS tank trundled past them towards the swarm of Russian infantrymen and squashed the scuttling brown uniformed soldiers under its heavy tank tracks. The shrieks of men mixed with squealing tank tracks.

"The Lord has Salvation planned for us," gloated Jesus, staring at the SS manned heavy Tiger tank.

"That was close," said Luke realizing that there wasn't going to be an easy escape from this one like Jerusalem.

"We need to go back to Adolf's bunker," said Jesus. "The Underworld is up to something."

"Wait, hold on now Jesus," said Luke. "Hitler and the Klan are on the same side."

"So am I," said Jesus, "but there is a time-warp that is happening and its threatening to change history even as we know it."

"Hey, remember I'm a KKK Grandmaster," said Luke, but then he caught sight of that SS General Heinz Wolf driving up in his Mercedes and he ducked for cover.

"OK, maybe we're not in the same league as the Germans," he said, as Jesus suddenly ran out into the open.

"Come on, we have to get to Hitler!"

Luke noisily sucked in his breath through his teeth. That guy was going to get him killed, as he gripped his automatic rifle, gritted his teeth and chased after Jesus.

Ronald Trump with Melanie

Melanie and Trump are sitting in their bedroom and its been a long time since they have been so relaxed since the Nuclear War.

"Ronald why don't the aliens attack us?" she asked worriedly, as these giant ships sat as if they were waiting for something to happen. She clutched her cross with Jesus on it and fingered the man on it. He was so brave to have sacrificed His life for Humanity, and then she turned to gaze at Ronald who had fallen asleep now and his considerable stomach heaved as he snored in his restful sleep. He seemed to take an interest in the paranormal now as his left hand held the swastika, while the *Mein Kampf* on his table seemed to radiate a strange power. She was worried for her son, Michael, who was growing up fast, but in a terrible and devastated world. He was getting military training with the US Army, while already a great shot with the rifle, and taking after his elder stepbrother, Ronald, Jr.

Anyways, there seemed to be another human who seemed to be the main focus for the alien invasion of Planet Earth. Whatever it was, the fate of the planet seemed to be entwined with this human's destiny. Then she fingered her cross again. Jesus would save. She trusted him, while remembering her small beautiful village in Northern Slovakia, and wondered when would she ever visit it again. But with her woman's intuition she knew that she would never see it again, and sighing returned to her gold embroidered sheets with Ronald's monogram imprinted on each of them.

14

LOS ANGELES

"It feels great to be back in L.A again," said Xander.

"Yeah, and this time there's no pesky LA Mayor to betray us," said Tor, remembering his murdered sister for the first time since the nuclear war had started. The last few weeks had been such frenetic chaos, where they had lost most of French Company.

Kim now observed the *Screaming Eagles* in their Humvees speeding towards their motorcycles, and he felt like Chuck Norris ready to fire with his blasters at the ready. They had to do some tedious detective work in LA trying to locate Hillary and her loyalists who were now all under termination orders.

A General from the *Screaming Eagles* got out of one of the humvees in battle-fatigues and sunglasses and walked over to Tor who stood stiffly at attention. "General," he saluted.

"At ease Special Operator Tor," he said, and nodded at the rest of French Company, while acknowledging their salutes.

"We have cordoned off L.A, while our drones are relentlessly patrolling Los Angeles. *Ex-fil* for Hillary is impossible, so gentlemen your quarry is here alright."

"What about manpower?" asked Tor, aghast to be combing through Los Angeles without any back up. "The Democrats could be packing serious heat in the town."

The General laughed.

"Hey Democrats in California believe in gun-free zones," he joked, but French company was not laughing. The he whispered conspiratorially.

"They didn't tell you, but Klan death squads are already liquidating undesirables in LA."

"Oh no," groaned Tor and Xander together. They had just escaped from the humorless Klan Army and here they were back with them.

"The Klan specifically requested for you guys. Apparently, you made quite an impression on them."

"Let me guess, a guy called Captain Samuel of North Dakota," groaned Kim.

"Yes, he's been promoted to Colonel for these Special OP's here," said the General and he began to walk away.

"So yeah," shouted Tor. "Walk away while we get our hands dirty."

The General shrugged, but continued walking.

Suddenly, a helicopter's rotors beat above their heads.

Thwack! Thwack!

A new prototype with the new Klan Army insignia on it —— the KKK twisted into a swastika, which landed quickly with its nuclear thrusters powerfully bringing it to bear near their motorcycles. Whoever had said that war didn't advance mankind needed to have his head examined.

A man in a black uniform and shiny boots accompanied by bodyguards strutted forward.

"Well look who it is," shouted young Samuel with his new KKK insignia on his right shoulder.

"Fuck, are you some kind of a sadist?" demanded Tor. "I thought you didn't want to work with us."

"We haven't been able to find Hillary and her Democrats," he said. "Time is of the essence since aliens are already here in L.A with Hillary to sign the surrender document."

"Well if you weren't so busy shooting Mexicans, then you'd have found her by now."

Samuel smiled now.

"Shiiieet, it's even better than shooting niggers," said Samuel with an evil smile. French Company didn't say anything.

"This time, we're going to have the country just like we really wanted," said Samuel.

"Yeah, heard your Grandmaster Luke died," said Tor.

Colonel Samuel's face fell.

"We can take casualties," he said. But the disappearance of the architect of the Klan Army was disturbing indeed and a very hard loss to replace.

"Get to work, scum!" he screamed suddenly. "Your official orders will be transmitted to you." He stormed back inside the helicopter which quickly blasted into the skies. Welcome to Los Angeles, as French Company downloaded marked maps on their HUD's and gunned their motorcycles to roar down the highway into interdicted L.A. Where the hell could Hillary be hiding anyways?

Zyk's Underworld

It was a dark and cold place as he descended the staircase draped in thick red carpet, and Zyk gaped at the low-lit ambience, while the velvet ropes ahead displayed a sign saying to wait. Very mysterious. A woman giggled in the darkness and then stepped forward wearing a green and shimmering leather overcoat with long black patent leather boots.

"I always told you that you never knew your power," she said merrily as she lifted the ropes for him. "Remember?"

Jura! *The platinum haired Lithuanian from Chicago!*

"This is how you'd picked me up from the club *Soundbar*," she giggled again as she pressed her tall body against his. But the leather was frozen as were her cheeks. What was he thinking? That it would be cozy here in hell? He shook his head as he kissed Jura on her cheeks. She was a loyal woman indeed and he knew he could trust her dead or undead, as he gazed into her ice-cold blue eyes.

"Anyways, all your fantasies are going to be coming true here," she said. She knew him well enough, so he wondered which fantasy was coming true.

She pointed in the distance where an SS man stood with round glasses and as he took off his peaked hat, his identity was unmistakable.

Heinrich Himmler.

"Hello!" he shouted striding over in his shiny black boots. "I'll take care of his entry." Apparently, she was still working the ropes, even here in hell, while she stared forlornly at Zyk.

"Come back and see me."

Zyk nodded and hurried away with Himmler. Always on the move was Zyk.

"It's about to start," Himmler said tersely, as they entered a long dark corridor, where suddenly pounding music began to thump through the wall, and heavy distortion guitars filled Zyk's ears.

"DJ Adolf is about to start his gig," said Himmler. "He hates it when we're late."

Zyk nodded. Just like 'ole Hitler, as an SS guard saluted and opened the door to a hall filled with well dressed people and with Adolf Hitler on the DJ console. Hitler's sharp eye quickly noted Himmler's presence along with Zyk. He permitted himself a rare smile as he turned the record on the turntable and pressed play.

Thundering guitars again hit the hall and now the drum set hit. Ah, acoustic drums.

Nice.

"We're going backstage," said Himmler. But of course, Zyk didn't expect anything else.

More SS guards saluted, while acting as bouncers too for the thronging crowds. Zyk scanned their faces. Europeans, with Germanics in the majority. After all, who would have the balls to make it to the Underworld anyways? Only acid heads.

"Come on, Zyk," said Himmler, making it up to the stage, where Adolf was wearing headphones and spinning music on the heavy metal turntable. Zyk got up to the stage and an SS soldier came hurtling with a guitar. Zyk stared at it. It was a Flying V painted in red with SS lightning strikes all over it.

"Come on!" yelled Hitler. "Let's give them a little bit of Blitzkrieg!"

Zyk looked at Himmler who seemed to think this was all normal. Hitler was even wearing his favorite AKG Austrian headphones.

Another soldier came running with a guitar pedalboard fitted with an assortment of heinous looking distortion pedals. A fuzz pedal with a swastika on it. Only God knew what kind of horror that pedal would unleash.

Zyk plugged the lead into his guitar from the distortion pedalboard, while another soldier clipped on a Telefunken microphone to the guitar's shoulder strap. Now Zyk stared ahead at the hall which had suddenly become quiet. Hell, he didn't even know if the guitar was tuned.

"Hit it!" screamed Hitler, cranking the amp's crunch level to full. Jesus, he could blow everyone's ears away with that SPL. *But then this was the Underworld.*

Zyk switched the pedalboard on with his left foot and then hit the swastika fuzz pedal. Instantly, a whine of electricity cut through the air as Hitler looked happily on.

Now to strum the dam thing. He wasn't really good at the guitar, but he didn't want to disappoint Hitler.

His nails slid over the strings causing a howling noise that rose from the bottom of the earth. Hitler quickly turned to switch the metal plate reverb on his console. The hall was now filled with the moaning of the devil himself. Amplified fuzz which created a wall of sound as Zyk really got into it, thrilled to feel the power as he strummed a chord. But it was no chord that emerged, at least one that he didn't know, and the sound rose to a crescendo of a tsunami till it hit the audience like a tidal wave.

Hitler took the mike now.

"Wilkommen to the Underworld!"

Everyone roared back, as Der Führer programmed a bass line with heavy beats while layering chords through a Roland synthesizer. It was the same one that Zyk had owned, the JD-XA.

Zyk now played in a frenzy, as Hitler tuned the beats and synth to the guitar as Zyk continued to plunk a piece of hell into the air. He could see nothing but flashing lights and a darkened hall. He wanted to see the audience as he walked around with his guitar careful not to ensnare the wires.

"Sing!" shouted Hitler, now coming towards Zyk and fixed another mic to his leather jacket. Zyk wracked his brain for a song and then he opened his mouth.

"Another day for you in Hell!" Zyk shouted.

The audience roared. *Oh yes!*

"Gonna last forever they said!"

"In the horror of the night!"

"Gonna love the redness of it all"

"The blood flows and the demons rejoice"

"The smell of fear and sorrow,

This is where we live,

They'll never find us,

Since we'll take their souls and make them weep.

They thought they knew more than us, but we get the last laugh!

Let the demons Rejoice,

To party till the Kingdoms are no more and we shall be free.

Till we rule the skies and galaxies,

In the horror of the night
Gonna love the redness of it all

A tear in the fabric of time,
The vision of the damned,
Terrible fear fills your heart,
Where're ya gonna go?
Nowhere to run,
Darkness and fear are your friends,
Demons that roam your soul,
Ready till your debt is paid,
Whisk away your soul!

In the Horror of the night,
Gonna love the redness of it all

In the Horror of the night,
Gonna love the redness of it all

Been there so many times,
That I feel at home,
To remain here till eternity!

Welcome to the Underworld!

Zyk finished it off with a few more heavy strings and Hitler glanced at Himmler to see if he was rocking to the beat and was elated to see that Himmler had been joined by the stuck-up Heydrich. The audience was ecstatic that DJ Adolf, who like any good DJ, knew how add a guest appearance to stir things up.

"Ladies and Gentlemen, that was Zyk!"

More applause as Hitler now left the stage and shepherded Zyk away backstage.

Jesus enters Hitler's bunker

SS soldiers stood guard at Hitler's bunker as Russian guns advanced ominously towards the bunker firing 155 mm shells into Berlin with it's crumbling and burning buildings. Hitler Youth fought on from destroyed alleyways and fired from any position available causing the battle to be no less apocalyptic than Stalingrad, but with German teenagers doing most of the dying here as the men of Germany lay dead.

"Just how do you think that we're going to enter Hitler's bunker?" demanded Luke.

"I don't know, but someone is parting the dimensions here and we have to stop him," said Jesus closing his eyes and trying to see deeper. A music concert somewhere but after that blackness.

"Use your SS uniform," commanded Jesus. Luke muttered under his breath as he approached the guards.

"We have urgent business with Adolf," shouted Luke, as Jesus grinned at the stony faced tall Leibstandarte guards.

"Fuck off," growled one of the soldiers.

"Let us in please," said Jesus. "Something is happening inside the bunker."

Now Luke noticed that the air had changed a little bit and the guards somehow seemed bigger and meaner than before. A gleaming Mercedes now suddenly stood besides them.

Smoke appeared.

"Jesus, this looks spooky," Luke said tugging at Jesus's sleeve.

Now the soldiers leered at Jesus.

"Alright snowflake, what's the fucking password?" one of them demanded now with a grin.

Jesus wracked his brain now for an answer.

"Err... Heil Hitler?"

"Wrong answer," said the guard. A shell just then crashed nearby, and a ton of dust swirled around them.

Jesus grabbed Luke's jacket and they nicked into the bunker in the confusion. Luke gaped at the red interior. What the hell?

A tall blonde stared at them in surprise inside and there was a velvet rope just below the stairs.

"Are you guys on the guest list?" she asked sweetly.

Jesus and Luke gaped at her. Just outside were teenagers fighting for their lives and here was Hitler running a *noir* nightclub in his bunker. Well if that wasn't Chutzpah then Luke didn't know what was.

"You just tell Hitler that the game is up," huffed Jesus.

"Yeah," chimed in Luke also aghast that the Supreme Leader of the German Armed Forces was partying inside, while Germans and Russians were desperately trying to kill each other just meters outside.

"Yeah, like do you even know what's going on outside?" demanded Jesus.

"I just work here," said Jura rolling her eyes. She always got the occasional oddballs and she looked behind. The usual SS bouncers were missing, and she was on her own here.

"Well if you know Hitler, then I think that I can let you in," she said smiling at these long-haired blondes who probably were musicians too. They didn't pay her nearly enough to argue at the door anyways.

She lifted the velvet rope as if it was the entry through the pearly gates of Heaven itself. But Jesus shook his head at Luke as they went by Jura. He had seen Heaven and sure as fuck didn't look like this with this ominous red light. *Trust Hitler to have a crib like this.*

Jesus quickly followed the thundering music and strobe lights that flickered to give anyone an epileptic attack and which led to the hall. The SS guards stared at Jesus suspiciously but then relaxed noting Luke's SS jacket. Luke's jaw fell open when he recognized Hitler on stage and his face was on the giant tv screens everywhere.

"Oh my god," gulped Luke. He was in the same room as Hitler.

"Dude check the guitarist out!" said Jesus pointing to the tall guitarist in black jeans and a leather jacket.

"Those are some insane guitar riffs he's got," said Luke appreciably. Awesome distortion guitars, just like the music that he loved.

"No, you idiot, he's got this dark power around him," said Jesus. "He's probably the guy causing the energy disturbances here in Hitler's bunker."

"Is he Aryan?" asked the KKK Grandmaster now squinting to see Zyk better.

"Oh yes, he is. That's the problem," said Jesus. "An ancient Aryan."

"Well then I have no problem with him," said Luke.

Suddenly, the show was over.

"Ladies and Gentlemen, that was Zyk!" announced Hitler and then he left the stage with Zyk.

"Come on," said Jesus." Let's find out where they're going."

LA Democrats

"Come out with your hands on your head, Democrat scum!" shouted a Klan trooper as he held a flamethrower's nozzle pointed towards a house. There was no response. French Company gaped as the soldier proceeded to pour fire into the two-story wooden house. People screamed from inside the house as searing fire quickly leapt into the house and the trooper moved to the next house. The Klan was building a new America, where there was no place for anyone who didn't agree with the Klan, while not even the Republican Government had much control over this *State within a State*. Ronald Trump was working with the Klan as he didn't have any other option. For now.

French Company was sickened by these execution style killings.

Kim shook his head as Jane looked frightfully back to hear the screams. *Macabre*. To think L.A would ever be like this. Whole sections of minority communities had been labeled as *Democrat and* marked for deportation from USA to giant concentration camps being set up across the *Rio Grande* river in *Mexico*. Those that resisted were being ruthlessly eliminated.

"Alright gentlemen, we have a mission," ordered Tor, and everyone turned their attention to reality. *Hillary was negotiating with the aliens.*

"Her last known location was on Hollywood Boulevard," said Xander sending an annotated map on French Company's HUD. Jane was afraid of the KKK and the only one she really trusted was Kim, even though he looked more like a ZZ Top band member than Delta Force. But then behind that bushy beard and sunglasses was a very kind and considerate man. Not like the Klan soldiers who would've probably shot her if they knew that she was a Mexican citizen, and the worst part was that the Klan soldiers were all so young but filled with ideology. Professional soldiers like French Company never brought their personal views or politics into their mission and that was usually a relief, even though she thought of her life with the brutal looters who had tried to kill her. Fuck 'em. There was simply no kindness left in the world, and she shook her head, and glanced sharply at a grinning Xander who flexed his biceps mockingly at her.

"Alright, let's ride," said Tor checking his coordinates and gunned the Kawasaki now nicknamed by French Company as *The Ghostrider*. It had a cold fusion nuclear engine with a range of 3,000 miles before its Lithium nuclear fuel rod needed a recharge.

"Yeehaw," screamed Xander chasing after Tor's dust. Drew and Kim followed closely behind them, with Jane full of trepidation at what lay ahead.

"According to the NSA's satellites, we're seeing a lot of body heat inside a Beverly Hills' mansion, but the Klan isn't operating so far from there," said Tor into the com. "Let's hit it before they do."

Their motorcycles charged towards the location. They wanted to get the hell out of LA. *Mass executions.* No had foreseen this level of savagery to ever hit the USA, but after the aliens and the nuclear war, the gloves had come off. There was no traffic save for Klan Army patrols and ominous Klan Police trucks carrying death squads from suburban counties, as French Company blasted by them on their nuclear Kawasakis.

Zyk meets Jesus

Adolf Hitler ushered Zyk into his private chamber where were gathered some old cronies, Theodore Eicke, Heydrich, Himmler, Goebbels, and Sepp Dietrich. Upon seeing Zyk, Dietrich burst out into a loud laugh.

"So, we finally meet!" Sepp said, leaping up and clasping Zyk's shoulder with that infectious smile, while the humorless Heydrich and Himmler looked on. "This guy has written so much shit about me."

Hitler smiled at this.

"Yeah, about me too," he agreed nodding.

"So, Herr Zyk, what brings you to the underworld?" asked Heydrich coolly, while lighting a cigarette on an ivory cigarette holder.

Zyk shook his head, while still shocked at what was going on.

"I think that I'm dead or something," replied Zyk sadly.

Hitler laughed along with Himmler, while Sepp stared at Zyk in amazement. "You mean you don't know!"

Zyk stared in surprise now at the audience. He was still holding his distortion pedal board with those hideously colored and disfigured guitar pedals. They had some power and they made him hold onto them.

"We were all summoned here by you," announced Heydrich drily.

"Yes, you saw my Mercedes outside," said Hitler. "I was in the middle of gardening when I received your message."

Zyk gawked at these men. Goebbels' shrewd eyes darted now as he chewed over the situation.

"Only a leader of the Underworld with vast powers can summon us," he pronounced.

Zyk appeared perplexed.

"But why would you all come if I summoned you? After all, who am I?"

Hitler waved his hand.

"Oh, come off it," he said. "You've been summoning us all your life. It's just that you're getting more powerful at choosing the location."

Theodore Eicke pulled out a small steel flask. A flash of recognition. With Justine and Ozzy in the desert.

"How is that little Jew?" SS General Eicke asked wickedly.

Zyk looked away.

"You must have killed her by now," he said with a smile.

"Well, not because she was a Jew."

"You see much more than even us. Remember that," said Eicke with a smile playing fiendishly on them. "But you choose to let your Doppelgänger carry out your darkest deeds."

Zyk really felt bad about her.

"Relax, it was not to be," said Heydrich now. He was irritated to have been summoned like this to discuss a Jew's death.

"There must be another reason that we are all here," insisted Himmler.

Sepp nodded.

"If nothing else, then at least we have met our man, Zyk," said Hitler and shook hands again warmly with Zyk.

There was a scuffle outside and suddenly the door burst open with two long-haired blonde men.

"What the...?" demanded Heydrich, drawing his Luger and aimed it at Jesus and a terrified Luke, who gaped at Hitler.

"The game is up," said Jesus with a flourish. "Look at them. All sitting around like nothing is happening in Berlin."

Luke stammered his agreement.

"You idiots are in a different time reality," said Heydrich putting the gun to Jesus's temple.

Eicke came over to sniff Luke.

"You shouldn't be here."

Hitler came over now smiling.

"You know you look like Jesus with that hair," he chuckled, as Zyk felt for his guitar distortion pedals. He wanted to make sure that whatever happened he kept those pedals close. An intuition told him that they were going to come handy. "We met briefly outside, and you still think you are Jesus!"

"Well, I am," said Jesus throwing his hair back.

Heydrich was suddenly enraged.

"Someone is playing tricks on us!" he screamed waving his Luger. "They send this weak fool to waste our time!"

"I don't think that I am here to stop you," said Jesus suddenly closing his eyes. In his mind's eye, he saw Zyk on another planet with spaceships and soldiers marching.

"That man there!" shouted Jesus. "He is the one I have to stop."

Now Heydrich looked perplexed as Himmler's frown deepened.

Hitler paced the room now.

"Now look here, Jesus, what do you really see?" he asked as everyone's attention turned to Zyk.

"He's a spy!" shouted Goebbels pointing to Zyk, who looked quite worried now as all eyes turned to him. Even Heydrich now turned with his Luger pointed at Zyk, who rolled his eyes. The theatre of the absurd.

"His name is Zyk," said Goebbels turning to Jesus, who ran that name through the Old Testament, but drew a blank.

"Why did you really come to us, Zyk?" demanded Heydrich. Hitler, Sepp, and Eicke smiled now. Hitler nodded.

"Heydrich, we were already in Zyk's mind in the desert," said Hitler. "We saw his darkness, don't forget that."

Heydrich nodded slowly and then turned to Jesus.

"What are you trying to prove?"

Jesus shook his head. "This is all new to me too. I am just the messenger from my Kingdom."

"Well fuck your kingdom!" snarled Heydrich and rested his Luger on Jesus's temple again.

"Come come, Heydrich," said Hitler. "There is more to this mystery, and if we shoot Jesus then we will never know the answers."
 Luke nodded gratefully at Hitler.
"Zyk, tell us something that you might know. Obviously, Jesus has seen something in your future."
"I'm just an Artist."
"Don't lie," said Eicke. "You're also a bleeding medical doctor."
"Yes, that too," smiled Zyk finally looking into Jesus's eyes now, who laser locked into his eyes, and Jesus suddenly grew startled.
"He wants my kingdom," he suddenly stammered. "He holds the darkest demons in his mind. So much darkness in there."
"Stop whining like a baby," growled Heydrich now putting away his Luger. This was beyond a pistol bullet now. "Guards!"
 SS guards came in.
"How did these clowns get in?" he demanded. "Take them away!"
"Wait!" cried Jesus. "Don't you want to stop Zyk? He will become your enemy too. I have foreseen it!"
 Everyone in the room laughed now.
"Get him out of here!" screamed Hitler now, who had also lost his humor.
"Jawohl, Mein Führer!" saluted the soldiers, while grabbing Jesus and Luke.
"Shall we execute them?"
"No, just throw them in jail," said Himmler hastily. No point in executing a high-profile VIP like Jesus.
 Hitler turned to Himmler sarcastically.
"You were always so circumspect."
 Himmler nodded while remaining seated. Sane heads were what were needed right now, and he too could see a little into the future.

French Company

"Ok, we'll go in from the front and you guys enter from the rear," ordered Tor, as Xander and Drew with DARPA blasters drawn, went around the large house and jumped over the wall. But what they saw caused their jaws to drop. *In the middle of Klan executions happening in the backdrop of a nuclear holocaust in Los Angeles, here there were scores of people in all white sitting and meditating in a smartly spruced garden with fountains and waterfalls.* Just then Tor came racing through the front door. So far, no gunfire. Jane waited outside with their bikes.

The hippies sat with closed eyes. French company scanned the serene faces for Hillary and the democrats.

Tor raced up to Xander, whose mouth was trying to ineffectually ejaculate some profanity.

"Fucking snowflakes," growled Tor contemptuously.

Rows of meditating young people in white Indian clothing sat cross-legged and pointedly ignored French Company.

Xander went over to the teacher, a blonde with closed eyes and stuck his blaster in her face with the barrel touching her lips.

"Hey honey, wake up," he said gently.

The blonde scowled now.

"Can't you see that we're in the middle of Prana Yana," she said scolding the Delta Force Operator in a full AWS suit.

Xander wanted to push the barrel deeper into her mouth. Tor came over worriedly.

"The Klan has just told us to clear the area. They're coming here."

Xander turned to the hippies.

"Listen up, girls and boys, time to snap out of it!" He fired his blaster in the air. That got a few eyes open and suddenly the girls started to scream, and people began to dart all around the garden.

"I think we just saved their lives," said Tor, when Drew came running.

"Tor, I think that Hillary is here in the basement of this house," he said, while transmitting a drone video to Tor, who viewed it on his HUD, as Xander entered the palatial L.A. mansion. It was fancy inside, real fancy, like stuff you never saw in Louisiana, and Xander wondered when the hell would he ever get to lie in a couch like this, as he stopped by a luxuriously appointed divan with ornate gold plating.

Gunfire!

Xander snapped out of it. Apparently, Kim and Drew were already in the basement before him. He took the stairs and heaved down till he heard the tinkle of a grenade pin dropping somewhere on a floor. He dived down the stairs headlong and prayed that it wasn't a tactical nuclear. Fucking DARPA!

Ka-BOOOM! A small heatwave flew overhead. His HUD showed conventional infra-red readings with multiple readings on the staircase. Somebody was armed in this facility. Xander's helmet had taken a blow to the chin and he straightened the modular helmet, when there was an ominous roar behind him, and something crashed into the rear of his helmet.

He was out cold for god-only-knew-how-long, when he saw Tor's worried face.

Probably a few seconds.

"Xander, Kim and Drew are not responding," he whispered worriedly. "It looks like the aliens are here too. They shot the Klan chopper out of the skies, so this seems to be an important operating base of their's."

Xander rubbed his head groggily and got to his feet.

"Who turned off the lights?" he asked peering into the dimly lit staircase. Great. They had stumbled into a heavily defended alien base looking for Hillary.

"Secure your helmet," said Tor. "Things are going to get hairy." He descended downstairs, as Xander got his helmet and blaster together, switched on the FLIR to plunge the basement into bright green, and then followed Tor into the eerily quiet basement.

Zyk comes clean

"Ok, how about you start telling us about this book?" demanded Reinhard Heydrich, while taking out a copy of *SS DEATH STAR*. "What the hell am I doing in a distant galaxy fighting aliens?"

Sepp Dietrich laughed as he lifted the copy of the heavy book.

"Oh, it has an awesome cover story!" he said. "Though I haven't read it."

Zyk took the book from Sepp and looked at it.

"I don't know," he said. "Its just a fictional book."

No one believed him there.

"Look, we have plans for the Valhalla and you have written all about it," said Heydrich. "Its like you're writing our future."

Hitler nodded.

"Yes, what exactly do you want from us, Zyk? Probe your mind."

Zyk flicked through the pages. God dammed space aliens had turned out to be true alright and they were on Earth now. He had written *SS Death STAR*, many years ago just for fun. *Fiction, right?*

"It looks like whatever you write turns out to be true," said Goebbels imagining the possibilities of publishing propaganda through Zyk.

"Yes, except that I was just the medium," replied Zyk tersely.

"That guy Jesus saw something in your mind that scared him," said Hitler. "You have to look into your subconscious. It's where my power comes from too. The most primal beast lurking down there will power you to great heights if you listen to it. The whole point of religion and Christianity was to shield you from your *doppelgänger.*"

"Yes, the collective horror of the writhing soul," said Heinrich Himmler, a great believer in Yoga and the concept of the soul. "It can be very stressful if you are opened to it's collective weight. The *Untermensch* has long hidden and run away from these realities, while cowardly preferring the comforts of a loving Father-God, than to become the responsible Man-God. *The Übermensch.*

Sepp's eyes glazed as he understood nothing about this psychological jumbo-jumbo. He was a General of war and used to action. All this thinking made him restless, but the war was over, so he unclenches his hand and observes the blood return to his knuckles. He remembered that he was a Werewolf, at least in Zyk's books, and he hastily covers his hands as his nails turn to claws. Fuck.

Somebody knocked on the door.

"Enter!" said Adolf Hitler.

A man in a trench coat entered and Hitler's mouth twisted into a sneer.

"Edouard Daladier!" proclaimed Hitler. "You come late, but yet you come."

Daladier, the ex-French Premier stammered.

"I was summoned here," he replied flummoxed to be suddenly surrounded by top Nazis.

All eyes turned to Zyk.

"He is a stupid Frenchman," snarled Heydrich fingering his Luger again. "Why is he here?"

"Defeatists!" shouted Hitler. "Their project to ruin Europe is still happening. The French swine are gutless scoundrels."

"Well anyways, I'm trying to sort out my mind," replied Zyk, aghast that he'd somehow summoned the ex-Prime Minister of France. "Take a seat at the table."

The Frenchman sat trembling next to Heydrich, once the most feared man in Europe, or *Hangman Heydrich,* and rumored to be the father of the Holocaust.

"Please don't summon anymore *auslanders*," growled Heydrich now with a dangerous glint in his eye, as he lit another cigarette and blew smoke into the sweating Frenchman's eyes.

"Daladier only escaped SS execution in that *Battle of Castle Itter due* to some *Wehrmacht* traitors."

Hitler shook his head. In the end, some of the Wehrmacht had sold out to the Americans. But so had the SS, and he gazed at Himmler who gulped knowingly.

"Anyways, there is a new future in the galaxies for the SS and the Wehrmacht," said Zyk reading from the book. "We would be very foolish not to seize the untold treasures that are controlled by alien empires across the galaxies."

Zyk's words fell like a bombshell on the people gathered at the table.

Suddenly, there was a knock on the door. Heydrich rose with his Luger drawn. "I think that our SS guards need to be severely dealt with," he complained, as he opened the door to confront a very large woman with large and sad eyes.

"Hello there," she nodded, and with her considerable girth, she pushed a gaping Heydrich aside to enter.

Zyk and Himmler jumped to their feet.

"Madame Blavatsky!" they shouted in astonishment. Hitler vaguely remembered this Russian-American occultist, while Goebbels furiously began to write in his diary of the bizarre happenings —— even by Underworld standards.

Heinrich Himmler, the SS Reichsführer, now helpfully brought a chair over to the table, where she sat down and the wooden chair creaked under her considerable weight. But her eyes burned bright as ever.

"I see that you are with this *Storyteller,*" she said mischievously glancing at Zyk who blushed now.

"We were just discussing that, madame," said Adolf now summoning a SS guard.

"Would you like some refreshments? I'm sure your journey here must have made you tired."

An SS orderly entered smartly.

"I'll have an iced tea," she said.

"What about the rest of you?"

"Beer," replied Heydrich, as did Theodore Eicke.

"Beer," echoed Zyk, hoping to sample some high-quality wheat beer.

"Beer for everyone, and iced tea for me and the madame," ordered Hitler, as the SS orderly dressed in impeccable white jacket and black trousers, scribbled furiously. There could be no mistakes here.

"Well yes, its true," said Zyk settling in now that drinks were coming on the house. He didn't really have any money on him, but here Hitler nodded at him as if he would settle the bill. Phew. Didn't want to owe the SS money. No sir, no trifling with that crowd, as waiters quickly brought their drinks in and now stood besides them to serve some more. Looks like the party was just starting as Zyk lifted the heavy *stein* to his lips. Thick blonde beer and it tasted like the nectar from the heavens itself.

"A toast to the führer," proposed SS General Sepp Dietrich. Everyone stood up including Blavatsky.

"To the führer!"

"While we're at it, I also propose that we make Zyk an SS Obergruppenführer," continued Sepp, one of the lead creators of the Waffen SS. "He will serve us well in the galaxies. We can see it in his books."

Eicke protested.

"But he has no military experience! We can't make him into a bleeding General!"

"But neither did we. Every single one of us learnt on the job. Well mostly," countered Sepp. Heydrich blushed now, as he had never seen combat even as a General.

"Its true," said Hitler turning to Himmler, who nodded.

"If Zyk is to help us, then we shall open the doors of the underworld Reich for him," said Hitler, turning to an SS orderly.

"A paper and pen," he ordered. "And my seal."

The orderly returned quickly. Hitler now turned to Zyk, who put his beer mg down quite reluctantly. Becoming an SS General wasn't something that he'd ever aspired to be.

"Zyk, I now pronounce you as a General of the Waffen SS," said Hitler, while retrieving a red and black ribbon with a golden swastika attached to it from his draw and pinned it to Zyk's shirt under his leather jacket.

Obergruppenführer Zyk.

Everyone clapped, including Goebbels and the Madame.

She stared at him. She had taught him so well and here he was carrying out her fondest wishes, without him ever realizing that she had guided him for so long and from so far away, yet so close.

French Company in L.A.

A hellish nightmare, thought Tor, as he advanced with Xander behind him. It was pitch black. Someone had cut the power mains, as FLIR lit up the area on his helmet visor.

"Warning, alien presence detected," announced the computer's worried female voice. *"Alien infestation. Terminate with prejudice."*

"Easy for you to say," snorted Xander pulling alongside with his blaster sights glued to his visor as they entered a very large basement.

The men were sweating profusely —— someone or something had burrowed in deep over here, while the temperature shot up as they descended. Their AWS's air conditioning strained to cool them, while battery health plunged below 50 percent. *Getting hairy fast.*

"Kim and Drew are still not responding," said Tor as he descended. Whoever had taken Kim and Drew had burrowed deep and fast.

Xander pointed up ahead.

"There is a hall down below, but its filled with a purplish gas according to the computer."

A few figures stood ominously down below.

The computer's voice cut in.

"Suspect positively identified," announced the computer. "Hillary Fenton confirmed. Orders to terminate immediately. Purple gas is alien in nature."

"Calm down," said Tor, realizing that something was very wrong here. He zoomed in his FLIR vision and it was Hillary alright, but then she was talking to someone, and as he zoomed in some more to realize that she didn't have any eyeballs and in the purple gas looked quite sinister. Fuck!

"You see what I see," crackled Xander's voice over the com.

"Let's toast them!" roared Tor realizing that that there weren't any humans here. "Fire!"

Intense laser blasts sounded as Hillary was suddenly struck down with heavy laser blasts along with her companion.

"Target is down!" heaved Xander running over to Hillary's remains, as Tor blasted away at the computers that stocked the room. It was really a command and control facility with Democratic flags everywhere and old posters of *Bernie 2020!* plastered on the walls.

"Looks like Hillary never recovered from the election," laughed Tor.

"I don't think she was ever herself," said Xander tersely. "Tor, you gotta see this."

Tor leaned over Hillary's dead body.

"Look, her body parts aren't human," said Xander, as her gaping abdomen revealed bizarre and malformed organs.

"Dude, she was just old as fuck," argued Tor. "Let's get out of here first. Mission is over. Order the Heli-VAC, computer. Meanwhile, we're going to search for Kim and Drew."

"Understood," said the computer. This place gave them the creeps. But all in all, it appeared to be a buried Democrat party command and control structure allied with the fiendish aliens.

"Look, there are some posters of this human that the aliens are looking for," said Xander pointing to a bunch of plastered posters on the wall.

"*Zyk.* Wanted dead or alive," read Tor, and sent an email of Zyk's photo to the DARPA number as they headed back towards the surface. But now as they ran upstairs, what they found was that there was nothing upstairs but endless black corridors.

Dark synthetic texture lined the walls with one small window cut-out like they were on a plane, but when they peered outside, they saw nothing but dark space and then the blue Earth lit so prettily by the sun which burned like an untiring yellow lamp.

15

Trump's Plan

"General Schwartzkopf, what's the latest update on Hillary?" demanded Trump as Schwartzkopf burst into the room.

"Sir, French Company just reported something unbelievable," he said breathlessly.

"What?"

"You know the location where we tracked Hillary to was some sort of an alien base?"

Trump nodded as Schwartzkopf continued.

"Well Delta Operators Tor and Xander were inside when the entire basement took off into the skies."

Trump thought about it as Schwartzkopf played Drew's drone video for him. On the screen a breathless Drew exclaimed, "There were explosions and suddenly we saw the entire basement just take off into the skies! We just lost our commander Tor and operator Xander."

Drew appeared forlorn alongside a stoic looking Kim along with Jane.

Ronald Trump shook his head now. The Democrat treachery was worse than even he'd suspected. Talk about being hand in glove.

"General, I want every last one of those traitor Democrats found and deported to Klan camps," he snarled.

Schwartzkopf nodded and left as suddenly Trump thought about the aliens and why the hell weren't they moving? Not even crawling. Just static, hanging in the skies. Like a Venus Fly Trap. Waiting for their prey to enter. Just then a photo flashed on the giant screens of a human. *Wanted, dead or alive*

The Oscillator

More beer was served and Zyk stared at the foamy liquid bubbling in his large ceramic cup full of gothic inscriptions. Now this was life. Careful, he didn't want to get too drunk as he would only make a fool of himself. In font of the teetotaler Hitler, it would be quite disgraceful, especially that he'd been given a sealed paper saying that he was a General in the SS now and even as he drank, a Hugo Boss designed SS uniform was being stitched for him.

"But you know he's not going to stay here," commented Blavatsky, and Goebbels nodded. After flipping through his books, he'd realized that Zyk was quite the country-hopper. *Just like a Jew, who couldn't be trusted.*

"He's in his 40's and unlike us is unmarried," continued Blavatsky. Zyk now had a sheepish grin on his face. Well marriage and women were a completely different matter as he sloshed his beer mug down.

"There is too much conflict in his being," she said. Everyone nodded as Hitler pondered over this and more beer was poured into Zyk's beer mug. Then much to Zyk's delight, SS waiters came with plates and began serving food, while his stomach rumbled appreciably. Steak tartar was his favorite as he cut into the filet beef, while Hitler, the vegetarian, sipped a leek soup sparingly, but the rest of the the SS crowd dug into the beef with gusto.

Now Zyk lifted up a fork into the air.

"I have new ideas for powering galaxies with exotic energy," he said. "In the course of my writings, I have glimpsed new wave oscillator technologies that can be used to power us through the galaxies."

"General Zyk," said Sepp smiling while using his new rank to address him and that gave Zyk no small measure of joy. "You have mentioned Dark energy as powering the galaxies." Sepp held up Zyk's book.

"Yes, but I have not the faintest idea on how to harness dark energy or dark matter, but what I do know is that energy is being transmitted as waves across the galaxies at a particular frequency and if we build suitable receptors on our space ships then we can harness this cosmic energy continuously."

Heydrich interrupted now.

"But General in your book, *SS Death Star,* you mention nuclear fusion energy."
 No Zyk grew irritated. He actually had no answers.
 Hitler interrupted.
"Look he's not a physicist, but we must think of ways to power our new empire in the future."
 Now Blavatsky smiled.
"The Americans up above on Earth have already started using cold fusion technology under Ronald Trump," she said triumphantly and Zyk looked up sharply. Of course, the blasters those Klan soldiers, Travis and Phillip had carried contained cold fusion reactors along with their powerful AWS suits. Blavatsky smiled.
"So restless," she said staring at Zyk fondly. "You don't know this, but I was watching you read my book, *From the Caves and Jungles of Hindoostan.*"
"Yes, of course," replied Zyk getting served another half-kilo of steak which he began to dig into enthusiastically.
"Remember the Raj Yogi," she said. "The one who can see all. I was referring to you. I had already foreseen your birth and rise."
"The Raj Yogi could talk to tigers and other animals too," argued Zyk.
"Yes, and speak many languages, while knowing the goings on in the world intimately," she said. "What I'm trying to tell you is that you are the Raj Yogi I was writing about in my book."
 Zyk tore into his steak to cut out a healthy bite of medium-rare steak and laughed, though a little tipsy from the beer now.
 She stared at him with her large and doleful eyes.
"But you are also going in the right direction with your Oscillator energy," she said. "I have seen the galaxies being powered by these waves and this auxiliary energy."
 Zyk's head began to swim now with all this talk.
Hitler turned to Zyk.
"We will need this fusion technology from Ronald Trump."
 Zyk looked up at Adolf Hitler now.
"I am ordering you, General Zyk, to bring this technology back to us in the Underworld."
 Zyk realized that as a Waffen SS General now, he had to obey orders now. Something that he'd never done before.
 He found himself getting up from the chair.
"Yes sir!" he saluted a little drunkenly and then sat down to finish his steak.

Heydrich began to talk now.

"You don't know your importance to the movement," he said, watching Zyk tuck into another juicy medium-rare steak.

"Why is that?" Zyk asked with his mouth half-full of steak, which he washed down with a frothy mug of beer.

"You're the only one who is actually alive here," he said, and Goebbels nodded.

HItler turned to Zyk.

"You must get us the nuclear reactor," he said.

"It's only one life," said Blavatsky turning to Zyk. "Don't let it go. How I thirst to be back among the living, to be normal, but here we conspire to build Empires just to live again."

"Come come," said Zyk. "That life above can sometimes be so boring and stifling."

"There are always options," said Sepp. "Live well."

"I know, that's why I write."

"That's my point and with your music, too much of your time has flown. Irreplaceable," said Blavatsky remembering her own quick life, as reflected Hitler and Himmler. Zyk was single and Blavatsky was angling for him to have female company, while Heydrich felt the grenade blast that had killed him. Ah, Zyk now was suddenly losing his appetite. *The Underworld now had expectations from him.*

"But we will not send you empty handed," said Blavatsky.

"Yes," chimed in Eicke wickedly, who had been so quiet all this while. "Those are wicked condemned souls trapped inside those guitar pedals. Beware especially of the *fuzz pedal.* That's good old Otto in there."

Zyk stared at the pedal wiggle ominously on the board. Jesus, he had had too much to drink, as the guitar pedals began to twist and writhe like demented beings. One by one, they opened their eyes to smile nastily at Zyk now.

"Ok, I think that I better be on my way now," said Zyk hastily as a mini-panic attack rose in his breast. He needed to get back to his world now as he drunkenly saluted and left.

Jesus and Luke

"Alright, you clowns are free to go," said an SS soldier with his steel helmet gleaming under the red light, while his silver breastplate had a sinister dull shine. *Military police.*
"Luke, get up," said Jesus with his eyes shining.
"We're free to go," he said, and Luke bounded up forgetting his sleep. The SS soldier led them to a processing station where the two were fingerprinted and photographed.
"Even in the underworld?" asked Luke. *Talk about bureaucracy.*
"We're German," replied the policeman stiffly.
"Let's go get Hitler!" yelled Jesus, as Luke groaned in dismay. The idiot still hadn't come off it.
Now the policeman seemed genuinely amused and laughed.
"You think you clowns can touch old Adolf," he said. "He's the sharpest cookie in town."
"Well, they haven't seen my powers," boasted Jesus.
"I'm letting your sorry ass out of jail," said the SS policeman now picking up a thick ham sandwich and proceeded to wolf it down. "Don't push it."
"They nailed me to the Cross," said Jesus proudly. "But I'm still here."
The policeman filled his mouth with the seasoned meat and thick brown bread.
"Well, I'm not supposed to tell you, but we just traded you for that Zyk guy," he said conspiratorially.
"Traded me?"
"Yes, old Himmler just sold you to the aliens," said the policeman. "Its very hush hush."
Jesus was outraged.
"For 30 pieces of silver?"
"You see Himmler is trying to build his own empire in space and he needs to cut a deal with the aliens for raw materials," said the policeman without a care in the world. Luke knew that this could only mean one thing. That they were marked for execution. At least that's how he had operated in the Klan. How many people had he confessed to before shooting them? Ah, the dead tell no tales. Just then the clanging of steel. Doors being opened. Monstrously large beings with dreadlocks with a swirl of purple gas around them enclosed in a translucent bubble.

"Oh shit!" shouted Jesus, as the aliens suddenly stood before them.

"Hello, we're Pzyklos," said the taller one of them. "My name is Commander Terl and I am in charge of security."

"What?" demanded Luke now. "Pzyklo sounds a bit like Zyk."

"Believe it or not, but we're looking for him too," said Terl now stepping forward at 7 feet tall and cut an imposing figure.

"Bullshit!" said Jesus. "We're trying to stop Hitler from resurrecting the Third Reich in space with the help of Zyk."

"That's not my problem," said Terl smiling now. He was built like a bear and with red eyes. Not a very pretty face, but with the wolfskin draped around his shoulders and with the animal's head resting balefully on his, he didn't seem someone to argue with. "And we just heard your story of thirty pieces of silver."

The SS policeman and the aliens burst out laughing, as Jesus again simmered at the thought of betrayal.

 Terl approached Jesus and Luke.

"Where are you taking us?"

"Somewhere safe —— to our home planet Pzyklo," said Terl, as the 'cuffs snapped into place and sealed with a blue flash of light on their wrists.

"Zyk is very dangerous," said Jesus. "And you let him go for me."

"We wanted you in our Museum of Natural History," laughed Terl. "And don't worry about Zyk, Himmler just gave us his location too. It's only a matter of time before we eliminate him. But we actually paid money to get your friend here." Terl turned ominously towards Luke, who appeared shocked.

"For the murder of Lt. Zadoz in cold blood while they were negotiating."

"That was no negotiation, he was trying to kill me," protested Luke hotly as he remembered shooting the alien in the cave. Fear gripped his heart as the SS soldier nodded, and the Pzyklos prodded Luke and Jesus to start moving.

French Company

Tor and Xander had been through the worst combat zones in Delta Force, but now on this alien ship, their jaws fell open like schoolboys, as they examined the metallic walls and the strange material on the floor. Just then they heard voices approaching and they hid in a corner.

 A door opened and they saw two blonde men being escorted by horrifically large aliens, just like the alien that they had stolen the ship from in Mexico.

"Shit, that guy looks like Jesus," whispered Xander.

"Shut up," hissed Tor, but could *the lord* really be here held prisoner on this alien ship as it hurtled away to some god forsaken place. They were in major trouble now.

"Let's follow them," said Xander, as Terl led the handcuffed prisoners away.

"Well we don't really have anything else to do on this ship, except not get caught," said Tor, scanning the metallic ceiling for cameras. So far so good.

"Well we need some weapons first," said Xander.

"We have our DARPA blasters," said Tor, but then he followed Xander. It was always handy to keep upgrading weaponry. That was the way the Delta Force operated. *Overwhelming fire power.*

Zyk returns to the forest

"Won't you take me with you?" Jura had asked reproachfully, as Zyk had glanced at his fiendish guitar pedal board slung across his chest. The *Fuzz* pedal grinned hideously at Jura, but it was the *Compressor* pedal that had been the scariest to look at for Jura. It had the biggest ears that she'd seen made of pure skin. Like it was partly a human stuffed clumsily into a guitar pedal.

"Why are you so weird?" she'd asked him finally.

"Take a god dammed look around you," replied Zyk finally, unhappy to be unable to take Jura with him for the second time. "There's the whole *Third Reich* sitting inside the club there, a bunch of demented Jewish angels waiting for me outside, and I think that I might have just killed my most recent girlfriend."

"I can look after myself too," protested Jura hotly. "Don't you see my power here in the Underworld?"

Zyk knew she was right; she was powerful and had Underworld *street-cred*. But where he was going only the most terrible of damnation lay there. Visions of horror in space filled him. About what he himself was going to do. The Nazis feared Zyk's unrealized power and were no fools who they courted. It was no surprise that he'd lost Justine and this horror would've eventually killed her anyways in the process of Zyk's becoming.

"Don't think too much of yourself," Jura cut in with tears. "You need to get over yourself." With that she turned away sobbing to return to the Underworld.

Zyk beat a hasty retreat. He was an SS General, though he hadn't waited for his uniform. Couldn't really be walking around in an SS uniform looking like a ponce. Everybody was looking for love, these days, but none were satisfied. The grand Karmic joke of time, he thought, while grieving for Justine. For her to have died by his own hand or mind.

By the tree, he saw the angels hanging around for him. Blast! There was Gabriel and Elohim.

"We can take care of 'em," said the *Fuzz* distortion pedal looking up with hideous red eyes, while an evil mouth displayed a row of small sharp teeth.

"Yeah, just switch me on!" shouted the *Compressor* pedal.

"Yeah, put me in the chain, then I'll exterminate all of them!" screamed the *Delay* pedal.

The Angels loitering around now looked suspiciously at the guitar pedal board as Zyk neared them.

"Ok, those are straight up demons in those pedals," said Elohim suddenly recognizing the nature of the beast, and the old angel fearfully took a step back.

"Back Jew!" screamed the *Compressor* pedal.

"Scratch that," said Gabriel taking a step back too, as the *Wah* pedal let out a howling scream.

"Don't you like us anymore?" demanded Harut and Marut, the Arabs. "We are your ticket to Allah."

At this the pedals screamed with laughter, and the Fuzz pedal couldn't hold back and let out a torrent of white electricity that blasted through the angles sizzling them in seconds.

"You just killed two angels!" screamed Elohim.

The pedals chuckled as the angels stared at the swastika on the pedalboard. *Ah, Nazi demons.* All of them. And Zyk was safe with these horrible pedals. Maybe, he was in on it with them.

"Well, we're going," said Gabriel staring forlornly with his big eyes at Zyk. "But the aliens have got Jesus and its the Pzyklo empire behind it."

"So?" demanded Zyk who couldn't give a farthing for Jesus or the smoldering and quite dead Arab angels.

"Well, your name is Zyk and their empire is called P-zyk-lon," said Elohim caustically. "Ring a bell, ding ding?"

"Well," said Zyk hesitantly.

"Let us come with you," said Gabriel.

"Never Jew!" screamed the *Wah* pedal.

"Shut up," said Zyk. "There are other matters at hand."

"Nothing that we demons that can't take care of," grumbled the *Wah* pedal.

"Let me remind you that you are now a General of the Waffen SS," said the *Compressor* pedal. "Any deals with enemy Jews is treachery."

"What?" demanded Elohim.

"Yes, its true," said Zyk staring at his willful pedals.

"Adolf Hitler personally just appointed him," giggled the *Fuzz* pedal readying a blast of electrical energy.

"Never!" shouted Gabriel.

"Our backs are turned to you Nazi swine!" shouted Gabriel feeling betrayed.

"Forever!" chimed Elohim.

POOF! The angels disappeared.

Zyk began to walk deeper into the forest, while the guitar pedals giggled with malicious laughter as they gloated over their victory over the Biblical angels.

"Did you see that when I shot the two Arab angels?" shouted the *Fuzz* pedal.

The Reverb pedal clucked its tongue.

"Why, if I had fired my reverb energy, they would've been trapped for a thousand years in reverberating time."

"Pooh, that's nothing," countered the Delay pedal. "If I'd had put them in my delayed reality, then I would've unglued their very atoms."

Zyk realized that these Nazi pedals were packing some serious firepower. How happily he'd slung this pedalboard across his shoulders not realizing its demonic nature. *Former SS Death Camp Kommandants trapped in the pedalboard.*

"So General, what are your plans?" demanded the pedals, as the old woman and the fair maiden once again approached Zyk.

"For goodness's sake keep your mouths shut this time!" whispered Zyk fiercely, as the blonde approached him with a wide smile.

"The General wants to get laid!" snickered the pedals evilly. "We'll have to get rid of the hag then."

"Oh, I'm so glad that you made it out of that club safely," cried the fair maiden, while giving Zyk a surprise hug.

"Well, hello hello," muttered the pedals. The slim maiden stared at the assortment of pedals noting their red eyes and sharp fangs.

"Ah, you bring back German demons with you," she said worriedly. The old hag caught up with the maiden.

"Did you see what just happened?" croaked the hag. "They just took Jesus on an alien ship. It just took off."

Zyk remembered Jesus and Luke from Hitler's HQ. What did he care what happened to them?

Now the pedals started to kick about.

"Which aliens?" demanded the Fuzz pedal glaring with its baleful eyes.

"Well you know the tall furry ones," replied the hag.

"Pzyklos!" swore the Fuzz pedal.

"Who cares?" demanded Zyk. "So what if they have the same name as me?"

"This story goes deeper into the future than you think," snarled the Compressor pedal.

"The Pzyklos have an Oracle who has seen into the future!" guessed the Reverb pedal as it searched deep space for reverberating events and peered for hundreds of thousands of light years away into the future. "But I'm running into a blank."

"Well now," croaked the old Crone now shrewdly. "Why didn't you say so before that you needed an Oracle? Donay, my fair daughter is an oracle too and for the right price, she will tell you your fortune and future."

Zyk looked into the girl's eyes. Her green eyes sparkled merrily in the forest sun.

"Well how will we know for sure?" demanded the Fuzz pedal. "How much money do you want?"

Zyk suddenly landed back to reality with a thud. He was stone cold broke and couldn't pay the girl.

"It's alright, you can pay me later," Donay said sportingly and took Zyk's hand into her hand.

"No!" swore the old woman. "Nothing doing till we get paid. We have to live too you know."

Now the pedals started to warm up and everyone stared at the gruesome pedals that swelled into giant caricatures of the pedals. They were indeed growing larger as they growled fiercely.

"Do you know that you talk to an SS General?" demanded the Compressor pedal. "He can have you lot executed."

"Are you really a General?" demanded the old woman paling.

"He has recently been appointed," said the girl peering deeper into his hand, while Zyk grew uncomfortable, but the girl had already seen deeper into him and now her eyes were closed.

"I say," said Zyk trying to change the subject. "What's her name again?"

"Donay is the name of my darling girl," replied the hag.

The pedals were muttering amongst themselves. Sounded more like a mutiny.

"We will need a ship," said the Fuzz pedal. "We'll have to get that no-good Jesus back before he blabbers about you and gives the Pzyklos a visual on what you look like. We can't risk it. Heinrich Himmler is up to his old tricks again when he sold Jesus to the aliens. No doubt a lot of money was paid."

"Wait, I see something," Donay said now as she swayed while gripping Zyk's hand. "Empires, ships, wars and great danger."

"Tell us something that we don't know," sneered the Delay pedal.

"A security chief by the name of Terl will seek Zyk and try to kill him," she said. "He will be successful if we don't alter the future."

"See I told you," said the Distortion pedal now. "We must stop Terl."

"We must rescue Jesus from Terl to preserve Zyk's identity," agreed the Fuzz pedal. "But we will need this Oracle to come with us."

"Never!" howled the old hag and conjured up a magic spell to turn into a horrifying large serpent, and it giggled now, as it opened its jaws wide. Donay screamed to let go of Zyk's hand and took cover. She knew that the old hag was a terrible and powerful Witch.

Suddenly lightning strikes in the shape of twin SS lightnings into the serpent which tears off the serpent's tail, but which quickly regenerated like a lizard's, but the Delay pedal started terrible reverberations along with the Reverb pedal, and before Donay's horrified eyes, the ground began to tear open with a giant gaping mouth. The earthquake continued till the splitting ground caught up with the slithering serpent into which it fell —— deep into the very bowels of the earth. Suddenly, the reverberations stopped, and the earth became whole again squished tightly together by the Compressor pedal.

"No!" screamed Donay now in dismay. "That was my mother!'

"Well then let it be a warning to you then," snarled the Compressor pedal. "Don't mess with us Germans, especially gypsy scum like your mother."

"I don't think Donay is gypsy," noted Zyk.

"No, she adopted me," said Donay, who didn't seem to be the least like the old hag.

"Donay is Aryan," said the Delay pedal appreciably. The Distortion pedal agreed.

Zyk turned to comfort her.

"Well the Witch was going to kill us," he said, and she nodded.

"She had made up her mind to kill you in the forest since the very beginning," she confessed sobbing, and the pedals howled again.

"See General, we made the right call!" they gloated, as Zyk took a distressed Donay's hand and led her deeper into the forest.

Terl interrogates Jesus

"Spill it, or you're dead," growled Terl now lifting Jesus by his neck to his seven feet height. Luke trembled as Terl held him there.

"Tell him, Jesus," implored Luke. He didn't want to die over Zyk.

"Alright," struggled Jesus. He didn't like all this dangling business ever since he had been nailed to the cross by the Romans for like a week. Certainly not for Zyk who was out not to join his kingdom but usurp it into some twisted dystopian Nazi future.

"Alright," gasped Jesus with tears springing into his eyes, while Terl's horrific red eyes seemed incapable of pity.

Terl handed him a headband with a probe built into it.

"Wear it and let the operator search your memories," he said. "We will then generate Zyk's face and quickly find him."

Jesus wore the probe.

"Why is he so important to you?" Jesus asked, puzzled why such a powerful alien was looking for an earthly Zyk.

"We have the same problem," smiled Terl wickedly. "He's trying to take both our kingdoms, but luckily a mysterious Oracle warned us about this Zyk."

"Well, I've met him and read his thoughts," said Jesus. "He is dangerous and a sleeper agent, manifesting only when he is activated. Someone else is controlling him."

"Hey!" said a pleased Terl staring at an image of Zyk. "There you are!"

"Yep," nodded Luke. "That's him alright."

"I'm sending this to all our ships on earth to send out probes to get him," said Terl.

"Well you won't find him," Jesus shook his head. "The power of your ships means nothing where is he."

"Why?"

"He's in the Underworld, in another dimension," smiled Luke.

Terl now glared at these humans who smiled stupidly at him, but Terl already had a secret deal with SS Reichsführer Heinrich Himmler, who the mysterious Oracle had introduced him to recently.

A camera watches Tor and Xander enter a secluded part of the ship, where they furtively make their way through the cold and dark ship. A silent alarm is activated and Terl's watch beeps with a video image. He finishes glaring at Jesus and Luke to glance at the hologram. Humans!

"Ah, we have stowaways!" announces Terl thinking quickly. "They must have been that team that attacked Hillary's HQ."

"What, you're in cahoots with Hillary?" demanded Luke now outraged. He was her sworn KKK enemy.

"Well we were supporting her till she became too ill, so we had to do a body transplant for the elections," admitted Terl. "We were trying to find Zyk quietly through our agents in the Democrat party. But then they lost the election and thus we planned Earth's invasion."

"Oh my god!" shouted Luke. All this while he'd been quiet feeling out of his league, but here was red meat and it threw his memory back to the fateful 2016 elections.

"Lock her up!" rang the chants in USA. Well they hadn't been wrong.

"Where is she?" asked Luke.

"These very stowaways killed her, while attacking our base with nuclear grenades and caused us to take off a little prematurely," said Terl. "And now these American criminals are onboard my ship!"

He turned to tap the glass screen on his watch. A squad suddenly stood ready and this is when Jesus and Luke realized that the Pzyklos didn't talk much but communicated digitally. Pretty much like the millennials on Earth.

"Let's go and get these animals," Terl grinned evilly as he wore his combat helmet that secreted purple gas.

"How come you guys are wearing purple helmets?" asked Jesus.

"Our secret Pzyklo gas is very volatile and isn't stable in deep space, thus we have to wear our masks," scowled Terl. "But in high concentrations it gives us a super adrenaline kick like your cocaine on Earth." He glared at the animals, who were getting too big for their boots. Well, he was going to bump them off now anyways now that he knew what Zyk looked like.

Terl abruptly then turned to deal with the stowaways.

Zyk builds a spaceship

"Well how the hell are we going to catch up with the aliens?" demanded Zyk, walking with a very reluctant Oracle, who glared at the sniggering pedals on the steel pedalboard that Zyk so effortlessly slung across his chest. He must be strong, she realized, while reminded of her own frail shoulders. Her adopted mother had always seen to it that she grew up without hardship and had always said that she would be a better bride for royalty that way. She had been bred only for the Witch to become rich, but now these demented pedals had killed her. Zyk appeared to be innocent, but then these demons were his slaves or his masters? She would soon find out.

"Well think, you're the intellectual doctor," replied the pedals snarkily, as Zyk peered into the dark forest. It never got light enough here for it not to be a dark forest.

"Well there is a crashed space-ship at some distance from here," said Donay, who had grown up here in these haunted woods. "But there is great danger too there."

"Leave that to us," chortled the pedals. "We're Germans."

Zyk turned to the Oracle and she saw kindness in his eyes. But then why was even Jesus so fearful of this man? And the aliens desperately looking for him? It just didn't make sense. But then maybe he was rich, thought Donay, and she was dismayed that even though she was an Oracle, she couldn't see her own future. Though Zyk didn't seem too interested in throwing those lavish and expensive Royal balls like her stepmother had told her stories of. Anyways, maybe he could be turned but his eyes were somewhere else like he was communicating with other dimensions. She put her hand on his shoulder as if to steady herself, but then slipped into his mind to enter a very dark place with nothing but a humming sound. A machine. *An engine of thought.* But few humans were so blank inside. Not even the stupidest oafs that she had trained on. In fact, no one and not even including the witch had such silence in their mind. A terrifying silence that grew on her causing her to take her hand away. Zyk turned and smiled at her half-apologetically. She now knew why he wasn't married. The *Abomination of Desolation* lived within him —— an isolated mountain from where he would descend occasionally. Not exactly who she wanted to spend her life with.

"Woman, pay attention," snapped the Distortion pedal. *"Schnell!"*

She came crashing back to reality away from her dreams. Hopefully, the swamp monsters would get these nasty pedals.

In the inky darkness, the pedals now threw an arc of electricity that illuminated the swamp in front of them, and Donay put out her lantern —— she would save her oil for another day.

"Look snakes!" shouted the pedals. Donay knew them alright. They were the witch's sisters and they would be looking for revenge alright while in the distance lay a golden sword buried in stone.

"Go and see if you can pull that magic sword out of the stone."

Zyk stared suspiciously at her and the serpents that swam around the crashed spaceship. How the hell were they even going to get the ship out of the water? The entire clean-up process would take too long, and how was he going to pull a sword out of stone?

"Easy," said the Fuzz pedal. "Directing all firepower at that stone!"

A crackling beam of energy smashed into the giant rock. After the smoke settled, the serpents were now circling the stone. It had cracked but hadn't broken open.

The Reverb pedal now sent out an earthquake that split the earth all the way to the sword and everyone now had their hearts in their mouths as the earth opened up with a huge yawning gap. The sword going to fall into the earth.

But then the rock that held the sword was solid rock that extended deep into the bowel of the earth.

"Look! All the serpents have fallen into the earth!" cried Donay disappointedly, as Zyk gazed at the writhing snakes disappearing into the bowels of the molten earth.

The Distortion pedal now shot out a burst of black light that smashed into the crumbling rock and the sword now moved. But now all around the sword lay gaping earth with burning molten lava at its mouth. There was no way to the sword.

"That's a tough proposition now," said Zyk, but he also noticed that the swamp had been drained by the split earth and the ship now lay on a dry bed. "No, you don't understand, that sword is very powerful," argued Donay pointing with her slender finger towards the sword longingly. Zyk looked at it. Bah, it seemed too much work, but then the pedals were bucking by his waist. He looked down and they grinned eagerly.

"What she says is true," said the Compressor pedal, and Zyk gazed at the blazing red landscape with the solitary sword wedged into the mysterious piece of rock that emerged from the earth's depths.

"Well we can't fly," said Zyk and turned to the ship. Now that could fly. Donay appeared dismayed that her trap had failed as she trailed him and his demented pedals. There seemed a weird psychic energy all around this place and it felt familiar. That energy had a smell to it, no, a taste, like a personal energy. Someone was influencing everything here, and not just the pedals. Her senses told her to investigate Zyk deeper, but for that she would need to be alone with him and without those nasty pedals protecting him.

Terl catches his quarry

Xander and Tor are now on the bridge where everything is deathly quiet. Suddenly, there is the hissing of gas and purple gas appears on the bridge.

Luckily Tor and Xander still have oxygen in their AWS, while the computer readings cause an alarm to go off.

"Warning alien hazardous material detected. Warning," said a worried female's voice on their HUDs.

"They're trying to poison us," whispered Xander into the com, and Tor nodded. A dirty trick.

"Assume defensive posture on the bridge," ordered Tor. "I'll scout on ahead meanwhile."

"You got it," said Xander, as he unhooked a tactical nuclear grenade and grinned, as Tor exited through the sliding doors. Nobody was getting Xander. At least alive anyways. No alien experiments on him. No sir. That just wasn't how he was constructed. Suddenly, the floor went out from beneath him and he crashed down below with a sickening thud. The nuclear grenade rolled out of his hand, as heavy boots suddenly surrounded him and the last thing that

Xander remembered was a grinning seven-foot bear with long hair and red eyes, who smashed a boot into his helmet.

Ronald Trump

Trump's eyes are on the giant screen in the White House, displaying a ship rapidly taking off from Beverly Hills, LA, while the last feed that they'd received from Tor and Xander's *body cameras* was of Xander falling into a black hole, where the hideous Terl smashed his boot into Xander's helmet before their video feed was cut off.

Trump released his breath, which sounded like the hissing of air from a gas balloon. Schwartzkopf stared in shock, and he was still coming to terms with the fact that Hillary was an alien. *Had been an alien all this while.* Phew! Whatever next, as he mopped his forehead with a handkerchief.

"General Schwartzkopf, it is clear that we are up against a diabolically clever enemy," said Trump clearing his throat now. "An alien that can deceive us for their own purposes."

"Well sir, that's the definition of a parasite and we have plenty of those in the Democrat party," managed the General now with a grin.

Aliens in the Democrat Party. No wonder they had been so against Trump's wall.

"French Company has conducted itself with magnificent bravery and I want them all to get the Medal of Honor," said Trump. "Xander and Tor will be posthumously awarded."

"What about Hillary's remains?" asked Schwartzkopf.

"Let the Klu Klux Klan handle it," replied Trump. LA was under the Klan's jurisdiction anyways.

"Yes sir," said Schwartzkopf saluting and leaving the Oval Office, while Trump now grieved for the loss of his brave Delta Operators. Tor had been the best of the best. These sacrifices had not been in vain. But there was something about this Zyk fellow. He had been having dreams where Zyk and a pretty blonde were flying in a spaceship, and he shook his head. When would Zyk really make his move? What was he waiting for?

Or was he simply planning to abandon Earth?

Zyk checks out the damaged ship

The wind blows through Donay's long and lustrous hair, but Zyk doesn't notice, while the demonic guitar pedals only chuckle evilly among themselves. She misses her stepmother, even if she was a witch —— and had looked after her well, though only to market her well to some wealthy suitor. Instead, she had found a disinterested Zyk, who craved adventure in the galaxies and skies. She had seen into his heart. There was no desire for a warm hearth or the luxury of soft comfort. Only the cold and passionless drive for the *Fifth Reich.* He was being manipulated too by others, but he seemed oblivious of that, though his demonic pedals respected him, and grudgingly obeyed him. That part of a further hidden agenda in Zyk's breast was blurry and beyond her youthful powers of soothsaying, and she shook her head as her visions ended. Someone powerful was protecting him.

Donay reluctantly found Zyk on the ship's bridge, inside the metal hull of the ship where it seemed intact inside though it gave her the creeps —— cold and metallic. But Zyk then quickly sat at the console, where one of his guitar pedals tapped into the computer's mainframe.

"Throw in some electricity," he ordered, and the Fuzz pedal obliged with a loud fizz. Donay was stunned to see the ship's computer jump to life with numbers and multiple displays lighting up.

But the language was foreign as Donay tried to peer deeper into the screen to comprehend, as Zyk chuckled in the echoing interior.

"Its in Sanskrit, an old ancient Aryan language," he said and also tried to read it but couldn't fathom much. He placed his hand on a fingerprint reader and was pleased to see the language switch to English. Donay grew scared as suddenly a hologram appeared of the ship's log minutes before it crashed —— showing it being pursued in space by alien ships who eventually shot it down and it had crashed thousands of years before into the Underworld here. Time was such a mystery.

"Look it has Analog to Digital circuitry," said Zyk, as he unscrewed the main console. The pedals had meanwhile tapped little wires into the ship and were running their own diagnostics.

"The main nuclear reactor is offline," said the Distortion pedal eventually.

"Come on, Reverb," said Zyk. "Plug in your power."

The Reverb and Delay pedals pushed in power and the ship began to hum with energy and quickly lifted off the ground.

"We need an Amplifier for the voltage," said the pedals, as the Fuzz and Distortion pedals mashed in their energy too.

"Its working," said Zyk, and Donay grew frightened as the ship lifted higher before her very eyes.

"But the windscreen is shattered," she countered wondering how this ship would ever fly without windows.

Zyk and the pedals belatedly realized what she said was true.

"Well let's get that sword first," said Zyk, and steered the ship with his hands on the joystick. It glided right over the sword.

"Donay, can you get the sword?" asked Zyk, while holding the ship delicately over the sword. Burning fires raged below in the cavernous maw of the earth and smoke rose as young Donay's heart leapt to her mouth, which opened and closed like a fish-mouth's till the Fuzz pedal snarled at her.

"Hurry up," it growled revealing a red mouth with vicious fangs and it seemed to be in mammoth pain as it struggled to power the ship.

Donay hurried to the open ship's hatch, where a hot wind blew furiously outside, as she pushed her long hair back, and then stretched out her hand to grab the sword's hilt that stood tantalizingly close to the hovering ship. A howl erupted from the bowels of the earth as she gripped the leather handle. It was her stepmother.

"Avenge me, daughter!" howled the old hag from the fiery earth. Tears appeared in Donay's eyes, as she realized the pain that her stepmother was in. She gripped the sword and pulled with all her might. The ship jerked and the sword suddenly came free in her hand. There. She held the sword and wondered who to blame. The pedals. They had killed her mother but then it was all Zyk's fault in the end. *If only he hadn't crossed their paths.*

"Kill Zyk!" howled the voice again from the fiery insides of the earth causing Donay to shudder, and she hurried inside into the lurching ship. There was relief in Zyk's eyes when he saw her with the sword, as he flew the ship again back to the dried-out swampland to set the ship down.

16

Security Chief Terl

"Wake up, animal!" snarls Terl smashing a fist into Xander's mouth as he sits tied to a chair. Xander grimaces and spits out blood. That punch had rattled his skull like never before.

"Fuck you," managed the Delta Operator, as he painfully realized that Terl was wearing a helmet filled with purple gas.

"What's with the purple haze?" snarled a bleeding Xander now seeing red. This alien was so dead if he ever got his hands free. "You look like my dog wearing a helmet."

"We're aliens, asshole," grinned Terl, and now smashed another huge hairy paw into Xander's stomach causing it to flatten as he gasped for air.

Terl turned and left as Xander struggled with the metal restraints on his limbs. A metal door slammed shut and the sound reverberated through the cell —— a pretty big place guessed Xander in the darkness. But then he grinned in the darkness. Tor was still out there somewhere and free.

Tor, meanwhile, had gotten off the bridge, but in the next room he had run into a room of aliens. His eyes had widened with horror, but instead of being aggressive, the alien women all had welcoming smiles on their faces. He looked around suspiciously. They were all wearing pink lipstick. An uglier bunch he had never seen, maybe Michele Ovadia on Earth, but then at least these were smiling. It looked like some kind of an *alien brothel* as Tor grimaced and tried to avoid their welcoming arms. He grinned now as he took a glass of what smelled like wine and took a swig of it. Hmm, tasted pretty nice, fermented. Probably some alien fruit. He drank some more as more alien hands caressed his uniformed chest. His helmet was still on, but then one of them was trying to take it off. He pushed the broad away and tried not to look at her alien tits. But then there was some fascination there and he tried to imagine being with an alien. A feeling of revulsion grew in his stomach, but then the drink began to take hold of him, and he started to lose strength, while the 6 feet tall hairy alien women now began to swim on his vision much to his dismay. This was what an alien gang-rape looked like as he felt his clothes being taken off.

 Much later he woke up with a headache, naked though with his body still intact, and he wondered what had passed between him and the alien women. *Jesus Christ.* He saw his clothes and bounded for them which he quickly donned and took his weapon to quickly dash out of the room, but he also swiped a pink wig that one of the women had left behind. That would help to disguise him from the ceiling mounted cameras. He picked up his blaster, when he realized that he wasn't wearing his helmet. *But how was he still alive?*

This was very perplexing. Either the Pzyklos were suddenly breathing oxygen or he was breathing their purple gas.

Zyk

"Hey Donay, give me the sword," said Zyk as they disembarked from the ship. This had been the shortest ride ever. Donay reluctantly handed over the sword to Zyk who marveled at its gold and thick steel construction. They had descended to repair the windscreen which the pedals were trying to figure out, meanwhile.

"It's a Christian sword," she said, and Zyk nodded. Not that he gave a *rat's ass,* but it was good to know the history behind it.

"Actually, its a fallen Knight of the Templar Order's sword," she said touching the sword and saw visions of ancient and bloody Jerusalem.

"This particular Templar Knight had murdered thousands and had made a pyramid of skulls in Jerusalem, before he was condemned and hung by the Pope himself on trumped up charges of Blasphemy."

"That's awesome," said Zyk, and for the first time she saw a glint of excitement now in his eyes. The mass murder and blood had stirred his blood. Signs of a true psychopath. And on top of that the demonic pedals claimed that Hitler himself had made him his General, realized fair Donay.

Zyk grasped the sword and suddenly dashed inside the ship. She could now foresee the long journey in space and was strangely excited about it as she foresaw that she would be in love, *though she couldn't see with who.* But she had seen the marching armies and empires that Zyk was going to seed and begin thousand-year wars. Zyk would have to immortal for that, and maybe that's why Jesus and the Aliens were afraid of him. But first they needed supplies. Food. Lots of food if she was going to be on this ship. Meat, vegetables and she wondered if the ship had a larder. She would return to her house and bring back the honey and thick loaves of bread that her stepmother had recently made. The most delicious honey ever and she wondered if Zyk would appreciate it as she headed inside the ship. To her surprise she saw that Zyk had suspended the sword on a wire like a clothes' line and the pedals had connected themselves to the wire. Then the guitar pedals hooked their output to the ship's nuclear engines by more wires.

"What have you done to the sword?"

"Oh, its our energy source," said Zyk, as he started to paddle the sword around, and a buzz of blue electricity shot into the demonic pedals and then into the ship's nuclear reactor.

There was a roar and the ship shuddered heavily again.

"We have just started up 90 percent of the nuclear reactor," announced Zyk happily.

"Are you a nuclear engineer too?" asked Donay amazed.

"We just need lots of water," said Zyk playing around with the ship's controls. "There," he said. A hose shot out of the ship and snaked its way towards the almost dry swamp.

"Fill 'er up," said Zyk, as the ship greedily sucked in the remaining swamp water. A few thousand gallons and the reactor was good to go.

"Err... I have some supplies at home that I'd like to take with me on the ship," she said. Zyk turned towards her as did the demonic pedals.

"She might be up to some tricks," said the Compressor pedal.

"A snare," added the Fuzz pedal accusingly.

Donay glared at them.

"Oh yeah, what are you going to do for food?"

"Well since this ship crashed, I'm sure that there is food aboard this ship," said Zyk confidently. He pressed a few buttons and brought up the inventory.

"Look half full of freeze-dried meals," said Zyk, though wondering how old the food really was. Thousands of years at least, and who knew the physical laws of the Underworld?

"Well, I'd still like my honey," she said firmly.

"OK, we also need some sand to repair the broken glass and a welding machine to close the damaged hull on the rear," said Zyk nodding. The blasts on the ship were critical and needed to be closed to make the ship space worthy.

"Let's go," he said, and Donay felt grateful, though sadly, they were never going to be alone as the suspicious guitar pedals were watching her every move. She wondered if Zyk was attracted to her, but if he did, his eyes didn't show it. She knew that she was beautiful. Her stepmother had told her everyday about that and from the surrounding villages in the forest, many men had come for her hand. But the stepmother had held out, knowing that a Prince would one day marry her. Now the witch lay dead, and she was being kidnapped by the Nazis into the skies.

Ronald Trump

The Klan had cleaned out L.A to quite an extent, while the wall was coming up nicely. So, it had taken a nuclear war to bring a Klan fantasy to California and then to have his wall built. But this was no ordinary wall, but a self-aware wall with its own defenses and parameters with machine-gun emplacements, along with poison gas zones to prevent any mass attacks. The entire area around the wall was heavily mined too ——— an interdiction zone from now on. Automatic gun towers with lasers ready to zap heavier vehicles and tanks were also thoughtfully being placed. A video live feed of a Mexican being zapped had also been helpfully added by *Georgia Securities,* the company awarded the contract. Trump was impressed as the Mexican turned into a green fireball. *Kinda like the electric chair.* But who knew how many felonies that illegal might have already committed in the United States? Not that it mattered anymore, but Trump was also trying to build a new America, not as radical as the Klan's, but a legal America. With a clean slate. Sometimes that's what it took for real change.

Xander

Two more guys were thrown into the cell along with Xander who stared at the new curious folk. One guy appeared to be in a Nazi uniform and the other blonde was dressed in long robes like Jesus. Maybe they were gay and Xander stared at this kinky couple suspiciously.

"Hey, are you American?" asked Luke noting his Delta Force insignia and the US flag. Xander was relieved to hear English. Then Jesus spoke up too.

"We are all Terl's prisoners and we watched you on the tv cameras getting caught," said Jesus." That's how we already know about your mission in L.A."

Fucking L.A. It had been a trap or something. Now here he was jetting out to some alien planet, but then thought of Tor and brightened up.

"They are looking for your companion as we speak," said Jesus. Xander's eyes jerked at the mention of his commander, well, Tor was a wily one and wherever he was, he was probably outsmarting them. Tor was a survivor.

Tor, meanwhile, crept under a camera and evaded its radius but still had the alien female wig on just in case they were tracking him. He needed to find a safe place and reassess the situation. His com was still working but Xander's was out. He had meant to go back and find Xander but after the alien girls, he'd found himself in a different room, and completely disoriented.

Zyk rescues the Norwegian

"The nuclear turbines have started to fail," announced the Fuzz pedal feeding on the fluctuating oscillator power of the spinning sword. "There is a glitch in the feedback system of the ship's nuclear reactor."

"What do you mean?" demanded Zyk, as he spun the sword around frantically snagged on the line of wire.

"Its enough power to hover around here on earth, but the Fusion generator onboard is damaged and keeps switching off. We need a real good continuous source of energy. Of metal strings," said the Compressor pedal.

"You mean like a guitarist?" asked Donay suddenly. Everyone looked at her amazed.

"Yeah, and a better one than the General here," commented the Delay pedal. "We need someone who can play really fast and for hours on end. That way the energy oscillations will keep us going real good to juice the nuclear reactor even if it fails."

"And I know just the guy," said Donay quickly. Zyk and the pedals regarded her suspiciously. She was after all a witch's stepdaughter.

"Who?" demanded the Fuzz pedal.

"A guy called *Varg* who's been in jail for the last 20 years," she said. "He's in the Norwegian village of *Bergen* beyond the river. Legend has it that he was drawn to the devil when he set a Church on fire in some satanic ritual and managed to kill twenty people."

"Is this guy the only guitarist around?" demanded Zyk. "I don't want psychos around me in deep space. We have enough problems with these demons here." The pedals chortled.

"The devil you said?" giggled the Fuzz pedal. "Why, when I was in human form, I had executed entire divisions of Jews.

Zyk turned sharply to the pedals.

"Like *Einsatzgruppen?*"

"We were all hung for our crimes, but our spirits were trapped into these guitar pedals by Himmler for you. My real name is Major Otto Ohlendorf, head of *Einsatzgruppen D.*"

Zyk noted Donay's horrified expression.

"Between us pedals, we have about half a million people dead and rotting," boasted the Fuzz pedal. "And *Obergruppenführer,* as a General of the SS, don't think that you wouldn't do this. An Oracle called Maria Orzic has already prophesied you to lead the Fifth Reich where we will all be resurrected and massacre Alien Races through the galaxies till the Aryan Race is supreme."

Donay recoiled in horror as she realized that she was surrounded by German mass murderers.

Zyk turned away. *Maria Orzic.* Such a familiar name. But it had always been Kali in his dreams. *Or Madame Blavatsky.* Well someone. But the answers lay in Space and not on Earth anymore. He had wanted to meet Ronald Trump, but here a bigger destiny was calling. Sepp, who was supposed to be his character in his book, but had set up Zyk to become a General in the SS. Then the Aliens and Himmler. Complications at every level. He stared at the fiendish pedals who bared their fangs at him. As far as he knew, Otto had been a reasonable guy, as he stared at the impish Fuzz pedal. Once in Human form, he knew that he could turn Ohlendorf back to his command again. He was the Obergruppenführer here anyways.

"Right, lets get your boyfriend," said Zyk, as he fired up the nuclear reactor to full power causing the ship to levitate. There was a roar and Donay quickly got into a command chair and strapped herself in.

"He's not my boyfriend!" protested Donay hotly over the engines with her pale cheeks in full blush causing the pedals to snicker. Donay sulkily pointed in the direction of the imprisoned Norwegian.

A rescue of a *Black Metal* head.

Jesus

Jesus thought about the recent events that had taken place and none of which he was controlling. *Maybe Dad.* Didn't put too much faith in his absent Dad, though people always thought that his Dad was perfect and shit. Jesus laughed sardonically. Tell me about it, as he gazed at his his nail scarred hands and feet. Some Dad.

"Xander, tell me something," said Jesus turning to Xander who was looking for a way out of their prison. But it was built for really strong Pzyklos. "Do you believe in God?"

Xander turned to this blonde fruitcake.

"Yeah, and the tooth fairy too," he grunted, as he searched for crevices behind the door's hinge. But it was all solid carbon steel. The hinge didn't budge. "If He gets me out of here and back on Earth, then yes I'll start going to Sunday Church."

Jesus laughed. Fat chance of his dad doing anything like that. Unless you died and were reborn. That's what Jesus had done. But it was all so complicated.

Luke looked at Xander.

"Hey man, this is Jesus here," he said. "I'm serious. The real deal."

Both of them were Christian fanatics, realized Xander. Jesus stared sadly at Luke and shook his head. Sometimes people weren't ready for the truth. He put on his best martyred look, but it wasn't working as Xander continued to look for alternate exits in their smooth carbon metal prison, which appeared to be made of one long sheet of alien metal.

Tor looks for a way out

Tor, while still wearing his pink wig, snuck into another control room. He'd taken off his helmet and it was so much easier to walk around the place without it. He headed over to the console that sported a few buttons which said something in an alien language, but Arabic numerals, and he pressed a button. On the screen, suddenly, a flight map appeared showing the distance to the other galaxy that they were headed to. His blood ran cold when he recognized the units of distance that they were using was in Light years. *About 12.5 billion light years.* They were never going home again. He realized that the ship was weaving in and out of wormholes, like booster shortcuts and the journey was being completed fast. He needed to send this map back to earth for any hope of a rescue and gripped a large and black joystick to move it around. It panned a zoomed-out view of the map of the galaxies and wormholes. He took pictures with his helmet that he still carried with him and then transmitted them over his video feed as a general broadcast on Ultra-High Frequencies. This was DARPA Mars mission-tech that allowed for Deep Space micro radio-waves to travel quickly. God only knew when Earth would receive this, but Tor also decided to leave a video message as he faced his helmet.

"SOS. If someone is receiving this, please follow coordinates to alien planet Pzyklo for rescue attempt. SOS. Repeat US ARMY Delta Force Operator Tor being taken to Planet Pzyklo. SOS."

A noise startled Tor suddenly and it was the bridge's hatch opening.

He ducked under the console as someone also came in from the other side of the ship's bridge. *Trapped!*

Tall aliens thundered into the room.

"Ok animal come on out!" boomed a voice in English. "We know you're here. It was stupid to send a transmission from our ship because that triangulated

your location to over here, and you certainly saved us the bother of searching for you. We'll also invite your President Trump formally to come and visit us."
Tor realized that he was ringed in and he groaned.
"We have your friend too, Xander," coaxed Terl. "A lot of other humans to play with too. Come out immediately."
Tor flinched at the mention of Xander. Well that settled it.
He stood up and walked out into the open and his mouth dropped open to see Terl at over seven feet tall with red eyes. *Certainly not as pretty as the Pzyklo women.*

Zyk and Donay

The ship flew steadily over mountains and rivers that lay scattered amongst the foreboding forests, while offering themselves for viewing only when the thick canopies would clear. But on the whole, a dreadful fog hung over the forest, as the ship switched on its space-arc lights to navigate through the soupy mix.
"Well Donay, this is not some of the most cheerful country is it?" smiled Zyk.
Donay knew these lands quite well, but then the darkness was where she had grown up and it was home.
"Just over there on top of the hill is the village of Norway."
"Ok, and this Norwegian village has its own jail?" demanded Zyk. Preposterous, this naming of a village after a country. She nodded.
"Yes, land her in the middle. There is only one policeman in the village so it should be easy to get Varg out," said Donay confidently.
Zyk stared at her as she flicked her sandy hair across her face and smiled now sweetly for the first time.
"Varg," said Zyk playing his name thoughtfully. *Very interesting.* The guitar pedals powered down as the ship touched down, and Donay felt relieved to be on solid ground again. It wasn't going to be for long, as she dashed out, with Zyk and his pedals following after her. She really was in love with this prisoner apparently.
In the small police station, there was an old policeman sitting with his boots on the desk, while eating lunch. A piece of thick black bread slid from his

hands, as he gaped at Donay and Zyk, who had burst into his quiet police station with young Donay quite flushed.

"Release the prisoner, Varg," ordered Donay imperiously. Zyk stared at the Fuzz pedal, which bared its teeth at Zyk.

"What are you looking at me for?" snarled the pedal.

"Show us where the prisoner is," ordered Donay, grabbing a sword that lay near the policeman's desk. Donay was feisty, nodded Zyk. If the men weren't going to help her then she would have to take matters into her own hands as she placed the sword on the old man's neck. Zyk came forward and took the bunch of keys that lay on the desk.

"Give me the sword," he said. "You go and get your boyfriend."

She flushed but released the sword and hustled away deeper into the police station, when there was the sound of metal on metal and a cell creaked open, from where a tall, and thin man with long and dirty hair emerged wearing all black. He had a matted blonde beard but Donay appeared thrilled to bits with him.

"Guys, I haven't had a good meal in three years," Varg complained to his liberators while shooting a blistering look at his jailer.

Donay turned to Zyk.

"We can load up supplies from the village bakery and the general store here," she said and dashed out, while dragging a weak Varg by the hand.

"Don't forget to get his guitar," said Zyk after them.

The policeman now turned to Zyk.

"He's a murderer," he complained bitterly.

"Well we're going to give him a chance to redeem himself," said Zyk.

"On whose authority?" demanded the policeman.

The pedals now puffed themselves up.

"You dog," said the Fuzz pedal. "Do you know you talk to a General of the SS."

"Maybe, but who has no authority in Norway," replied the policeman calmly.

"Norway was occupied by the Nazis, and technically the Germans still rule Norway, at least, in the Underworld," retorted the Fuzz pedal in his best legal voice.

Now the policeman thought about it.

"Well if he can give me a legal paper with a sign and stamp," said the policeman.

The Fuzz pedal now looked at General Zyk.

"Open the pedalboard," the pedal said. "Inside lies Nazi stationery and your stamp, Herr General."

Zyk quickly unslung the pedalboard and cracked it open. Inside indeed lay money, stamps, a swastika armband and stationery with Zyk's name on it.

"Well, I'll be damned!" swore the policeman, as Zyk tied the armband around his left arm. The policeman sprang to attention and saluted.

"My General!" he saluted.

"Release the prisoner into my custody under wartime German Army occupation laws of 1943," ordered Zyk. How did he know all this, as he hastily scribbled a few lines onto a piece of paper without thinking?

Then he took out the stamp which was basically an eagle clutching a swastika in its talons and smashed it down on the piece of paper which read,

"In the name of the Führer, Adolf Hitler, Supreme Leader of Germany and all of its occupied lands in the Underworld, I, SS General Zyk order the release of convicted Norwegian prisoner Varg Viks into my custody and henceforth assume command of this Norwegian subject. I would also need supplies and I order you to assist me in procuring supplies from the village of Norway for a mission of the utmost importance to the Reich and its Volk."

Signed
Obergruppenführer Zyk of the Waffen SS
Leader of Underworld Special Forces of the Reich
Heil Hitler!

The old policeman quivered at the menacing *swastika* heavily stamped on the paper and thought of the Underworld. At night, the terrible screams from the forest beyond were frightful and he had no intention of ever visiting it. The Nazis ran a roaring nightclub there and it was a popular haunt of Hitler's ever since he had taken a fancy to Dj'ing. He trembled at the thought of running into the SS there or drawing their attention to his peaceful village and dashed out to help Donay and Varg get more supplies and stock the ship well for an intergalactic voyage.

Hopefully enough for them not to return.

Ronald Trump

"Well General Schwartzkopf, what on earth are we supposed to do with this map?" demanded Trump as he stared at the map of the sky on his screen.
"Beats me, sir," said Schwartzkopf. "But Operator Tor is requesting a rescue from Deep Space."
 Trump shook his head helplessly. He hated leaving good Americans behind, but it looked that this was the end of the line for Operator Tor and Xander.
"Close the map and terminate this operation. We will no longer be monitoring these Operators," said Trump, and walked out from the operations' room as Schwartzkopf cut the Deep Space com link, but then thought about it, and forwarded the video to DARPA.

Tor meets Xander

"Hey, never thought that I would see you again!" shouted Xander, as he helped Tor up from the floor of the cell, who had just been thrown in roughly by a gloating Terl.
"Guess there's no rescue then," rued Xander, but still glad to see the A-Team OP leader.
"Yeah, the damned cameras," said Tor shaking his head while taking off the pink wig.
"The good news is that the air is ok for us to breathe," said Jesus.
"Who the hell is this guy?" demanded Tor.
Luke stepped forward.
"Sir, its an honor to meet with you," he said. "Grandmaster Luke of the Klan Army."
Tor stared at him distastefully. He was no fan of the Klan after what he'd been through with them since North Dakota and California.
"Who the hell are these aliens?" demanded Xander.
"What we've heard is that they're called Pzyklos," relied Luke thoughtfully.
"And they're after a guy working for undead Nazis called Zyk.
"The human the aliens are after is called Zyk?" asked Tor.
"Jesus!" swore Xander.

"This sounds like a bad hollywood movie. Zyk and Pzyklo," said Tor thinking about it.

"They came to find their Dad?" demanded Tor incredulously. All of Earth had been laid waste just to get this Zyk.

"Well they were also making sure that no future threats from Earth will ever emanate again," Luke said. "Actually, once they get Zyk, they plan to destroy Earth in totality."

"Jesus, talk about daddy issues."

"You keep taking my name," said Jesus now with a sickly smile. He was still popular with humans.

"This guy is another piece of work," snarled Xander, and took Jesus by his lapels. "How would you like a knuckle sandwich, creep?"

"Come on, he's just a nut. The intergalactic journey has probably fried his brain," said Tor, and Xander suddenly grinned and put Jesus down. Luke wisely decided not to say anything. Jesus had already gotten him into so much trouble, and he was here all because of him anyways.

"Looks like we're going to find out just what the hell Zyk did to piss his kids off so much," said Tor, as he decided to lie down and get some shut eye.

Jesus closed his eyes to meditate. Zyk seemed to be just like his own Dad with his kids all pissed off at their absentee Father.

Zyk's ship

Varg returned with Donay, along with the policeman carrying armloads of supplies, while Zyk's demonic pedals were contemptuous of this need for food.

"Are you going to eat all that?" demanded the Compressor pedal contemptuously. The Delay pedal also made eyes at all the brown bread and cheese, as Zyk made an inventory of the food outside in the thick snowy village of Norway.

"Would you look at the jam and dried meats?" swore the Fuzz pedal. "That used to be my favorite before they hung me at Nuremberg." There was a wistful note in Major Otto Ohlendorf's voice.

"I will eat for you," said Zyk with a twinkle in his eye.

"Thanks," said the Fuzz pedal, but his tone was softer now. Zyk was making friends with the pedals now. He was also their commander. But Ohlendorf now inside the pedal felt Zyk's soul. Warmth. After so many years someone understood and remembered him. Otto Ohlendorf still lived inside Zyk's memory. The pedal sullenly looked at Zyk with new respect. Maybe he would make a good General. Well that would be seen only in battle and so far, this new Waffen SS General was untested.

"Varg, come here," cracked Zyk's voice, and the long-haired Norwegian stared at Zyk. The pedals grinned now expectantly. *First contact.*

Varg stood in front of Zyk now, who wondered what to make of this strange looking man in a leather jacket, black jeans, and boots. He even had a pedalboard slung across his chest, but the pedals on it were all demonically alive. A chill went up Varg's spine.

"Varg Viks, you are a convicted criminal and murderer, but we have need for your guitar skills onboard our ship," said Zyk coldly. "Let it be known that I don't like criminals, and in the Waffen SS, we would have executed you."

Varg nodded sullenly.

"Do you agree to follow all orders given by me?" demanded Zyk.

Varg nodded. But Zyk didn't seem like the shooting kind and a sneer rode his lips.

"Any insubordination or infraction and my demonic pedals will eat you alive," said Zyk, and now all the pedals leapt up with their terrible red fangs and almost snapped Varg's head off. Varg fell back into the snow in surprise. Ok, these guys were really bad news.

"Get onboard, Donay," ordered Zyk, as she and the old policeman scurried inside with the supplies. "There is a larder behind the ship's bridge with plenty of frozen food already stocked there." Donay felt bile rise to her mouth. Thousands of years of old food. And the ship had been without power for that long too. Zyk could eat that if he so wished.

"Well, I'm not going to be eating any of that," she retorted while entering the old ship, and the old policeman couldn't wait to get back into his warm police station. This ship was dark and cold. Exactly as he pictured a Waffen SS ship would be. But what the hell did they need Varg for? He didn't seem to have any skills apart from Donay having the hots for him. Well his was not to argue and wordlessly he deposited all the food in three trips and the deed was done.

"Right, old man," said Zyk at the ship's entrance hatch. "You've done well, and the Reich thanks you."

The old policeman saluted with his arm out and said as stiffly as he could, "Heil Hitler!"

"Heil Hitler!" roared back the pedals before Zyk could reply. Oh, they were diehard Nazis alright, as Zyk sighed while pushing the button to close the hatch. The old policeman stood at attention, as snowflakes piled up on his face, till the metal hatch firmly snapped shut and only then did his heart stop hammering.

Heil Hitler, indeed thought the policeman and he hoped he'd never see this devilish crew again.

Terl visits

"Get up animals!" Terl snarled. The prisoners got to their feet and were herded out by fearsome guards who butted them with their mammoth blasters.

"What's the rush, Terl?" demanded Xander causing Terl to cuff him on the head for his impertinence.

"You get that every time you address me like that," roared Terl, while Xander shook his head as his vision swam. Some cuff.

"Alright, we want to show you today what our glorious planet looks like," said Terl jovially, as the metal doors of the prison opened, and Tor was grateful to stretch his legs. Jesus stared at Terl reproachfully.

"Maybe we can spread the word of God over there in your heathen lands," said Jesus happily with his eyes shining. His father would be so happy, when suddenly a hairy mitt crashed on his ear that sent him flying into the wall. Tears and stars greeted his vision, as Jesus recovered slowly from that blow, while everyone laughed including Xander. Luke came quickly to help Jesus back to his feet.

"Why don't you keep your damned mouth shut?" demanded Luke sullenly. "This is not a fight that I want to be involved in."

"Even you, Luke?" asked Jesus with hurt in his eyes. Luke joined the others as they strode off, while the guards roughly prodded him back to his feet with their boots.

Jesus shook his head and rejoined the group, which was being given some kind of a guided tour of the ship and then an audiovisual presentation of Planet Pzyklo. Well, Jesus would escape and then try to covert the lot of them to

Christianity, no matter the odds. The Jews had nailed him. Let's see what the Aliens could do to him. His Father might just protect him this time, and he could feel it in his aching bones.

Ronald Trump

The President is considering another round of the DARPA nuclear shield, while gazing at the giant 10-meter-high OLED screen in front of him. He is in the NSA HQ where they're trying to figure out the latest Mothership maneuvers. A lot of them have descended lower into the Earth's atmosphere like they were closing in on the mysterious Earthling.

"Run a search globally on who the hell this Zyk guy is," ordered Trump, watching the live video feed from Tor's helmet cam. He couldn't believe Jesus was alive and with them gazillions of miles away in a spaceship blasting towards an alien home planet.

"Sir, we don't have most of our internet resources and many servers are down," said NSA chief Davis. "But the Israelis have a backup of all our data in Tel-Aviv."

"Well, get the Israelis on the job then."

"Yes sir," saluted Admiral Davis and got on the phone with the MOSSAD. If they couldn't dig up any dirt on this guy Zyk, then no one could.

"Yeah Avi, this is Director Davis," he said into the phone. "We need an urgent favor about a lead that we have. I'll be sending our request thorough an official email. Yes, I'll send it right away. The President of the United States sends his best regards to you."

Director Davis put the phone down to turn to Trump who simply nodded and strode away from the operation theatre.

Varg realizes

"Who the hell are you, anyways?" demanded Varg, gathering strength after a hearty meal quickly prepared by Donay

Zyk stared at the murderer coldly.

"Look he was just a kid when that Church burning happened," protested Donay coming to his defense and Zyk nodded.

"Just a stupid kid, right?"

Zyk pointed to Varg's guitar.

"All you have to do is play the guitar and you'll get food and money as a soldier. If you try anything funny on this ship, then we will execute you on the spot. There will be no mercy, prisoner Varg."

Donay paled at Zyk's words, while Varg nodded slowly as the message sunk into his brain.

Just then the Fuzz pedal threw out a bolt of lightning into the ship's console. The ship's computer suddenly crackled to life, while the lights flickered all across the ship.

"Hello," said an eerie voice.

"What the hell did you just do?" snarled Zyk at the Fuzz pedal.

"My name is Devus and what are you people doing on my ship?" asked the disembodied voice causing Zyk's hair to stand up on his neck. "Anyways, I have run a ship systems' check and we need to replace the broken windscreen before any space journey. Welcome to my ship, by the way, Zyk."

There was a thunderstruck silence. Even the pedals stopped their perpetual grunting and snarling at each other.

"Were you eavesdropping?" demanded Zyk realizing that this computer knew way more than it should.

"I come from the planet Pzyklo and we know all about you, Zyk," said Devus eerily.

Donay and Varg exchanged glances. This was way over their head.

"Zyk's future lies on another planet in my visions," she told Varg who grunted and nodded. Varg didn't seem to be so interested in Donay, while apparently busy fighting demons inside his head. He needed work, realized Zyk staring at his own demonic pedals. Were they even real? Was this all a giant hallucination?

"Varg," cracked Zyk's voice. "Start playing the guitar."

Varg's face brightened up as he brought out his trusty handmade mahogany electric guitar —— with its heavy embedded signature pickups —— luckily still at home from where he had retrieved it. His parents were long dead, but his guitar had kept him company for most of his life, and Varg plugged in the lead from the Fuzz pedal's mouth causing his guitar to suddenly sizzle to life. The overdrive pedal kicked in along with the compressor pedal all connected in series, while Donay was thrown off balance as Varg erupted with passion. The electrical energy went straight to Zyk's digitally constructed amplifiers on the computer's mainframe, which multiplied the energy a million times more. "A very clever energy source," commented Devus, as Donay listened aghast at the terrifying distorted howl of Varg's guitar.

"Nuclear reactor firing at full capacity," announced Devus, as Zyk dashed back into the supply room and heaved back a large package that Devus had highlighted in the storeroom on the screen. When he opened the package, it had bacterial bots that would construct the new windshield organically and hermetically seal the hull too

"Fuzz pedal crack the old windshield some more," ordered Zyk, and the Fuzz pedal shot out a bolt of electricity that almost melted the glass into sand. Zyk then placed the windshield glass containing bots all around the old clamps which automatically clutched the nascent and soft windshield from the bottom. Then the genetically modified bacteria began to spin out new glass rapidly from the old and melted glass. Within twenty minutes they were done.

"Ok, testing the windshield density and tensility," said Devus and did a tensile strength test on the windshield. It held. The hull, meanwhile, had also been repaired by metal excreting bacteria. Genetically modified bacteria were now repairing damaged spaceships in mid flight without the need to land.

"Yeehaw!" shouted Zyk and smashed a fist onto the ignition button. The ship suddenly lifted up and rocketed into space.

Terl on the ship's bridge

"Now animals, we will show you the wonders of *Pzyklo City,*" announced Terl proudly turning on the giant screen to display impossibly high towers stretching into the clouds above the city. He panned into superhighways one on top of each other, while thick with cars that seemed to move like roller coaster rides.

"Wow, those cars are just sitting on the highway," gasped Tor.

"The cars don't move, the highways do," replied Terl.

"Kind of like an open hyper-loop," marveled Jesus. He was sure now that his Father had nothing to do with the Pzyklos. They were on their own, never to be saved.

"What does this guy Zyk have to do with the Pzyklo planet?" demanded Xander, and now Terl turned glowering to hit him hard on the head which sent him flying into the bridge's console. Apparently, that was something that Terl didn't want to talk about.

"Our civilization flourished despite other Empires that tried to bring us down. We have defeated them all."

"So why are you after one man?" demanded Jesus, seeing some parallels with his life after being hunted by the Jews —— now Zyk being hunted by Pzyklos. Was Zyk also on a mission from his father? He felt the solid wallop of Terl's paw that sent him flying too in the direction of Xander who softened his crash into the console.

"Thanks man," said Jesus to Xander who smiled at him ruefully.

"Anytime."

"You animals need to realize that you cannot interrupt me," snarled Terl feeling some of his thunder stolen.

"We just want to put things in context," said Tor going to help Jesus and Xander up.

"You will know everything once we land on planet Pzyklo," said Terl, and the humans worriedly stared at their new home on the screen. A gigantic planet thirty times the size of Earth hidden in a swirl of purple gas.

Devus

Everybody is now safely strapped into their seats as the ship hurtles into deep space with Devus now doing the navigating.

"Did you guys have any idea where the hell you were going or were you just blasting into space?" demanded Varg staring at Zyk. Even the pedals were quiet as they stared at the sun.

"I can fly my own ship very well, thank you," said Devus now appearing to be in command.

"I am commanding this ship," countered Zyk, looking up at the ship's speakers placed in the roof of the ship.

"Gravity stabilizers engaged," said Devus.

"You said you crash-landed in New York a week ago, but wee Donay here says that your ship had been there for hundreds of years," said Zyk. Devus remained quiet for a few moments.

"I have no idea. I was offline and have run a systems' check but the date of my crash and today's date show a difference of one thousand years. All that I remember is that I was shot down above the Earth's atmosphere and here I am. My surveillance cameras were also offline."

"Well that's *time* for you in the Underworld," said the Fuzz pedal also in deep thought. "Someone is able to play tricks on all of us."

"Damned business when dealing with Demons," muttered Zyk. "But Devus, I want you to know that I am in command of this ship."

"Yes, of course, Zyk. After all, it was you who designed the previous *Devus I and II generation* ships," replied Devus.

Another round of thunderstruck silence. Donay fearfully glanced at Zyk who stared back with an equally amazed look. The pedals giggled.

"So General, is there anything that you're not telling us?" asked the Fuzz pedal.

"I told you there was something about our guy," said the Delay pedal. The Reverb pedal shook its head.

"This is ridiculous even by Underworld standards."

Zyk stood up unhooking himself from the seatbelt.

"Look Devus, I don't know what you're talking about."

"My memory banks had been partially destroyed and I cannot clarify my statement, but Dr Zyk here is the original programmer of the *Genesis* microchip that is embedded in all Devus class ships."

"Wait a minute," said Varg turning to Zyk. "Are you like the father of the Pzyklo empire?"

"Come on, look at me," said Zyk. "Do I look like an alien?"

The pedals giggled.

"Well your hand tells me that you have lived a lot more than your years on Earth," said Donay. Zyk looked away wracking his brain. There had to be answers somewhere and he couldn't remember anything just like Devus. A sudden flash of armies and explosions lighting up dark space like a sun. A call for help in deep space. A crash landing and then blackness. Zyk shook his head.

"Devus, take us to planet Pzyklo," said Zyk. There would be answers there for sure.

"I'm sorry but I cannot."

"Explain."

"My memory banks have been fried," replied Devus. "It was a rather bad crash and my inter-galactic mapping systems are offline, sir."

"Devus, you're not helpful at all," replied Zyk. "We're lost in space then."

"Yes sir."

Zyk turned to Donay.

"Come on then," he said. "Use your oracle powers."

"Fuck off," she said angrily. "I'm not telling you anything till you tell us who you really are! Because of you, my mother is dead."

Zyk realized that she still hadn't forgiven him for that. Not that it was his fault. It had been a fair shootout.

"Look all you need to know is that I am an SS General and I give the orders around here," said Zyk sharply. "All of you including Devus are under my command by the authority of the German Reich."

"Affirmative," replied Devus toadily, and Donay looked up to glare at Devus.

"You who can't conveniently remember anything?" she demanded.

"What do you really remember, Devus?" asked Zyk turning to Devus again.

"What is your primary mission?" interrupted Varg, getting straight to the point.

"To safeguard the children of Wotan," replied Devus. Everyone shook their heads.

"Secondary directive?" asked Varg.

"I don't remember."

"Can you communicate with planet Pzyklo?" asked Zyk now desperately searching the ship's data systems for maps.

"Negative, I don't remember the call frequency," Devus replied.

"We may as well head back to Earth then," said Zyk frustrated at this failing mission. He would be laughed out of officer-cadet school with this level of planning, though this had all been very ad-hoc SS style. Improvisation was the name of the game for much of the SS armies' success on the battlefield.

Terl

During the screening of Planet Pzyklo, Tor had secretly turned on his helmet cam for a continuous video transmission now into deep space. Terl didn't see any threat from Tor wearing his helmet again, though he thought it was to avoid getting hit by Terl's massive paws. He grinned evilly. Well, he was known to have a very heavy hand.

"Is this some kind of a time machine where you come back to set things right in the future?" asked Tor.

Terl glanced sharply at him.

"No, this is the present and Zyk is a threat predicted by a powerful Oracle. That's all. I don't know who and how he came to be named Zyk."

"And you pulled your whole Pzyklo fleet to come and deal with Zyk."

Now Terl laughed.

"Why we have hundreds of these kinds of fleets. You have no idea of the power of the Pzyklo Empire. We have survived for thousands of years and seen off many other empires. As security chief, I identified Zyk as a clear and present danger because so far, our Oracle's predictions have never been wrong —— so far."

"Right," said Tor nodding.

"Hey Terl, how old are you?" asked Xander, as he tore off a piece of his shirt to wrap a cut on his forehead and Jesus helped him with that.

Terl glared at him again but then shrugged.

"I don't know, but more than two hundred years," he said realizing that he'd never kept count.

Everyone including Jesus looked shocked.

"Why even as the son of god, I've only lived a few dozen years myself," he roared now speechless with rage at his father who seemed to be more pathetic by the moment.

Terl grinned at him.

"How's that Christianity working out for you? At least those German swine in the *Valhalla* are not Christian."

"What Valhalla?" demanded Tor now, and Terl rolled his eyes and walked out of the room. He was done with this rabble's questions. The guards were watching their movements, and everyone knew that escape was useless.

Xander hobbled over to Tor.

"Do you think that the Valhalla is real?" he asked.

"Enough for Terl to take it seriously."

"Do you think that this Zyk guy has some connection to it?"

"Damned if I know, but we need to get to planet Pzyklo and find out more."

"We need help."

"I know. Hopefully, someone on Earth is listening."

Trump at NSA

"Hopefully, someone on Earth is listening."
Trump turned with his eyes glittering. First proof that there was life after death.

"Sir, but this Valhalla's existence would make it racist," argued a Jewish aide, who seemed appalled that some Aryan Hitler mythology actually existed out there.

"What do you wanna do about it?" asked Trump with a glint in his eye. The aide hastily retreated into the shadows.

"Sir, we don't have the resources to take on this Empire. Hell, our Space Marines don't even have ships as yet that are space worthy," said General Schwartzkopf. "Our Space Force is quite grounded, I'm afraid."

Trump only nodded.

"I think that I've heard enough on those tapes," he said. "General Schwartzkopf, come with me to the White House war room and assemble all the top Pentagon and Air Force Generals ASAP." With that Trump with his golden mane strode out of the room.

General Schwartzkopf mopped his forehead and stared bug-eyed at the NSA agents.

"You heard the President!" he barked, and the aides scuttled to their phones. President Trump had a plan.

An hour later, all the good men of Virginia were assembled in the War Room of the White House with Trump projecting slides on the screen.

"Ok, we have a very audacious plan of attack," said Trump. "What I have noticed is that they don't breathe the same gas as us."

"Yes, we saw that purple air, but the humans were breathing it normally," protected General Schwartzkopf.

"Yes, but what does that tell you?" asked the President triumphantly.

"That they breathe different stuff from us, but we can handle it," replied General Harry Schwartz of the newly formed Space Force.

"Ok, what I have in mind are small Space Marine teams that will hijack their ships and then blow their air supplies."

Everyone looked admiringly at Trump, who now rocked on his heels feeling like a military genius now. Who on earth could come up with a plan like this, except Trump? Schwartzkopf felt his heart do funny summersaults, while General Schwartz marveled at Trump's chutzpah having never attended military school except as a schoolboy.

"What do you think?" demanded Trump. "I hope you didn't forget that I went to a top military academy for high school."

Yes, that was it. Trump was literate in military matters till only a GED level, while the Space Force General remembered his own decades long military education. But it counted for nothing in front of Trump who was now getting into an enthusiastic swing of things.

"I want you to come up with a Space Force hijack plan by 0600 hours," ordered Trump.

"But sir, that's in less than 15 hours," protested General Schwartz. There went his anniversary night celebration. His wife would be livid at this surprise order.

"Does the world National Security mean anything to you?" demanded Trump. "Schwartzkopf, get me up on all the T.V channels tonight for an emergency broadcast.

Schwartzkopf gulped and wondered what Trump wanted to tell the American people today as the President walked away leaving a gaping bunch of Generals and aides.

Hijacking aliens!

17

DEVUS

He was thinking hard. *Sanskrit.* But he had not built this ship. He didn't know any. This was all a grave misunderstanding.

"Otto," he said to the Fuzz pedal, who seemed surprised to be addressed by his old name.

"Something very weird is going on and I have no memories of any of this. Hell, I don't even have any special abilities."

"Whatever it is, Herr General, we are there for you," replied the Pedal, though even the Fuzz pedal felt that they were going to find out sooner than later.

Devus suddenly spoke.

"We have a transmission from Earth," he said. "A T.V broadcast that you might like."

"Are you crazy, Devus? You want us to watch fucking TV while we are lost in space."

Devus didn't care, as suddenly Ronald Trump filled the ship's screen.

"My fellow Americans!

Greetings and as our country limps back to normal, I would like to assure the population that emergency laws suspending our constitution will soon be removed and USA will become a normal country again. We are also facing the scourge of aliens who have ulterior motives

against our planet, and we have received a broadcast from an alien ship where we have a Delta-Operator still transmitting onboard."
Zyk excitedly turned to Varg. His eyes shone now as he waited with bated breath to hear what Trump was going to say next.
"Embedded in this transmission is the tracking frequency of our Delta-Operator. Good luck and God Speed."
Then a video of Trump taking questions from the press, with CNN taking the lead.
"Shit turn it off," swore Zyk. "I can't stand CNN!"
The picture disappeared as Donay turned with large eyes to him.
"What is CNN?"
"Something horrible in our World that we thought had been destroyed in the nuclear wars," said Zyk, though even the pedals and Varg had no idea about CNN.
"Devus, did you get the coordinates?" demanded Zyk.
"On it, Captain," Devus said. "Locked."
"Ok Varg, hit the guitar again," ordered Zyk, as Varg happily took his guitar and blasted out some ghastly black metal tunes that scarred Donay's soul, but the guitar pedals happily sucked it in. The reverb pedal took it in and sent out massive earthquake shuddering waves through the demonic delay pedal. Suddenly the fabric of space began to fold into waves.
"Look, we're surfing through time and space now!" shouted Zyk staring at the tidal wave of space charging towards them. These demonic pedals were worth their weight in gold, decided Zyk, as the ship hurtled through the space fabric.
"I've never seen anything like this," said Devus, who had been looking for the nearest wormhole, but here was an entirely new technique of folding time and space into mere cloth.
"Told you we were special," chuckled the Compressor pedal as he began to compress time and space. Suddenly everything began to shrink in front of them.
"Are you really compressing everything into a smaller size?" demanded Devus now. All those thousands of years of useless time journeys.
"Yes, but not our ship. We just got a million times bigger, so we accelerate a million times faster through space."
Donay was watching with her mouth open. Varg now riffed a shrill guitar tone that the Fuzz pedal distorted, while Zyk's amplifiers kicked in to multiply the amplitude of the sounds waves hundreds of millions of times.

"Sir, our nuclear reactor is running at top speed and I am powering down the reactor capacity to avoid overload, otherwise it might blow," said Devus. "A new small leak has been detected in the Nuclear steam turbine room."

"Ok, how much are we leaking?" demanded Zyk.

"20 percent of power, sir," replied Devus.

Varg had closed his eyes while shredding his "V" guitar like he was meditating and Zyk liked Varg's dark tunes. Scenes of a dark and frozen Norwegian forest floated in front of his eyes, while Donay sighed as she realized that Varg didn't look at her with that same passion. She glanced at Zyk, also completely focused on the mission. Well she didn't blame him with the aliens after him and that *destiny* that she'd seen for him —— far bigger than any Prince that her stepmother could have wanted.

Planet Pzyklo

"Animals prepare to land," announced Terl, as the guards came and clamped them with magnetic restraints to the metallic prison wall.

"This is for your own safety, as when we land, there will be heavy shearing forces," said Terl as he slammed the door shut behind him. The ship then landed heavily on the tarmac of planet Pzyklo, and Tor thudded into the metallic wall as the momentum caught up with him. Jesus was ecstatic —— another planet to proselytize and for him to spread his Father's Gospel! His reward would be in heaven. Then he caught Xander sneering at him as they landed, who knew what he was thinking. Well it wasn't hard, since he was Jesus.

Eventually, the guards escorted them out into the open, where everyone gaped at the sight outside, a city in the clouds. Thousands of shiny metallic roads, one on top of each other, layered, and snaking around buildings that were constructed on top of gigantic towers. As they looked beyond, they saw the clouds swirling down below.

"Why are you living up above?" asked Xander and dodged a cuff from Terl expertly. He wasn't in the special forces for nothing.

"There is nothing down there," said Terl grudgingly.

"A natural disaster?" asked Tor noting how defensive Terl was. Now Terl growled and caught him hard on his helmet. Tor winced from the blinding blow and he staggered to his knees.

"Don't forget yourself, animal," snarled Terl. The guards remained impassive. Apparently, they were used to seeing Terl getting his hands dirty, as Luke and Jesus helped Tor back to his feet.

Terl motioned towards a flying cargo car that resembled a freight elevator into which everyone trooped into, including the three Pzyklo guards. The humans were strapped into seats and then the elevator whisked away at breathtaking speed towards Terl's dreaded Security Headquarters in Pzyklo city.

Ronald Trump in space

"General, are the Space Marines ready?" demanded Trump gazing out of the window at the American secret facility on the dark side of the moon, where the shadow concealed an American Space Marine base on the frigid section of the moon that lay blanketed in moon dust and cold darkness. President Trump and his entourage had secretly rocketed up to the facility last night to put into motion the most dangerous phase of their plan.

General Schwartzkopf ran a worried hand through his hair. Who the hell was going to lead the mission to hijack alien ships and blow their gas tanks? So far Trump hadn't picked a commanding General, but this plan was so crazy that only Ronald could've come up with it.

"We also don't have anyone volunteering for this mission," argued Schwartzkopf, wiping the sweat off his brow just thinking of the harebrained plan.

"I have a feeling that something will come up," said Trump fingering his swastika. He was Christian, but something about the Aryan symbol told him that there were Underworld forces outside the control of Jesus working here. Kali had come in his dream even last night to tell him to trust in his intuition, and he stared at Schwartzkopf hard now.

"Look, if they're all gutless then I'll lead the mission!" growled Trump, and he was strangely excited at the thought of leading a mission, though in his mid-seventies, and still craved a Big Mac. The liberal press would have such a cow, he thought, and toyed with the possibility of tweeting it. But for now, the Reality Star turned President had far more important matters on hand.

"Sir, I'm going to look for a Space Marine General right away!" quaked Schwartzkopf, now imagining the overweight Ronald in a space suit, and charging alien ships. More sweat appeared on his brow.

Zyk

Zyk's ship rode the waves of space and time all rolled into a soupy fabric. This was not the way to travel but the Delay and Reverb pedal were distorting time with their giant waves. Truly demonic pedals. But who had caused them to have such energy? A thought suddenly dropped into Zyk's mind as he stared at Donay mooning at Varg, who played without a care. Trump had sent out a space transmission with the coordinates of the planet, but maybe he expected a reply. He got on the microwave radio.

"Devus," he said.

"Yes, Captain?"

Zyk hammered out a statement on the keyboard.

"Transmit this to Earth as fast as possible," he said.

"Yes sir," said Devus and sent the message via deep-space microwaves. Zyk was learning fast the ways of Deep Space, realized Donay. But then she glanced at him. *He'd built it in the first place!* But then he had no recollection of doing so. Varg seemed so normal now compared to the sinister SS General Zyk who seemed to be a man with many faces, a past that lay in the future. She shook her head at the concept of time and her Oracle powers told her that Time was the play of demon gods.

"Hey Donay, how about a sandwich or something?" asked Zyk now putting up his feet on the console, which Devus quickly blanked out helpfully. There, his heel was resting on the otherwise hot nuclear ignition button.

"Make your own sandwich," snapped Donay taking the men by surprise. Even Varg was startled out of his guitar haze.

"Hey, I'm hungry too," said Varg, and now Donay quickly calmed down and disappeared to rummage through the pantry. *A sandwich for Varg.* Why, she would fix him the best dam ham sandwich that he'd ever had. Zyk and Varg exchanged glances and smiled. *The power of a crush.*

Zyk switched his mind back to the screen and observed the waves of space-time that were being created in front of him by his pedals. Absolutely throwing all the Physics out of the window that he knew at least.
"Devus, run an analysis of the physics that we are using to fly through space."
"Captain, these are not natural physical laws. Demonic quantum principles are more like it," said Devus, sending a chill down Zyk's spine. Well scratch that then. So, you needed Demons to really coast through space. Faster than even aliens.
"Devus, how long will it take us to get to the Pzyklo coordinates?"
"At our approximate speed, we will be there in the next two years," replied Devus. "Planet Pzyklo is 700 Trillion Light Years away from us currently." Donay had returned and dropped the tray containing the sandwiches on the ground.
"What!" she screamed, hearing her young life vanishing. Two years was almost like a death sentence. Zyk looked ashen now and only Varg smiled for the first time that Donay could remember. Well what did he care? He was in it for life anyways.
"Devus, there must be other ways to that alien planet," said Zyk. "After all, we were only two days behind them."
"Yes, there seem to be some secret wormholes that have been wiped out of my memory bank," said Devus apologetically.
 Everyone looked up at the speakers to stare suspiciously at Devus's words. Maybe he was leading them into a trap.
"Devus, tell the American President that we need marked waypoints of that alien journey if we are to follow them in time."
"Affirmative captain," said Devus shooting another deep space email through extremely short wavelength microwaves.

Pzyklo

"In the year 35,690 of the Pzyklo Empire, we had a nuclear war, and everything was destroyed on planet Pzyklo. Even till today the ground down below is contaminated beyond redemption with radioactivity. All Pzyklos were forced to live high up in the atmosphere which has been artificially purified and is safe for Pzyklo citizens," said an interactive video. "It is so even today."

Jesus put his hand up.

"Question," he said, while Xander stared at him contemptuously. *What a cuck.*

"Yes?" paused the computer helpfully.

"Any renegade citizens down below that need saving?"

Everyone groaned including Luke. Jesus was still trying to find a role for himself.

"That is a classified question and is forbidden to be answered on the grounds of Pzyklo Security Chief Terl's directives," replied the computer. Aha, apparently this Empire was very secretive.

"And where does Zyk fit into all this?" asked Tor.

"Classified again," replied the computer. Aha, so they were asking the right questions at least.

"Who is Zyk?" asked Xander finally.

"A progenitor male sentenced to 3,000 years of hard labor down below on Planet Pzyklo."

It was like a thunderclap had hit. *Zyk serving hard time?*

"Is he here on this planet?"

"No, but he will be," said the computer laconically.

Just then the door opened and in walked Terl.

"Well animals, I hope that you've satisfied your *Zykian* curiosity," chuckled the security chief. He seemed to be in a very good mood now.

"What's got you so happy, Terl?" asked Tor sensing something.

"Well, we now know for a fact that we didn't have to find Zyk," crowed a triumphant Terl. *"He is already on his way to Planet Pzyklo!"*

Tor thought about his transmissions. The coordinates must have been picked up by none other than Zyk.

"Yes, animal. He is walking into a trap, thanks to you."

A chill descended even Jesus's spine, as Terl let out a monstrous laugh.

"And so now we can destroy your stupid Planet Earth once and for all. They have been attacking us, but we held our fire. Now your pathetic planet will see the power of the Pzyklo Empire."

Tor and Xander looked alarmed as Terl pulled up an image of thousands of motherships now descending on their planet, while their purple bellies began to open up ominously.

"Jesus fucking Christ!" shouted Tor, and Jesus looked alarmed too.

His name would die too along with the planet.

Ronald Trump on the Moon

"President Trump, the Motherships are up to something!" shouted an alarmed General Schwartzkopf and turned on the screen to reveal the Motherships closing in on Earth with their fat bellies opening up to reveal ominous purple lights.

"Where is our attack?" demanded Trump, as bone-chilling terror set in that mixed in the the despair of the condemned. He knew when he saw a super-predator. In his almost 75 years of life, he had rarely lost, but today a feeling of utter desolation descended on Trump. Who had he been kidding when he had taken on the aliens?

"Sir, threatening levels of electromagnetic energy being recorded by our sensors!" screamed Schwartzkopf as he stared fearfully at the screen. Trump walked over to him and put his hand on his shoulder.

There were tears in Schwartzkopf's eyes.

"We fought a good war, General," said Trump drawing himself to full height. There was only one way to die for an American. Boots on and tall and proud. The blinding blue light that coalesced together caused the screen to black out and suddenly there was fire like never before on earth.

Zyk fights back

Zyk was sleeping, when suddenly there was an alarm on the ship, and he woke up with a start. It was Devus.

"Red alert!" blared the computer. Suddenly on the screen, small specks of light appeared — and they were moving fast.

"Pzyklo fighters!" said Devus, and suddenly their ship zapped out lasers. Devus was taking matters into his own hands.

"But Captain, you will need to man the turret guns once they get closer," said Devus as suddenly a hatch opened above their heads. Varg nodded to get into one of them.

"How many fighters?" demanded Zyk, as suddenly hundreds of fighters appeared, and he felt his heart sink into his boots. "We need more hands on the guns!"

Devus zapped out hundreds of lasers and took out quite a few of the lights. But more and more swarmed closer.

"Release us!" cried the fuzz pedal. "You know we are humans trapped in here."

"Ok, as SS General Zyk, I hear-by release SS personnel Otto Ohlendorf, Arthur Nebe, Paul Blobel of the Einsatzgruppen. Wehrmacht General, Kurt Student, and Party leader Rudolf Hess."

There was suddenly a large flash and bang that caused young Donay to scream. When she stopped screaming, there stood men in German uniforms, who looked mighty pleased to be back in human form. Hess still looked depressed though, but Zyk needed all his men fighting fit right now.

"Ok boys, you know what to do," he commanded. Devus quickly lit up the gun port exits with different color schemes and everyone picked their favorite color to race towards their gun port. Meanwhile, laser blasts and torpedoes blasted past the ship with Devus taking crafty evasive action. Without Devus, they would've been goners. So much for him being captain, thought Zyk wryly as he settled into the turret drive of the laser blaster. He pushed a pedal and the turret shot out of the ship extending for about twenty meters above the ship. Now that gave him quite an elevation from where to pick off the fighters.

"Automatic targeting," droned Devus's voice as Zyk put on the headphones that rested on the gun.

"Multiple targets sighted," said Devus, as Zyk pressed the trigger to emit a tremendous barrage of lasers.

BLAM! BLAM! BLAM!

With each barrage Zyk felt himself smashed back into his chair, and he wondered how his SS demons were doing. Hundreds of Pzyklo fighters were going up in flames. But then this was a Pzyklo ship too.

"Pzyklo Death class," cut in Devus helpfully.

"You can read my thoughts too," said Zyk accusingly.

"Well, once you're strapped into the gun, its all on thought control," replied Devus, and Zyk swiveled suddenly to send out a barrage of lasers, lighting up the dark skies.

ZAP! ZAP!

"Threat levels?" demanded Zyk, as the swarm of Pzyklo fighters began to thin out. Devus was still firing his lethal torpedoes that would blast among the fighters, but now since they were approaching closer, Devus had stopped firing the nuclear torpedoes. Instead, laser blasts began to hit the ship which began to rock. In the background, Zyk could hear Donay screaming.

"What kind of damage are we taking?"

"Sir, our shields are up," said Devus. Zyk felt stupid now. Yeah, shields up.

"But not for long if we take more hits," added Devus helpfully. Zyk increased his firing rate.

BLAM BLAM BLAM!!!

The ship was surrounded by fighters, but Devus was running many programs all at once, and Zyk marveled at his processing power. *To think that he had built such a computer or at least had something to do with it in the future or the past?* He shook his head as he blasted a few more flies out of space. The *Pzyklo fighters* design was odd, something that he wouldn't build himself. The aesthetics of the fighters were all off. Maybe something that the Russians would build. Fat, heavy, and slow. Not fast and agile at all. These fighters were more like bombers. Bullies, while expecting little resistance. Obviously, the Pzyklos had not thought much of him to send such fighters. Or maybe it was all an elaborate trap. *Bah!* He blew out two more fighters before swiveling to the left and took out three more fast moving bogies. The SS gunners on his gun cam blasted dozens of these drone fighters out of space. So much for the Pzyklo attack, thought Zyk triumphantly as he stared at a fireball hurtling below the ship.

Pzyklo empire

Terl now had the attack live on his screen and an open-mouthed Jesus, Tor, Luke, and Xander now stared at giant motherships pouring purple laser into planet earth.

"Already, animals, most of your planet is overheated, but we will fry the core inside till it explodes like a giant supernova," gloated Terl. The humans could only feel sadness to see their only home being so cruelly destroyed.

Xander swore that he would rip off Terl's head the next chance he got, while Terl seemed to enjoy their helpless feeling —— the only humans still alive.

But then Jesus thought of Zyk. He was alive and coming to get them. Still some hope.

"As for your friend, Zyk," said Terl. "I have established communications with the computer on board, who is deviously now guiding Zyk into a trap as we speak."

He laughed now as he flipped screens and there, they saw Zyk's ship surrounded by enemy fighters.

"But look, they're blowing away your fighters!" countered Tor quickly doing a battle analysis. It looked like the Zyk's dense laser fire was more than a match for Security Chief Terl's forces.

"Watch this, animals," he gloated.

Suddenly, a giant Mothership appeared out of nowhere on the screen.

"Using a cloaking device," announced Terl. "We have teleportation technology that the animals are no match for even though they are using some kind of demonic propulsion."

Jesus shivered at the mention of demons. He remembered Zyk meeting Adolf and Himmler. Zyk was in with the Nazis. But now Earth had ceased to exist. He shook his head as he felt tears spring to his eyes. Where was his Father? God? Art thou in Heaven?

"The trap has been sprung," roared Terl, feeling this his moment had come as the Mothership opened its belly to fire at Zyk's ship. Purple light began to light up space and the surrounding area.

Zyk understands

"Oh my god!" shouted Zyk. "Devus, where did that Mothership come from?"

"I have no idea," replied the computer smoothly. Zyk was out of his pod and racing back to the bridge, while yelling for the SS soldiers to return to the pedals.

Breathlessly, he hit the bridge and he needed the pedals to use their fearsome energy to blast the alien ship first. But too late, he saw it preparing to fire as the SS soldiers returned to their pedals.

Donay was screaming while Varg held her. Everyone felt their last moment had come and terror filled everyone's hearts.

"Its too late," whispered Zyk, as the guitar pedal began to take their human souls in again. It had all been a trap and he looked up at Devus.

Just then a barrage of laser blasts filled the space around them, and the Alien Mothership erupted into a fireball of flames, which began to disintegrate into small particles. A fearsome weapon had hit it. But as Zyk scanned the skies, he drew a blank.

"Devus, what the hell was that?" demanded Zyk with relief filling his voice. Suddenly, hundreds of dark and agile fighters filled the skies blasting the remaining Pzyklo fighters out of existence, while following them was an Armada of gleaming white ships. Some kind of teleportation realized Zyk.

Their radio crackled, while Zyk waited with bated breath to hear who their rescuers were.

"Heil Hitler!" announced a German voice triumphantly. "The Reich welcomes General Zyk and best wishes from our Leader, Adolf Hitler."

Wagner's triumphant *Ride of the Valkyries* filled the airwaves.

Zyk hugged Donay and Varg in a group hug.

"Oh my god, we are saved!" shouted Donay happy to have been rescued even though it was by the Nazis. Varg just stared at the Swastika bedecked white Motherships and the red Messerschmitt space fighters that screamed all around them.

"I don't know what magic Hitler pulled, but he just saved our goose!" shouted Zyk, as now a Nazi Mothership quickly engaged the Traktor beam and captured their ship. Devus was strangely very quiet.

"Please disengage your nuclear engines," ordered a cool voice over the radio. "You no longer require its services."

"Devus, I think that he's telling us to switch off our engines."

"Disengaged," was the quick reply from Devus. Oh, he was cooperating fully now.

Suddenly, another voice came online.

"Hello, this is Reichsführer Heinrich Himmler and we thank you for your brave service to the Reich. We will be going into teleportation mode to the Valhalla, where the Führer is expecting you."

"Oh, yes please!" shouted Zyk feeling relief still flooding into his mind and his body began to relax.

Terl

 Terl's face had turned color and he looked like a hunted animal as his jaw fell open and gaped at the Nazi swastikas filling up the screen.
"How did the Nazis jump into space?" he demanded, with his mind whirling, while filled with questions. "How did the Nazis escape from the Underworld on Earth?"
"I think that you did that, my friend," said Tor now grinning as he realized what might have happened. "You destroyed Earth and freed their trapped spirits."
 Terl roared with anger. He had just unwittingly freed his most deadly enemies and now the prophecy was coming true.
"Zyk is now going to come after you!" shouted Xander triumphantly. Terl now gnashed his teeth and took out his blaster.
"You're dead, animal!" he screamed.
"Fuck you, Terl, the human race will still win, and I will go to the Valhalla!" shouted Xander, as Terl squeezed the trigger and blasted Xander out of existence. Tor, Luke, and Jesus screamed, but only a burnt skeleton remained.
"Fuck you, Terl!" screamed Tor furiously now waiting to join his friend. But Terl had already dashed out of the room. A red alert now sounded throughout the Pzyklo building with the doors slamming shut automatically.
Jesus now looked up into the heavens. His Father had indeed spoken, but through Hitler.

The Führer bunker in the Valhalla

 Zyk and Donay enter Hitler's bunker set now in a cold and far away Nebula, where lay the mysterious Aryan Valhalla planet orbiting a series of giant stars. The released demonic guitar pedals are busy getting dressed as is Varg, who is being processed into the Waffen SS as a soldier. He will have a new pardoned future, while an award ceremony has been planned for them by Himmler, but Donay is not happy at all.
"You know you're a fool, Zyk," she swears bitterly. Zyk stares at her in surprise. After that spectacular rescue, they were now on a hi-tech planet filled with humans. Well Germans, but still alive, nonetheless.

"We were *the bait* all along," she said replaying the events in her mind.

Zyk was startled. He thought about the meeting and his promotion to Obergruppenführer. *All for the final act of getting Terl to destroy Earth.* It was horrible. Such a diabolical plan. Who could've thought so far?

"I mean you fell for the oldest trick in the book!" shouted Donay thinking of her dead stepmother. *All for nothing.*

"Look, I didn't know that Hitler and his hounds were swinging this for their own good," said Zyk. But then what was the role of a soldier but to sacrifice?

"If Adolf had ordered me into this situation then as a loyal General, I would've done it anyways," said Zyk. *Loyalty Honor and Courage* played in his mind. Donay stared at him.

"Then you're a bigger fool than I thought," she said. A tool for Hitler.

"Millions of Germans died for Germany," countered Zyk.

"But you're not even German," cried Donay.

Zyk thought about it.

"Aryan," he replied. Somehow there had always been mental clarity about what he had to do in this world. No confusion and everything had worked out just like that.

"I would never stay with a man like you!" shouted Donay.

"But I never asked you too," howled Zyk in surprise. "Besides, I think that Varg is the better man here."

"You fool!" she shouted again and burst into tears.

Bah, this was beyond ridiculous. Zyk would deal with the SS any day versus the vagaries of women.

Suddenly a lot of saluting and the doors opened.

Himmler and his entourage.

"Heil Hitler!"

"Heil Hitler!" shouted Zyk snapping to attention, while Donay stared at the ridiculous proceedings in front of her. *Boys playing solders.*

"At ease, General," said Himmler.

"Jawohl, Reichsführer!" shouted Zyk for effect and to scare Donay a bit.

Himmler shook hands with Zyk.

"That was magnificent," he said smiling." A master stroke."

"How was everything timed?" asked Zyk now with wonder in his eye. To have fooled an empire so large as the cunning Pzyklo was quite an achievement.

"You see we had a double agent all along," said Himmler. *"Maria!"*

In walked a stunning blonde in a black neoprene suit and patent leather boots. Very futuristic. She even had a blaster slung low on her shapely waist.

"May I present *Maria Orzic* to you?" bowed Himmler while taking her lovely hand. "The Oracle."

Zyk mumbled while Donay now felt quite small. Another woman in the picture. Of course. She was just a lowly village girl.

"Ah, Zyk," she said cooing a bit and Zyk felt the estrogen in her voice. "Finally, we meet."

"You're the Oracle that set up the Pzyklos," said Zyk desperately trying to sound intelligent in front of this goddess.

"Oh yes," nodded Maria. "Himmler, Zyk is clever."

Himmler and his SS soldiers turned scarlet at him being addressed so informally. Donay also wanted to disappear at that moment. She felt so out of place.

"Well how on earth did you know how the Underworld works and that the annihilation of Earth would free the Germans?" asked Zyk.

"Well we have a powerful ally, who guided us into these temporal matters," said Maria, and Himmler stiffened now. "Madame Blavatsky."

"Oh yes, we just met her recently," replied Zyk in awe now. Himmler nodded and looked around uneasily.

"Yes, she appears at her will and does as she pleases in the Universes," said Himmler now. "A bit too often."

"Oh Heine, she's lovely and she just saved your soul," coo'ed Maria. "I meditate and she guides me through the Universes. That's how I got into Terl's dreams and we played such a trick on him."

Maria giggled.

"Terl?" asked Zyk.

"The Pzyklo Empire's security chief."

"But he still destroyed our planet," said Pzyklo.

"Yes, but the Madame can turn time and change many realities," said Maria. "There are many planes of existence in this Universe and entire civilizations appear and disappear within a slice of space time. You see time doesn't flow like water or sand. It exists as Dark Energy waves. So yes, right here, right now in the Valhalla, our planet is destroyed, but we are billions and billions of light years away from Earth in a time, when the Earth couldn't even exist due to its natural lifespan. But we need only to escape this box and into the other box where the Earth still exists."

"Sounds like confusing Quantum realities," said Zyk. "Ah, it's all a game. Death is nothing but fleeting."

"Oh Heine, he's gonna fit right in with us," she said sizing Zyk up with a naughty eye that sent Donay into a tizzy.

"But Terl is very clever and will renew his resolve to destroy us, so we don't have time to lose," said Maria worriedly now. "Excuse me, the Führer has summoned me."

She exited to leave Himmler with Zyk.

This Terl guy was bad news. Every ointment had its fly. Karma.

"Hitler is already organizing everything. You see we got here a few hundred years ago before you in this quantum reality. But we have already set up our Mercedes, Porsche machining units, and organizing into the Wehrmacht and SS branches of the Reich's Space Forces. Maria has her powerful Vril organization."

"Yes, I can tell," said Zyk nodding, as he remembered the Nazi rescue ships. Really well machined into an organized space navy.

"A new future awaits us now," said Himmler and nodded as he exited leaving Zyk with Donay.

To be Continued...

Psysword Publications

Please look for our other exciting titles in your nearest bookstore or online portal.

OTHER BOOKS PUBLISHED BY PSYSWORD PUBLICATIONS

BLACK SHARK VALLEY
SOLOMON: DEMON KING
THIRTEEN WITCHES
SS DEATH STAR
FLIGHT 777 TO ATLANTIS
'82 BEIRUT
BLUE I.C.E.